Damaris

Damaris

A ROMANTIC HISTORICAL NOVEL

JANE SHERIDAN

ST. MARTIN'S PRESS
NEW YORK

CONTENTS

Prologue
LONDON,
1815

The town house of the young Marquis d'Egremont was large and magnificent, his bedroom airy and spacious. But he was a gallant lover, and when he received his mistresses he had a care for their privacy and took them to a small, secret room that he had built especially for this pleasure. The ceiling of this room had been painted for him by Claude Baptiste, the famous émigré painter, with erotic scenes in the Italian style. There were silken wall-hangings, a dais, and upon the dais a huge bed said to have belonged to Madame de Pompadour. On this bed one warm afternoon lay young Damaris, tipsy from drinking champagne, warm and flushed with love-making.

D'Egremont, with a silk dressing-gown wrapped about him, leaned against the bed-post and smiled down at his lovely favourite. Although their affair was of several months' duration, his pleasure in it was still intense, and he was amazed by the fervour of his own emotion. Handsome, gay, and rich, he was much spoiled by women. Making love had been for him the most pleasant of pastimes, but this was different.

He never tired of gazing at this woman—or girl, rather, he reflected, for she was barely twenty years old. Since she came to Town she had been the reigning beauty. Even the Prince Regent pursued her, though she was very different from the fleshy matrons who were his usual choice. His Damaris was slender and elegant. Seeing her like this, a man could truly appreciate how exquisite she was, with her narrow hips and deep bosom, fine bones, and delicate curves.

Her beauty was in the true English style: her hair was smooth and dark, her face fair with classical features, her eyes as blue as the rich silk counterpane that lay tangled at her feet. It was a beauty normally cold enough to freeze a man, but in Damaris . . . ! Just then her body had a sheen and glowed like porcelain warmed by candlelight. She smiled up at him and his heart turned over. He had never intended to fall in love, least of all with an Englishwoman, he told himself with a slight sense of foreboding, yet he could not be sorry he had permitted himself this luxury.

He longed to take her in his arms again, but they were not alone in the small room, nor was he the only man delighted by Damaris's glowing body. Claude Baptiste was sitting at his easel, working on an almost finished portrait of the woman on the bed. He was happy with his subject and only cursed the inadequate daylight that came through a tiny window high in the wall. Massed candelabra had had to make up its defects.

Still, the blended light gave the portrait a luminous quality. For all my trouble, he thought proudly, it will be my masterpiece. A thousand pities that it is only meant for the eyes of the Marquis. But he remembered the amount of gold he would receive and went on to complete his work, humming to himself. The song he was humming, without realizing what he did, had come over the Channel from France and celebrated Napoleon's victories. The Marquis, recognizing it, gave the artist an amused glance.

When Baptiste had put the finishing strokes to the portrait, he called the Marquis over to admire it. D'Egremont was delighted and bade the subject take a look.

'Come, Madame—regard what this genius has wrought!'

Damaris caught up the lace shawl which she had so eagerly cast aside earlier that afternoon. She covered herself as much as possible and, without enthusiasm, glanced at the painting. She admired the artistry of Claude Baptiste but was hardly as pleased as the Marquis—perhaps not pleased at all.

'It is well done, M'sieur Baptiste,' she said in her usual gentle voice.

The Marquis loved her voice, low and sweet whether she spoke French or English. He wondered if he could have fallen in love if she spoke like most Englishwomen, in those high, piercing tones that surely came from the hunting field. Damaris was perfect in all things. He looked again at the smiling, alluring figure in the portrait and felt himself to be a happy man.

Damaris was not smiling. It would be of no use to complain to the artist, she thought; the fault was her own. When she consented to sit for a portrait at d'Egremont's urgent request, she had expected the pose to be conventional. But Claude Baptiste was a painter of nudes, and the Marquis, with a thousand protestations about the safety of the portrait and the utter discretion of the painter, had overridden her objections, as he always could.

D'Egremont, who had succeeded early to his father's title and wealth, with his looks, air, and blood—blood equal, the d'Egremonts always claimed, to that of Louis himself—was the leader of French society in London and the adored darling of the English ladies. The outwardly cool Damaris had always longed for love, even before she knew what it was, but when it came it threatened to shatter her carefully constructed life.

To her the portrait showed, accusingly, a naked, abandoned woman, so undeniably herself, and she shivered as though someone were walking over her grave. She blushed, remembering how d'Egremont had first brought the painter into the little room, just two weeks before, when she had been weak with pleasure from an afternoon spent in love and was able to refuse him nothing.

D'Egremont had taught her love—but he had made himself her master in the process. She knew well she should never have consented to this portrait, yet she could not speak. When she failed in courage and daring he would mock her by calling her an English prude and praise the valour in love of the great ladies of France and of French ladies now in England, until jealousy—another new emotion!—made her leave caution far behind. But now she had to turn her head from the portrait and wonder miserably how she had come to this.

D'Egremont opened another bottle and gave the painter a glass of wine.

'Ah, that is good, Baptiste,' he said exuberantly. 'I wish it could be hung in my gallery so that all London could see it!'

'Jean-Philippe,' Damaris protested.

He laughed. For the first time his gaiety, which had been for her his great charm, was not enchanting. He saw her expression, understanding her fears very well, for he had had too many mistresses not to know the ways of women. For himself, he had little faith in the discretion of the artist, nor did he believe any of the comforting tales he told her. Yet he thought she need not fear. The Marquis d'Egremont was in a fever of excitement that only increased his desire for love. And he wanted Damaris to be happy.

His dark eyes were brilliant with laughter, mischief and something she did not recognize.

'Do not worry, Madame,' he said teasingly—it was often his pleasure to be formal even in their most intimate moments—'the portrait will be hung in this room. *Certainement,* this should make you easy in your mind. I could hardly bring any other charming friend here when you are so obviously in possession. My fidelity is now assured.'

Damaris, who was not at all certain of his fidelity, had to laugh. The laughter brought back the faint colour to her cheeks and tumbled her hair. D'Egremont gave her more wine, drank to the painter's triumph, and sent him on his way. The Marquis had important business to take care of before the day was over and should have been off himself. But almost without volition, he brushed the dark curls that fell about her neck and shoulders. Her body was warm under his hands. Silently, breathlessly, they made love again, and for the moment Damaris was happy, flushed with her young ardour and the warmth of the afternoon sun. And yet the question she had asked herself was not forgotten and soon echoed persistently in her mind. How could she, who had been Damaris St Cloud, have come to this?

Book One

ENGLAND,
1794-1815

1

The morning was dark and wintry. Young Captain Lord Edmund St Cloud looked out of the window at the cold rain as it drove across the fields, and felt heavy-hearted. He was dressed in his uniform; his equipment was ready, and his horse already saddled. There was nothing for him to do before rejoining his regiment with the Duke of York in the Netherlands but to say good-bye to his wife.

Yet he hesitated. She had fallen asleep just an hour before, and it seemed wicked to wake her. Certainly she needed her rest; she was heavily pregnant and she was not well. Not well at all. For the first time the words of his father, the Fifth Duke of Camberly, dead now over twelve months, made sense to him.

'A soldier, sir, has no business being married,' he had roared when the youngest of his three sons had told him that he wished to marry the lovely Griselda Mayne.

Younger sons with no fortune were not expected to marry unless they married money. Certainly the Mayne family, although their blood was as good as any in the kingdom, were poor, and the girls had no dowry. Griselda had been expected to marry only because of her looks; her sharp-featured, red-headed sister Augusta was already considered a spinster. But he had persisted, against his father's wishes, and the Duke had given the young people a small income, and they had been happy in the intervals of the campaign when the Captain had come home.

Then the Duke had died. His eldest son succeeded, to become the Sixth Duke of Camberly, and he had immediately cut off his youngest brother's allowance. While the Captain was fighting at Hondschoote, his wife gave up their comfortable home and moved to this house, little more than a cottage, that she rented from one of the farmers who leased land from her brother-in-law.

The only servant was a girl who came daily from the village. She would not arrive for hours yet, and the house was cold. The Captain found paper, sticks and coals and lit a fire in his wife's room. She was coughing in her sleep. He looked at her with painful anxiety and felt a hatred for his brother, who would do nothing for Griselda, weak and vulnerable as she was. She needed a comfortable house, good fires, and a carriage to take the air in. But with what he himself could send her, she could hardly live as a lady at all.

She was still lovely, he thought, looking at her delicately-cut features and her dark hair tumbled over the pillow, but she was far too thin. The thought of the disease of the lungs, which ran through generations of her family, weighed upon him so that he wished he could resign his commission. But he could hardly do that with the campaign still raging and the French advancing in the Low Countries.

Footsteps approached in the passage. Not the village girl as yet. The door opened quietly, and his sister-in-law Augusta, Lady Gratton, fully dressed and buttoned into her widow's weeds, stood before him. She looked at his sleeping wife and then motioned him quietly outside.

'She needs to rest,' he said.

His sister-in-law was holding an oil lamp, and she preceded him down the dark, narrow stairs.

'She will want to say good-bye for all that,' she remarked. 'You have had no breakfast?'

'I will get something at the inn later,' he replied.

He cared little for food. The campaign, he knew, would be long. In his years of soldiering he had had few fears of his life, but now he found himself reluctant to go. His wife so weak and with the hazards of childbirth before her—he made to speak to his sister-in-law, but she went before him into the kitchen.

Lady Gratton, who had been the proud Miss Mayne and in spite of her family's poverty had certainly never been below-stairs, had that morning lit the stove and set coffee boiling. The smell struck him agreeably as he entered the small room. Her ladyship had sliced bread, found butter, and cut up the remains of the pork from their last night's dinner.

'Eat,' she commanded, and he obeyed. They were of the same age, he reflected, but Augusta had always made him feel like a boy.

The hot coffee heartened him, but the worry remained.

'You will stay with her, Augusta, until the child is born?'

She nodded. 'I will not leave her, and there is nowhere I could take her.'

Lady Gratton did not speak her thoughts to the young soldier, but the knowledge that death had removed most of their choices was in both their minds. General Mayne had been killed at Mouvaux; his wife had died before him of the consumption she had brought into the family and that had already carried off their only son. Sir Hubert Gratton, the elderly baronet whom Augusta had married shortly after her sister's wedding to St Cloud, had disappointed his wife by dying of a lingering complaint of the stomach. He had left her nothing but her jointure, on which she had been making shift to live by sharing a house with another widow with two children in Kensington, not a fashionable part of Town but the best that the society-loving Augusta could manage. The Kensington house was too small to accommodate her sister for her lying in, and so in Hertfordshire, in this miserable hovel (as she termed it to herself), they would have to remain.

The Captain looked at his sister-in-law. He had never liked Augusta; her sharpness had not softened with widowhood and straitened means, but her cool kindness and steadfast friendship touched him. He swallowed, wishing he could express what he felt, but Augusta's ironic green gaze was a bar to sentiment.

'I couldn't talk to Griselda as she is about—about things,' he said. 'But I have spoken to my Colonel. He is an old friend of my father's and he knew General Mayne. He has promised me that if I should be killed and the child is a boy, he will take care of him and see that he gets into a good regiment when the time comes.'

'And if it should be a girl?' Augusta said matter-of-factly, not from any hardness of heart, but merely from a long habit of viewing facts with as little emotion as possible.

'Let us hope it is a boy,' St Cloud said. 'At this time I don't know what I could arrange for a daughter—unless the Duchess could be induced to do something.'

Augusta's sniff said plainly that she expected little from the present Duchess of Camberly, a small, plain, mean-spirited woman with a growing family of her own.

A voice, weak but clear, came from the upper room.

'Edmund! Edmund, you are not leaving without saying goodbye?'

He rushed up the stairs and knelt by the side of his wife. She had struggled up on her pillows. In the lamplight he could see her eyes filled with tears, but she was smiling—her familiar entrancing smile that still caught his heart.

'I was just telling Augusta about the arrangements for the child,' he said, stroking her head. 'It is not very likely that I will be back in time for the birth of our son.'

'Do you have to go yet?' she whispered. 'It is still dark.'

'It is morning,' he said. 'The sky is overcast.'

'You'll have a wet journey.'

Her frail white hands clung to him as they talked quickly, as if to fend off the moment of parting.

'It will clear later,' he said. 'The sunset blazed like fire over Grundison wood last night.'

She shivered. 'Don't talk to me of fire. I've been dreaming all night of cannon—oh, Edmund.'

They held each other as if they knew that they would never meet again and that neither of them would live to see the year out.

'Take care of our son,' he said indistinctly, 'and Augusta will take care of you.'

'Augusta,' she said, and tried to smile. She did not want his last memory of her to be a tearful one. 'The women are the strongest in our family. I think the child will be a girl. I will name her for my great-great-grandmother. She was very rich and lived to be ninety-five.'

She laughed, and her husband thought how wonderful it was to hear her laugh.

'Her son was a gambler and in dreadful debt and was always waiting for her to die, but she outlived him at last—it was left to her grandson to gamble away the family fortune. Her son said she was possessed of the Devil and called her "The Damned." '

'But what was her name?'

'Damaris.' She smiled up at him as he prepared to go. 'But our Damaris will have no fortune, no Devil, and certainly will not be damned.'

And her soft laughter accompanied him as he went away.

2

Captain Lord Edmund St Cloud was killed at Pont à Chin in the '94 campaign, but if he could have seen his sister-in-law fifteen years later he would have thought her little changed. She had left off her widow's weeds; there was a little grey in her red hair, but she was in vigorous health from leading a quiet but comfortable life, which she disliked, on the Angelhurst estate in a remote part of Somerset.

Lady Gratton, a woman meant for the pleasures of society, could hardly be happy shut away in a house where she saw almost no adults except the servants. But she had made her bargain; she knew it was the best she could do for herself and her niece, and tried to be content. On a warm afternoon in late summer she was watching from an upstairs window, not the incredibly rich green of the fields nor the majesty of the oaks, still in full leaf, that formed a barrier between the small park and the farm, not even the tall, elegant figure of her lovely niece, Damaris St Cloud, who was cutting roses for the table that night. Lady Gratton was eagerly awaiting the servant she had sent to the post.

The post for many years had been Lady Gratton's chief link with the world. She corresponded regularly with her girlhood friends and all the ladies she had met as the baronet's wife during her two seasons in Town. She was a good correspondent with a vigorous style, and her friends were pleased to get her letters full of gossip and humour. It was not, she told herself, as if she were quite a recluse. By many exertions of economy, every two years she gave herself a short season in Bath, not too far away. Prices had risen shockingly in the years since the death of the baronet, and her jointure was worth little now. Fortunately, her personal expenses at Angelhurst were few. She kept no carriage—there was nowhere to visit within forty miles except the vicarage, and the vicar had married a woman too low-born to be visited by the baronet's widow, who had been, after all, a Mayne.

Damaris saw her aunt at the window, looked up, and smiled.

Lady Gratton stood quite still. For a moment, as she smiled, the girl in the simple white dress and shady bonnet looked so much like her mother, like Griselda Mayne before illness and pregnancy had worn her to a shadow, that the sensible Lady Gratton had a moment's confusion. It seemed as if she were back at the Mayne house in Leicestershire and her sister Griselda was in the garden, smiling as she waited for the young St Cloud, a lieutenant then, son of the ducal house that in those days Augusta had hoped would make all their fortunes.

She sighed, wondering why the man she had sent to the post—on a horse borrowed from the farm, to the annoyance of the Duke's steward, who grumbled that the beast could not be spared—had not returned. Her niece had gone back to her task, clipping away with her neat fingers—not really like her mother, Lady Gratton reflected. Griselda had been quick and impulsive, always eager, always impatient. The basket of roses would have been left half-full while Griselda ran off to some other occupation. It was her eagerness and impatience that had overridden all objection when the Duke forbade the match and the Mayne parents had warned her against it. To marry into a rich ducal family was a fine thing—if the head of the household were willing to receive her. But a Miss Mayne with no fortune could hardly live on the pay of a lieutenant's wife—especially a lieutenant in an expensive regiment with a position of fashion to maintain.

But the young people would not be denied. Griselda had flown eagerly down the aisle, and all that was to come had followed in train. Lady Gratton had done her best to bring Griselda's daughter up to be very different. Damaris had not been indulged. From the first, she had known the truth of her position. The only other children about the place had been the children of the farm. Until she was five years old, Damaris had been allowed to tumble about with them in play, but after her fifth birthday she was taken from them and brought up as a lady, even though that meant she was almost in seclusion. The great families of the county, aware that the two females in the small establishment were not accepted by the Duke and Duchess of Camberly, held off. Damaris grew up used to solitude.

Lady Gratton had spent money she could ill afford to have good masters for her niece; the girl had not only the accomplishments of a woman of fashion, but if the very worst should happen, she was learned enough to teach others. But *that* Lady

Gratton was determined to prevent. Damaris was a beauty. If the Duchess could be persuaded to give her a Season in Town when she reached eighteen, she was certain to make a match even without a fortune.

Hooves sounded along the road. Lady Gratton, all pleasant expectation, left her room and made her way down the fine flight of stairs through the well-proportioned hall to the morning-room where she sat in the day-time. Eager as she was, she would wait until the man took the letters round to the back and they were carried in properly by the housemaid.

Everything at Angelhurst was done as it should be. Her retirement had not caused Lady Gratton to fall into slipshod ways; no great lady was more demanding of her household. From the beginning she had been determined that it should be so. She had been with Griselda when she died, shortly after the news of Captain St Cloud's death, and had played her cards well. Certain that the Duchess intended to do nothing for the child, Lady Gratton had sent a short, peremptory message saying that she herself was returning to London and that the infant would be sent to Camberly with a nurse. The Duchess had reacted as Lady Gratton had known she would. She had had hysterics at the idea of giving shelter to the child of her sister-in-law. The Duke had been told to do *something* to fend off this disaster—but not too much.

The Duke's agent, Mr Crawford, a sensible man, had taken care of everything. He had proposed to Lady Gratton that she accept the use of the Duke's small property in Somerset—a good long way from Camberly!—and bring her niece up in a healthy country situation. He had made inquiries, and he knew that Lady Gratton could hardly support herself in Town on her small jointure. Angelhurst was really not much more than a large farm and the few cottages that comprised the village, but the house was definitely a gentleman's residence, by no means a farm-house, and was set in a small but pleasant park shielded by great old oaks from the sight of agricultural activity. Lady Gratton had hesitated, and Mr Crawford had pointed out that the rent of the farm, of course, would go to the upkeep of the establishment while aunt and niece were in residence.

It had served, Lady Gratton thought now. Her niece, her basket full, entered the house quietly. She would take the flowers to the garden room, put her pruning shears away, and wash her hands before she joined her aunt. Lady Gratton smiled, knowing that

Damaris was as eager as she was herself to have news of the letters—such a small event was a large one in their lives—but she was pleased that the girl had learned her lessons so well. Damaris would be biddable; *she* would not rush down the altar with a handsome but penniless young man, causing pain and grief to those who loved her. A miniature on the table beside her showed Griselda at eighteen. Like Damaris, yet unlike. Both had fine and delicate features, like so many of the Maynes, but Damaris's eyes had the vivid blue of the St Clouds, and her aunt hoped that she had their robustness.

The maid brought the letters in on a tray. Lady Gratton was pleased to see the respectable pile. There were some bills from tradesmen, of course, but there were half a dozen letters from her old friends—some of them living in the country like herself, but others still in the world of fashion.

Damaris came in quickly after the maid, her step measured, her greeting to her aunt as it should be, but the blue eyes sparkled with pleasure as she saw the letters. None, of course, was addressed to her, and she made no remark, but seated herself in her usual place and took up her work. She was making new covers for the dining-room chairs, and her needle flashed in and out of the canvas, her head bent demurely, before her aunt took her ivory-handled letter opener and began on her post.

Because of Damaris Lady Gratton now had a special pleasure in her correspondence. Although her niece was so young, she was already fully formed, and her beauty had the elegance of maturity. Perhaps because she had hardly been allowed to be a child, she had grown quickly to womanhood. Already she could grace a drawing-room and a ball-room. The music master said she knew almost all that he could teach her, and the master who had instructed her in the classics had made her a scholar superior to some of the young men attending the universities.

And so of late Lady Gratton had been paying particular heed to any mention in her friends' letters of young men who might be eligible and rich enough to take a poor but well-born wife. These thoughts, in fact, occupied a good deal of her time. The girl was so lovely now, she reflected. In spite of their country life, she had been careful to keep her from the sun, so that her complexion was as fair and dazzling as any in England. It was a pity she could not be presented this year. But her looks would last. Lady Gratton had no doubt that if she had a season, at eighteen Damaris would almost certainly be the beauty of the year. To make quite certain, the careful aunt had brought down expensive masters to teach Damaris every dance now fashionable in the salons—even the waltz, with many a stern injunction about the occasions suitable for this new and, Lady Gratton thought, rather daring favourite of the ball-room.

If only she could be sure the Duchess would give the girl a Season! That was Lady Gratton's chief concern. There was no way, with the means at her disposal, that she herself could manage it. And certainly, Damaris's chances would be improved if she were presented under the aegis of the ducal family. But the Duchess had girls of her own, already of presentable age and, Lady Gratton feared, dull plain girls like their mother, hard to move on the marriage market, even with their fortunes.

The letter of her friend Mrs Clare, of Clare Park in Hertfordshire, close to Camberly, brought information. The summer had been quiet in that part of the country, as the Duchess had taken her two eldest daughters to Brighton after they had been presented at one of the Queen's last Drawing-Rooms that spring. 'So we are very dull,' Mrs Clare had written, 'but we expect great things this autumn. The Duchess had been busy, and there are rumours that a marriage will take place. Lady Honor is to marry young Devereaux, the eldest son of the Earl of Fosters, and a very good match it is. Just between us, I am rather surprised. Honor is a good enough girl but small and dark and not very pretty, hardly likely to be the belle of the ball-room. The Duke must have come down with something handsome.'

Mrs Clare had gone on with other Hertfordshire gossip, but Lady Gratton looked up.

'It seems your cousin, Lady Honor, is to be married this autumn,' she told Damaris. 'She must be nineteen. The Duchess was slow in taking her to Town, but not in arranging the match.'

The Duchess had been wise, she thought. If the marriage was being arranged by the families, there was no point in taking the girl to have an uninspiring season before the arrangements were complete. The Duchess was much safer in the less formal air of Brighton—even Lady Honor might look intriguing as she disappeared into a bathing machine.

'Whom is she marrying?' Damaris asked with a lively interest.

'The eldest son of the Earl of Fosters. They have a big place near Derby and a good house in Town.'

'But what is he like?' Damaris asked.

Lady Gratton had never met Devereaux, but she knew of him by reputation. He was in his thirties, something of a rake, something of a gambler, yet not of a kidney to ruin himself. His mistress was the well-known lovely actress, Sylvia Garden. The 'something handsome' that the Duke was prepared to give would probably not come before it was needed.

'It is not a marriage of love,' Lady Gratton said, 'but it should do very well.'

She added enough, carefully phrased, so that her niece would understand. It was necessary that Damaris be familiar with the ways of the world. A girl, upon her marriage, was expected to make the leap from total innocence to wisdom; Lady Gratton believed in a more rational scheme. A girl beautiful, well born, but poor must not expect life to be too pleasant or romantic.

'I don't suppose that Honor will have all her husband's affection,' she concluded. 'But certainly the Duchess has brought her up to conduct herself with dignity. And her situation will be grand.'

Damaris listened patiently. But though Lady Gratton had taught her to be anything but romantic, she was not at heart as practical as her aunt might wish. She had read Greek legend and Roman poetry, and she knew the songs the troubadours had sung. Romance was not part of the real world, she knew, yet she had her dreams and longings. But of these she knew better than to speak. Her needle worked a design of a maiden and a unicorn, and she nodded her head to her aunt's words.

Satisfied with her lecture, Lady Gratton went back to her post. There was a letter from Crawford, the Duke's agent. Usually he corresponded directly with the steward of the Angelhurst property, but sometimes he wrote to her formally on matters concerning the estate. She put that aside and went on with her personal letters.

An old friend, Mrs Crewe, now a dowager in Scotland, had written complaining of the damps, cold, and general misery of that country. She wrote of pains here and there and trouble with her teeth—for all the world, Lady Gratton thought, as though she were an old, old woman, not a recent widow in her forties. And Dorothea had been such a gay girl, the toast of many a mess. She had come out the same season as the present Duchess of Camberly—Miss Arkwright, she was then. How jealous she had been of

Dorothea—just as later she was jealous of poor Griselda. But Miss Arkwright had been the richest girl on the marriage market, and she was chosen to marry the eldest son of a duke. Dorothea had married well enough and had been happy until she was widowed and left in the backwater of the dower house.

Lady Gratton made some sage remarks to her niece about the necessity of a woman's being able to live on her own resources.

'One never knows when one may have to live in retirement, and if one cannot occupy oneself without a whirl of people,' she lectured sternly, 'what a miserable life one leads.'

Damaris, who had never known any society other than her aunt's, nodded in sober agreement.

Most of the letters told of the pleasures of Brighton. Ladies who had been there six weeks and had returned to their country homes, however reluctantly, now had time to write. Mrs Farthingale, a very old friend and a wonderful gossip, was even more faithful and wrote from Brighton itself.

Prinny is still here and all is gay as ever. Lady Hertford is still very much in favour, although everyone knows that he is also granting Mrs M—— the benefit of his affections. Mr M—— can do nothing—he and Prinny have been gambling, much too deep for Mr M——, and the Prince is holding IOU's for far more than M—— can pay. It is all the buzz of the dandies, quite outshining the match of the season—but you know about that, of course. It has not yet appeared in the *Gazette,* and for a long time we were not sure it would come off. The Duchess did the best she could, but Fanny was never a good manager. She not only brought Honor but also Wilhelmina, who is as big and fair as Honor is small and dark. We are very tolerant in Brighton, you know; many a girl who could not shine at Almack's looks well upon the Steyne in the sea breezes. But alas! The Beau saw them together at a small dance given by Lady Trevor, and someone *would* ask him what he thought of the St Cloud ladies. I fear he was unkind—he put up his quizzing-glass, looked from one to the other, and said in that way of his that he always thought Camberly *so* depressing, so drearily flat in some places, so unexpectedly bumpy in others: Hertfordshire altogether, he said, was wearily dreary, and so the young bucks took to calling the girls Miss Dreary and Miss Weary, and young Devereaux, who had not been greatly *épris,* tried to withdraw. After all, a thing like that does hang on. The

mammas were called in, with powers plenipotentiary—it
was like a great conference of treating empires, and I suppose
a few provinces were thrown in to sweeten the bargain—and
the Earl of Fosters threatened Devereaux that if he balked,
the Earl would not pay his debts. And so I think the match
is made. But I have news of closer interest: I was at a great
supper at the Pavilion, and the Duchess was there talking to
Prinny—boring him, I fear—when suddenly he looked at her
and said, 'Duchess, whatever happened to your beautiful
sister-in-law?' She was so angry she nearly fell over her train.
Poor Griselda, dead all these years—Fanny must think she will
never be finished with her. But of course, I remembered that
poor St Cloud had been in Prinny's regiment before he
exchanged and Prinny had known Griselda well. So like him
to think she would still be about, somewhere, when he
deigned to think of her again. But a word to the wise—I
would not expect any fine Christmas presents from the Duchess
this year to Angelhurst.

The Duchess had never sent presents to Angelhurst, but Lady
Gratton did not inform her friends about that lady's deficiencies—
family was family, after all.

The Duchess was so vexed, and there have been rumours
floating down to us that your niece is growing up just like
Griselda—I really think Fanny would do you an injury if she
could. So take care—keep your little beauty hidden away
until the time is ripe. Mrs M——, who is not very reliable, has
told me that the Duchess grumbles to her about expenses,
that Angelhurst is a drain on the ducal pocket, and hinted
that perhaps with her cousin married, Griselda's daughter
might make herself useful in the home of the future countess.
But Mrs M—— can be malicious—I would not worry about
that if I were you. Have you seen the new fashions in your
Somerset fastness? Bosoms are cut lower than ever—we will
soon look like Princess Caroline. I understand she calls her
costume 'à la grecque' and bares her bosom entirely—and
it is not the most *attractive* bosom about. Poor Prinny—one
really cannot blame him there, in spite of all the fuss.

The letter went on with more gossip, but the sheets fell into
Lady Gratton's lap unheeded. She felt disturbed, very disturbed.
She knew the Duchess better than her friend, and the jokes that
had seemed so funny to Mrs Farthingale were serious matters for

Angelhurst. The unkindness of Beau Brummel, the foolishness of the Prince, could have done much damage to Damaris's future.

Damaris worked on carefully, watching her design, unaware of the darkening of her aunt's expression. As soon as there was something amusing to be told, Lady Gratton would tell her, she knew—unless it was not fit for a young person's ears. Lady Gratton might have been her only companion, but as far as wit and general chattiness went, she was a satisfying one. And if her aunt had not shown much affection to her as a child—for Lady Gratton was simply not the kind of woman to be fond of children—Damaris was not conscious of any lack. She knew no other way of life than the one they shared.

Lady Gratton, with her sense of foreboding growing stronger, ignored the rest of her friends' letters and took up the one from the Duke's agent, ripping it open more quickly than her usual deliberate manner would allow.

The letter was not long and stated simply:

> Dear Madam: His Grace the Duke requests you be informed that due to increasing family expenses at this time, it has been found necessary to dispose of the Angelhurst estate. Arrangements are going forward, and His Grace requires possession by the first of the year. Regarding Miss Damaris St Cloud, His Grace realizes that it may not be convenient for you to continue to provide a household for her. The forthcoming marriage of Lady Honor and Lord Devereaux was announced today in the *Gazette* and will take place in early December. Lady Honor, at His Grace's request, is willing to take Miss St Cloud into her new establishment. His Grace tenders his thanks for your excellent stewardship of his property and your care for his niece. . . .

The last few polite words, made up, Lady Gratton was certain, by Crawford and not the Duke, soon faded from her attention as the matter of the letter occupied all her mind.

Some sound must have escaped her lips, because Damaris looked up.

'What is it, Aunt?'

'Only a letter about your cousin Honor's wedding.'

'Are we invited?' Damaris's eyes were wide with hope.

'What nonsense!' Lady Gratton said coldly. She had decided not to tell Damaris as yet. The full autumn season was before her—

she must think of something. There was no use making the child unhappy before it was needful. But there was no point in her having false expectations either.

'Have I not told you, Damaris, over and over, not to expect any notice from the Duchess? She has four daughters of her own, and three still to marry. Certainly she will not want any more girls about the place. And she was hardly a friend to your mother. These things must be accepted with dignity and never, do you understand, be discussed outside the family.'

Her aunt was so stern for no reason, Damaris thought with a rare flash of rebellion, that she was almost tempted to answer. After all, there was no one she *could* discuss anything with, unless it was her maid Betty. And even a child knew, she thought scornfully, that one does not complain about one's family to a servant. But she saw that her aunt was upset, and her anger subsided.

They went in to dinner as though nothing had happened. The next morning Lady Gratton wrote to the agent and said that his instructions would be carried out. She said nothing about her niece, and when these matters were reported to the Duchess that lady was satisfied.

CHAPTER

3

For the next few days Damaris went about her usual occupations. Her aunt kept her hard at study; for exercise she walked with her aunt in the shrubbery and along the paved walks of the park, and on fine mornings she rode out on her old pony in the company of the man who served as groom to the ladies but also worked on the farm.

Her rides were the most exciting part of Damaris's day, because she did see some people—the labourers who worked in the fields. Already they were picking apples in the orchards; not just the men, but women too were helping, and the children running about. Damaris recognized some of the young people with whom she had played years before. She still remembered the times when she had escaped from the house to run in and out of the cottages and sit down with the other children to great dishes of cake and clotted cream with all the fruits of summer. Only one of them was still close to her, her maid Betty.

Damaris's young eyes were sharp, and she watched how the young men and women lingered together, losing themselves among the trees. One morning she saw Betty herself with her arm about Jem the cowman. That night, when Betty was getting her ready for bed, she couldn't resist teasing her a little.

'So you are courting with Jem the cowman, Betty,' she said as Betty's strong young hands were brushing her hair.

'Now, why do 'ee say that, ma'am?' Betty blushed and bent her head downward so that her young mistress would not see her blushes reflected in the looking-glass. 'T'ain't true.'

'It looked as though it was true when I rode past the three-acre this morning. The road is high by Danewich corner; when I looked down I saw you two in the trees.'

'Picking apples, we were,' Betty said stoutly. 'The crop's so big Mr Tinkerty needs all the help he can get.'

Damaris giggled. The steward, Tinkerty, was not allowed to call on the female servants of the house for help. She wondered how Betty had slipped away—the younger servants were not allowed to 'gad,' but they managed now and then. Betty laughed too, but unwillingly.

'Now, don't you be saying anything to her ladyship,' she urged, 'or I'll be losing my good place. And there won't be any banns read for Jem and me, after all.'

Suddenly, a tear trembled on Betty's pale eyelashes. Damaris felt abashed. She was sorry she had spoken. A little love-making among the young people from the village was not condemned severely. The banns were read, the marriage took place, and if sometimes the young wife gave birth at seven months, the gossips enjoyed themselves, but people were charitable. It was natural enough.

'It is all very well for such people,' Lady Gratton had explained long ago. 'The common people can marry as they please, just as nature's fancy takes them—as with the animals of the fields. But you will notice, Damaris, that with *valuable* animals matters are not left to chance. Horses, beef stock, dairy herds, and even pigs are bred most carefully. Your little cat and my pug have long pedigrees. People of rank must have matters properly arranged also.'

Damaris had thought with a sigh that it seemed altogether more desirable to be a field animal or a village girl, but she had been brought up to know her place and had not demurred. Now she saw that even for village girls there could be problems.

The stout Betty was pouring out her troubles in the intervals of hearty sobs. 'Jem and me, we always had a fancy for each other. And my mother's been asking when is the banns to be read, and she spoke up last Sunday to Vicar. And Jem, he said nought to me, but he tell Vicar he be courtin' with a widow over by Baldicott Lake. She do have her own cottage and four acres freehold land. And she do have no children, and she has gold put by. Jem said it be his mother and father do want him to marry the widow, but I can see his eyes big for that land and gold. So don't you be losing me my place, Miss Damaris,' Betty urged, sniffing. 'I don't think I'll ever take a fancy to another man. I shall be in service all my days.'

She brushed the tears away from her cheeks with a quick rub of her wrist. Damaris assured her warmly that she would always keep her place at Angelhurst.

'I hope it be so,' Betty said, brightening, and then her face was shadowed again. 'Yet they do say—I heerd from Mrs Beeson, who had it from Mr Tinkerty himself, that there be talk of His Grace selling Angelhurst and a lot of foreigners coming here among us. And if the new master should enclose common, Lord, what will become of the village?' Betty said, and cried again.

Damaris assured her that she knew nothing of these dreadful tales, but next morning at breakfast she asked her aunt directly. It was another lovely day, with the sun flooding the small parlour where the ladies took their breakfast. The air was full of the scent of roses; two fat, lazy robins sat on the window-sill looking for crumbs. It seemed impossible that the normal order of things could be changed, yet Betty's fears needed to be put to rest. But when Damaris posed the question, her aunt did not reply immediately.

'Your Betty has been disappointed by Jem the cowman, I hear,' she said.

'Yes.' Since her aunt knew, Damaris was not betraying a confidence. 'That is why she is anxious—'

'I hope that is the only reason she is anxious,' Lady Gratton said dryly. 'Even in her station in life, a young woman must be careful of herself and know the man she means to marry. It is just as I was afraid it would be, with the village people running after that Methodist that came round preaching in the spring. People flocking from different parts of the county; restlessness and disturbance. That's where the cowman met his widow, and now you see the result.'

'I am sure you are right, Aunt,' Damaris said, knowing Lady Gratton's dislike of the Methodists, 'but can I tell Betty that her place is safe?'

Her aunt gave her a long, measuring look.

'I am afraid, to a great extent, that will depend on you.'

'On me, Aunt?' Damaris did not attempt to hide her surprise.

'The time has come,' Lady Gratton said deliberately, 'when you are to begin taking up your responsibilities.'

Damaris noticed that Lady Gratton's eyes were dark-circled. She had not been sleeping. The girl was struck by a chill, but she was silent, waiting.

Her aunt had been considering how much to tell Damaris so that she would understand the seriousness of her position and act as Lady Gratton thought best without being frightened into a dejection that could ruin the plan. For Lady Gratton had formed a plan.

Several wakeful nights had pushed her to a desperate gamble. At first, she had looked coolly over all the possible alternatives. Her preference was to return to Town. There she could lodge with an old friend at comparatively little expense, but she could hardly afford to support Damaris; and even if she did, living so obscurely without means to enter Society, the girl would be entirely thrown away. And once Lady Gratton died, her jointure, of course, reverted to the Gratton estate.

She could stay in the country, dismiss all the servants except Betty, who could stay on as maid-of-all-work if she wasn't pregnant, and live in a cottage in a style lower than that of a moderately successful farmer. She herself would be miserable, and Damaris would be equally thrown away, her only opportunity for marriage a farmer or a minor clergyman.

Then there was the Duke's offer. If he had consented to take Damaris into his own house, Lady Gratton might, reluctantly, have considered the matter. Damaris could meet some eligible men at Camberly; she would have the protection of her uncle, the Duke. Even so, with the Duchess's jealousy it was more likely that Damaris would be kept in the background, an unpaid drudge to the family. But what he had actually proposed was far worse. It was, of course, the Duchess's idea and not his own that Damaris should live with the Devereauxs. Lady Gratton thought, in near despair in the small hours of the morning, that the Duchess must indeed be vicious, then tried to tell herself in the light of day that the woman was perhaps uncommonly stupid.

Damaris, as an unwanted, unprotected poor relation in her cousin's house, would be in a dangerous situation indeed. Lady Honor had neither the age nor the sense to be a suitable chaperon for such a beauty; nor, brought up by her mother, would she be likely to care very much about the charge. Damaris would not be safe from her own brother-in-law: Devereaux was a rake; he would never be able to resist the charms of such an innocent young beauty under his roof. Obviously, there was no one to step forward if the girl was ruined; the future Lady Devereaux would merely turn her out of doors.

Lady Gratton shuddered. Such a thing must never be. She had only a few weeks in which to work; her niece was really too young to be brought out, but all niceties would have to go by the board. Already her plans were set in motion. She was going to do what she had never done; she was going into debt—and heavily. If she failed in her endeavours, she would give up a good part of her future income: she had signed papers that could make her a pauper. She smiled to herself grimly—it was Griselda who had been considered the reckless Miss Mayne. It seemed the gambling fever was in her blood also.

But as she looked at the girl before her, whose eyes were dark with adult concern in that young face, Lady Gratton knew that she could not turn her over to a clod or a Devereaux. The chance would have to be taken.

'I have written to Bath for lodgings for six weeks this autumn,' she said. 'We will have to see about your clothes straight away.'

Damaris's lips were parted in wonder.

'You will come out there instead of in London,' Lady Gratton went on unemotionally, 'and before the Season is over, it is necessary that you will have found a husband. I hope that that is quite clear.'

Despite the heavy responsibility that had been put upon her, Damaris couldn't help being delighted with Bath. For the first time she was surrounded by all the delights of a town: shops, concert halls, the play, the Upper and Lower Rooms—and people, people, and more people. It was sheer delight just to look out of the window of their exclusive lodgings in Milsom Street and see the carriages go by—even the carts and drays. She loved to hear the cries of the newsmen, muffin men, and milkmen and on rainy days to hear the clink of the ladies' pattens.

Lady Gratton had always enjoyed Bath, but this year her pleasure was overlaid by much anxiety. In some ways, their visit had done all she had hoped: Damaris was certainly the beauty of the season. When they had first arrived, she had put the girl in the hands of a clever dress-maker recommended by Mrs Farthingale, a wizened old Frenchwoman who had once made gowns for the ladies of the French court.

Lady Gratton had made no bones about their condition to this worldly-wise dame.

'The girl must make her mark at once—it will be her only Season. She should seem a little older than she is, and she must stand out.'

The two women had regarded Damaris as dispassionately, she thought with wry mirth, as Mr Tinkerty regarded the cattle to be shown at the Agricultural Show.

'*Belle* she is, *par exemple*,' the old woman muttered, 'but she must be *distinguée*.'

'Damaris has distinction,' her aunt said.

'It is not the same.' The dress-maker shook her head. 'You must realize—so many young ladies in Bath, so much sprigged white muslin in the ball-rooms—we must do something else!'

For once Lady Gratton looked uncertain.

'Not wear white? A young girl? Madame Mathilde—'

'*Les beaux yeux,*' Madame went on, not heeding. 'Such a blue I have not seen. Not the cold light blue I see all round me.'

'It is the colour of a flower called the periwinkle,' Lady Gratton said, smiling faintly. 'It grows wild in these parts. One little flower alone on a stem.'

I have become countrified in my years at Angelhurst, she thought with some annoyance. Lady Gratton in her days in Town would not have babbled of botany.

But Madame Mathilde had pursed her lips and looked satisfied.

'That is what we wish. One flower alone on a stem—I will find you silk of this colour; do not ask me where and how. And everything Mademoiselle wears, it will be blue or trimmed with blue—we will bring her forward,' she explained. 'She will be noticed.'

Lady Gratton looked worried.

'But a lady must not be—too noticeable. My niece is not an opera dancer.'

Madame smiled.

'Trust me. I have dressed the greatest *femmes du monde* the world has known—perhaps will ever know.' She sighed for glories past. 'This *sacré Empereur*—he told the court ladies to cover their bosoms. The man is a peasant at heart. I will make Mademoiselle *distinguée, élégante* to catch the eye, but with such discretion! Not the most fierce papa, the most jealous husband, could object.'

Nervous, but with a sense of reckless necessity, Lady Gratton consented and gave orders for a wardrobe that caused Bath to open its eyes and meant certain ruin for her if her plan should fail. 'The beautiful lady in blue' became the focus of attention in the town. As she was niece not only to the baronet's widow but also to the Duke of Camberly—a fact that Lady Gratton made sure was known everywhere—the attention was very respectful. As Damaris was driven through the streets in a smart, if hired, barouche, wearing her blue promenade dress, the shopkeepers came to their doors to gaze.

Men had crowded about her in the Upper and Lower Rooms; she had had dancing partners to spare. The two ladies had been invited to more dinners and evening parties than they could possibly attend. Yet Lay Gratton was not satisfied. She had done all she could, but fate was against her, she thought. For though Damaris had been all the success that she hoped, the gentlemen at

Bath suitably impressed—yet there simply had not been *enough* gentlemen of rank in the town.

Bath was not what it had been, Lady Gratton believed. The Prince did not favour it—Society, the *bon ton,* spent their time elsewhere. London and Brighton were now the playgrounds of the fashionable. Bath was becoming the resort of the dowdy. Families that could no longer afford to live in Town could be important there at less expense. Too many invalids were taking the waters. Such was the excitement Damaris had stirred that she might have married anyone—as long as he was *there.*

One morning towards the end of their stay, Lady Gratton stared out of the window through a light rain. The same *chink, chink* of ladies' wood and metal overshoes that pleased Damaris irritated her aunt; the wet weather had kept many travellers from coming to the West Country that season. She had been scanning the newspapers for the new arrivals for days, but no young men of fortune had appeared and the season for Bath would soon be over.

She and Damaris had been invited to a luncheon at a house set in some pretty gardens not far outside Bath. The hostess, Lady Herter, was a woman of some importance in the fashionable world, and the invitation had been accepted; but now the worry was too sharp in Lady Gratton's mind, and she could not face the talk and gossip. She had sent her excuses and let young Mr Ruthven take Damaris, in the company of her maid Betty, of course, and instructed him to bring her back as soon as luncheon was over. She did not want Damaris lingering in wet gardens and catching a cold—nor did she wish her to linger with Mr Ruthven.

Mr Ruthven was obviously in love and would no doubt make his offer before they left, but Lady Gratton was not eager to accept. He was an unexceptional young man, attractive enough in his person, but although his family was quite good, he was a younger son. Lady Gratton was not fond of younger sons. He was intended for the church and was to be ordained in preparation for a suitable living becoming vacant. The match would be better than none—and certainly better than the Devereaux house!—but how that young man could pay off the debts she had incurred Lady Gratton could not imagine. And Damaris as the wife of an obscure if well-connected parson would be very much thrown away.

Two men had already offered for her niece, and neither of them had been as yet refused. There was Mr Barnaby, a widower, a man of substantial means. But his money had been made in the

City. He *was* a gentleman, though no one in particular, greying and balding, his appearance neither striking nor prepossessing. It was again better than no match at all, but the woman who had been the proud Miss Mayne thought Mr Barnaby very forward to aspire to the hand of her niece. Certainly he would not have done so, she reflected, but for the news of her fortune and prospects which had followed them to Bath. Word had gone about quickly that the 'beautiful lady in blue' had not a penny of her own and that her uncle, the Duke, would do nothing for her—that in fact the Camberly family was estranged from this youngest branch of the St Clouds.

Mr Barnaby knew all this, for he had told her so quite plainly when he made his offer—certainly with no encouragement from her niece. Mr Barnaby must have known that he could not attract so young a girl, and Lady Gratton privately thought his eagerness for the match rather disgusting. But she received him politely and sent him to wait with the words 'of course, the family must be consulted.'

Sir Alastair Cripp, on the other hand, was of fine old family and not more than thirty-five. He had a place of his own in Yorkshire —heavily mortgaged. He had inherited a good fortune, but most of it was frittered away in gambling and on women. There was little he had now to offer her niece—in fact such a marriage for him was absurd. He needed a woman of fortune to put him to rights. But he spoke wildly to Lady Gratton of his passion and said that the love of this pure young girl would cause him to make a complete reform. Lady Gratton reflected that it was too late for this medicine to do the patient much good; and besides, though she might command her niece to marry Sir Alastair, she could hardly command her love. Sir Alastair was a weakling and looked it, with moist eyes and drooping lips—the thought of those two living in all the seclusion of straitened means on the Yorkshire moors brought no relief to her worried mind.

The more she considered Sir Alastair and Mr Barnaby, the more eligible young Ruthven seemed. Yet she had doubts there. Some new acquaintance had told her recently that Ruthven had been on the point of an engagement when he came to Bath, an engagement very much wished for by his family with a young woman of birth and fortune. Damaris would not be welcome even in the poor life that awaited her there—and then, suppose the young man's proposals were accepted and later his family persuaded him to break off the match? It had happened before when a girl had so little protection.

The carriage drew up at the door, and Ruthven helped Damaris down. By the expression on his face, no diminution of his love had as yet occurred. He brought Damaris up to her aunt and, after bowing to her, spoke to Lady Gratton.

'Miss St Cloud will no doubt wish to tell you some family news. May I have the honour of calling on you this evening? I would like to see you for a private word, if I may?'

She bowed her head graciously. 'We will expect you.'

'I have a dinner engagement, but I can be here before ten.'

She smiled. They all knew what his mission would be. Damaris did not look unhappy. He certainly was the best of the three suitors but . . . Lady Gratton determined to think about it later. Her niece was all agog with something she had to say. Instead of going to her room with the patiently waiting Betty, she took her bonnet off in the drawing-room, giving it to the maid.

'You will never guess, Aunt, who was at Lady Herter's.'

'I don't suppose I shall,' Lady Gratton said caustically. 'Perhaps you will inform me.'

'I think Lady Herter is a little cross with you—we were two ladies short because an extra man arrived. He is a connection of hers—I wonder if you knew?'

Lady Gratton regarded her niece. It was not like Damaris to be such a rattle. Her colour was a little higher than usual—something out of the way had occurred. A suspicion crossed her mind—had Ruthven been making love to her? Certainly not in front of Betty, her common sense told her.

'Who, Damaris?'

'Lord Devereaux. My cousin's future husband. Lady Herter was telling us before he arrived that his father is gouty and Lord Devereaux was coming down to make arrangements for his reception. Not, she said, that Lord Devereaux is usually so dutiful, but he hopes for an increased allowance from his father on his marriage, to match the fine fortune that my cousin will bring.'

'A most improper conversation for such a company,' Lady Gratton said. 'Such matters should only be spoken of in the family circle. And I am sure that Lady Herter can hardly know what goes on in Lord Devereaux's mind.'

'Of course, Aunt, it was improper. But I don't think that Lord Devereaux is a—a pleasant man.'

It was the nearest she had ever come to gainsaying her aunt, and Lady Gratton was surprised.

'I have never met Lord Devereaux and only know him by repute,' she said. 'What sort of man is he?'

Damaris hesitated.

'He is well looking enough—very fashionably dressed and not unhandsome. But he is very bold in his speech and—and unkind.'

'Why, what did he say?'

'When we were introduced—we were already at the table—he realized who I was and stared and said, as if I weren't there at all, "Damme, who would think it? The chit is not sixteen." '

Lady Gratton did not curse, even in the privacy of her own mind, but if she did, in the first flush of annoyance she would have damned Devereaux. She had been at pains, without actually lying, to give the impression that Damaris was at least seventeen—prospective suitors should avoid the opprobrium of courting a schoolroom miss. But on second thought she decided that no harm had been done. No new suitors would arrive. By the week's end she and Damaris must return to Angelhurst. The three present suitors would not be so easily put off; they were too far gone for that.

'And he went on,' Damaris said, her colour deepening. 'He said I was a fine girl for my age and he kept staring at my—my figure.'

Her hand went to her bosom and she looked abashed. So like a man of Devereaux's type to make a young girl self-conscious. Of course, Damaris could not know that to see her blush was a pleasure to such a jaded and determined rake. And her dress of heavy blue silk had been cut to emphasize her splendid figure.

'Hold yourself up, miss,' Lady Gratton said sharply. 'The impudence of a gentleman should never make a lady careless of her deportment.'

'I don't think Lord Devereaux is a gentleman,' Damaris said with some heat. 'All through the luncheon he was whispering to Lady Herter, and they were looking at me and smiling, and Lady Herter laughed. And as soon as luncheon was over, Lady Herter began to talk to Mr Ruthven, flirting with him, Aunt, and she took him off to the back drawing-room to show him the view of Castle Rise. And when the other guests went to the gardens through the covered walk, Lord Devereaux asked if he could escort me.'

'So what did you do, child?' Lady Gratton looked at her niece keenly.

'I went after Lady Herter to the drawing-room and made my apologies and said that I must leave. And Mr Ruthven said that he must bring me home, although she asked him to stay most particularly.'

Lady Gratton smiled grimly. Her niece was not a fool. Deportment she had taught the girl, but her brains were her own. Frowning, she collected what she knew of Lady Herter. She would not be the first aging beauty to keep herself surrounded with men by acting as pander. Yet her reputation was high in her own neighbourhood. Devereaux must be a special favourite. At all costs, Lady Gratton felt, Damaris must be kept from his house. Even Sir Alastair or Mr Barnaby was better than that. From what Damaris had so graphically described, Devereaux had been ready to make love to the girl while she was still under her aunt's protection.

Young Ruthven was coming tonight. What should she say? No one seeing the upright Lady Gratton could have guessed the frightening whirl of thoughts in her head. But she was a woman to handle each problem that came in its turn. Betty, the stolid, freckle-faced maid, stood waiting to accompany Damaris to her room. Betty had always been plump, but it occurred to Lady Gratton that she had put on weight since they had come to Bath—a good deal of weight. She glanced at her waistline, disguised by a dress hanging full, and sighed.

'I will speak to you, Betty, as soon as you have finished with Miss Damaris.'

Betty stared at her, put her hands to her belly, burst into tears, and ran from the room.

'What is all that?' Damaris stared after her.

'Nothing,' Lady Gratton said firmly. 'Nothing that need trouble you now, at any rate. Look, Damaris, the shower has stopped. I can see the sun coming out. Put on your hat and let us go for a walk. I have not had a breath of air all day.'

She did not add that if she stayed indoors any more she felt she would go mad. Betty would have to be sent back to her family, who most certainly wouldn't want her. Damaris would be upset—and she should not be upset just now. There were too many things to be decided. Lady Gratton determined to ask the girl her preference. That alone would not decide her, but it would help in making the decision. Almost certainly, Damaris preferred the young, attractive Mr Ruthven. Yet that match seemed such a poor, uncertain thing. And the girl was not in love, that was obvious. Lady

Gratton thought little of love; still, she supposed it might be some consolation for a life without the pleasure of society—for a time, anyway.

They walked through the pretty streets with the sun quickly drying up the pavements. All the consequent bustle and noise raised the spirits of the aunt and soothed the agitation of the niece. They looked longingly in the windows of the shops, but they knew their shopping days were over.

'Do look at that turban, Aunt,' Damaris said at a milliner's window. 'Is it not the most cunning thing?'

'Much too old for you, child,' Lady Gratton said. 'Besides, it is a fashion I dislike.'

It was still very pretty, Damaris thought in silence. Two young ladies walked inside the shop, and one of them tried on the very turban she had admired. Yes, she was buying it, the beautiful blue turban that seemed almost Damaris's own property. And the young lady was sallow and much too plump to wear it.

She was reminded of her buxom Betty, and her distress.

'Are you going to scold Betty, Aunt? She did all you bade her, but of course, she could not stay with me in Lady Herter's dining-room. Naturally, she was sent below.'

'She is not to be scolded,' Lady Gratton said. 'However, we must think of future plans now that we are leaving Bath. But we can talk of that later.'

Damaris looked as though she wanted to speak then, so Lady Gratton hurried her along. 'Look at this window, Damaris.'

The next building had a shop front like the others, but the only exhibit in the window was a portrait, already framed, with a small label indicating that the portrait was sold.

'Lady Elizabeth Harkaway,' Lady Gratton said. 'Painted before her wedding. I am surprised that the Harkaways allow it to be exhibited in this fashion—but then, Mansart is such a success he can do as he pleases.'

While the ladies were looking and admiring, the painter himself appeared. The paint-spattered smock he wore proclaimed his occupation; otherwise the thin man with his grey hair brushed back modishly had an elegance equal to that of any gentleman they had met in Bath. But he cheerfully addressed the ladies, unknown to him, as a gentleman would not, commenting on the sudden brightness of the day.

'Now I have the light to work, I would rather, like yourselves, stroll about the streets. At least, I stand here and take the air—unless'—Damaris had turned from the window, and he saw her full face—'I am to have the pleasure . . . ?'

Lady Gratton shook her head decisively.

'No, I am afraid we are merely admiring your work. We have not come to commission a portrait.'

The painter looked disappointed. He put on a pair of spectacles and peered at Damaris closely.

'What a pity! What a pity! I would really like to paint *this* young lady.'

'Perhaps later on.' Lady Gratton was gracious. 'But now I am afraid we are taking up your time.'

The painter, still staring, did not seem to hear her.

'Now would be the moment,' he said softly, 'before the dew has dried.'

Lady Gratton prepared to walk on.

'Just a minute,' the painter said. In his eagerness he caught Lady Gratton's arm, to the interest of two ladies in an open carriage driving by.

'The young lady is Miss St Cloud. I have heard of her—the lovely lady in blue. You must be Lady Gratton.'

Lady Gratton nodded, stiff at the man's familiarity.

'Lady Gratton,' he said persuasively, 'allow me to paint the young lady. You need not buy the portrait. I will take it with me to London.'

'We must refuse your kind offer,' Lady Gratton said. 'Miss St Cloud's family would never allow her portrait to be displayed like this.' She indicated the unfortunate Lady Elizabeth Harkaway in the window. 'And certainly it could never be offered for public sale.'

A ray of sunlight, almost horizontal, broke through the cloud to illuminate the two ladies.

The painter gazed in fascination as Damaris's skin caught the light and her eyes sparkled. Under his intense gaze her colour rose, just a little, and she looked up, smiling.

'My lady!' he cried. 'I must do this portrait, on any terms you wish. I will take it to my atelier, and it will never be shown except by your express permission, and it will be offered for sale only to the husband of Miss St Cloud upon her marriage.'

Lady Gratton could find no further objection. A portrait by Mansart was very fashionable. The painter was successful and rich enough to choose his clients, and to be his choice was a mark of approval equivalent to a compliment from the Beau.

She explained to the painter that they were leaving Bath at the end of the week, so there could be few sittings.

'It does not matter—I will put everything else aside! With your permission, ladies, we can begin now. The dress of Miss St Cloud is perfect. She will remove only her hat.'

He led the curious ladies upstairs as he talked, and before Lady Gratton could raise more difficulties, he had Damaris seated in a chair before his easel and was already sketching with great deftness and speed. The room was full of novelty for aunt and niece. It comprised the whole floor at the top of the house; the walls and ceiling were mostly glass, and the place was suffused at the moment with golden afternoon light. The smells of paint and turpentine were pungent but not disagreeable.

Mr Mansart had considerable address. As he worked he charmed Lady Gratton by relaying all the gossip of Bath, London, and Brighton—he was a better informant than even Mrs Farthingale—and he told her such tales of the Prince as he could before a young lady, with looks to show he could tell much more, which made Lady Gratton resolve to see him privately before she left Bath.

So well amused was she that by the time a young boy brought up refreshments, Lady Gratton was most agreeably soothed and for a time cast aside all her troubles with money, her niece's suitors, the wicked Duchess, and even the pregnant maid. The chance meeting with the painter seemed to be a happy one. What difference it could possibly make in their fortunes she did not know, yet somehow she felt it was lucky.

She sipped her wine, ate the very delicious little cakes that Mansart had provided, and admired the sketch. In such a short time, he had caught Damaris's very look—delicate, innocent, yet with an eagerness behind the modesty in her eyes. Lady Gratton sighed and expanded a little in the warm, bright room. Perhaps, after all, there would be a miracle. Perhaps everything would, somehow, come right.

CHAPTER

5

It was as well that Lady Gratton had found cheer, briefly, in the painting of the portrait. Soon after, she regretted her consent to Damaris's sittings; they took so much of the final week of their stay, and she felt that the time could have been better employed. But how? she fretted. Except for Devereaux, who had had the impudence to call twice, asking to see his young 'cousin,' there had been no new arrivals of gentlemen of quality.

Mr Ruthven had appeared to ask formally for Damaris's hand. Alone in the small parlour of their first-floor rooms, Lady Gratton frowned, sighed, and paced about—her pacing afforded little relief, as she had to be careful not to bump into the profusion of chairs, tables, and bibelots. There was no comfort in life at all, she thought bitterly, without money—and a good deal of it.

She had almost settled in her mind on accepting Ruthven's offer —if he had been prepared to marry straight away. He was a good, honest, trustworthy young man: she had been ready to tell him the truth; between them something could have been fashioned to take care of the crushing debt. Though *that* would have been much better handled by Mr Barnaby. The City man had quickly found out her predicament and had bluntly offered to pay. But he seemed so gross for her Damaris—she could not bear the way he looked at the girl. Like Sir Alastair, he seemed indecently eager.

But Mr Ruthven, unfortunately— She scowled. Devereaux seemed to have ruined that chance. Young Ruthven was not only intended for the church, he was apparently well suited to it: a model of propriety. When asking for Damaris's hand he had referred to the incident at lunch.

'I had no idea,' he said gravely, 'when I planned to make my proposal that Miss St Cloud was not yet sixteen.'

He paused, and the rest of his thought was politely unspoken: why had Lady Gratton brought out a girl who still belonged in the schoolroom? Neither Mr Barnaby nor Sir Alastair would have cared about it, she thought bitterly—quite the reverse.

'There were family reasons,' she said calmly, 'for Miss St Cloud to be brought out early. She has the form and sense of a woman.'

'Of course,' Ruthven replied courteously. 'And perhaps in the circumstances, it will work out for the best. I will be ordained in three months, but it is unlikely that the living on which I have set my hopes will fall vacant that soon. The present incumbent is ill, very ill, and will not recover, but the illness is of a lingering kind. If Miss St Cloud and her family accept my offer, we could set the wedding date in a year's time or, say, after her seventeenth birthday, when almost certainly the living will be in my possession.'

Lady Gratton had regarded him in despair. She and Damaris had hardly two months' tenancy left at Angelhurst. But she decided against telling Ruthven the truth. He was so very proper and parsonical. If a man of his age was satisfied to wait over a year for his wife . . . ! And if she persuaded him against his judgement one way, who was to say that later his family could not persuade him in another?

She had sent him off with the same words she had given the other two suitors. It looked as though it must be Sir Alastair or Mr Barnaby. But the usually decisive Lady Gratton simply could not make up her mind. They were to leave the day after next, their trunks were being packed, and still she was undecided. Damaris, aware of the situation, looked gravely at her aunt, but Lady Gratton did not speak. Damaris was a good girl; she trusted her aunt, and because of that trust Lady Gratton found it impossible to act.

One bit of fortune came her way. While Damaris was having the last sitting for her portrait, accompanied by Betty—to whom Lady Gratton still had not spoken, since there was obviously no urgency in the situation—Lady Gratton took her afternoon walk to see the shops and was pleased to meet her suffering friend from Scotland, Mrs Crewe, now looking quite well and triumphant.

Her complaints had been successful, and her son had sent his mother on a visit to Bath for her health. The expense of the journey was dreadful, Mrs Crewe told her, but rooms were cheaper to come by now with the season almost over. She had quite a good set, though not on a fashionable street, and she took Lady Gratton to see them.

She was most grieved that her old friend was leaving the next day.

'For I find, Augusta, that there is no one I know in Bath these days. It is not what it used to be. And then, I am so remote up in

Scotland—I am quite out of everything. Pray, Augusta, do not let your lovely niece—yes, I have heard of her, she is all the talk of Bath—pray do not let her throw herself away in some dreadful remote country. It is the ruin of one's entire life. . . .'

She babbled on, just as Dorothea Lalingly had done so many years before. Lady Gratton smiled and listened, but the chief outcome of this meeting was that Mrs Crewe offered her friend the use of a small cubby-hole of a bedroom to stay and keep her company, at least for a week or two.

'I am afraid there is not room for the young lady, but perhaps after she leaves, you might care to stay, Augusta?'

For a few moments Lady Gratton tried to contrive how she could possibly fit Damaris into Mrs Crewe's rooms and life, hoping that something—anything—would happen, and that their choice would be less drastically small. But it could not be done. There was no money left. The carriage was given up. The weather was changing; if they stayed, her niece would need more clothes which could not be purchased. And there was little likelihood of any interesting new arrivals. Also, Devereaux was hanging about in a most unseemly fashion—yesterday he had waited for Damaris outside Mansart's studio in his new, shiny curricle and offered her a ride home. Fortunately, as the faithful Betty had reported, he was frozen and repelled by Damaris herself, and by Mansart, who always accompanied mistress and maid downstairs and on this occasion walked with them to the very door of their lodgings. Mansart, the painter, was a gentleman, Lady Gratton thought, which was more than she could say of certain noblemen.

She sent Damaris, subdued and anxious, back to Angelhurst in the care of Betty and one of the menservants from the estate whom she had summoned to act as escort. Damaris asked few questions, and Lady Gratton only told her that matters had to be gone into before her marriage could be arranged. Knowing that it must be Mr Barnaby or Sir Alastair, Lady Gratton tried to prepare her by explaining, thoroughly this time, their actual position. When the aunt unemotionally spoke of the home offered to Damaris by the future wife of Lord Devereaux, the girl looked up once with a long, steady look, and Lady Gratton knew that she would accept without a word whomever her aunt chose as husband. For some reason Lady Gratton remembered that in Roman Catholic countries girls of good family who could not make suitable marriages sometimes took the veil. It had always seemed to her a barbarous custom; now, for the first time, she almost wished it were the thing to do in England.

As soon as Damaris had left, the three suitors pressed Lady Gratton for a decision. She put them off from day to day, sheer weariness of mind preventing any action, and she claimed she had not as yet received letters from the Duke. Sir Alastair and Mr Ruthven offered to go and see the Duke themselves; Mr Barnaby, more shrewd and worldly, at least knew better.

Lady Gratton was not, after all, good company for her friend Mrs Crewe. She had no heart for the Rooms, the concerts, or shopping. She spent most of her day in the parlour of the rooms on the unfashionable street, looking out of the window, ostensibly trying to decide, actually letting her mind idle where it would.

On Mrs Crewe's insistence, one afternoon she walked by the milliner's and the shop that had housed Mansart's studio. The portrait of the offending Lady Elizabeth was no more to be seen; the shop front was shuttered.

'Oh, did you know?' Mrs Crewe said. 'Mr Mansart left last week, as soon as I arrived, naturally. I have come here only to be dull after all. Everything is over. Lady Herter told me last night that that was her last card party this season. She is closing her house and going to Town until Christmas. She cannot bear Somerset, she told me, once the leaves are off the trees and her gardens dun colour. I understand,' she whispered, not to sully the ears of a postilion who was riding by, pulling a handsome coach with arms on the panel that Lady Gratton felt she should recognize, 'that Lord Devereaux is leaving—her late husband's cousin, you know.'

Lady Gratton knew. She had heard all about the long standing *affaire de coeur* between Lady Herter and her husband's cousin from the invaluable, gossiping Mansart, in delicious, whispered intervals while Damaris changed into her blue gown behind a screen. The portrait was a masterpiece, and Lady Gratton had hated to leave it in the painter's hands. She supposed that Mr Barnaby would buy it if he married Damaris; Sir Alastair might not afford it—she did not know. The thought of money was depressing. Payment was due for the first of her bills, and she had no way of meeting it.

When the ladies went back to their rooms, the post had arrived. Lady Gratton saw the missive addressed to her in a small, crabbed hand and knew very well what it was. She turned it over and over, unable to open it—the reminder of her obligation. Slowly she walked to the writing-table. There was no use putting off her decision any longer; matters would not change. Miracles did not happen. She, Augusta Gratton, most practical of women, was being childish. She must write at once to Mr Barnaby or Sir Alastair. Both of them, like young Ruthven, were still in Bath, waiting for her word.

There was another reason why she must settle matters that night. Now she must return to Angelhurst. If Devereaux was leaving Bath, what was to prevent his stopping at Angelhurst on his way to Town? Nothing was beyond the evil nature of the man. Alice Garden, Lady Herter, his other mistresses—these were not enough, it seemed, but he must wish to ruin her niece, cousin to his own future wife. He was a scoundrel and should be whipped. But neither Sir Alastair nor Mr Barnaby was likely to thrash the powerful Lord Devereaux. If Lady Gratton, pen in hand, her letter paper before her, preparing to write the all-important communication, had been a woman to cry, she would have done so. As it was, she felt an unaccustomed constriction of the throat and a sharp pricking in the back of her eyes.

Her friend saw nothing of this.

'Why, we are not so dull after all!' she exclaimed. 'Someone has called on you, my dear—and how exciting!'

The ladies, looking at the cards, stared at each other, Mrs Crewe curious, Lady Gratton puzzled. The cards had been left by the Earl of Malfrey. Now Lady Gratton remembered the coach that had passed them in the street. Of course she should have recognized the arms belonging to the Earls of Malfrey; the Heron family was one of the oldest in England, their title and ownership of their estates going back to time out of mind. And the present Earl was a great man in his own right; he had held government office and was consulted on affairs of state. Lord Malfrey had just been arriving: there was no announcement in the papers yet. He had called on her immediately at her undistinguished little lodging. But she had never met him and was not personally acquainted with his family.

Then she noticed the message on the card.

'I am sorry not to have found you at home. I will call later this evening on a matter of importance. Malfrey.'

The two ladies gazed at it, wondering. Then Lady Gratton

slowly, deliberately put her pen down. She did not know what was happening, how it could be, but all her instincts told her that her miracle had come.

CHAPTER

6

To Damaris at Angelhurst, the news of her splendid match did not seem miraculous at all. She had been waiting nervously for her aunt's return to learn what her future would be. Though she was not in love, she had hoped that her aunt's choice would be Mr Ruthven; at least he was young, pleasant, and not distasteful to her. She also believed he was a good man, if slightly priggish. As for her other two suitors, she was not confident of their goodness, and distasteful they certainly were.

When Lady Gratton arrived unexpectedly, having travelled post without thought of the expense, full of her news, excited in her contained way as Damaris had never seen her, the girl's first feeling at the announcement was one of dismay. She was not to marry Mr Ruthven, whom she had come to like, but a man, according to her aunt closer to fifty than forty, whom she had never seen.

'It is a great match, a great match!' Lady Gratton said ecstatically, beaming even at the unfortunate Betty, who brought her tea and whose condition was showing deplorably.

'You will be Countess of Malfrey! Malfrey House in Town, one of the finest and very private; Malfrey Abbey in Kent; Great Heron, the principal seat, a huge house on an immense estate. And one of the largest fortunes in England. You will be a great lady. Your cousin Honor's match is nothing to it.'

Seeing that her niece's enthusiasm did not match her own, she added, 'And it is very romantic. Just imagine how it came about, such a strange chance! That naughty Mansart,' she said indulgently. 'After all his promises, he couldn't resist showing the portrait to such a connoisseur as Lord Malfrey. And having seen it, he fell in love at once.'

'It would be more flattering,' Damaris said, sounding for once like her aunt, 'if he had fallen in love after seeing me.'

'He will, child, he will. We are not living fifty years ago; of course you are to meet. It is for you to accept Lord Malfrey's proposals or refuse them.'

The marriage agreements were being prepared, and Lady Gratton's debt had already been paid, but she saw no need to mention that yet. She was sure, with the matter presented to her sensibly, Damaris *would* accept, and gracefully. It was fortunate that the Earl was not only an impressive but also a well-looking man.

'Lord Malfrey will be here in a few days. He went to Town to see his man of business. He *was* going to the Duke, but I assured him that I am your legal guardian. We will have to ask the Duke and Duchess to the wedding,' she said coolly, 'but they will have no *extra* mark of respect. We thought of your being married from here, Damaris. Just a small family affair, and you will be in Town before Christmas.'

This arrangement seemed most suitable in every way. There would be little expense on Lady Gratton's part; the purchase of most of Damaris's trousseau could reasonably wait until she went to Town; and on the part of Lord Malfrey perhaps it was preferable, in the light of his bride's extreme youth, that the marriage become known to the polite world as a *fait accompli*. Meeting the poised young Countess, few people would think of her as a child from the schoolroom.

Lord Malfrey had been told the truth and had raised no objection. And even if he was of an age with Mr Barnaby, Lady Gratton did not find the Earl's eagerness for the match unseemly, though Lady Herter, hearing of the news goodness knew how, had delayed her journey to Town long enough to call on Lady Gratton and repeat some very unsavory gossip. Lady Gratton put little value on the opinion of a woman of birth who was content to share a lover with an actress. The baronet's widow was a woman of the world and would not have expected a man of Lord Malfrey's age and position, unmarried, to be free of all feminine association. He had caused no open scandal; for a gentleman that was enough. And any small irregularities in his conduct would doubtless be smoothed out by his marriage. It was a heaven-sent opportunity, and she rejoiced.

The meeting between the two contracting parties soon took place formally in Lady Gratton's drawing-room at Angelhurst. Lady Gratton had Damaris wear the blue gown of the portrait, and when the Earl was ushered in he saw the girl seated in the very pose. Lady Gratton smiled, sure that Damaris would be favourably impressed by Lord Malfrey's height, his commanding presence, his good figure, and his countenance, which would be thought handsome by many and certainly had nothing to disgust. But Damaris looked timid, though composed, and did not give Lord Malfrey the special, entrancing smile her aunt had hoped she would. Damaris said nothing, then or ever, but her first look at the Earl made her inwardly shiver—it was an enduring chill.

On Lord Malfrey's part, all was satisfaction. Damaris rose to greet him—he could not but admire, Lady Gratton felt, the girl's form and grace. And when she spoke, her low, quiet voice caused him to lean a little towards her, and despite his impassive features Lady Gratton could discern that he was caught by the girl's charm.

To Damaris, his expression was not altogether impassive. The conversation was about small things. Lord Malfrey remarked that the name of the estate was charming. Lady Gratton said it was believed that the name *Angel* came from the Romans, impressed with the blue-eyed maidens of the country, so different from the small, dark people further westward. The inevitable compliment was made. Then he admired the view. Lady Gratton took the opportunity to send them both to the window to inspect it further. As Lord Malfrey stood beside her, Damaris was aware that he gazed, not at the shrubbery and the park stretching off to the line of oaks, now brown and sadly faded, but at the lines of her neck and the rise of her bosom; and she caught a look in his eye no different from what she had seen in Mr Barnaby and Sir Alastair. But it was gone in a second, and his cold grey gaze, shielded by his drooping eyelids, was resumed before he turned back, with some polite phrase, to Lady Gratton.

He left for London in half an hour; he was required to make a speech in the House. Damaris found that as she had not blurted her refusal in his face, it was assumed she had accepted his offer. She made no demur that day but went to bed unaccountably depressed, and that night she woke from her sleep in a sweat, gripped by nightmare—vague, confused, but terrifying. Her cries brought Betty to her, and soon her aunt.

Betty herself was not looking at all well, her complexion green in the lamplight. For once her kind young mistress, now in a storm of tears, didn't notice her condition, but Lady Gratton certainly did. She sat on Damaris's bed, and when the girl sobbed that she could not marry the Earl, she stroked her head soothingly. Then she sent Betty to bring her a hot cordial and, practical as always, told Betty what to drink herself to steady her nausea.

When the cordial had been drunk and a fire lit in the hearth to provide cheer as well as warmth, Lady Gratton dismissed Betty, waited for Damaris to be settled, and then spoke to her frankly.

'And so the only possible choice came to Mr Barnaby,' she said. 'I was on the point of writing to him when Lord Malfrey arrived. You could hardly have wished for that. Now your duty to yourself, as well as to your family, is quite clear. And there are other considerations. There is this unfortunate girl. Not that I consider myself responsible for the loose behaviour of a country maid, but she was most grievously disappointed. Tinkerty has had a word with the cowman, but he is not to be moved. He is willing to lose his place if necessary to get the widow's land and gold. And the vicar cannot influence him, for Jem declares himself a Methodist. All this freedom for Dissenters,' she said, and shook her head. 'I knew what trouble it would lead to. In all events, I mentioned the matter to Lord Malfrey, and he said if you are attached to the girl you can keep her with you. She can go to Heron for her lying-in, and the child will be taken care of by one of the cottagers there. Lord Malfrey is used to a great household and all its hazards,' Lady Gratton added, 'and makes no large affair of it. You would have found it quite different with Mr Barnaby, or with that priggish young Mr Ruthven'—for although Damaris's future was settled, Lady Gratton still held a grudge against that cautious young man.

Damaris, her nerves calmed by the cordial, the warm room, firelight, and candlelight, forgot her nightmare. Her aunt's stroking of her head had been inexpressibly soothing. Lady Gratton, so cool, unemotional, and always formal, had hardly ever bestowed a caress upon her niece in all her life, other than the most perfunctory kiss sometimes, in greeting. Damaris had grown to young womanhood without knowing the loving touch of a hand. Now she felt comforted, almost happy, without knowing why. Her spirit expanded, and generously she wanted to help her maid, her aunt—

she would do what was so manifestly her duty, and she gave her consent.

For the short time that remained before her wedding, her aunt wisely kept Damaris busy with preparations: the ordering and fitting of the bridal gown and things needful for her honeymoon. Madame Mathilde, flushed with triumph, was brought to make the gown. From Heron Lord Malfrey sent a veil, some old and precious lace, together with a heavy rope of pearls with a clasp of sapphires that caused Madame and Lady Gratton to exclaim and made Damaris feel like an animal in a halter.

But she was too feminine not to enjoy the elegant bustle, the congratulations of all the people on the estate, and she shared Lady Gratton's rather vengeful pleasure in the very cross letter of acceptance from the Duchess—for even the Duchess of Camberly would not want to offend a man so great in the land as the Earl of Malfrey.

And if, in the late hours of the night, Damaris woke in some fear about her fate, she knew, with a calming if not exhilarating knowledge, that she must continue on the course set for her. The people she had known were few; her affections rested where they could. Betty's fate loomed large in her mistress's mind, and she was the only person who could help her.

Damaris did not share her aunt's aversion to the Methodists—most of the people about the farm had swarmed round the itinerant preacher when he came down to give a sermon in the open air on the common, though many of them still went to the village church. But Betty had told her dolefully that 'all the new preachin', it made folk mortal angry against sin. My father, he gave me a terrible beating and said he was fair shamed, and if it wasn't for my place up here at the house, it would go very bad. Old Vicar was never so hard on country girls,' she went on, sniffing. '"Suffer the little children,"' he said, and told the young men they should make things right in the eyes of the Lord. But that Methody preacher, he be away in foreign parts, and Jem do tell his widder woman that my child be none of his.' And she had cried until her face was red and swollen and her eyes looked drowned.

Before the ceremony, Lady Gratton, who had never believed in mincing words, explained to Damaris her duty as a wife, which was to bear a son to be the heir of Malfrey, and what her behaviour should be in all circumstances. Damaris, brought up on a farm, had shown no surprise. She was more familiar with the farm than her aunt suspected, for as a child she had become adept at slipping away from the house. The cowman had taught her to milk, and she had watched the women make the clotted cream for which the area was famous. She had seen the cider bottled, and she had scratched the backs of the young stock. With the other children, she had stood by the barn when Benjy, the prize bull, was taken out for service. And so Damaris had merely bent her head and said 'yes, Aunt' to everything, and if she had an inward chuckle, comparing the terrifying Earl whom she had seen in his gold-tasselled Hessian boots, his elegant coat and trousers, his stiff white cravat, with old Benjy, her aunt never knew it.

She went through the wedding as if in a dream. The Duke and Duchess had arrived at Angelhurst the night before, and if the Duchess was waspish, the Duke was unexpectedly genial. The Duke was not a bad man, though too easily led by his wife, and now was pleased that his brother's child was making not only a respectable but a brilliant match which reflected glory on Camberly. The earldom of Malfrey was far older than his own dukedom, and the earls had been great powers in the land while the St Clouds were private country squires. The Earl's prominence in the House of Lords added to his lustre, and the Duke smiled upon his niece who brought this good into the family without any money put down on her behalf—for the sum he was bound to pay over to Devereaux was a grief to him. Lord Malfrey himself stayed on the other side of Angelhurst village, with friends who had never called on Lady Gratton. The head of this family served as groomsman for the Earl, and the Duke gave his niece away.

The village church was small, and it was crowded with villagers come to shower good wishes on their own Miss St Cloud. Rumour had gone about that if the Duke sold Angelhurst, Lord Malfrey would buy it for his wife, and that they did not need to fear strangers coming among them. So the church was filled with happy faces, and Damaris, after the small wedding breakfast given at Angelhurst for the gentry, went out into the great barn where trestle tables had been put up for the usual feast for the servants and the village. The long boards were covered with beef, mutton, great pies, and the farm's own beer, and the merriment was loud. The health of the Earl and Countess was drunk heartily, and Damaris left the home of her girlhood with praise and good wishes ringing in her ears. Lady Gratton was pleased that the girl's wedding day was happy and that the sun shone on her.

7

The honeymoon was to be short, for the Earl was needed in London. It was to be spent at Great Heron, and there they went as soon as Damaris had changed her dress. Lady Gratton was closing the house at Angelhurst in preparation for her visit to her old friend Mrs Farthingale in Town, and she was to take Betty with her and leave her at Malfrey House to begin her new duties in the kitchen. Damaris, as Lady Malfrey, would have a new personal maid used to dressing a lady of fashion. And so Damaris arrived at Great Heron, a bride alone among strangers, except for the almost silent Earl.

The journey had been long and tiring. Lord Malfrey had taken to Somerset not only his grooms and outriders but also two female servants to attend his lady, and they had brought Damaris refreshment from the inns where they paused, but there had been no time to alight. It was dark when they came to Heron; the moon was mostly obscured by cloud, and Damaris could see little of the surrounding country. For the most part they seemed to be driving mile after mile through narrow paths between great trees.

She asked Lord Malfrey about this hesitantly, as he seemed little inclined for talk, and he replied that they were traversing the ancient Forest of Heron, once royal forest. Great Heron lay at its centre. She was glad when they came at last to the park gates. The gatehouse was lit up, and the tenants of Heron lined the way to the house, carrying lanterns to give her welcome.

Tired as she was, Damaris knew her duty and bowed and smiled. Great Heron itself was ablaze with light, and the household was assembled to greet the new mistress. The young bride made a good impression on the old servants, standing straight in her blue travel-gown, her head held high as though she had not had an exhausting day and half a night. Rumour had come that she was beautiful, and later the servants confirmed that the new Countess of Malfrey was one of the loveliest ladies in the country. She addressed them courteously in her low, sweet voice and

smiled on them. These were to be to her as Betty and the household had been at Angelhurst, and she wondered if there was anyone she would come to love as she had loved Betty. They did
seem elderly. She longed to bathe and change, but a supper had
been prepared by Lord Malfrey's order, and she was expected to
eat it; so she allowed herself to be taken to her room, which she
hardly had a moment to see, and merely refreshed herself slightly
before going down to face her husband at the table.

They ate in the small dining-parlour, where the table would
hold only a dozen people, she at one end, Lord Malfrey at the
other. In the candlelight the room looked gloomy, with dark por-
traits on the walls over black oak panels. Outside, the wind tapped
branches against the window-panes—Heron seemed almost swallowed up by its own great trees. The well-trained men served food
she didn't want. Damaris usually had a healthy appetite belying
her delicate looks, but that night she would gladly have settled for
a bowl of broth in her bedroom.

Instead she did as she was brought up to do and ate some of
her food and drank her wine and conversed politely with the Earl,
at least as long as the servants were in the room, for he was a man
hard to talk to, with his long silences and few remarks of his own.
Some questions about the estate and the history of the house,
which talk seemed to depress him, took them through the meal
and when the cloth was cleared and the port brought in Damaris
declined tea or coffee and went to her room.

There was a huge fire there, and her bath was already steaming
in front of it. She was thankful to be relieved of her clothes and
bathed by two old women as if she were a baby. As they put on
her night-gown of fine lawn and lace, she looked round curiously
at the heavy old oak furnishings—some of them looked as though
they had been there since Elizabeth's time. She had seen such
pieces stored in the coach house at Angelhurst, put away when the
house had been new-furnished.

Her room was always occupied by the Countess of Malfrey, the
servants told her. In the years when there was no countess, it
remained unused, though it had the best aspect of any room in
the house. She would see in the morning. There was a vista
through the great avenue, and on a clear day one could see for
miles—unlike most of the rooms, which were shaded by trees or
shut in by shrubbery.

'Not even Lady Cassandra, his lordship's sister, was ever allowed to use that room,' one of the old women said in a confidential tone; the other, even older, gave her a steely look, and she subsided.

Damaris felt sorry for the poor Lady Cassandra, who had not been allowed to enjoy the only pleasant aspect of the house. She was impressed by her noble if heavy surroundings, but not awed. The food and wine had done their work and she was feeling, though not happy, tolerably composed.

But nothing had prepared her for what was to come. From her husband's manner towards her, she had expected neither romance nor any pretence of love. In spite of Lady Gratton's words, she had already decided that he had married only for an heir, and that a healthy young woman of a ducal family had seemed to him a suitable mother. His liking her looks had caused him to offer, but no affection had come in train. On their journey he had seemed bored with her company and from time to time had studied papers with an official stamp.

When he came to her room shortly after she had retired, his manner was the same as it had been. He was not an ill-looking man—his form was strong and neither fat nor thin—but his coldness made him repulsive to his young bride. His brief passion, unwelcome and painful to her, at least brought no surprise after her aunt's careful teaching. Damaris, in whom an imp of humour lurked, thought disrespectfully that Benjy the farm bull had managed better—he looked more dignified and seemed to please the cows.

But almost before Lord Malfrey's passion was over, while his breath was still hot on her cheek and his heavy body still crushed her own, he pulled away with a start and she saw his face in the light of a single candle. Afterwards, she tried to tell herself that she had been mistaken, that the flickering light had been deceptive, that the moving shadows had played her false. But she soon learned that she was not mistaken, for the pattern was repeated every night she was visited by the Earl. Once their bodies parted, not only was his manner cold and distant as it had been before, but his face looked upon her with an aversion amounting to disgust.

Damaris was horrified and hurt, wondering what was wrong, longing for her aunt to confide in, then feeling she was too ashamed to speak. Gradually she became inured to the manner of their lives; in the day the Earl was coolly courteous, at night incomprehensible. But each night of her honeymoon, after the Earl had left her side, alone in her room in the Great House of Heron, Damaris would weep hopeless tears.

CHAPTER

8

When Lord Malfrey went to Town, he left his young bride at Heron. Damaris was surprised, as the plan had been for her to go to Town and be presented at the first Queen's Drawing-Room after her marriage. But Lord Malfrey decided that as the Christmas holiday was so near, Damaris might as well stay and get to know her new home.

If she was disappointed at not seeing London, she was also relieved at being free of her husband. With him gone her youthful spirits soon reasserted themselves, and she sprang from bed the first morning, eager to explore. The Great House of Heron, which had come to be called simply Great Heron, was very unlike Angelhurst. Instead of being small, light, and well proportioned, it was huge, rambling, grand, and gloomy. The housekeeper told her they could make up fifty beds—though she added that she could not herself remember having done so.

'The house hasn't been full since the old Countess died, my lady, and that was a long time ago. Not that she was old, either, poor woman, for she died when his lordship was born. After she was gone, his lordship's father had no fancy for people about the house. He spent most of his time in Town. But he kept on the old servants, and people thought a rare lot of him for that, for times were hard for the poor.'

'And what of Lady Cassandra? Did she entertain?' Damaris asked, remembering what she had heard of the Earl's sister. She wondered if Lady Cassandra was living; she had not come to the wedding, nor had her name been mentioned.

The housekeeper looked at her with the same expression that the elderly chambermaid had worn.

'Lady Cassandra has never had her health,' she murmured. 'Excuse me, my lady.' And she made to leave Damaris's room, where she had gone for instructions as to the day's meals.

'Just a moment, Mrs Crump.'

The sun was shining; Damaris could see the long vista through the avenue leading down to the gatehouse—she had found on her first morning at Great Heron that the maid's words were true. She did have the best and brightest outlook, a feeling of space and freedom, with the illusion that the park gates were not so very far away. Looking out of her window once Lord Malfrey had gone, she would find herself humming happy little tunes as she thought of showing her aunt this and that, and the old maids looked at her and smiled.

If she wanted information, she knew she would have to ask directly.

'Is Lady Cassandra married? Does she live close by?'

'Lady Cassandra never married, my lady,' Mrs Crump said, her face without expression. 'She is too sickly for that. She hardly goes out of doors. Lady Cassandra lives a good ways off; we don't see her at Great Heron. Is that all for the second service, my lady? Usually there is apricot tart and almond pastry for dessert, if I might be so bold as to make the suggestion. His lordship likes it to be served.'

Damaris, controlling her amusement, gave her assent. Her husband was not expected home for dinner, no one but herself would be there, and yet Mrs Crump gently insisted on her ordering the most huge meals. Lady Gratton had told her to follow all the customs of the place, certainly until she had been there long enough to understand its ways and be able to weed out the bad from the good. 'And remember,' Lady Gratton had said, 'many customs should not be changed, even if you personally do not care for them. People are attached to their old ways, and there might be virtues in them that you don't understand.' Great Heron followed the old way with two services for dinner, each at least a dozen dishes, and a profusion of desserts to follow.

At first she had thought company was expected, but of course no company had called during their honeymoon, and since Lord Malfrey had left she had received no callers. Only the vicar had come one day while she was out exploring the shrubberies and walks, going as far as the park gates. The gates were locked and barred.

'You would not want to go out on foot, my lady, and unattended,' the lodge-keeper had said civilly, but in some surprise at seeing the Countess of Malfrey roaming about alone. 'We are deep in the forest here. You could be lost or hurt on the rough paths.'

Damaris looked through the gates. There seemed to be quite a wide path. Tomorrow, she determined, she would order the carriage and take a drive. When she had returned, she was disappointed at having missed her visitor. The vicar had come by the north lane from the other side of Heron, where the vicarage stood, close by the church.

'A good house, the vicarage,' the maid who was attending her told her that night as she brushed her hair. 'My cousin Alice works there for Mr Poyntz, the vicar. But it's old and not cheerful; Vicar has no wife, and a house needs a lady to brighten it up.'

'Perhaps he'll marry,' Damaris said pensively as she watched her own face in the glass. It looked a very young face next to that of the wrinkled servant. Damaris had an inward flash of amusement, thinking of the fairy-tale princesses who lived alone in enchanted castles except for kind but gnomish servitors.

'Oh, Vicar's too old to marry now. He's very set in his ways,' the maid said positively, and Damaris sighed.

There would be no young and feminine company from the vicarage, then. But Lady Gratton would be at Great Heron within the week, bringing Betty, who was close to her confinement, with her. With these two companions the quiet of Heron would not be burdensome, though Damaris regretted that no one else had come to call. At least she wouldn't be faced with those huge dinners and no one to eat them. What happened to the food she didn't know, but she supposed it was enjoyed in the kitchen.

For the next few days she rambled about the house happily enough, looking at the old drawing-rooms, dust-sheeted, the dining-parlours, the morning-room, the breakfast-room. She peered into Malfrey's study and examined the library, where it looked as though damp was destroying the leather of some of the bindings. She ordered fires to be lit there whether the house was occupied or not. Her masters had taught her proper respect for books.

She examined all the bedrooms with the housekeeper, and finding a pleasant one in the back of the house that looked down onto a small flower garden, she ordered it to be made ready for

Lady Gratton. The housekeeper gave her an odd look, she thought, but did not demur. In a burst of energy and vigour, Damaris went on to order that the suite of drawing-rooms all be opened up and a general extra cleaning and polishing take place to make the house ready to receive her aunt. The servants did not seem to resent her orders; she thought they enjoyed the look of life coming to the place.

She asked that a room be made ready for Betty. Mrs Crump, who had been informed of the circumstances, pursed her lips and sniffed but said at last that Betty would find herself comfortable. Damaris asked the head gardener to bring in such flowers as he had in his succession houses for decoration. He did as gardeners were apt to do and brought in just what he was willing to bring, very few bright blossoms and a great many green branches. When she and the maids had arranged flowers and foliage about the place, she looked at her work and wondered if she had actually made the place more cheerful—it looked rather as though she had brought the forest inside the house; there was no escaping it.

Still, it would soon be Christmas. There would be yule logs burning, presents, and, she hoped, carollers coming to call. The Earl had been very generous; he had left ample funds at her disposal. Even better, he spoke of buying Angelhurst from the Duke: her villagers would be safe. She ordered roaring fires everywhere— her aunt must be comfortable—and she consulted Mrs Crump, for she was ignorant of shops and warehouses where she might find all the good things she planned to buy.

She was so busy with her preparations that she did not have time to be angry when, asking for her carriage, she was told the family coaches were being repaired and refurbished down at the coach house and were not as yet ready for her ladyship. They had not been used for many years—his lordship came down in his curricle. New carriages were being built in Town, the coachman told her, but she would not have to wait for the London tradesmen. His men were working as fast as they could.

Damaris wondered, a little crossly, why one carriage shouldn't have been made ready before she came; there were certainly enough men about the place to attend to it. She strongly suspected that Lord Malfrey preferred her to stay where she was. The ladies of Great Heron didn't seem to have much freedom. What kind of conveyance could the Lady Cassandra have used with the family coaches, according to the man, gathering dust since the late Countess's time?

She knew that nothing would be said about Lady Cassandra by the servants, not even the most ordinary remarks. Mrs Crump had not told her that the room she had chosen for Lady Gratton had been Cassandra's. Looking in a chest, Damaris had found some of her lesson books, some embroidery, neatly done, an old sash, and a jar of pot-pourri, its contents faded and crumbled to dust, with hardly a hint of fragrance remaining.

Looking at the remnants of girlhood, Damaris could only imagine that her husband—that man of such unaccountable and painful dislikes—disliked his sister, and that his servants, who were loyal, kept their silence about the lady. When she finally received a visitor, even though it was only the vicar, she thought she might learn a little more, but she was disappointed.

Mr Poyntz was as old and crabbed as she had expected him to be, a respectable old man, no doubt, a little hard of hearing, with rheumy eyes, a red nose, and a sad trail of snuff down the front of his coat. He still wore a wig, and looked to the girl like a relic of a former time. He accepted some Madeira, but his conversation was not enlivening. Damaris asked about the parish. He discussed the state of tithes and the iniquity of the Methodists.

'We don't have the troubles they have in some parts, Lady Malfrey. Things are quiet and orderly on the Malfrey land. On the Malfrey land. We don't have a lot of damned Methodistical parsons—I beg your pardon, my lady; as you see it's been a long time since we had a lady here—stirring people up, dragging them out in the open like the pagans they all really are, and filling them up with unsound doctrine and unholy excitement. Excitement! Humph!' He dipped into his battered old snuff box and left a further trail upon his black coat. 'Those parsons, they don't like the Forest of Heron. They won't come down here. Not down here.'

Damaris was fascinated by the wicked-looking vicar and his odd way of repeating his words as though he were afraid that his original phrases had lost themselves in some strange limbo. She wondered why he thought the Methodist preachers feared the forest. Was he implying the villagers would set upon them? Most country people she had known respected the teachings of Wesley and Whitefield. Or was he relying on some demon of the forest to assault the Evangelicals? Then he himself must be a pagan, a snuff-spattered, pagan parson. She wanted to giggle but controlled herself and asked how long he had held the living.

'Fifty years,' he said, 'and I expect to hold it another score—we Poyntzes are long-lived. Long-lived.'

He didn't sound enthusiastic.

'Then you knew Lady Cassandra,' she said pleasantly.

He finished his wine and shuffled his feet as if preparing to go, but she nodded to the manservant to fill his glass.

'A delicate young lady,' he said, sinking back in his chair. 'Rarely went to church. Kept to her room, her room.'

'How sad,' Damaris said. 'And she never married. I expected to find her at home,' she added which was of course a lie, but she hoped to provoke the vicar into saying *something*.

'Home,' he muttered. 'She is at home. Doesn't live here, why should she? Place half closed up. Bein' taken care of. An invalid. An invalid.'

This time he struggled to his feet.

'You're young yet, Lady Malfrey,' he said gruffly, 'a young head. You need to be careful, listening to what people say. All this toleration of Dissenters—it is the ruin of the church. Ruin of the church. Good day to ye, my lady. Good day to ye.'

And he shuffled out. Damaris did long for Betty so that they could have had a good laugh. She wondered what Mr Poyntz was like in the pulpit. A Bible verse could stand repetition, she supposed. And at a marriage ceremony? 'I now pronounce you man and wife. And wife.' But she pulled a face. The thought of weddings was not pleasing to her.

Mr Ruthven, she thought suddenly, would look well in the pulpit. John Ruthven—for a time she had thought of him that way. He would be a good speaker and, her mind rushed on, as a husband he would not—the thoughts came against her will—he would not have looked upon her with a lasciviousness that turned to disgust. As she sat alone she felt warm, blushed and fidgeted and got up and walked about the room. After her first shock and dismay, and the torturing ideas that had followed, she had assured herself that it was not her person that was disgusting, but something strange about the Earl that made him think so. Her confidence sometimes failed. At its highest it could not make her happy; at its lowest she was afflicted by thoughts that became a physical force causing her to toss and turn at night or to pace about, finding relief only in exercise during the day. Now she resolutely put such thoughts from her. What was done was done. Tomorrow her aunt came.

Briskly she called a man to inquire as to the state of her carriage, and in a slow and formal way word was brought her that a chaise could be ready that very afternoon and at her order the horses would be put to. Delighted, Damaris ran upstairs to get her bonnet and cloak, to the distress of her maid, who could by no means move as fast. But at last Damaris was allowed to be properly attired, with gloves and muff, and she went off in the late afternoon, well admonished not to stay out above an hour, as darkness would fall and she would be trapped in the forest with great risk to horses, carriage, her servants, and her person.

It was wonderful to feel free, to be driven down the avenue and have the lodge-keeper respectfully open the park gates, but soon she was sadly disappointed. The path that had looked so promising merely led for mile after mile through the great forest, with the trees, although nearly leafless, so high and dense overhead that she could hardly see the pale and wintry sky. She was still held in the clutches of Heron. After they had driven for about an hour, over the muttered objections of the coachman, she asked how much further they had to drive to get clear of the forest.

The coachman shook his head.

'You couldn't do it in a day's ride, my lady, not on this road. Fair dreadful, it is. His lordship, he talk of doing summat with road, but it seems hardly worth it, so few carriages coming down. Whom so be built the Great House, he had no mind for visitors, nor for ladies driving out in their carriages. And if you will forgive me, my lady, it be much too late for a lady to be out in an open carriage with the night air coming on. There be a clearing close by where horses can make the turn, and I think we should go back, ma'am.'

Damaris gave her reluctant consent, considering the lords of Heron a most unsociable tribe. Why could they not have built their manor-house on the forest's edge? She wondered if her husband had spent his youth there—but of course, a boy would go to school. It was the unlucky daughter of the house who would have been immured. No wonder she had taken to her bed.

When they came to the small clearing of which the coachman had spoken, Damaris saw another path leading westward. As they came about, she noticed on that path, distant but just visible as it stood right on the lane, a small house that didn't have the look of a cottage. She had just a fleeting glimpse, but it was enough. There was a house—and a house within the range of visiting.

'What house is that, coachman?' she asked.

'House, my lady?' he said, busily shouting instruction to the grooms about proper care and not scratching the new varnish.

'The house we passed, by the clearing.'

'Don't know of any house, my lady,' he said, intent upon his business. 'I think that there left trace be loose, Dick. As soon as we get back to stable, look to it. Beg your pardon, my lady. There be a few cottages about the forest. People working on the estate, wood-cutters and the like.'

The house, so briefly seen, had seemed of more importance than a mere woodsman's dwelling. She had had a decided impression that it was a gentleman's residence and hoped it housed people of quality. But perhaps it was just the house of a steward or superior agent of some kind. It was very annoying.

A bird, startled from an overhanging bough, fluttered by her ears with a raucous cry. A little further on, she was unnerved by the stare of an owl, bold with lack of dealings with humankind. The forest was eerie with dark coming. She wondered what happened when Great Heron entertained—of course, the guests must stay the night. There was no doubt in her mind that once Lord Malfrey was in residence they would be called on by the great families of the county and normal social intercourse would follow. In the meantime, the next day would bring Lady Gratton and Betty, and the young Lady Malfrey went home happily enough to dress for her absurd dinner, where she counted the dishes to be able the next day to amuse her aunt.

9

Lady Gratton came, but she was in no mood to criticize the domestic arrangements at Great Heron. Lord Malfrey had been most courteous, calling upon her at Mrs Farthingale's, and had sent her down in his own coach, with Betty, now enormous, in attendance. Damaris's greetings to both were joyful, if restrained as always under the eye of her aunt, but she promised herself a little chat with her maid when they were alone.

The baronet's widow listened indulgently to Damaris's tales of the horde of old and mostly idle servants, the tremendous profusion and waste, but she pointed out to her niece that what was wasteful in the household of a person of lesser rank and wealth was only proper to a personage such as the Earl. The table must be ready for hospitality; the servants were needed when the house was full, and it was a good master who gave them steady employment.

She did not add, though she might have done, that for herself, a woman who had hardly ever known what it was to have money enough for her needs, to be in a household conducted on such prodigal lines was very pleasant. Her niece as yet had little knowledge of the careful management it had taken to ensure Damaris the education and modest comforts she had known at Angelhurst. Their table had been limited to the products of the farm, and Lady Gratton had no objection to being served such delicacies as Damaris described. Her appetite was keen, for Mrs Farthingale, her old friend and hostess, had made large displays at her entertainments but, when the ladies were alone, was inclined to suggest coddled eggs on a tray—'Quite enough for two old ladies like us, eh, Augusta?' Augusta, polite as always, had not demurred but had thought rebelliously that she was not too old to eat a good meal.

Now she enjoyed the roaring fire in the morning-room and the 'small collation' that was brought in to stay her until dinner: soup, meats hot and cold, fruit, and cake; and she realized, as Damaris did not, the excellence of the old Constantia wine that she was served.

After she had eaten, Damaris showed her the house. Where Damaris had seen only gloom, Lady Gratton saw the richness and the splendour of the house and the furnishings, and felt she had done well indeed.

'We travelled more than a day through Malfrey land, my dear,' she said. 'We spent last night at Goodacre Inn, in the forest itself, and travelled on this morning. It is a noble estate indeed.'

The mere thought of her nephew-in-law's possessions gave her a comfortable feeling of security. Though she had had to leave the excitements of Town, she found herself happier at Heron than she had been since she was a girl. Even then, Miss Mayne, who had sense, had been confided in by her parents and knew all their financial worries, so that her girlhood had not been without care.

When the ladies went to dress for dinner, Damaris had a happy reunion with Betty. Betty was as glad to be at Great Heron as Damaris was to see her there; she had been cared for by the Malfrey servants in Town, but their manners had been coolly civil. Her time of sickness was gone; she was not afraid of her approaching confinement, and she begged to be able to serve her mistress in the country as she had before. Damaris gave a qualified assent, with reference to the wishes of the absent Earl. Privately, she was certain he would let her have her way. His treatment of her aunt, his liberality with money, brought her the understanding that whatever was amiss in their private life, the Earl was giving his Countess respect, even honour.

Lady Gratton relished the sumptuous dinner, quietly served, and when the cloth was drawn and the ladies retired to the great red drawing-room for their tea and coffee, she was content. Damaris laughed at the dim old splendours and was reproved.

'It is all very fine, my dear. Such carpets as these and the stuffs in the curtains,' she said approvingly, 'could not be replaced—not while that wicked Napoleon is rampaging all over the Continent. You are not used to it—we had nothing so fine at Angelhurst, though the house was very well in its way.'

She looked round judiciously. 'It could use a lady's touch—no great changes that would perturb your good husband. Men think that they don't like changes. Of course, they do—no one wishes his house to become shabby and quite out of the mode—but a lady uses tact and makes her changes little by little. In Town, of course, you will find matters quite different. It is the custom these days for great ladies to new-furnish whenever they choose—though I hope you will not indulge in *some* of the excesses I have seen. Young Mrs Carroway has turned the fine old Carroway house into I don't know what. The drawing-room had been one of the most noble in London. Now it is so hung about with silk and glittering with new gilt and marble sphinxes and the like—well,' she said indulgently, 'perhaps I am old-fashioned, but I do not like it.'

Aunt and niece had much to talk about, and Lady Gratton gave much sage advice about the management of the household. When Damaris went to her room she was aware that she had not spoken to her aunt on the matter that had so much occupied her mind and caused so many tears. She felt an unwillingness to speak, partly from a sense of shame, partly from another reason. With her aunt and Betty present, two very tangible evidences of the Earl's good faith, she felt the stirring of a new loyalty and was reluctant to defame a man who was, after all, her husband. She did not quite decide to say nothing, but she thought that the matter could wait.

Lady Gratton was considering the same subject. While she was in Town, in all the gossip she had heard at Mrs Farthingale's, there were rumours about Lord Malfrey that she could not ignore. She had wondered if her niece was having problems and decided to talk to her during her stay at Great Heron. Now she changed her mind. Her niece looked well, even blooming; she seemed happy, and her impish humour was manifesting—a quality that Lady Gratton always endeavoured to restrain.

She went happily to sleep in the very comfortable bed in the pleasant bedchamber, having been waited on by the two maids assigned for her personal needs, enjoying the well-banked fire in the hearth and the plate of sweetmeats left by her bedside lest she be overcome by hunger pangs in the night.

The next morning they visited the portrait gallery. Damaris had not been interested in the long, dignified row of ancestors dimmed by heavy brown varnish, but Lady Gratton was enthralled. She knew each and all of the great families of England, and as they went down the row she lectured her niece with tales of which bride had come to such a one, be he a nobleman, soldier, or prelate, to the further distinction of the Heron family. Damaris had long lost interest in the worthy wives and was about to descend the staircase at the gallery's end when Lady Gratton called her back.

'Do look at this, Damaris. How interesting!'

Damaris sighed, sure it was not going to be interesting—unless this last ancestor had been beheaded or died of drink. Her aunt was examining a portrait at the very end of the gallery almost hidden by the corner, where little light fell. She sent for candles and examined it with rapt attention. This portrait was not brown and soupy; it had a lighter, more modern look. But it was the subject that caught her eye: a young girl, with startling blue eyes, dressed in simple sprigged muslin. The tiny waist and billowing skirt were in the style of Lady Gratton's own youth, but the painter had caught the timeless look of innocence in the girl's young beauty. The shining hair was pale gold; except for that the face could almost have been that of Damaris.

'Who is that lady?' she asked Mrs Crump, for the housekeeper had accompanied the men who brought the candles.

'That is Lady Cassandra, the Earl's sister,' Mrs Crump said without expression.

Lady Gratton was fascinated. She thought the resemblance remarkable, though Damaris, she saw, did not observe it. The difference in fashion in the gown and the coiffure was a barrier to recognition for the young. As she gazed she decided that the resemblance, apart from the freshness and innocence of youth, was in the blue eyes and dazzling complexion—Cassandra's bones had not quite the fineness of the Maynes. She thought furiously of all the gossip she had ever heard that might touch upon the Heron family and the St Clouds. A memory touched her, and she smiled. Then she shrugged slightly; she could be mistaken. Such looks, though uncommon, were not unique. But she gave the portrait one more glance as she turned away.

'It was sad that Lady Cassandra could not come to the wedding,' she remarked as the party descended the stairs.

'It was better she didn't make the attempt,' Mrs Crump said. 'Her ladyship's nerves are too delicate.'

'She lives on the Heron estate, does she not?' Lady Gratton asked.

Damaris observed with wry amusement that her reticent housekeeper could not avoid answering her formidable aunt.

'She lives at Greystones,' Mrs Crump said. 'It is a fair way off from here.'

A long way off, the housekeeper had told her. And Lady Cassandra had not called. She mentioned this to her aunt when they were alone.

'The servants are loyal to the family,' Lady Gratton said with approval. 'I understand that Lady Cassandra is quite a recluse: her health and nerves were always bad. Lord Malfrey, it is well known, takes excellent care of her. He is a kind brother. He visits her regularly, but she sees few other people.'

Lady Gratton had heard more about Lady Cassandra's illness, but she did not intend to alarm the girl who was to bear the future heir to Malfrey. The trouble was not hereditary, which was all that mattered. If Lord Malfrey was keeping his young wife and his ailing sister apart, it was the most sensible thing he could do.

The Christmas holidays were more successful than Damaris had hoped. Lord Malfrey arrived in gracious mood, unbending to Lady Gratton, with whom, his wife noticed, he could make easy, though heavy, conversation. Lady Gratton, though mostly a social woman, had a concern for the politics of the day and was genuinely interested in what the Earl could tell her. Their family party was genial, though little enlivened by outsiders. 'Of course, Damaris,' Lady Gratton said, 'Christmas is a family holiday. Visiting really stops until the New Year. Every great house in the country is filled with relations.'

The vicar dined with them one night, and Damaris had the pleasure of seeing a twinkle in her aunt's eye at his toast to 'the families of Heron and Gratton, Gratton.' If Lady Gratton wondered that Mr Poyntz was the only guest at the Malfreys' country seat, she did not express her wonder to her niece.

On Christmas Eve, after the family dinner at which Damaris counted thirteen dishes at each of the two services, and three desserts as well as the plum pudding and mince pies, presents were exchanged according to the custom of the house, before the yule log burning in the great front hall.

It was a pleasant occasion. Damaris, knowing her aunt's love of finery, had ordered dress lengths of the finest silks, laces, and muslins that could be bought, and all the most fashionable trims. Lady Gratton was delighted and expressed her pleasure with almost as much openness as Betty had shown for her more modest gifts—Damaris knew she must not show Betty to be too much a favourite or put her in danger with the other servants by making her too fine.

She had ordered for Lord Malfrey a snuff-box for his collection, engraved with the arms of the Heron family impaling those of the St Clouds. Having heard of her husband's interest in old books of military history, she also presented him with three volumes on the American war that had belonged to her Mayne grandfather, annotated by him with references to campaigns in which he had fought. Lord Malfrey was obviously pleased with these gifts, his usual cool courtesy melting to something like warmth as he turned the pages and made out General Mayne's criticism and comment. He waited until Lady Gratton had distributed her presents: the miniature portrait of her mother for Damaris and a fine new riding whip for himself. Then two menservants brought in a ponderous iron chest with heavy locks, and Lord Malfrey motioned them to place it beside him. He himself unlocked the chest, which was lined with velvet and fitted with many drawers.

First he took a pair of earrings, large pear-shaped emeralds, and presented them to Lady Gratton.

'For you, Madam,' he said, 'for giving me a brighter jewel, my Countess.'

Lady Gratton for once was speechless. She put the earrings in her ears and swung her head gaily, and the sparkle of the jewels brought a corresponding green glimmer from her eyes. For the first time Damaris realized that her aunt had once been young and had had the comeliness of youth.

Lord Malfrey, with great stateliness, brought out the family jewels of the house of Heron, which he now gave Damaris, and which would be hers to wear throughout her lifetime. Lady Gratton's eyes, still sparkling, went wide—the Heron jewels were magnificent and impressive, if somewhat old-fashioned in their setting.

'These are all family jewels and can be reset if you wish,' Lord Malfrey told Damaris. 'They should have been given to you after the wedding, but I preferred to go to Town and bring them down myself. And at the same time I had something made for you alone.'

Damaris looked with interest, not so much for the sake of the jewels, which she had not yet learned to value, but because of the care and thought shown by her husband. Perhaps he felt some affection for her after all—or perhaps this was one more example of the courtesy shown by the Earls of Malfrey to their wives, whether they loved them or not.

He produced a magnificent collection of pieces set in the most modern style: sapphires of the darkest blue surrounded by brilliant-cut diamonds, rings, bracelets, earrings, a necklace, and a magnificent tiara.

'Put them on, my dear,' Lady Gratton urged, and Damaris obeyed, glad that she was wearing a gown of white twilled silk with a blue sash. The servants, who had been called in, all showed their admiration quietly; they received their gifts from Damaris and murmured to each other that she was a very proper Lady Malfrey. Christmas punch was served to the family and the upper servants all together while the waits sang Christmas carols. Then the waits were taken downstairs for further merriment in the servants' hall.

The family retired to the drawing-room for coffee, and Lady Gratton stood by Damaris in front of an old gilded looking-glass, handsome but rather cloudy, that hung above the chimney-piece.

'See how you look,' Lady Gratton said, beaming, a trifle flown from the wine and punch, feeling that as guardian she had done her work well indeed. What a splendid countess her niece made, to be sure!

Damaris looked. The jewels were certainly handsome. Damaris, she told herself, if Jem the cowman were here he would think you had won first prize. But she stifled her giggles, behaved with perfect propriety, and the holiday went off happily for them all.

On Christmas Day they went to church, and Damaris felt the eyes of the village upon her. The villagers themselves looked swarthy and small in stature to a girl accustomed to the big, flaxen-haired people of Angelhurst. The vicar called at the house between services, and at dinner Lord Malfrey and Lady Gratton were still deep in talk. Damaris toyed with the Christmas goose on her plate and enjoyed a private joke: it was a pity that Lord Malfrey had needed to marry for an heir; he was much happier with Lady Gratton, nearer his own age, with a liking for the same dull things—politics, whist, and cures for rheumatism. He unbent enough to enjoy a little gossip; they happily deplored the wild Lord Langley, who, when prosecuted for driving his curricle into a crowd, rode the horse into the courtroom, claiming it was a witness.

'The young Caligula,' Lord Malfrey said grimly, to Lady Gratton's satisfaction.

Dreamy, Damaris imagined them in a happily married state, until she was roused by a sharp glance from her aunt. A lady, that glance said, always takes a proper part in conversation. Damaris exerted herself again. 'And what did Mr Canning say?'

And on the talk went.

Lord Malfrey left after a few days, saying he would soon return. To his young wife he looked more at ease when he left than she had ever seen him. There had been no tension between them; he had not visited her room. Damaris did not know that Lady Gratton had made certain inquiries of Betty and her other personal maid and had reported the results of these inquiries, smiling, to Lord Malfrey. During the entire holiday, he had only once frowned and relapsed into his habitual frosty silence. On New Year's Day when Damaris had come down dressed for church, she had met her husband and they had waited together for Lady Gratton. To fill the time, she had pointed out the present she had received from Lady Gratton, handing him the miniature for his close scrutiny—the young Lady Edmund St Cloud.

'Aunt says I resemble her in form and feature,' Damaris had said, and Lord Malfrey had nodded gloomily. It seemed as though he was as depressed by her mother's looks as he had been by her own. Perplexed, she wondered why he had admired her portrait, why he had married her. There were so many young and well-born girls; he did not have to marry a penniless, obscure St Cloud. Lady Gratton had warned her that gentlemen could be strange in their ways: she was certainly right. But when her aunt descended, happy in the crisp, bright day with the sun reflecting from clean drifts of snow, Damaris joined her in pleasure and forgot the peculiarities of her lord.

10

The snow hung from the boughs of the trees, making that usually gloomy forest look like a children's playground. With Lord Malfrey gone, the ladies took their walks and carriage rides, Lady Gratton finding as much to make her happy as Damaris had found dull before she came.

The great extent of the forest, which Damaris found confining, gave her aunt pleasure as she calculated the value of the woodland. She knew much of such things and told Damaris that the villagers of Lesser Heron were woodsmen, forest folk different from the farmers of the county. Some said they were part Welsh, others that they had intermarried with the gypsies, but they were a breed apart.

'Your servants, you will notice, think poorly of the village,' she remarked. 'Nor do they like the poor vicar, who is a gentleman but perhaps has some of the village blood.'

'Why do you say so, Aunt?'

'Because when he came to dinner, I noticed his glass wasn't filled as often as it might have been. Servants always have a way of making their feelings known.'

Lady Gratton did not add, for she was chary of giving praise, that Damaris seemed to have earned their approval. And soon would do better, she thought with satisfaction.

The coachman turned to the ladies and pointed with his whip to the side of the path.

'You see the pond there, my lady?'

The small pond was frozen over and half-hidden by a drift of snow.

'These woods be full of ponds. Some go deep. Treacherous after dark for a body walking. It is always best to stay on the path, even in daylight.'

His words gave Damaris the feeling again of being enclosed, shut in, but Lady Gratton, who was no explorer, remained unperturbed, and her attention was soon drawn away.

She put up her quizzing-glass.

'Coachman, what is that house?'

They had come to the clearing where Damaris had been before. In the light of day the house along the side-path was well in view, not large but substantial and well proportioned, its grey stone façade almost giving her its name before the coachman spoke.

'Greystones, my lady.'

'The home of Lady Cassandra?'

'Yes, my lady.'

Lady Gratton was satisfied, but Damaris was curious. Lady Cassandra was said to be a recluse, but there was a coach and a curricle outside her house.

'Perhaps we should call, Aunt.'

Lady Gratton shook her head and gave her niece a glance—it was a matter to be discussed out of the hearing of the servants. That night, when Betty was dismissed, Lady Gratton came to her room.

'Lord Malfrey does not wish you to visit Lady Cassandra. Company, except for people she has known all her life, is too upsetting for her. Change of any kind, her doctors say, must be avoided.'

Damaris thought about this, gazing into the fire-light.

'Is she mad, Aunt?'

'Certainly not. There is no madness in the Heron family. Rest assured, Damaris; I have made careful inquiry. Lady Cassandra was always delicate and had a breakdown many years ago before she could be presented. She perhaps was disappointed in some girlish love affair, but no one knows. The doctor who attended her went to another part of the country and has been dead for many years. The vicar knew her, of course, but he would never discuss the family. I tell you all this, Damaris, because I think you should obey your husband's wish, and also because, in the present circumstances, I do not wish you to worry.'

Damaris understood her aunt's reference. She had said nothing herself; it was too soon to be sure. But from her disinclination for her breakfast the last morning or two, her aunt's guess was probably right.

'Lord Malfrey,' Lady Gratton said, 'will send a doctor from Town.'

Lord Malfrey himself did not appear. They both received letters; he was busy with matters concerning the army estimates. Lady Gratton, knowing that the lovely Lady Ramage, his mistress, had recently returned to Town, did not expect him back too soon.

At the proper time the doctor arrived, and all Lady Gratton's happy anticipation proved correct. Damaris was with child. Lord Malfrey came down; he and Lady Gratton radiated a discreet approval; a new coach was ordered for Damaris, especially sprung and cushioned so that no jolt could possibly disturb her morning rides. The coachman was given special instructions by Lord Malfrey as to the direction and duration of these drives, and Damaris was cautioned to walk no further than the shrubbery.

'We cannot,' Lord Malfrey said, his usual seriousness intensified, 'be too careful.'

Damaris was full of rueful mirth that she must not express: she was being treated like a valuable brood mare. Her husband no longer approached her room on any of his brief, formal visits to Heron. To her regret, she found there was no plan of taking her to Town. All *that* must wait on the production of the heir. Damaris hoped heartily the child would be a boy; she believed that once the heir was born her marital duty would be done and she would be free to lead the life, discreet but pleasant, of a woman of fashion.

Her disappointment was tempered by the help she could give to Betty in her confinement. The other servants could not show disapproval while Damaris was there to protect her. Betty's child was born, and Lady Gratton found a decent village family who were willing to take it. Damaris rebelled, demanding that Betty be allowed to keep her child, but Lady Gratton told her that would be the end of domestic peace; the other servants would never accept such a thing. And Betty herself agreed with Lady Gratton.

'Better I be like the others, not different and them always knowing it,' she explained to her mistress before she had recovered from childbed. Damaris sat with her in her attic room, clean, whitewashed, and getting some sunlight. 'Besides'—Betty looked at the cradle with no affection—'baby, he do remind me of that Jem.'

Damaris would have outfaced Lady Gratton if Betty wished it; the baby seemed a fine little fellow. But Betty obviously did not; she pursed her lips when Damaris took the child on her knee, and fretted about her gown. Betty knew that some ladies were quite foolish about babies—that came from not having to nurse them, she supposed.

It was as well Damaris did not need to quarrel with her aunt, for she was being very kind. Lady Gratton had given up her return to Mrs Farthingale's, and all the delights of Town, to be with her niece in her seclusion. She was delighted with the speedy fulfillment of the marriage and decided that much she had heard of the Earl must be false. She was glad she had not alarmed her niece with the gossip and felt she had covered the subject discreetly by saying one night after dinner, as they sat in the drawing-room, that though gentlemen might sometimes be odd in their ways, fortunately nature took its course.

Damaris, who was not feeling well, at the moment could not think it so fortunate. She wondered what Lady Gratton had heard; the hint implied she knew something. In all events, she hoped devoutly that Lord Malfrey's oddities were no longer her concern. Betty had been at Malfrey House long enough to hear the talk and had alluded guardedly to Lady Ramage. She would have told more, but Damaris, with her sense of privacy, could not discuss her husband.

The next morning Damaris was cheered by some news. Lady Gratton beamed and told her niece she had received a most interesting communication from the Duchess of Camberly.

'From the Duchess!' Damaris interjected.

It seemed she had heard that her niece was *enceinte*.

Lady Gratton read aloud: '. . . and Great Heron, I hear, though a magnificent seat, is very remote in situation, with not a family to visit within a day's ride. I fear that Lady Malfrey may be lonely, especially with her husband so occupied in Town. Just now I have staying with me another St Cloud niece, Gregory's daughter Margaret, who is fifteen and not, as yet, out. Her mother doesn't need her at home at this time, and it seems a good opportunity, if Lady Malfrey is agreeable, for Margaret to visit her cousin.'

'A very good notion,' Lady Gratton said with enthusiasm. 'Most certainly, Damaris, for you to entertain your cousin will mean that the breach between the members of the family has been healed. And young Margaret will be excellent company for you. From all I have heard, she is a very pleasant young girl.'

And if Lady Gratton's social instinct told her the Duchess was hoping Damaris would take her cousin to Town later on, she thought such a manoeuvre perfectly proper. Besides, it was convenient, for it meant she could escape for a while from the magnificent but very quiet Great Heron for a little gaiety in Town. Damaris was not the only one to be suddenly receiving notice: now that Lady Gratton was known to be aunt to the Countess of

Malfrey many of her old friends, previously remiss, were showering her with invitations.

She stayed until Margaret arrived and was very pleased with the quiet, timid young girl, very much not *out,* obviously a St Cloud with her pale golden ringlets, blue eyes, and brilliant complexion. There was a family resemblance to Damaris, but of course Margaret did not have the delicate beauty of the Maynes. Then she went off to Town and all its pleasures, certain her niece would not be lonely. And if she heard more in Town of Lord Malfrey and Lady Ramage, she also heard that he had completed the purchase of Angelhurst, which he was making over to his wife on the birth of their first child, and she could think very little ill of him.

Damaris enjoyed the company of her young cousin. It was strange for her to meet another young St Cloud, one who had basked all her life in the approval of her family. The girl, though sweet-tempered, seemed to her very spiritless, and Damaris soon found that Margaret's education by no means equalled her own. She had been taught the accomplishments of a lady, and nothing else. Damaris began to realize, in an adult way, how much she owed to her aunt, and gratitude warmed her heart. She determined to do her best for Margaret; she read with her and played and sang, determined when they went to Town to obtain masters to instruct Margaret in languages and history.

'Mamma says it does not do to be learned,' Margaret said, her eyes wide when these plans were made known to her.

'Just because we are females, we don't have to be fools,' Damaris said firmly, and Margaret, in the first flush of something like hero-worship, solemnly agreed; but Damaris was afraid that Margaret would have agreed to anything, even if she had suggested a carriage race through the depths of the Forest of Heron.

The two were content together, and if Damaris missed Lady Gratton's incisive manner and tart humour, her great superiority of mind, she had for the first time the pleasure of being able to give as she guided her cousin's taste in literature and poetry. They were happy when spring came and they could walk beyond the shrubbery and drive a little further than the church in one direction or Greystones at the other. Damaris's time of sickness passed, as Betty had told her it would, and she had hardly noticed the absence of Lord Malfrey, which had lasted two months, when he sent notice of his arrival and appeared in the house at dinner.

He came down with Lady Gratton, who thought what a pretty

pair the cousins made. Damaris's condition showed but little under her high-waisted gown, and the fair St Cloud cousin at her side, though reduced again to timidity at the appearance of Lord Malfrey, lost none of her charm by *that* in the eyes of the older woman.

It was not surprising that Margaret was rendered speechless by the Earl, Lady Gratton thought privately, for his manner was even more distant than usual. They had conversed cheerfully enough in the coach as they came from Town; they had spent the night at an in, and he had borne it well—he had sent his servants ahead to make sure that all was comfortable and a good dinner ordered. He had shown no sign of irritation or temper or disturbance of spirits —in fact he had seemed happy, for the government was taking his advice in army matters. 'We must have the strength to beat Napoleon by land as well as at sea. The money must be raised.'

But the man who could plan to defeat the Emperor, the Conqueror of Europe, was reduced to glacial silence by the addition to his family circle of one schoolroom miss. Lady Gratton had long suspected that Lord Malfrey's real trouble was shyness, especially with young women—he would not be the only great man so afflicted. His cool manner could well be a shield for that shyness. But his behavior that night was marked, and she knew that above all things Lord Malfrey hated being remarkable. He spoke little; he ate less but drank rather more than usual, emptying each glass as it was filled by the attentive servants.

Although Damaris was accustomed to her husband's moods, she was cross with him for undoing her hard work in inspiriting her cousin. When the ladies withdrew, both she and Lady Gratton, by an understanding that needed no words, cheered and made much of the girl. Damaris asked her to play and sing, and Lady Gratton heaped praise upon her until her cheeks turned pink. When they were joined by Lord Malfrey, Lady Gratton firmly kept him beside her while the girls poured tea and coffee.

But Damaris's crossness at the table was nothing to her confusion when her husband, large and pale, loomed at the doorway to her room that night and demanded that she send her cousin away the next morning. He gave no reason but merely repeated, for all Damaris's shocked inquiry, that she had to go.

Damaris was aghast. Not only was she losing a valued companion, but the insult to her cousin was gross. Lord Malfrey had ordered her to tell Margaret of her dismissal that night so that she could be packed off first thing in the morning. Damaris sat before her glass quite silent and looked at Betty, who had been putting her things away. Mistress and servant were equally dismayed.

Damaris rose. She was Countess of Malfrey, but in this matter she simply did not know what to do. Slowly she made her way to her aunt's room, knocked, and was admitted. Lady Gratton had removed her wig. Damaris had never known that she wore one. Her aunt's own hair was still fairly abundant, though somewhat faded and streaked with grey, but a little scalp shone through at the crown now her hair was disarranged.

'It is easier travelling,' Lady Gratton remarked, seeing her glance, 'as I don't take a maid of my own.'

She spoke casually, though she guessed that it was no small matter that brought her niece to her at that time of night. She was not totally unprepared for the subject of Damaris's confidence either, but she was quite outraged at its extent.

'Tomorrow morning? But that is impossible!' Lady Gratton said, deeply disturbed.

Damaris explained. Lady Gratton was not a woman to interfere between husband and wife, host or guest, or to argue with the master about the conduct of his own house. But this was different. This was a family matter of great importance. Where Damaris saw the injury to her cousin, Lady Gratton saw the insult to the whole St Cloud family. She knew her duty. Replacing her wig and tidying her person, she left Damaris with a word and went swiftly to Lord Malfrey's chamber.

She demanded admittance of the surprised *valet de chambre* and received permission from Lord Malfrey to enter. He had not retired but was standing fully dressed, his back to the fire-light, gazing out into the darkness where the spreading great oaks shrouded his window.

Lady Gratton drew herself up and in a few words said what she had to say. No one would have been aware, seeing her manner, that only a few months ago she had had to apply to Lord Malfrey for money to pay her debts or become a pauper. She, however, was sharply and painfully aware of this; nevertheless she had to remind him of his duty. It was true that the girl had been invited without his knowledge or consent, but custom dictated that a lady could invite such unexceptionable company without permission from her absent lord.

'Margaret was to have made a long visit. If it must be ended, at least let her remain a few weeks so that her parents can be informed and send for her—Damaris can write that poor health is keeping her too much confined to her room to be cheerful company for her cousin.'

The Earl had not turned to receive her; nor did he show in any way that he had heard her remarks.

'Lord Malfrey,' she urged, 'if Margaret is turned out of doors like this, the insult to the St Clouds and Camberly will be such that the two families will be estranged through all our lifetimes, and beyond.'

At last he turned. His face, usually pale, looked livid by candle-light, his prominent grey eyes opaque.

'I am sorry, Madam,' he said abruptly, 'but my instructions remain. The girl must go tomorrow.'

And he gestured to his valet to show Lady Gratton out.

For the moment, to the outraged Lady Gratton, his face seemed unpleasantly sneering. But as she walked slowly and reluctantly down the long passage to her room, it struck her that his features were distorted by some unbearable inner torment.

CHAPTER

11

Lady Gratton was nothing if not practical. Before returning to her niece, she had realized that there was nothing she could do about the expulsion of Margaret and all that would follow in its train. But Damaris was Countess of Malfrey; she would be mother to the heir. It was necessary that the rift between husband and wife be lessened as much and as quickly as possible.

She returned to her room, ordered the kitchen to send up a soothing posset, and put her niece in a comfortable chair by the fire. Wife and widow talked through the night. Lord Malfrey was unreasonable in this matter, she told her niece calmly, but they must not judge him. He had been upset by Margaret's presence—perhaps his upset had reference to some loss in his early life. They could not know.

Yet, she went on, he was a far better husband than most. Lady Gratton thought she was being fair in saying so: certainly compared with her own late husband, the elderly widower, Lord Malfrey seemed fine indeed. Sir Hubert had been a cheese-paring, grudging man who had married the young Augusta Mayne simply because her sister was daughter-in-law to the great Duke. When it became obvious that no advantage was forthcoming, the baronet had shown his disappointment all too plainly, and he had softened not at all during his illness, when Augusta had nursed him with all the devotion her sense of duty made imperative.

She recalled her niece to this sense of duty that she herself had inculcated in her. 'You must think of your child's future and your own,' she said. 'You have given your oath to love, honour, and obey. Honour and obedience you *must* give, for it is in your power to do so. Love you must try to give, for your own sake, and not waste your thoughts on matters you cannot help.'

Then she turned her mind to how the blow to Margaret could be softened. Go she must, but excuses must be sent with her. Lady Gratton caused Damaris to write to both Lady Gregory and the Duchess of a serious outbreak of fever at Great Heron, of a most alarming kind. The family were vacating the house, and as Malfrey House was not ready to receive them, they were accepting an invitation of long standing to stay with friends of Lord Malfrey. In the circumstances, it seemed best and safest to send Margaret back to her family while the fever wore itself out. Lady Malfrey hoped to see Margaret again soon, perhaps in Town.

'That taradiddle won't deceive the Duchess, Aunt,' Damaris said gloomily. 'If only Lord Malfrey *would* allow me to go for a visit—but you know he will not.'

'Quite true, I'm afraid,' Lady Gratton said, sighing, 'but I fear it is the best we can do. I expected that Lady Gregory will find the truth out also, but at least it will serve, I hope, so that Margaret won't suffer. Let us pray that Lady Gregory will hold her tongue *there.*'

Next morning Lord Malfrey did not come down to breakfast. Margaret, bewildered but fortunately very fearful of the fever which she was told had broken out in the night, was sent off with great ceremony and many gifts hastily assembled by Damaris and many hugs and kisses to prevent the girl from feeling dismissed.

Timid as always, Margaret, although willing to kiss her cousin and Lady Gratton, drew back from any proximity to the servants, whom she suspected might have been contaminated. She was driven away in Damaris's new carriage, shrinking into a corner.

Damaris had to smile, but Lady Gratton could not. The truth would become known, the insult felt, and Damaris would once again be cut off from her father's family. It was not a tragic matter, as it had been before, but it was serious enough. A girl's family was her background, as foliage is to a flower.

Lady Gratton looked at her niece and sighed, with a touch of something cold at her heart. Damaris looked what she was— young, lovely, and rich; even the wakeful night had not taken the sparkle from her eyes, and the spring sunshine could find no blemish in that face. As she watched Damaris standing on the steps in her blue morning-gown, waving good-bye to her cousin, Lady Gratton thought of her words to Madame Mathilde: 'a flower alone on a stem.' Damaris in her splendour seemed so much alone —her husband had already departed, without a word to anyone— even with the child in her womb.

She sighed again. Her plan had been to return with the Earl in a few days' time. She had engagements to be fulfilled in Town—but they must be cancelled. She must stay with Damaris a few weeks longer to comfort her and make sure the breach had healed.

Her task was easier than she had expected. As Damaris had never thought her husband reasonable, she was more hurt than shocked by his rejection of her cousin. The animosity of the St Clouds she had known all her life, so its renewal could not affect her as it did her aunt, and Lady Gratton's company was certainly superior to poor Margaret's.

They entertained Mr Poyntz, were amused at his oddities, and speculated why the servants disliked him. Damaris even went so far as to ask Betty, but Betty reported that the Great Heron servants were a closemouthed lot, unlike the gossips of Malfrey House, and they considered her an outsider and told her nothing.

'But Mr Poyntz isn't part of the family,' Damaris said.

Betty shrugged her plump shoulders.

'He be gentlefolk. It be all one to *them*.'

Damaris considered this and was afraid that her maid was having an unpleasant life downstairs. But when she spoke of it to Betty, that stout young woman told her not to trouble herself.

'I be maid to your ladyship; and I be trained in kitchen and parlour work. There are those that do think I might be house-keeper one day, and they pay me respect.'

And she brushed her mistress's hair with vigour.

Damaris, laughing, told Lady Gratton that Betty seemed to be building up her power and influence with the same dogged deter-mination and absence of frivolity that Lord Malfrey had in gather-ing political support in both Houses of Parliament and in those private meetings where policy was made.

'Let's make a wager, Aunt,' she suggested, 'on a race—I wager that Betty becomes housekeeper before Lord Malfrey is prime minister.'

Lady Gratton, amused herself, nevertheless reproached her niece for levity. She was relieved, however, that Damaris had weathered the turbulence about Margaret and that her interest in the Heron household had not diminished. So well were things going that she felt justified, a month after that unfortunate event, in leav-ing Great Heron for a long-anticipated visit to a certain Lady Rise, one of the great society hostesses in Town; she was tempted by the prospect of great dinners, visits to the theatre and Vauxhall Gar-dens, routs and balls—though Lady Gratton felt herself too old to dance, she still liked to gossip with the chaperons on these occa-sions and felt she could do justice to all the other delights.

So she bade farewell with promises to return, and Damaris was left to her now familiar, placid country life. For a time her preg-nancy brought a longing for sleep, and she spent much time in her room or lying on the drawing-room sofa. Betty kept her company and told her of life below-stairs and in the village.

'They do say, my lady,' she told her mistress one evening as she was helping her undress, 'that young Mary Bodger, who be kitchen maid at Greystones, be in the family way. Mrs Crump says it's no surprise to anyone, for she was always on the gad. And no one sure who be the father.'

Betty had the look of a proper outraged matron, for if she had been disappointed by Jem the cowman, at least she had been promised and her village had known the father of her child. Da-maris was amused to see Betty in her new role of worthy dame and asked some questions about the unfortunate Mary.

'Oh, his lordship will have it looked to. His agent do take care of all. His lordship knows that Lady Cassandra can't always mind her household as she should, poor lady. Not in health, is Lady Cassandra.'

'Lord Malfrey is a good brother,' Damaris observed.

'And she be rare fond of his lordship.'

'He seems to be her only relation,' Damaris said meditatively.

'Yes, miss.' Betty, when excited, would forget Damaris's new status and revert to her old title. 'And I hear it do play on her mind. Would you believe, miss—I had it from Mary Bodger herself —that just before your wedding, Lady Cassandra took a draught. Very ill she was, and the maids thought she might die. His lordship had to be sent for. He just left her to go straight down to Somerset for wedding.'

Damaris, while feeling she should stop Betty's gossip, was for a moment speechless.

'There was a rare lot of talk,' Betty continued, 'but Vicar, he bade 'em hold their tongues. He said 'twas the apothecary made a mistake in the sick lady's draught. But the village say she be terrible jealous of the Earl, my lady.'

Damaris longed to know more, and it was with great effort that she silenced Betty. That night she lay in her bed, wakeful once more, gazing into the moonlight that strayed into her room. So that was why her husband wished to keep her from his sister. Poor, sickly woman, how lonely and desperate she must have felt! Damaris had long fancied that Lady Cassandra had been neglected by her father, and no one knew better than Damaris St Cloud what it meant to be neglected by one's family. She wanted to know Lady Cassandra, to make her feel that she had not been replaced in her brother's life and that she could have a sister's place in her own and enjoy being aunt to the child about to be born.

The village could whisper, but it was plain enough to Damaris that any woman would seem strange, shut up in this remote, wooded country all her life. And Lord Malfrey—what must he have suffered! She herself had been unfair to him, imagining he disliked his sister when his emotion must have been all affectionate distress. No wonder he had been so strange and stiff at the wedding; he must have been in great agony of mind. Even his strange behaviour on their honeymoon—this might explain it, at least in part. A man tortured with concern over a loved sister might find it hard to love his wife.

Her eager young mind formed plan after plan of getting to

know the Lady Cassandra, giving her warmth and affection, and bringing her back to the family circle. Whatever her husband's orders had been, they were based on his fears; surely he would welcome her disregarding them if that made for family happiness and peace.

And with such cheerful thoughts, drowsiness overcame Damaris and she slept the deep, refreshing sleep of the young. By morning, her intention was unchanged. As she ate her breakfast, she considered how best she could lay her plans. Lady Cassandra, she had already learned, had 'spells', spells of ill health followed by times when she did receive some company—the vicar, Lord Malfrey's agent and his wife.

Damaris ordered her carriage, had herself dressed for out-of-doors in a discreet gown and pelisse that disguised her condition, and told the coachman to drive her to Greystones. The old man pushed his lower lip out, grumbled and muttered and made slow work of going through the forest path. Yet with the sun shining brightly, piercing through the branches with only small, tender leaves upon them, and the ponds glittering with light, he could hardly make an excuse of the danger to carriage and horses. Damaris was no longer a strange young bride; she was very much the mistress of Heron, and he couldn't disobey, though he looked doleful when he turned left at the clearing and approached the house by the roadside.

Damaris was announced and shown immediately into a front parlour where a woman, about the age of Lady Gratton but with a fretful air, waited to greet her. It took a moment for Damaris to realize that this was Lady Cassandra. The lady of Greystones, in all her mysterious seclusion, had so long occupied her mind that she had become a romantic vision; Damaris had seen the girl of the portrait, somewhat faded but still lovely, languishing on her sofa, only rising perhaps to take the air in her garden.

Now she saw a woman nothing like the girl of the portrait, tall like the Earl and quite stout. Far from sickly, she looked robust, if bad-tempered. She greeted Damaris calmly. The appearance of her sister-in-law was no surprise to her; she remarked that she had seen her often in her carriage as she passed by.

Damaris felt abashed. Suddenly it seemed immensely rude that she had never called before. But Lady Cassandra showed by her manner that she had not expected the visit. Nor did she show much interest in Damaris's presence now. She seemed to accept it as a matter of course and conversed of ordinary things. Her embroidery frame was by her, and Damaris admired her work, and Lady Cassandra allowed it was one of her pleasures.

'I like to sit here in the front, instead of in the back drawing-room, and see the passers-by.'

Damaris remarked that there must be few .

Lady Cassandra looked at her coolly, with an expression all too familiar—it was very like that of Lord Malfrey. 'Oh, for those of us born at Heron, there is much to interest. There are not too many great folk visit here since my mother's time, but I know the country people in these parts, and there is always something to see.'

She absently patted her little pug, which shared her sofa. There was nothing about her of the air of a woman who felt a lack in her life; Damaris, coming on her mission of mercy, felt nonplussed. Lady Cassandra seemed as calm and self-sufficient as Lord Malfrey himself and not in need of any help from her. Still, she invited her sister-in-law to visit her at Great Heron, only to be met with a firm refusal.

'I am a sad invalid, you must have heard, Lady Malfrey, and I do not visit.'

At that moment the servant came in with a decanter of port for Lady Cassandra—it was, apparently, her mid-morning refreshment. She offered a glass to Damaris, who hated port but drank it to be friendly. Then Lady Cassandra took her on a tour of the principal rooms of the house; it was a pleasant, small establishment, unremarkable, but lighter than Great Heron. Damaris, whose imagination had seen Cassandra imprisoned behind the grey walls, was ashamed of her foolishness.

How Lady Gratton would laugh if she knew! For the aunt had deplored romance even more than levity in her niece, and when she had learned that her niece was reading *Le Roman de la Rose,* she had instructed her master to put that dangerous volume away. The damage had already been done; in spite of her acceptance of reality Damaris still had a hidden longing for a knight of chivalry who came to her sometimes in sleep. But Lady Cassandra as a maiden in distress—she had been very off the mark there.

Her plump sister-in-law was flushed by the port, and though she moved with dignity, a small crumb from the biscuit she had eaten with good appetite still trembled in the corner of her mouth on what Damaris could only think of as a whisker. She averted her gaze quickly to repress a giggle. She was being shown the back drawing-room that overlooked the garden, an apartment of some dignity. A portrait was well placed to catch the eye: Damaris looked, first from politeness, then with a sense of shock.

The portrait was a companion to the one of Cassandra at Great Heron, of a boy instead of a girl. It was painted in the same light, clear style—perhaps that explained the young Earl, or Lord Heron, as he had been then, having a countenance so different from the one she knew. The boy—fifteen, sixteen?—looked so young and eager, fresh-faced, his mouth sensitive, his eyes frank and innocent.

Damaris stared at the boy who had become her husband, trying to imagine them the same person. Lord Malfrey had not become plain and commonplace like his sister; he was considered a handsome man by Lady Gratton. Certainly he was distinguished; he had the look and air of a man of importance, polished by all the graces of the *ton*. But the thin-lipped man she knew, with his cold stare and cutting sarcasm and a strange dark side to his nature, who used his wife as a brood mare with less interest than a stable stud in service, was far from this gentle boy. The two were further apart than the fretful country dame, who was complaining at that moment in great detail of her afflictions in many parts of her body, and the dewy, shy girl of the Heron portrait.

Damaris left Lady Cassandra, saying she would call again, which news that lady took with no interest whatsoever, and even before Damaris was shown out she was already back on her sofa by the window, placidly embroidering on her frame. The young Lady Malfrey felt silly indeed and almost resolved to go no more, as her husband had forbidden it and Lady Cassandra obviously was not in need of her chivalrous attentions.

But the days and nights were long at Great Heron; as the months went by and her desire for sleep left her, she had little to do and missed her aunt sorely. But Lady Gratton was in the full flood of the Season, and knowing her sociable nature, Damaris could not ask her to come away. And so her mind went back to her sister-in-law at Greystones, and her visit was repeated, again and again.

Lady Cassandra continued as she had been on Damaris's first visit; she accepted her coming as part of her normal, day-to-day existence, but no intimacy developed, no beginnings of the friendship which Damaris craved, even with this woman of such limited interests and such habit of confinement. Her conversation was of her ailments—she was doubtful of her liver and not confident of the good state of her female organs—and of tales of the village and the encroachments of poachers, with which she seemed very familiar. Damaris met no one at Greystones except Mr Poyntz, who looked surprised and not pleased to see her there; his 'good-day to ye, to ye' had a somewhat ominous ring. She wondered if he planned to tell her husband; he probably knew she was forbidden to call.

The young Lady Malfrey was puzzled. There seemed to be no reason why she should not visit her sister-in-law; Lady Cassandra was normal enough. Perhaps she really did have 'spells' or perhaps—Damaris remembered the decanter and glasses brought in regularly every morning. Could it be that Lady Cassandra drank? She wrote to Lady Gratton of her doings, justifying herself with reference to that lady's often repeated comments on the virtues of family ties.

In reply came, not a letter, but Lady Gratton herself, post-haste from Town, leaving her engagements in disarray. She stayed a few days with her niece, lecturing her sternly, warning her to cease from the visits that would displease her husband greatly.

'It is wrong, very wrong of you, Damaris, to thwart his wishes in this way,' she said.

Damaris was surprised by her aunt's heat and remarked, as she remembered the matter of Margaret St Cloud, that sometimes her husband's wishes were irrational and perhaps should be thwarted.

Lady Gratton looked exceedingly upset.

'That is unkind in you, Damaris. Lord Malfrey may have his little peculiarities, but he is a good husband, a kind man. The purchase of Angelhurst has gone forward, and it is to be your very own. Think what it means to the village! Any other purchaser, you know, would certainly enclose the common—it is really the sensible thing to do—but then the villagers would be poor indeed. Consider the young men, Damaris, forced to go north to the manufactories, leaving the old people in want and care.'

Damaris was somewhat abashed but still declared she could see no harm in visiting Lady Cassandra and offered to take Lady Gratton to see the Earl's sister herself.

'There is nothing wrong with her, Aunt—except that she is dull. She is so confined, you know, and spends her days in over-feeding herself and her pug—they have the same look about them, now I think of it,' she said, and laughed.

Lady Gratton regarded her with vexation and dismay. Damaris's laugh was so very like her mother's. The gay laugh of Griselda Mayne echoed through the years: Griselda, who would marry the handsome young lieutenant against the wishes of his powerful family. 'Well, they can't eat me, Augusta,' she had said, laughing at her serious elder sister. But Griselda had been wrong. The Camberly family had eaten her, after all. Her youth, health, and very life had been taken, and not one St Cloud had been at her funeral. Lady Gratton hoped that Damaris, so carefully trained to sense, was not growing up into her mother's high spirits and headstrong nature.

'You know little about her,' she said severely. 'I have spoken to Dr Renshaw in Town—he has been consulted on her case since she was a girl. He told me that her nervous collapses are severe, and the excitement of strange persons is always likely to bring one on. Lord Malfrey has a care for both of you, and that is why he has asked you to leave her in privacy. It would be very bad for Lady Cassandra to be over-excited into another nervous seizure, and it would certainly be bad for you in your condition to have to witness one. I have heard she can be somewhat—violent, in fact.'

Damaris was perplexed, because no one seemed more placid than Lady Cassandra. Yet there might be something in the tales. Betty *had* told her of Lady Cassandra's taking a poisonous draught on the eve of her brother's wedding. Servants could exaggerate, but they would hardly make up such a tale in its entirety —she allowed Lady Gratton to convince her. Lady Cassandra's company was only mildly entertaining, after all. Perhaps her madness was the kind that village people spoke of, which came and went and often coincided with the waxing and waning of the moon.

The doctor himself arrived the next day, sent by Lord Malfrey to attend his wife, and he was able to report to Lady Gratton that all was well. He prescribed certain noxious draughts that he assured the ladies would benefit mother and child. Damaris took them without complaint, which pleased him, as he had no idea that Betty, suspicious of the foul-smelling stuff, had thrown it away and substituted a home-brewed wine that she had used herself for the same purpose, with very good result.

Domestic harmony now prevailing, Lady Gratton deemed it safe to return to Town. She promised Damaris a long visit in the summer to keep her company until the child should be born. Her letters, full of cheerful gossip, were eagerly awaited by her niece, and Betty was a comfort to her lonely mistress. More than Damaris realized, she relished their talks in her bedchamber when she was being dressed and undressed and Betty would tell her all the village news and little things she learned of the history of the family. Damaris would have felt it undignified to have gossiped openly with her maid, but she did allow Betty to talk and only rarely stopped her with an admonition.

She learned that her husband's father had been a terrifying nobleman of the old sort, a hard, severe man with a fearful temper, a great pride, and a huge appetite for women. He had not been faithful to his countess, but he had loved her. She had been a woman of noble blood and good fortune, and her entertainments at Great Heron were still talked of in the village. But when she had died, after the birth of the present Earl, there had been no more entertainments. The old Earl rarely came down from London. The village had expected that Lady Cassandra, growing up, might entertain. Indeed, Betty had discovered that contrary to the fixed custom of the house, at one time Lady Cassandra had left her old nursery and moved into the Countess's chamber, which Damaris was using now. But it had all come to nothing. Lady Cassandra became ill, the old Earl returned, and everything went back as it had been before. Great Heron had remained unchanged to the present day.

Damaris made up her mind that once she had been presented, she would invite guests to Great Heron and the former glories would be restored. She felt certain that the Earl would not gainsay her after the necessary heir was produced. If only, she prayed heartily, the child was a boy! She felt well and was sure the child would be healthy and thrive. For the time she enjoyed her walks and drives in the woods, but the days were long and the coachman would only take her a few miles, never further than the church. The road beyond there, he stated emphatically, like the road to Greystones, was too overgrown for the safe driving of the chaise.

Damaris knew he was following the Earl's instructions, and she rebelled. She had been obedient indeed, but some *small* diversion she must have. Brought up so quietly, she could spend days with her books, music, and needlework. But the fine spring weather was so tempting, and here at Great Heron there was no farm she could escape to, away from the eyes of her household. The Home Farm was many miles away, half a day's ride on the other side of Lesser Heron, close to the small town of Woodbridge Mere. The village spoke of the farm people as foreigners, and there was little going back and forth.

And so one especially fine day towards the end of June, Damaris sent the coachman on an errand, then went herself to the coach house and ordered the groom to put a horse to the gig. The man, reluctant, could not refuse his mistress, who murmured something about a little turn about the park. He watched her drive off at a sedate pace and went about his business.

Damaris drove to the park gates, had them opened by the surprised gate-keeper, and was off down the path through the woods. Coachman had been talking nonsense, she thought. The path was no more difficult than it usually was. The full-leafed trees made a green canopy through which the strong spring sunlight filtered in a delicious, aqueous glow—she might have been driving under water, a mermaid in the sea. She laughed out loud in the exuberance of pleasure, enjoying the rapid motion of her light equipage—so much more fun than lumbering along in the chaise. She felt free and happy and sang to herself as she held the reins.

The forest itself seemed to be happy. Instead of the grim silence of winter, it was full of the song of birds, a happy, busy calling in this time of mating and nest-building. They were no different from herself, she thought, smiling—all bringing forth the next generation to enjoy the pleasures of these woods. Certainly the coachman had exaggerated the dangers of the path. Grass had grown up, and here and there were patches of king cups and forget-me-nots, but certainly not enough to hide the dangers—those outcroppings of roots that could lame a horse if the driver was careless. The light was certainly enough to make them out. Damaris sped along, intoxicated by the day, composing in her mind a letter to Lady Gratton on the delights that were to be had, still, in a country life. She plunged into a deep green tunnel fragrant with spring blossom, a carpet of late golden primrose stretching before her. There were no words, she thought, to describe her sensation—and then, in a moment, her mare whinnied and reared, the gig shook, the long green tunnel seemed to shudder and dance, and she was in terror for her unborn child.

She kept a firm grip on the reins. The mare calmed and steadied. Damaris's heart was pounding, and her palms wet. Dismounting, she walked forward to see what had so agitated the normally docile mare. The animal looked at her with its soft round eyes and whinnied again. Damaris patted her neck soothingly. Now she saw what had been hidden by the carpet of primroses—the twisting, gnarled roots.

The mare was raising her left foreleg, and Damaris slid her fingers over the injured fetlock. She hoped, she believed, that no bone was broken, but most certainly the mare couldn't walk, much less draw the gig. The young countess was deeply mortified by her own folly. She had been warned; she had disregarded the warning. The pretty bay mare was hurt and could have been killed. She might have hurt herself and lost her child. More than foolish, her actions now seemed wicked, and it was a downcast and repentant young woman who stood in the green tunnel and took stock of her position.

In all her imprudence, she had come out unattended. The only thing to do now was to walk. She had left the house in the early afternoon; now she tried to conjecture how far she had come and how late it was. Certainly, in her speedy travel she had come a good distance, too far to walk back before dusk. She had not passed the crossroad to Greystones; it could not be much further. There was nothing for it but to add to her sins and call at Greystones for help. Lady Gratton would be angry; her husband most certainly would hear of her folly—Damaris, rueful, considered braving the long walk back to Great Heron. She was not afraid of the dark. Then she felt her child move and knew she must not take the risk. She would have to bear her scoldings, which, she told herself, she certainly deserved.

The way to the clearing, which had always seemed so short when she was being driven, now seemed long. It was a relief when she came to the end of the tunnel of dense, overhanging trees, but even when the path cleared she thought she would never come to the end of it. She walked carefully now, her eyes raking the ground before she trod. It would not do to fall. After a time, her burden that she had borne so lightly began to weary her. She had had no exercise so strenuous in a long time, and although she grew impatient, she made herself sit down on a hummock and rest. Betty would cluck her tongue when she saw the state of her gown, inches deep in dirt and grass. Damaris, with all the riches of the Countess of Malfrey, still thought like the modestly reared, impoverished Miss St Cloud.

She walked on and on through the growing dusk. Soon it was quite dark, and she was thankful when moonlight came to light the path before her. At last she saw the pond glitter at the road's edge and knew she was near the cross-road. She hurried on carefully and soon turned off in the direction of Greystones.

Inside the house, the lamps were lit. Outside, to Damaris's surprise and to her dismay, was Lord Malfrey's curricle. Her heart sank. The exposure of her disobedience was closer than she had expected. She did not want to see her husband just then. Her gown so dirty and tattered—she could imagine his cold looks. What could he be doing there? She had had no letter, no announcement of his coming, and Lord Malfrey never arrived at Great Heron unannounced. She looked about, but even his groom was nowhere to be seen. Lord Malfrey himself and Lady Cassandra were in plain view in the front parlour, their figures silhouetted as they stood together near the window.

Damaris, full of anxiety of one kind as she hesitated outside Greystones, began to feel an uneasiness of a quite different sort. It stole upon her before she knew it, a strange sensation she hardly understood. Her husband and Lady Cassandra were deep in conversation. Damaris could not hear their words, but there was *that* in their manner she found disquieting.

Lord Malfrey was almost fully backwards to the window, but Cassandra's face was clear. She was crying; she was beseeching; her plump and usually peevish face was now alive with emotion. She clutched her brother and loosed him only to run her hands up and down his arms and back, plucking at his very flesh with a strange avidity.

Damaris knew little of love. Her marital relations with her husband had hardly the warmth of passion on his part; in the conjugal embrace she thought disrespectfully that he seemed possessed by a cold fit. Yet even the ignorant young wife recognized love when she saw it.

She stood, irresolute, unable to turn away from a sight she knew she should not see. Lord Malfrey caught at his sister's hands. His head turned from side to side in negation, but Cassandra, it seemed, would not be denied. Her arms were strong about his neck, and she drew his face down towards her own in a kiss that had nothing sisterly in it.

The night was warm enough, but Damaris shivered. She felt as though a shard of ice was lodged deep inside her. The child moved again, and she was overcome with shock, disgust, and nausea. Unthinking, she ran back into the wood, dragging her skirts through the pond's edge, losing a shoe as she ran, with no thought except to get far away, far, far away, back to the safety of her room where she could crawl into her bed and hide.

On and on she ran, startling small animals that fled at her approach, once disturbing an owl in a thicket so that it flapped about her. She screamed in some childish horror as though she had been touched by an evil thing; tears rained down her face; she stared up for guidance to the moon that came and went behind the scudding cloud.

She came to the tunnel where her mare and gig still stood. The mare whinnied hopefully at her approach; for a moment Damaris thought to stay in the comparative safety of her small equipage, but a night-bird called; the place was dark. Terrified, Damaris was driven further and yet further.

The wind rose; a shower tossed its drops between the leaves and fell upon the frightened girl; it grew stronger, and water collected in rivulets along the path, turning the moss to a slick treachery. Damaris stumbled, righted herself, and was off as though demons pursued her. Thoughts of home, her aunt, and Angelhurst flickered through her mind as a haven she must reach. She ran; her foot came down on a stretch of slime, slid, and slipped; she staggered, struck her head on the trunk of a great tree; she fell and knew nothing more that night.

The servants had long since raised the alarm for the missing Countess. The mare and gig were found, but Damaris, in her flight, had wandered from the main path to another leading through the forest to nowhere except an old abandoned cottage. It was dawn before she was found by a gamekeeper, and she was carried back to Great Heron only in time to begin her labour.

Word was sent to Lord Malfrey at Greystones, who summoned doctors and rushed to his wife's side. The nearest doctor came from the town of Woodbridge Mere, Lesser Heron having only an apothecary, and was long in coming; Dr Renshaw could not arrive until the next day. Betty and Mrs Crump stayed with their mistress, and in her long and difficult labour the Earl was never far away.

He sat by his wife until she fully recovered consciousness, but when she saw him she turned her head aside with a shudder. Lord Malfrey, rising, left her and went to sit outside her room, returning only when she had forgotten him, and he sat in a dark corner almost unnoticed by the women. The doctor arrived about the same time as the baby.

Lord Malfrey stayed at Great Heron until Dr Renshaw came from Town and could ascertain that the baby was healthy and would live, and that the mother was out of danger. He visited his wife, but they exchanged only a few conventional words. They did not then, or ever, discuss the incidents of her drive and flight, but Lord Malfrey guessed what she had discovered. As the husband and wife regarded each other, with the baby at Damaris's side, they both knew that any hope for their marriage was over. Still they were condemned to continue on as they had been. For a great disappointment had come to the Earl and his Countess. The fine healthy infant was a girl.

CHAPTER

13

Damaris was to spend another year at Great Heron, a place she now thought of as a prison, where she was visited by a husband whose touch, no longer a matter of indifference and a slight distaste, had become loathsome, inspiring a disgust so great that Lord Malfrey himself could not but recognize it. The work of creating the heir to the house of Heron and the Earldom of Malfrey was a penance to them both.

Lady Gratton came down regularly to see her niece and was grieved to see the change in her. The life and laughter had gone, and her aunt was dismayed by her listlessness. Damaris had said nothing to Lady Gratton of her discovery; it seemed too painful, too shameful to be spoken of, ever. The Countess was now the mother of the infant Lady Griselda; for good or ill she was part of the house of Heron and that much removed from her own relations.

Her aunt attributed the change to a difficult childbirth and hoped for a quick amendment, but as the months passed Damaris failed to improve. Lady Gratton, in consultation with Dr Renshaw, attributed her continuing poor health to her new pregnancy, and the physician and the lady hoped that the birth of an heir would bring about all the recurrence of health and spirits that they could wish.

This time Damaris was watched closely to see that she didn't escape on any adventure that could hurt her or the child, until she felt wearily that the only thing more her husband could do would be to order her tied to her bed with the door of her room barred and bolted. Even more distressing to the young mother was Dr Renshaw's edict that she not be troubled with her baby. As soon as her pregnancy was known, a wet nurse was brought in for Lady Griselda, and she was kept well away, in Lady Cassandra's old nursery, so that the mother wouldn't be disturbed by the child's cries. The baby would be brought to her to gaze upon twice a day, after her feeding, when she would fall asleep and, if placed in her mother's arms, soon howl for her nurse.

If little Griselda could be no comfort, Lady Gratton did what she could. She sat beside her niece as she lay under long fringed shawls on a sofa by the window, where Damaris liked to gaze out into the shrubberies, feeling like some caged creature. When Lady Gratton returned to Town the days were even more dismal. Betty, sorry for her young mistress and convinced she was in an early decline, mixed herbs in her wine at night to make her sleep, and Mrs Crump, her enemy, saw what she did but for once held her peace. The servants whispered. Some thought she would become like Lady Cassandra; some thought she would die of the next birth;

while some who had heard of the sickness hereditary in the Mayne family thought she might be sickening in her lungs. Lady Gratton feared this last herself and sent a doctor learned in such matters to Great Heron. He reported to the anxious aunt that there were no signs of pulmonary complaint but that the young mother was sadly out of spirits. He was wise in more than matters of the lungs, and he told Lady Gratton and Lord Malfrey plainly that he thought a rest from childbearing was necessary for his very young patient, and he prescribed a course of social life and amusements to raise her spirits. He seemed more French than English, Lady Gratton was later to observe to her cronies, and understood the virtues to the female system of balls over belladonna and fashion over physic.

Before these remedies could be tried there were still two months of pregnancy, and Lady Gratton went to stay at Damaris's side until her lying-in was over. For all the anxiety of the household, on this occasion events were predictable. The baby arrived at the proper time; the doctors were ready and waiting at Great Heron; Lady Gratton and Lord Malfrey were in attendance. Once again, the labour was long and difficult. Lord Malfrey insisted that Lady Gratton go to bed for a few hours of sleep, but he himself stayed in his wife's room as he had done the year before. Lady Gratton, observing him, thought once more that he looked like a man in torment. She was more right than she knew.

To Lord Malfrey, this night was like the night when his daughter was born; he had the same thoughts, he saw the same pictures swimming before his mind. On that night he had looked at Damaris when she was brought in from the woods, bruised and cut, half-conscious as her labour began, in an agony of mind almost more than he could bear. He had come rushing up to Great Heron when he had learned of the accident, whip in hand after urging his horses on to their limit.

My God, he had thought, catching sight of himself in the long looking-glass, I look like my father. That thought was almost enough to kill him.

All during the birth of his daughter, and a year later that of his son, he had sat, silent, among the shadows of the mistress's room at Great Heron. Hideous scenes forced themselves before his mental gaze, scenes he could not wipe out, could not turn from; figures flickered before him, shifting pictures, jumbled, chaotic, tormenting him through the long hours.

He saw himself and Cassandra. How like Damaris she had been—how like, how different. But he and Cassandra had been different from all normal people, though they had not known it. They couldn't remember their mother; their father they rarely saw. The old Earl had hated children, especially his own heir, the heir who had killed his wife. The children were almost abandoned; Mr Poyntz, the vicar, was tutor to the boy, and a governess was left to watch over Cassandra.

The young Viscount Heron and his sister were forbidden to know any of the people on the estate—they rarely saw them in any case, with the Home Farm so far away and only a woodcutter sometimes passing near the park gates. They grew up in a strange world where the boy learned only history and classics, and his sister deportment, embroidery, and music.

They were too cut off from all normal life to realize the strangeness of their own situation; they knew only each other, for Poyntz had his church and his parish and in his free time was endlessly engaged on a work that was to be his gift to the world, a compendium of all knowledge, far superior to the *Encyclopédie,* the notes for which occupied several rooms. The governess, more modest, quietly, secretly took to drink.

The house servants, by the Earl's order and in the tradition of Great Heron, had only a formal relationship with the family. They still spoke of a time when a young manservant had addressed his lordship, then Viscount Heron, five years old, without the words 'my lord' and had been flogged for his omission.

The present Earl, sitting in his corner with his wife's groans ringing in his ears, saw himself and Cassandra as two young people, ghosts still haunting the house together. They had grown into adolescence side by side. As children they had learned already to escape from the park and prying eyes, and they made the forbidden forest their playground. In the winter their adventures were necessarily curtailed, but spring was the herald of their delights.

Knowing no other life, they had never been unhappy, but one early, lovely spring brought with it a positive happiness, a sense of joy. They strolled and ran and played without hindrance; the governess was fuddled into daylong stupors, and Poyntz had no time for anything except his amassed notes, which at last were ready to be assembled into his colossal work. The young people spent whole days in the woods, climbing the trees, jumping across the ponds, hiding in the thickets, resting on the mossy ground already sprinkled with the golden buds of primrose.

Love and longing took them by surprise. He held Cassandra in his arms as he had often done; he had brushed her hair from her face and kissed her cheek while a woodlark sang its sweet and wistful song. Cassandra, the elder, had returned his kiss with something new in her intensity, and all the joys of nature and of youth gathered in a ferment in his body and in the blue and suddenly strange depths of Cassandra's eyes.

Their warmth and closeness, their safety from prying servants, made their desires easy to gratify. They learned how to love with some confusion but little sense of wrong. Brother and sister were all in all to each other as they had always been.

This happiness, sweetly protracted, came to a sudden end. The old Earl, in his usual arbitrary way, decided the boy should go to school. No sooner had he decided than it was done. Cassandra was left alone, and the boy who had known no playmate other than his gentle sister was thrown into the harsh and, to him, cruel world of school. The young Lord Heron survived the shock of the swift change. His physical courage stood him in good stead with the bully-boys of school; and if he inwardly shrank at the jeers of schoolmates to a new boy of his age, so unaware of all their ways, he took it outwardly with composure. It was then that his quick wit and biting tongue first came into play, a defense against a new world that threatened to overwhelm him. For there was one thing he had quickly learned from the coarse tongues of his fellows, and that was the exact nature of the sin he and Cassandra had committed.

During the winter, Lord Malfrey decided for the first time in many years to go down to Great Heron for some shooting, and he took his son with him. They arrived at the house to find the servants grim, the governess fled, Poyntz hiding at the vicarage in Lesser Heron, leaving his mountain of notes behind. Lady Cassandra had locked herself into her room, the room where Damaris now lay, and refused to appear.

'Gone to earth!' Lord Malfrey had roared. Unaccustomed as he was to refusal, he was instantly aware of something very wrong. 'Drag the vixen out!'

A groom had broken the door open, and as his gaze had fallen on his trembling daughter, despite her loose night-gown the reason for her hiding was very plain to see. Terrified, Lady Cassandra tried to shield her body with her arms, but nothing could hide the fact that she was heavily pregnant.

Lord Malfrey roared and howled in a passion of rage such as his children had never seen. Catching his daughter by the shoulders and shaking her till she screamed, he demanded the name of her seducer. The man would marry her or he would die. If it were Poyntz, that cringing clergyman, he would marry her and then die.

Cassandra's screams, Damaris's screams, rang together in the ears of the man who had been Lord Heron. Cassandra had been too terrified, or too loyal, to speak. The red face of her father, his wildly rolling eyes, brought her to her knees in fear but did not appease his wrath. She clutched at his top-boots, looking up at him piteously for forgiveness, but Lord Malfrey roared on like a madman.

His son stood back in horror and disbelief, half hoping he would wake from nightmare. He had courage enough to fight his own fear and tell the truth, but the truth would only make his father's rage against Cassandra greater. There could be no husband for Cassandra, only a more deep, abiding disgrace. His father stormed and raged, hurling questions at the upper servants, with his daughter moaning at his feet. But they could tell him nothing. Some, like their master, suspected Mr Poyntz but had no proof; others, if they guessed the truth, remained silent, for it would have been beyond the laws of sense to speak.

Frustration worsened the anger of the truly frenzied Earl. He pulled his daughter to her feet and once again demanded the name of the man. Cassandra, her hair dishevelled, her eyes huge with fright, was dumb. In a culmination of fury Lord Malfrey thrust his daughter against the bed-post, lifted his whip, and brought it down, singing, across her shoulders.

Screaming at his father, Lord Heron pushed forward and tried to wrest the whip from his father's grasp. The Earl was a strong man in his prime. He merely motioned to the grooms who stood in the doorway, and they came forward silently, grasped the boy, and held him still.

'Quiet, my lord,' one of the grooms, more kindly than the rest, whispered to him. 'There is nothing to be done just now.'

The whip rose and fell, rose and fell. It tore the fine lawn gown on his sister's back and made great welts across her soft white flesh. Cassandra screamed and sobbed.

Lord Malfrey stirred in his wife's chamber—was it Cassandra or Damaris who cried out?

The whip whistled again and again. Cassandra, bloody, groaning, fell across her bed, one cry following another, her body contorting, until the groom who had whispered raised his voice and spoke steadily.

'Mistress, she be giving birth, my lord.'

The Earl, his eyes glazed in madness, paused, and with one last swish of his weapon, turned from his daughter.

'Let's hope she dies, then.'

He strode off to the dining-parlour to demand his dinner and wine. He lingered there long into the night, drinking himself into a stupor, but not before he had destroyed everything in the governess's room and collected all of Poyntz's Compendium, with its mountain of notes and references, and made a huge bonfire, looking on with grim satisfaction as it disappeared into the flames. Before he fell asleep he swore that he would rid himself of every servant on the place and that all the women should be whipped.

When morning came and he woke, his first question was whether the vixen lived. A frightened servant told him that Lady Cassandra was living but that the child, a premature baby, was born dead.

Dead. Lord Malfrey, in his dream and confusion, wondered whether this child would be born dead and Damaris be another Cassandra—Cassandra, whom their father had confined to Greystones with only one servant to attend her. Cassandra was a prisoner. Lord Heron had been sent back to school and did not see his sister again as long as his father lived. He later learned that his father had sent her no doctor and had ordered her kept on short commons in the hope that she would die. Instead she had lived, but with a burden of ailments of mind and body. Her only friend was the vicar, who dared not see her; he was disgraced, forever cut off from hope of future preferment, and only kept the living of Lesser Heron, which could not be taken away. With his life-work destroyed, he had gone into a mild, premature senility. By the time the Viscount succeeded to the earldom and could alleviate his sister's condition, she was no longer the girl he had known. Her understanding had weakened, and from her lonely years she would have bouts of fits where she wished to show her scars. The only thing that did not change was her passion for her brother. The horror of her cries and groans, the memory of her wounds, scourged Lord Malfrey as he awaited the birth of Damaris's children.

All his own folly and evil seemed to gather about him, each episode like one bird of a flock that circled, touching him in turn with the brush of a wing, and he helpless to banish them. Cassandra's life had been stunted before he came to manhood. She would not even leave Greystones. Her pattern of life was set. There would be no change for Cassandra until she died.

In due time he had taken his place in the great world. The old Earl's method of rearing children had brought forth a noble son, Society had said in approval. He behaved as a young man of fashion should; his mistresses approved him and never knew they did not stir him and that the pleasure they provided was shallow, unsatisfying.

Lord Malfrey sighed and tried to think and dream no more, but the black flock of memories pressed close. Something had happened to the mind of the brother as well as the sister on that terrible night. Love and passion had become twisted, stunted, in him as well as in her. Bored with the *femmes du monde,* he had been drawn to the young dancers of the opera. A fresh young face, a blue-eyed glance, a shy yet alluring smile was his undoing. And yet, when he took the girls to the small, out-of-the-way house he bought for this purpose, almost empty of servants and screened by tall trees, his passion would play him false: the girl would look like the young Cassandra, and he himself would change from the young lover to the tyrant, mad old Earl. His gold paid for what they endured, and his life continued smoothly enough—that of the respected statesman and nobleman who, perhaps like others, had a dark side to his nature.

He had always known he must marry at last and have an heir, but he loved no woman and postponed his decision from year to year. When he had seen Damaris's portrait in Mansart's studio he had been strangely drawn—it was the face and form of his secret desire. Yet he learned she was a lady of rank: here, he thought, was his wife.

But his marriage had been misery. Here he found neither the boredom that overtook him with his elegant society mistresses nor the tortured rapture that came with his opera girls. He could not use his wife as he did the girls of no importance; nor did he wish to. For the first time since his youth the unfortunate man knew tenderness and the birth of love. His young wife's smile caught at his heart, and he longed to pour out his affection. Yet his manner was constrained and inhibited—when he touched his wife in love, her face would change to that of the young Cassandra on the pillows, and he would feel a loathing for himself.

His pitiful love grew; his wife's dignity, charm, and character were what he had never known in his young women of pleasure, but his ambivalent feelings froze the expression of that love and caused him to stay away as much as he decently could. His struggle was long and unremitting—when he had arrived at Great Heron and seen the young, fair, blue-eyed Margaret St Cloud, for the first time in his life he had broken down and behaved with a discourtesy that broke the rules of the *bon ton*.

His torment lasted as long as his wife's travail. Dawn came, the doctors and women were clustered about the bed; there was a cry of joy and the words came triumphantly:

'A son!'

'And a fine healthy lad,' the doctor added soon after.

Lord Malfrey rose. He did not look at the infant that was being bathed by the women, nor at his wife. He left her room, never to enter it again. He waited downstairs until the news was brought him—the mother and child were doing well. Then he mounted his curricle and drove away.

CHAPTER

14

After the birth of the heir, Damaris's return to health and spirits was so swift as to astonish her doctors and her household. The young woman who had seemed to be doomed to declining strength and nervous affliction, with the spectre of her early death troubling those who loved her, was up, about, and impatient for Society as soon as the child was christened in the church at Lesser Heron.

Plans were made for Damaris to go to Town, where she was to be presented in the last of the Queen's Drawing-Rooms that season.

'For then, you know,' Lady Gratton remarked, 'you will be able to meet the Prince Regent at Brighton. And whatever people say about Prinny it is the thing to be invited to the Pavilion. And for myself, I must own that I still find him charming.'

Lady Gratton, who remembered the young 'Prince Florizel,' sighed a little.

Damaris paid attention to her aunt, who was proving to be a most useful social arbiter. Her wardrobe had to be put in hand at once. A lady's maid was searched for and engaged by Lady Gratton.

'Can't I take Betty?' Damaris said.

Her aunt shook her head.

'Take her or leave her as you please—but she cannot be your lady's maid. It is essential that your maid be used to dressing ladies who move in the first circles. You must understand'—Lady Gratton imparted her wisdom with a most serious air—'that a position in Society is not a matter of course. Certainly, as wife to the Earl of Malfrey, with your Mayne and St Cloud blood, you have a place, a high place. But for the pinnacle, more is needed. Beauty you have; but beauty alone is not enough. Fashion is essential; distinction, charm—all help. Graciousness in hospitality and also a certain—something.'

Damaris listened closely. For although she laughed a little to herself at her aunt's grave mien, in truth she craved a new life and yearned to shine.

'A great lady is distinguished but never outré—except sometimes when she is old. But perhaps one as young as yourself should not aim at first for *any* difference. A smooth, splendid début is what we will look for.'

Lady Gratton didn't say that Damaris's extreme youth as the Countess of Malfrey and the mother of two children was something of an oddity in itself. She had no idea of making the girl self-conscious, but Lady Gratton knew that the Duchess of Camberly, restored to all her old animosity against Damaris by the treatment of Margaret St Cloud, had been busy all through the spring in putting out gossip relating to her husband's niece: the strangeness of the match with a child not out of the schoolroom; Lord Malfrey's failure to present her immediately after the marriage; her long seclusion in the country.

Lady Gratton had heard all the rumours, brought to her ears by all her faithful friends. The young Lady Malfrey was an invalid, cast into fits by too early motherhood or, some said, demented from birth, her husband finding himself horribly deceived and hiding his error in the gloomy shelter of the Forest of Heron. Other rumours, more frivolous, had it that Lord Malfrey had made his offer after seeing Mansart's portrait and when it was too late to withdraw had found her to be a veritable 'Flanders mare.'

That at least, Lady Gratton thought, would be quickly disproved. Damaris had never been more in health and beauty. Her complexion was brilliant; her deep blue eyes sparkled brighter than her jewels. The aunt's relief at her niece's improvement was so great that she troubled herself little about its cause and possible outcome.

As soon as her child was pronounced a boy, and healthy, Damaris knew she was released. No longer would she be kept a prisoner at Great Heron—even if Lord Malfrey wished to keep her there, he could not. The opinion of the world would be too much against him; a husband might keep his wife on his estates and refuse to allow her the pleasures of Town—but only if she had disgraced herself. Damaris had no idea of disgracing herself, but she was more than eager for pleasure.

Since the birth of the child, she had only seen Lord Malfrey at the christening. He had left strict instructions for the baby to be taken from his wife and put to a wet nurse. Damaris had been angry, but Lady Gratton soothed her. If Damaris wished to enter into Society that season, it was better so.

As a mother, Damaris had another inner struggle. Lord Malfrey had no objection to her going to Town; he only stipulated that the babies be left in the country. 'For,' he wrote, 'London is an unhealthy place at best, and as the weather grows warm there are stinks in the streets and children die of putrid fevers.'

Damaris, who was fond of the Lady Griselda and the young Christopher St George, Viscount Heron, in spite of the difficulties of their conception and birth, at first said rebelliously that it was just a trick of Lord Malfrey's to keep her at Great Heron. Lady Gratton disabused her mind.

'He is quite right, my dear. It is one of the misfortunes of Town, with people so close together. In the great houses, matters are arranged as well as they can be, but in the humble streets and along the stables and the mews, the stinks in warm weather are dreadful—people shut up their houses and go to Brighton or the country. Yet still many infants die. It is better, Damaris, not to expose the heir and Lady Griselda until they are older. You can come down to Great Heron to see them whenever you wish. One of the great pleasures of a good income,' she added, smiling, 'is that the expense of travel is nothing.'

Damaris listened and obeyed. The one disadvantage of going to Town would be the presence of the Earl at Malfrey House. But, she thought coolly, he had his political life and his clubs—she doubted he would dine at home more than two or three times a week. And she would keep her table full of guests; there would be no likelihood of têtes-à-têtes. He would want that no more than she did herself. As her first act in warding off such unpleasantness, she invited Lady Gratton for the length of her own stay at Malfrey House and then to join her for the rest of the season at Brighton.

Lady Gratton, nothing loath to launch her niece into Society and to reopen the doors of Malfrey House, accepted the invitation gladly. The question of Betty settled itself. Betty had become a power at Great Heron and certainly could not go back to the kitchen at Malfrey House. Damaris offered her the post of assistant lady's maid, but Betty begged to be left behind for a time.

'I like to see what be happening here,' she said grimly, fearful that Mrs Crump would regain her undisputed sway over the female servants. 'And I can watch those nurses and see they do what they should and not be poisoning the little things with draughts from the apothecary. I don't hold with physicking, my lady. My little 'un never was physicked, and he be growing tall and strong as a young tree.'

Damaris thought about it and felt the children would be safer with Betty in the house, though she foresaw many long and venomous battles between her maid and the nurses. And so, as quickly as she and Lady Gratton could get her necessary things together, she found herself at Malfrey House in Town, in all the noise, confusion, and bustle that might indeed have injured the nerves of a girl as delicate as Damaris looked, but in truth gave her only a simple rush of pure delight.

The girl who had been brought up so quietly, and who had lived as a bride so obscurely, found the noise and press of people stimulating, the shops and warehouses a treasure trove, and every play and concert an enchantment. Lady Gratton took her to call on the great ladies, and they went to a few quiet dinners. Once Damaris had been presented to the old Queen, the doors of Malfrey House were opened as they had not been since the death of the former Countess. Lady Gratton had planned Damaris's first dinner and ball to be the last great event of the London Season and the one to be talked of the rest of the year.

When Society clapped its eyes on the young Countess of Malfrey as she stood receiving her guests, all talk of disfigurement, nerves, or ill health was done away with forever. The gossip about the 'schoolroom miss' was dismissed as a matter of no importance.

'For,' as Lord Alvanley remarked, 'who could blame Malfrey for snatching up such a prize while he could?'

'And who,' Lady Jersey replied, with her little giggle, 'can blame him for hiding her until he had his heir? Very wise, I should think.'

Lady Gratton smiled at her niece's success. She stood slim and straight and seemed taller than she was, in a blue gown trimmed with silver and all her sapphires blazing. Yet it was Damaris's young beauty that dazzled; and the slight shyness that she felt became in her an added dignity.

'Blue-eyed Damaris,' the young bucks murmured, and in their way fell a little in love.

But the great and final accolade came from the Beau himself. Lady Gratton, together with the invaluable Madame Mathilde, had dressed Damaris carefully, determined to hold a mean between those ladies who still liked to appear half-naked, in their slit muslins and the sumptuous look coming back into fashion. Her gown hinted at more than it revealed; the rich silks yet had a lightness and simplicity. The quiet elegance of her dress, together with a slight aloofness in her manner that shielded without altogether hiding her youthful eagerness, won the approval of the great doyen of restraint.

A Mrs Hammersley-Beckwith, a great friend of the Duchess of Camberly with wealth much greater than her lineage, ventured to disparage the new beauty in his hearing.

'She seems very much up to everything for a girl so very young.'

The Beau put up his quizzing-glass and gave her a languid look.

'Ah, but *she,* Madam,' he said, to the delight of a clutch of dandies who followed in his train, 'she is to the manner born.'

He turned away and addressed Lord Mildmay.

'What a happy end to such a dull season! I am entirely at the feet of this cool countess.'

And Damaris was known henceforth as the Cool Countess, a *succès fou,* Madame Mathilde declared in rapture. When the Earl learned of this appellation of his lady, he was satisfied and thought it proper indeed.

CHAPTER

15

Damaris, in the joy of her triumph, was at first reluctant to leave Town, but she soon found that Brighton was merely London by the sea. It was brilliant with the assembled society, and the scarlet and gold of the Prince Regent's Hussars were everywhere, to Damaris's pleasure. Captain St Cloud had been with the Tenth before his poverty and exchange, and she loved to hear those who remembered him talk of the dashing, reckless St Cloud.

Lady Gratton, while enjoying the comfort and prestige of the grand house that Lord Malfrey had taken for his wife on the Marine Parade—he himself had not been able to get away—was not quite so happy to hear of the wild youthful doings of her dead brother-in-law. She had nothing to complain of in her niece's behaviour, for Damaris, though enjoying her new-found pleasures, was a model of decorum. But the tales of the Hussars reminded her that Damaris came from a set of heedless, reckless parents, and there was always a tiny shadow of fear. For the one thing the young Lady Malfrey must never be was reckless.

Lord Malfrey, Lady Gratton knew, would indulge his wife in every way, give her every advantage of money and rank. But he had a deep concern for his family honour and the welfare of his children—he would not tolerate wildness in his wife. She had heard his opinion given strongly on the matter of the young Mrs Carroway, wife of the heir to one of the great private families in the kingdom, who was disgracing herself and her relatives by open profligacy—a bride who had not yet produced a son. Lord Malfrey had said sternly that the disgrace of a divorce in such a case was far less than the disgrace of keeping such a woman in the family.

But it was folly even to consider such things, she told herself. Damaris was pointed out to young girls as a model of perfect breeding by no less than the patronesses of Almack's. She did not drive her own phaeton, as some young ladies were doing—it coarsened them, Lady Gratton felt, and the exposure would certainly ruin Damaris's complexion. There were far too many weatherbeaten Englishwomen about already. Damaris danced the waltz gracefully but with no look of abandon—her whole demeanour was a perfect balance between the modesty of a young bride and the dignity required by her position.

As an unattached married woman she had a flock of young men, Hussars, young bucks, and dandies to escort her to balls and routs, to walk with her along the Parade and the Steyne, to fetch her ices and carry her shawls. Her attitude towards them was just as it should be; she was gracious but inwardly amused, Lady Gratton knew.

Lady Gratton sighed, for life was easier and more pleasant than it had ever been, and she wanted to have peace and enjoy it and not worry about such seemingly baseless concerns. Yet she knew in her heart that *some* part of Damaris's marriage couldn't be happy. Lady Gratton believed that a young wife should not expect much happiness in marriage; she also knew the strength of natural impulse, and she watched her niece carefully to see if any of her escorts meant more to her than the rest.

She soon saw that Damaris was quite impervious to the charms of her admirers. The Prince's Hussars, with their constant public displays, seemed to her like toy soldiers, and she became proud that her father had transferred into a line regiment. To her taste the young bucks with their talk of racing and the stables were dull, and the dandies for the most part absurd. Damaris was not to lose her heart, but soon danger came from another direction.

The transformation from prisoner of the Forest of Heron to toast of the *bon ton* was heady. All of Damaris's youth and vigour cried out for expression, and sooner than she could have imagined, the daily social rounds grew tame. The season at Brighton was long, as the Prince Regent was in no hurry to leave the place he loved best. Damaris visited the Pavilion, marvelling at this strange oriental fantasy that sat, like an opium dream, in the old fishing village of Brighthelmstone.

The Beau presented Damaris with a lovely blue enamelled snuff-box from his collection because, he said, the colour was exactly 'Damaris blue.' The Regent, not to be outdone in gallantry by a man he had come to dislike, hung his ballroom in blue silk for Damaris's first visit, and Damaris Blue became a colour of fashion.

All these compliments pleased the young Lady Malfrey, but she found they did not satisfy. Yet what was unsatisfied she didn't know. When Lady Gratton had to leave for a few weeks for a long-standing engagement with Mrs Farthingale, Damaris wished she could have Margaret St Cloud with her—she would have liked to be to some young girl what Lady Gratton had been to her. But *that* was not permitted.

The Duchess of Camberly did not visit Brighton that season, but her daughter Lady Devereaux did, and her sister with her—her poor sister, who still had received no suitable offer. The names Weary and Dreary had stayed with them, and the young bucks made fun of Dreary Devereaux, so small, cross, and crabbed, they said, just like the Duchess—Devereaux had earned his money 'deuced hard.' Damaris scolded them soundly. It was no pleasure to her to find her cousins teased and tormented. Poor Weary—almost nobody remembered her real name, Wilhelmina—unfortunately so big and fair-haired, quite out of style, was really looking sad and dejected. The young men were frightened off, for the Duke, it was said, annoyed at having to come down with so much money for Dreary, was clutching the purse-strings tight.

'The old Earl of Fosters would take her,' Mrs Farthingale had reported. 'But Lord, what a mix-up that would be! The girl would be mother-in-law to her sister and grandmother to her nieces and nephews.'

'And a dowager, most likely, at thirty,' Lady Gratton had added.

Damaris would have liked to help poor Weary—she was sure she could do something to retrieve her social fortunes—but was well snubbed for her pains. And so she was left with her circle of young men, for the ladies of the *ton,* while liking and respecting her, found her reserve a barrier and did not become her intimates.

And so she was quite pleased to leave at last for Great Heron to see her babies and Lady Gratton, though the thought of the house in the forest could still put a chill on her heart. The two ladies arrived to find Lord Malfrey already there. Mother and great-aunt admired the children and spoke of their increased weight and growth. Damaris toyed with the curls on the nape of Christopher's neck and, to the deep disapproval of the nurses, retied Griselda's hair-ribbon and was rewarded with a rare, shy smile. Their father said little, but the next morning he asked Lady Gratton if she and Damaris would oblige him by making a journey to Angelhurst as soon as possible. He himself was not able to go; he had some important matters at Great Heron.

The two ladies went off, Damaris eager to see her old home, Lady Gratton rather disturbed. She said nothing to her niece on their journey, but she realized, as Damaris could not, that the pieces of business confided to her care were very trifling, nothing that the agent, Tinkerty, who had been kept on, could not manage.

She had seen Lord Malfrey's face as his wife, no longer a country girl but already an assured, though gentle-voiced, young *femme du monde,* played with her children. Lady Gratton did not pride herself on her knowledge of other people's minds and hearts; she gave herself no credit for any extraordinary perception, but what was before her she did see. Her impression had been quite distinct—Lord Malfrey had greeted his wife with pleasure yet did not like her to be near his children. His father, she had heard, had been a strange man also, of long neglects and sudden jealousies, and she wondered.

Damaris was happy with her visit; when they approached Angelhurst and she saw the Malfrey colours flying, she was pleased and gratified. Lady Gratton privately thought they looked somewhat pretentious on the simple house, but the people on the estate had meant the attention respectfully.

The servants, farmers, and tenants had made much of the young mistress, and in the delight of coming home as Lady Bountiful, she was unaware of her dismissal from Great Heron. *Now* she and Lady Gratton were called on by the ladies from the great families of the county and were invited to dinners and balls, and Lady Gratton gave it as her opinion that they should attend.

'It is not,' she said sagely, 'for the Countess of Malfrey to remember the neglect of Damaris St Cloud.'

In these pleasures the weeks went by happily. Damaris loved

the fresh simplicity of her old home and enjoyed the gossip of village and servants—Jem the cowman was still working at Angelhurst, for his wife, the widow, had proved bad-tempered and close-fisted, and Jem was a poor farmer after all. The village laughed at him, calling him a fool for not having married Betty, who was high in the service of Lady Malfrey, and Damaris felt poor Betty was avenged.

Christmas was near, and Damaris was ordering her things packed for their return to Heron when letters came from her husband. The political situation would keep him in Town through Christmastide, and he asked that the ladies join him there. It was a request that a wife could hardly refuse. Damaris was disappointed; she had looked forward to seeing the children again and had ordered many clothes and playthings that she wished to give them herself. Yet she was pleased to be going back to the excitement of Town.

'And we can always go down to Great Heron before the Season begins,' she told Lady Gratton.

Her aunt said nothing, but she made the journey to Town with fear in her heart. She believed Lord Malfrey would do his best to separate his wife from her children. And Damaris had so little family. Only herself. The St Clouds estranged, the husband such a shadowy figure in his wife's daily life—Lady Gratton had heard more than one of the young bucks refer to Damaris as the lovely Lady All-Alone. Without her children to bind her to domestic life, what would her niece become?

CHAPTER

16

The question was soon answered. Damaris became a brilliant hostess and was the most sought-after woman in Society. She was the great love of the dandies, especially those young men who preferred to yearn in public for a woman rather than to fulfil their longings. And when she tired of ordinary amusements, from an evening at the opera to supper in a box in Vauxhall Gardens, there was always the Prince Regent to urge her on to more heady delights.

The Prince, the dandies, and all the young bucks in Town were avid gamblers, and the ladies were not left behind. The play could be deep, and Lady Gratton entered a salon one night to find Damaris, cool to a stranger's gaze, but with a brilliance in her eyes that her aunt knew meant a great excitement, wagering on her cards. Apparently all her guineas were already on the table, for without hesitation she tore off her sapphire bracelet and threw it down.

The men at the table laughed and applauded.

'Damme, but I like a woman of spirit,' Lord Hallbury remarked; and the Beau, who himself was losing the last of his fortune night after night at Watier's, bowed and said, 'To the greatest of the goddesses, Venus and Chance, in the person of my lady.'

Lady Gratton was cold with shock and fear. If Damaris should lose her bracelet, Lord Malfrey's gift of great value, how could he be told? What would he say when he learned his wife was a gamester?

The hand was played; Damaris won; the evening ended in laughter and congratulation. But Damaris *was* a gamester, and a lover of deep play—she was certainly the daughter of Captain St Cloud. Only one thing saved her. Damaris, her aunt found, was lucky—lucky, that is, for a gambler, for her wins balanced her losses.

'Favoured by fortune,' the dandies said, but Lady Gratton, more practical, decided that Damaris's good fortune came from a head for cards, a head that was not dulled by too much wine. The dandies most often were fuddled.

Her niece's reputation remained high, and Lady Gratton's worries subsided. Lady Malfrey was well established now, and her aunt thought that as a substitute parent she could at last lay down her burden. And if her niece, always restless under her calm exterior, realized how far she was drifting from the young Damaris St Cloud, she only shrugged. The *bon ton* was not the place for Bath misses; the great world had its own rules and she knew all of them now—and how to bend them.

She could have taken lovers if she wished, but she did not wish.

In her heart she thought the Beau was right; she was cool indeed. Her girlish dreams had faded with marriage and then with her knowledge of men of the world. Here were no knights of chivalry, not the man of whom she had dreamed in her quiet sleep at Angelhurst. Now she went to bed in the morning, with the rumble of carts already outside in the streets, and slept the sleep of a *femme du monde* until she rose at noon.

The Beau, with his wild love of a wager, bet he could dress Damaris as a dandy and walk with her, undiscovered, down St James's, that street where ladies, by tradition, never appeared, even in their carriages. Damaris, in what her aunt would have termed her hey-go-mad mood, agreed. She sauntered with the Beau down the street, with an air that belied her consciousness of her trousered legs, and gazed through her quizzing-glass at half the men she knew, all puzzled at the appearance of this newcomer. The Beau took her to White's, and they sat in the famous bow window and watched the world go by. Later the Prince sent a message—who was the charming youth? But Damaris had already changed and escaped.

It was not the last time she was to disguise herself as a man. The girl full of health and spirits, having no real duties, so quickly bored with the usual life of a lady of the *ton,* was enchanted by the freedom she discovered when she donned men's clothes. After a time, she decided ruefully that the life of an elegant woman was like that of the hens at Angelhurst. The hen-runs of Town and Brighton and the country houses were gilded and sweet, but hen-runs nevertheless. And all the time men had the whole world to range in.

If she could not do most of the things that men did as a matter of right, at least she could enjoy some of their pleasures. Soon she took a set of rooms in an obscure neighbourhood where she could change her clothes, calling herself Desmond Midnight. Desmond had a very shy young sister, Marianne, but Desmond was not shy. His bold manner soon gave him the reputation of being a young rake, and Damaris enjoyed it enormously. Only cock-fighting sickened her, and she never returned after a first visit; but she went to Jackson's Boxing Saloon, drove once with the Whip Club, and became a habituée of the gambling hells and all the theatres.

One night, as she lounged outside the opera chaffing one of the girls, two ladies accompanied by a clergyman tried to pass. The disapproving looks of the ladies and their quiet, countrified dress brought out the imp in Damaris, and Midnight hailed them with the too frank admiration of the very boldest young bloods. She was ready to giggle at seeing them blush, when her eyes met those of the young clergyman and she stood stunned. John Ruthven, whom she had not seen since her Bath days, was before her. He was hardly six inches away and knew her instantly—perhaps, she thought afterwards, because he had once loved her. Certainly recognition was plain in his eyes, mingled first with shock and then, as his glance took her in from head to toe, contempt. Worse was the way he drew his ladies from her—his wife, perhaps, and his mother. He passed on without a word, leaving her standing, her hand foolishly clutching her sword, her face scarlet, to the amusement of the opera girls, who thought the young blood had been caught by his minister. Damaris had preferred young Ruthven to any other man; she had thought she might become his wife, and since her marriage she had sometimes thought of him with tenderness. Now she was ashamed and hurt, and the hurt went deep.

That night she tossed and turned in her bed, unable to fall asleep. Over and over she told herself that Ruthven was parsonical, provincial, narrow-minded, but it failed to help. At last, towards dawn, sleep came, and when she rose she was calm enough.

Soon she resumed her usual ways. Young Hallbury took her to the worst of the gambling hells, and she gave him no peace until they went to the most notorious den of all. Even he was doubtful of the wisdom of visiting the Beggar's Club. There the young gentlemen sat at long benches and ate from wooden bowls with knives chained to the table. Desmond Midnight laughed from bravado, but Damaris was really sickened when she saw an insect crawling in the bottom of a heap of food.

Going home that night, her party was held up in the fields by a gang of cutthroats. Suddenly she was terrified, more of exposure than of coming to physical harm, and was faint with relief when her young gallants, heated as they were with wine, overcame the thieves, leaving two for dead, and she escaped to her rooms to change.

That night she lay awake long, listening to the bells of a nearby church tolling the hours. She thought of the dead men lying in the fields, their eyes staring sightless at the skies. She remembered Ruthven, his shocked, disappointed glance at what she had become. What had she become? She did not like herself—nor Desmond Midnight. It was all too much; the game was folly, the chances she took stupid. Now she realized how much she wanted a different life and promised herself a real reform.

She had not seen her children since the previous summer. She would go down to Great Heron. Desmond Midnight's rooms would be given up. More than that, she promised herself soberly, she would try to deal better with her husband. He had been kind in his way, giving her all the support that a Society woman needed; though he never appeared in her bedroom, he could always be counted upon to be at her side in her reception rooms when she entertained. He had kept his part of the bargain with generosity, but she—although she had done her duty and provided an heir—had not been generous. If there could not be love between them, there could perhaps be friendship. They did not need to live as polite strangers in this great house. She would take an interest in politics, she thought, becoming eager. It would be good for the children as they grew to see their parents live harmoniously. Perhaps—perhaps there might be another child. She remembered her children as babies, pink, warm, with tiny clutching hands, and smiled as she fell asleep.

Fired with this new ambition, she rose early—and at once incurred the displeasure of her maid. Mrs Chambers, a grim, grey-haired woman who had waited up for her mistress the night before, was astonished to be called from her bed so soon. With the help of two yawning young assistants she got Damaris into a morning-gown with a look of offended majesty. Damaris hid her amusement, for she did feel guilty at rousing Mrs Chambers—if only she would not stay up for her! But Mrs Chambers knew what was correct, and if Damaris came home long after dawn she was always greeted by the impeccably correct Chambers. Ladies of the *ton* were expected to stay out late, but getting up early was an affront.

Damaris went down to the breakfast parlour, her good resolution causing a new happiness. She was going to be a real mother again. The maids were packing her things for Great Heron; she would take the carriage and go after breakfast to buy all manner of presents and little playthings for the children.

The breakfast parlour at Malfrey House was pleasing. The walls and carpets were light, and the morning sun found its way in agreeably. The silver dishes on the sideboard were warming the eggs and sausage, the kidneys and the beefsteak, and the smell blended with that of the coffee to give her a good appetite.

Lord Malfrey was at the table, and if he was astonished at the appearance of his wife, his good breeding did not permit his surprise to show. He greeted her calmly as if she had been in her place every morning, ready to pour his coffee. In return, she greeted her husband as sedately as he could wish. Her gaiety was undiminished though she thought irreverently that her husband did look his most terrifying in the morning, his manner even more gloomy and glacial than it usually was. But she would not be deterred. She had permitted this situation to go on too long.

Together with her youthful energy and courage she now had the assurance of success in Society. She was not a frightened girl. Lord Malfrey must be wooed into a little warmth; he must be coaxed into a little companionship. But as she ate and chatted, she was almost daunted by his manner; his gloom was really impenetrable.

When she spoke of going to Great Heron, at last he raised his eyes to hers. 'The plan, I had thought, was for you to go at the end of May.'

'But I go to Brighton, of course, in June,' she replied. 'The engagements are already made. I want to spend more time with the children.'

She was going on to say that as soon as Parliament rose, she wanted him to join her, but the words were never spoken.

His grey eyes rested upon her, for once hardly shielded by his drooping lids.

'I think it a bad plan. It is not good to upset the children's routine; they are thriving as they are.'

Hot, indignant phrases came to her mind, but although Lord Malfrey's manner was calm and measured, she had no chance to speak.

'Besides, my dear, I think you should rest before you travel. You look tired this morning.'

Damaris stared, for in spite of her restless night, she had woken in good looks—Chambers had remarked tersely upon this unnatural occurrence.

'And there is always the risk of infection.'

Lord Malfrey didn't trouble to raise his voice; he might have been discussing the fineness of the weather.

'The Beggars Club—hardly a healthy place. You would not

want to carry some disease down to the children. I do not interfere with your pleasures'—his words fell like drops of icy water on Damaris's spirits—'but we will not corrupt the children. I will take you down to Great Heron at the end of May, as we planned. You will stay two weeks before going on to your amusements at Brighton. I trust,' he said almost languidly, holding his delicate coffee-cup to his lips and taking a sip, 'that we understand each other.'

Damaris, shocked, sickened, and aghast, stared and then rose and ran back to her room. Thank God Chambers had vanished—she sank down on her bed and cried. He knew. There was nothing she could do about that. And he was determined to keep her children from her. But why? she wondered, in a new, sudden anguish. It was true that her exploits had been scandalous, but there was no scandal. Her reputation was of the highest. No—that was merely Lord Malfrey's weapon. Why would he want to keep her and her children apart?

As soon as she had gone, Lord Malfrey convulsively crushed his coffee-cup in his fist. He gazed down without seeing the broken mess, insensible to the sting of the hot liquid in his cuts. He was asking himself the same question. He simply did not know. There were his feelings, his terrible aversions, which he hardly understood himself. He could admire his wife in her drawing-room, he even loved her in his way; for his children he had a strong devotion, yet when he saw Damaris, with whom he had lain and begotten two children, with the little ones on her lap, he was torn with the same agony that visited him in her bed. It must not be. He couldn't understand his own anguish, but he could prevent it. His wife could have her own life, befitting the Countess of Malfrey. Great Heron, as always, was his secret, hidden place, and there he kept his own.

Damaris recovered in time from her shock at her husband's discovery—and its consequences. Her feeling for him hardened into
an immovable dislike and distrust. She remembered the scene
with Lady Cassandra, the two figures by the window, and a shudder of disgust passed through her. Now she knew more about the
sin that was the secret of Great Heron; it was not unknown in the
fashionable world, but even there it was spoken of in whispers,
and to Damaris herself it seemed the most degraded of passions.

Behind her cool, controlled manner, the young Lady Malfrey
with her soft, low voice and elegant manner, became increasingly
restless. She missed the lost freedom of Desmond Midnight. That
summer at Brighton she found herself hopelessly bored, and neither gambling nor the homage of the young men pleased her. Lady
Gratton left her for a country visit to Mrs Farthingale, who was
too indisposed to travel. Alone, Damaris searched for new amusements.

The Prince Regent, tired of his latest love, a too complaisant
lady, was publicly at her feet. The young men, finding him absurd,
urged Damaris on to flirt with him a little; the sight of the stout
powdered Regent, sighing in his stays, brought on an ecstasy of
mirth.

'One more sigh of passion,' Lord Hallbury said, 'and he will
burst his bonds and his pantaloons together.'

'He will do as he did with Mrs Fitzherbert'—the Beau gave his
opinion. 'Cut a vein—a very small vein—and lie piteously in a pool
of blood.'

Their party was walking along the Steyne, enjoying the sunshine, the fresh breeze off the Channel, and the sight of the town,
bright as a new toy, a perfect background for the flock of the beau
monde turned out as handsomely as dolls to play in it.

Damaris pulled a face. She wanted no talk of blood and fervid
passions, as her companions knew, and they turned to watch the
equipages of the fashionable ladies pass by. Mrs Carroway, who

was dashingly driving her own perch phaeton, caught the eye, especially when she paused to take up a gallant young Captain of Hussars.

Lord Hallbury was watching through his quizzing-glass.

'Dear Leila Carroway, she invigorates us all. *Such* an air of fashion—to think she married into the dullest family in England. Leicestershire huntsmen all. Venery means more to them than Venus, and the women wear skirts that fall off if they take a tumble from their mounts.'

'Better than being dragged by the pommel, Hallbury,' Captain Grosvenor protested.

The Beau was always bored by talk of hunting.

'Too much fashion,' he said languidly, watching the lady. 'It hurts the eye. A little more subtlety would be in order. And the Carroways, I am sure, would prefer not an air of fashion but rather an heir to the house.'

The men laughed, but Damaris watched the carriage behind the phaeton. A light, elegant chaise, it bore the well-known figure of Mrs Drummond Burrell, one of the feared patronesses at Almack's, who was observing the openly-flirting Mrs Carroway with a disapproving look. Mrs Carroway was making herself far too conspicuous, Damaris thought; the foolish girl, bored no doubt with her stout hunting husband, could find herself in deep trouble, and in spite of the warm sun Damaris shivered a little.

But that night was the great dinner at the Pavilion, the event of the Brighton season. The Beau himself, who was estranged from the Prince, was not invited, but Damaris, who had expected to go with Lady Gratton, had already accepted. She considered a convenient headache, but the young men urged her to go.

'The evening will be nothing without you,' Hallbury begged. 'The Prince is so ponderous with Lady Hertford! If he doesn't yearn, we will all yawn.'

Damaris hesitated, but at that moment Lady Hertford appeared, stout, powdered, and glaringly rouged in the morning sun. She was sitting up in a barouche landau with another lady beside her. Seeing Damaris with her party, she made a haughty bow. Her companion whispered something as they passed, and her reply came loud and clear over the clatter of the horses' hooves.

'But naturally Lady Malfrey would prefer to walk, my dear. In a carriage, you know, you can have only one man on each side, but promenading down the streets she can have a regiment about her.'

The men laughed at the display of pique; Damaris smiled without amusement. She had her revenge that night when she appeared at the Pavilion in a gown of plain white silk with one blue ribbon binding her breasts. This time the Prince Regent had hung his main salon in Damaris blue silk, which clashed with the colourful gowns of many of the ladies, and most particularly with the crimson and gold worn by Lady Hertford—the Prince could be malicious as well as gallant. He himself was glittering with diamonds—the Order of the Golden Fleece, presented to him by the Tsar on his recent visit to London commemorating Napoleon's defeat.

The dinner was long and rich. After it seemed that even this interminable meal was at its end, another dish was presented in Damaris's honour. A silver salver was placed before each guest, bearing a delicious pastry confection in which nestled the back parts of thirteen different kinds of bird. Someone whispered it was the Prince's invention, others said he had stolen it from the Beau, but it was the most expensive dish in the world. It was served with iced champagne.

The wines had been many and various. Damaris, who drank abstemiously, had merely taken a sip of each from politeness, but the meal had lasted so long that even her sips caused a little elation, and she hesitated when the champagne came round. But the Prince's eye was on her, and he murmured he was giving her his finest vintage. Damaris, finding she was very thirsty from the heat that Prinny loved, drank her glass down.

The company, except for the routed Lady Hertford, was extremely merry. Damaris laughed, for as she looked up at the domed ceiling, a fantasy sky of gold and silver, the painted birds, flowers and butterflies seemed to flutter and move over their heads. The Prince drew close and murmured he had made one more change in her honour—he would like her to come to view it. She was reluctant, but to refuse would be gauche. The Countess of Malfrey could manage the Prince. Lord Hallbury caught her eye as she rose and gave her a discreet bow, but with amusement in his eyes that was far from discreet; he was enjoying the discomfiture of Lady Hertford. Her crimson face was beaded with sweat. Not a breath of air penetrated the Pavilion, and the many heavy scents of the guests struck against Damaris, thick and cloying, as she tried to draw a cooling breath.

The fantastic rooms swam about her as she followed the Prince through corridors painted as tropical forests, peopled by Chinese figures lit eerily by strange lanterns of figured, coloured glass; up a staircase like a forest of bamboo, wrought in copper and glittering darkly; through a room of mirrors and tulip lamps of golden glass; and then into a tiny room where palm-trees, gilded, seemed to hold a painted ceiling on their branches. Golden dragons writhed on every lamp and hanging; the walls glittered with rich lacquer of the new Damaris blue. It could have been the dream of an opium smoker—it whirled gently about her, and the Prince solicitously guided her to a long satin sofa, the only seat in the room.

She sank down gratefully. The heat was intolerable; her senses reeled; the dragons whirled about her. She closed her eyes, moaned, and collapsed. At once she felt the added great discomfort of the Prince pressing upon her, his stout body crushing her frame, his breath hot against her cheek. Dimly conscious, she was only aware of the excessive physical unpleasantness; his heavy scent choked her, and his hand on her breast brought nothing but a feeling of annoyed surprise—a mistake was being made. She certainly had not intended this, but she was too ill to struggle more than feebly.

Her eyes fluttered, inspiring the Prince to greater passion and encouraging him to further exploration.

'Oh, no,' she murmured, so excessively ill that she resented the discomfort even more than the attack on her modesty.

'I am afraid, *mon Prince,* that Lady Malfrey has fainted.' A voice, full of sardonic merriment, came to her ears. 'Your efforts, I fear, will not help her. Perhaps I could call a servant?'

The Prince paused. Damaris, unable to speak, felt a sudden surge of relief as his weight was lifted from her recumbent form.

'D'Egremont!' He sounded furious. 'What are you doing here?'

'I returned from France this evening and, finding your kind invitation, rushed to join you. But I was late, I fear, and mistook my way. I have rung the bell—ah, someone approaches.'

'Yes.' The Prince's voice modulated into some semblance of good manners. 'I was showing Lady Malfrey the new lacquer, and I am afraid she has been overcome by the heat. Send for assistance, D'Egremont—I must go back to my other guests.'

Damaris only learned much later of the Prince's appearance as he marched off in defeat—leaving the field, she was told, to a better man.

She still could not look up. She was far too ill.

'A physician has been called, Madame.' The charming voice with the French accent was agreeable to her ears—if anything could be agreeable at that moment.

'And I am at your service—Jean-Philippe d'Egremont.'

But Damaris had no attention for him. She was being extremely sick.

CHAPTER

18

The next day it rained. The dark sky and the sudden downpours gave Brighton the look now of a toy left out in a puddle by a careless child. Damaris, nursing a very bad headache and an even more painful conscience, was glad to stay indoors and received no visitors until the afternoon, when the Beau and Lord Alvanley called.

These two old friends she could see, and she had tea served in her comfortable little boudoir. Damaris was lying down on a striped satin sofa supported by gilded sphinxes, wearing a loose white gown, with her hair swept up and forward in a style that had once been called *à la sacrifice*.

The Beau sauntered in, dressed as he might have been in Piccadilly in his blue coat, biscuit-coloured pantaloons, and high, starched cravat—no lessening of standards, no outré fashion for him because of the proximity of the sea. After a greeting, he put up his glass and scrutinized her.

'Ready for the executioner? Or are you a Magdalen today? I do hope not. Repentance is so vulgar!'

Damaris had to laugh, and recovered enough to pour the tea.

'But you are pale,' Lord Alvanley remarked. 'More, I think, than uthual.'

Damaris told them ruefully of the happenings of the night before. It seemed they had already heard some of the story.

'Hallbury ith a young fool,' Lord Alvanley said shortly. 'He thould never have allowed Prinny to take you off alone. We have theen him today—I had a word or two to thay to him.'

His usually slight lisp was accented today in his anger.

The Beau was examining a little snuff-box in his usual languid manner. He opened it with a flick of his thumb and peered at its contents.

'Ah, yes,' he said. Inside, instead of snuff, there were several small pills glistening against the gold.

'Hallbury, too, had a headache this morning,' he murmured. 'Did you know, Alvanley, that years ago, when we were friends, I gave Prinny a box like this? He was charmed at the idea of a pretty box for his horrid medicines. He promised me in return some bauble from Grey's, but then he cancelled the order—so like Prinny!'

He turned his gaze, bright with intelligence behind the assumed languor, to Damaris.

'So unlike you, my dear, to be overset by a little wine. It has never happened before?'

'No,' Damaris said, struck by a new thought. 'No—I thought it was the heat—and all those dragons—' She began to laugh. 'That opium den—'

'Indeed,' the Beau said softly. 'I believe the heat and the, er, dragons, have had such an effect on others—at places, too, where there is hardly a dragon to be seen.'

Lord Alvanley looked grim. 'We all know—' He broke off. 'But to a lady of quality! He needth a horthwhipping.'

'He knows no bounds—that is the tedium of the man,' the Beau said, yawning. 'What his father attempts in his madness the dear Regent does with sang-froid. He is to be avoided, like all things disagreeable.'

Damaris shuddered a little. All London knew that the poor mad King attempted to thrust himself upon any maid or Court lady that came his way, and often had to be tied up for their protection. Her escape from Prinny had been narrow indeed. She sipped her tea and then remembered the voice, the voice that had come to her rescue. The night before she had been too ill and too embarrassed to inquire about the possessor of the voice. She had been interested only in the ministrations of the doctor and the help of the maids and the shelter of her chaise as it took her home. The name of her rescuer came back to her mind.

'Do you know, who is Jean-Philippe d'Egremont? That is the gentleman who so providentially strolled by—'

Lord Alvanley beamed. 'D'Egremont! He is back—how delightful. Society has been tame without that young man.'

'He returned yesterday,' the Beau said idly. 'He called upon me while I was dressing.'

The Beau took many hours to dress, his efforts often lasting until dinner.

'We were to dine, but I remembered you were to be at the Pavilion with only that foolish young Hallbury as escort. D'Egremont had had a card, so I did just suggest—of course, d'Egremont is an idle, faithless wretch,' he murmured. 'Had you not taken his eye, my dear, I fancy Prinny might have had his way. But beauty will inflame these Frenchmen—'

He turned to Lord Alvanley. 'He has just left Louis in Paris. They have quarrelled again.'

Lord Alvanley shook his head. 'I feared it. That constitution— of course, d'Egremont finds it intolerable. He has been complaining for some time past that *le Desiré* has become *l'Impossible*.'

The Beau shrugged. 'May I have some more tea, dear lady? A most delicious blend. Oh, these kings—of course, Louis wants to keep his throne. Boney might be safe at Elba, but Louis has other enemies. He can't worry about the estates of a few nobles, however hard they may have fought for him.'

'D'Egremont,' Lord Alvanley said comfortably, 'ith at least more lucky than most. He is still rich; he has his home here; the other poor devils have suffered, not he.'

'But who is he?' Damaris asked again.

'How can you not have met?' The Beau raised an eyebrow. 'But you were in the country, and then he was off with Louis, inspiriting him at Hartwell, and he rode with him when he entered Paris. But surely you have heard of the charming Marquis? Why, all the women in Town adored him—he owns the house you admired in Grosvenor Square that Lady Ramage took last season.'

'Oh, the house with the beautiful staircase with the columns holding up the second floor—I remember,' Damaris said with interest.

'It has many charms,' the Beau said idly. 'The Marquis, lucky man, can afford it—' He gave the tiniest of sighs; he himself was very close to ruin though only his intimates knew it. 'The old Marquis escaped with much of his wealth—though not his wife, poor lady. She was killed by a mob, before young d'Egremont's eyes. He is not too fond of the people.'

He took out another small box, this one of flowered Sèvres, and put a pinch of snuff to his nostrils.

'But certainly you will become acquainted with him, my dear. I am sure he will call upon you very soon.'

And at that moment her maid came in to inform her that the Marquis d'Egremont was waiting upon her below.

'I am not at home, Chambers,' Damaris said.

Lord Alvanley laughed, his florid face growing more rosy. 'Ungrateful, Ma'am. You are not to thank your benefactor?'

'In good time,' Damaris said demurely. She felt quite restored, and ready for a little mischief. 'But I find myself weary of Brighton.' She looked down at her long, elegant fingers, her fine-boned ankles and high instep, in secret amusement. 'I am going into hiding for a little, gentlemen.'

'To the country? You will find it dull, 'pon my soul,' Lord Alvanley protested.

'You are not running away, dear Lady Malfrey,' the Beau murmured, eyeing her quizzically.

Damaris gazed at him over her fan, her eyes snapping wickedly.

'I always run towards, George,' she said, and they laughed with perfect understanding. Lord Alvanley laughed too, but he was just a little outside; for that happy peer life would remain undisturbed, and he did not share the recklessness underlying the calm of perfect breeding that was to utterly ruin one of his friends and carry the other further than even their minds could foresee.

19

The next morning was bright. The young Marquis d'Egremont, travelling swiftly in his curricle towards Town and some very private business, was enjoying the day. He had been a little disappointed in his failing to find Lady Malfrey at home—the Cool Countess of whom he had heard so much—but, always sanguine, he was sure he would see her again.

He did not have long to wait. Pausing at an inn along the way, he saw a lady setting off in her carriage as soon as her horses were changed. The carriage looked as though it was hired, but the lady in such a hurry had a most distinctive appearance—it could only be Lady Malfrey herself. D'Egremont was amused. Lady Malfrey was said to take no lovers, but this sudden, secret flight suggested an *affaire de coeur*.

His curiosity aroused, he followed her at a discreet distance. Once in Town, following became somewhat difficult. Though the beau monde was elsewhere, Town was still bustlingly full of people. He observed Lady Malfrey look about her—she was surprised to see the other world. There were not only the poor and the respectable shopkeepers and workmen in the streets, there were some well-dressed people in elegant carriages—but none that she would recognize.

She was avoiding the fashionable part of Town, and in the humble streets the summer stinks were abominable. The Marquis wrinkled his nose, but his curiosity grew stronger. At last her carriage turned into a mean street with a grimy little theatre, and he saw her jump out, pay the driver, and disappear into one of the houses. He could not know that he had found the lodgings of Desmond Midnight, and he drove on, oddly disappointed. It would have been amusing to be the first lover of the elegant Countess, but obviously he had been forestalled—by some swaggering lout of an actor, perhaps, sweating in his grease-paint. The Marquis was well aware that highly-bred women could be overtaken by *nostalgie de la boue*.

He could not linger to observe more. His business was waiting, and when it was over he had to return to King Louis in Paris. It was a month before he returned to England. The Prince and all his court were still at Brighton, but d'Egremont found himself making plans to go to Town. Much too soon, his friends protested, but his inclination drew him, and with d'Egremont his inclination was all. He had inquired for the lovely Lady Malfrey, but it seemed she had gone to the country. D'Egremont smiled to himself and was soon in Town, and it was not too long before he took to loitering about Cuckfield Street and its theatre.

He was rewarded one evening by the sight of a young country girl, her hair loose about her shoulders, hurrying along the street. Despite the warm day the girl wore a pelisse close about her to shield her from the notice of street gallants: the clerks from the shops, the carters and lounging vagrants. He drew back into a doorway to remain unobserved and smiled as the girl passed—her simple dress and coiffure could not disguise that face, and he wondered as Lady Malfrey disappeared into the stage-door of the Cuckfield Theatre.

Strolling round to the front, he gazed curiously at the large notice. Mr Arnold Johnson was presenting the Cuckfield Theatre Company in a performance of *School for Scandal*. The role of Lady Teazle was being played by Marianne Midnight. D'Egremont knew many of the actresses on the London stage; Marianne Midnight was not one of them. He bought a ticket for the performance that began very shortly, not without a certain regret at the thought of his dinner, which would be much delayed.

Once inside, the fastidious Marquis regretted his impulse even more. Of course, there were no people of fashion in the audience, only a smelly, grubby, roistering crowd who seemed more inclined to amuse themselves fighting each other for places than paying attention to the stage. But once the new young actress appeared they settled and became appreciative, and so, also, did the Marquis. Surely she was the most stunning Lady Teazle who had ever graced the boards! With her hair piled two feet high in Restoration fashion, and in the gown with its sweeping, wide-panniered skirt, she looked a great lady indeed. Her voice, though still seeming low and very sweet, somehow penetrated to the last roisterer at the back of the pit. The Marquis was enchanted.

Damaris had been enjoying herself immensely. She had had little trouble getting the part; Desmond Midnight in his hey-day had teased Mr Johnson with tales of his lovely sister Marianne until the manager had pleaded to see her. When the beautiful girl had appeared at last, he had been more than willing to take her on. His leading lady had just left for better things at Drury Lane, and there was not one handsome woman left in the company. The girl's voice, with its decided Somerset burr, was a problem; it was also much too low, and he had set the leading man to work with her. The aging actor was nothing loath; such an innocent would certainly become his new mistress before the run of the play was over, and his present inamorata, though a good, robust actress, was stout and far from young, with a complexion disfigured by long use of white-lead powder. In the event, he had found Midnight devilish slippery, though a hard worker and a good learner. But he comforted himself with the thought that he would try again when the poor little thing had got over her first stage-fright.

Studying with her sweaty, dirty, and amorous instructor had been the first real work Damaris had done since she had left her books at Angelhurst, and she found it a stimulant more potent than the gaming table. Acting came easily to her. She could hold the attention of the mob; and Marianne Midnight had enjoyed the applause and the curtain calls, which she felt she had earned, more than all the admiration of the *bon ton* in her first season. That had been purchased, at least in part, by Lord Malfrey's money and position. Marianne Midnight's triumph was her own.

But by the night of d'Egremont's visit to the theatre, the charm was fading. She still liked the acting, but there were problems she hadn't foreseen. Lacy, her leading man, had become sulky. It would not have mattered, but it had been Lacy who accompanied her out of the stage-door so that she could escape the crowd of too eager gallants always waiting in her path. One youth, who dressed in a clumsy copy of the dandies' elegance, was there every night. He was a burly fellow whose nakedly amorous looks were repugnant and a little disturbing.

Knowing she would have to go home unprotected, she made her plans. She slipped away while the others were still taking their bows, hid herself in a dark pelisse and close bonnet, and was out of the stage-door before most of the gallants had appeared. A fight had broken out in the pit, and it took most of the audience, including d'Egremont, some time before they could leave.

She walked swiftly down the street. Her lodgings were only a few steps away. Marianne Midnight, she thought, had better retire.

It was a pity—she had a sudden burst of professional pride—for she had had an offer to appear at Drury Lane. Then she laughed at herself—she was absurd indeed. Lady Malfrey at Drury Lane with all the beau monde in the audience!

Her laughter was short-lived. Before she reached the safety of her front door there was a hand on her arm, another hand clasped her shoulder, and the burly amorous youth's wine-soaked breath was on her face.

'Come, my beauty, Miss Marianne, you don't want to run from me!'

His strong, ugly face stared at her, all too plain in the lamp-light.

'By God, you're as lovely as you are on stage. Pretty as a flower —and those eyes ain't big from paint! John Willbrough at your service, Ma'am. Come, I have a carriage waiting.'

'Unhand me!' Damaris ordered with indignation. 'I have no need for your carriage or for you.'

He smiled. 'And you've had my flowers every night for a week! You have a need for my carriage, lady.'

His grip tightened on her waist. For the first time, Damaris felt a shock of real fear. This was worse than her night on the heath after her visit to the Beggar's Club. Then at least she had been surrounded by friends. Now she was alone—and this wretch would obviously think nothing of carrying off an unprotected young woman of no importance. For a moment she regretted her coldness to the kindly, if absurd, Lacy and wished he would sud-denly appear. If he could not fight this villain at least he might give her the time to escape. But she well knew that Lacy was sulk-ing over a bottle of gin back in the theatre.

Willbrough grinned insolently, and she struck out, her gloved hand making a resounding crack against his cheek.

'Why, you little—' Furious, he clutched at her hand but a sec-ond later had to drop it and step back, his jaw slackening ab-surdly. Someone had dragged him backwards, and he turned to face a young beau with a pistol trained on his head.

'Be off,' the stranger said shortly. 'If I clap eyes on you again, I'll whip you within an inch of your life.'

Willbrough hesitated. The elegant young man before him was slender, graceful, and of a height a little below his own. Yet the handsome beau, with his dark eyes flashing in the lamplight, had an air that quieted impudence, and his expression suggested he would not hesitate to use the pistol. With an oath, the disappointed seducer turned away, leaving the others to regard each other with a variety of emotions.

Damaris's rescuer put up his pistol. He looked at her pale face, with its cool dignity in spite of her inner turbulence. Gracefully, he took her hand and kissed it, just where her wrist met her glove.

'*Exquise comtesse*,' he murmured, 'allow me to present myself—again.'

She looked up, shocked, but saw that his eyes were full of mischievous laughter. 'Jean-Philippe d'Egremont, at your service—as always.'

Her horror at discovery faded in the devil-may-care warmth of his regard. Damaris, Countess of Malfrey, once Damaris St Cloud, looked at him smiling, and there in the lamplight, on the narrow, smelly little street, the two were rocked by a sudden burst of joyous, heady laughter.

CHAPTER

20

The next morning found Lady Malfrey sedately travelling to Angelhurst, in a manner befitting her station. Her encounter with the brutal admirer of the stage-door and her rescue by the fascinating and gallant young Marquis had left her exhilarated but thoughtful. Her imposture had become too dangerous—she felt she could trust young d'Egremont, but nobody else must learn of this escapade. She had sent an excuse to Mr Johnson and thought philosophically that after all Lacy's mistress would enjoy playing her role and would do so with more gusto if less elegance than she had herself.

After the night's happenings, the magic of the theatre, small, crowded, and dingy, had faded, and the applause of the audience, brutes and vulgarians for the most part, had lost its glamour. The

Countess must be careful; her friends believed her to be at Angelhurst, and so to Angelhurst she went. And she had other reasons for wanting a little quiet contemplation. Sitting back in her chaise, with the first autumn leaves drifting by the window in the country lanes, she smiled to herself. A quite unfamiliar sensation possessed her. She felt her wrist where the young Marquis had kissed it—she could still feel his lips lingering there. It was a sensation sweet and exciting, and she knew again what she had realized the night before, lying in Desmond Midnight's humble bedchamber—that for the first time she was responding to a man's caress.

She had lain in her bed all night between sleep and waking, in a delicious drowsiness that contained no wish for deep sleep or a fuller wakefulness, but with a rich content that she had never known, to half dream, half recollect the pleasure of the moment and the embrace.

She had risen with her determination unmoved; she must leave London. It was a wrench, but she gave up her rooms, paying off her obliging and discreet landlady with a purse of gold—a reward for service, but not enough to cause greedy speculation. She had visited the shuttered Malfrey House as though she were breaking her journey from Brighton. Her husband was at Great Heron, for which she was thankful. Collecting a fresh supply of clothes, she left with one of Chambers's understrappers to attend her, before the sun had reached its height in the heavens.

The long journey and the two nights she spent at the inns were not wearisome. Not wearisome at all; and when she reached Angelhurst and followed her usual routine of walks and rides about the farm, visiting the poor in the village and entertaining and being entertained by her neighbours, she felt, underneath her sedate manner, a joy that she didn't care to examine too closely.

But at night her thoughts went back again to young d'Egremont as he had stood on the doorstep of the house in Cuckfield Street and begged to see her again. He made no claims for having rescued her not once but twice—his bold eyes made claims of quite a different sort.

The Cool Countess had withdrawn, murmuring that they would meet again, no doubt, in Society—but beneath her studied manner she was not cool at all. D'Egremont was different from any man she had known. He was a dandy without looking foppish. He was vibrantly masculine without the whiff of the stable that so wearied her with the young bucks, who aped their own grooms in speech and dress.

He was, in fact, a man who was dangerously attractive to women, and Damaris found herself pursuing her usual vocation with a strange, sweet undercurrent in her feelings. Her dreams were confused; she remembered her old girlish longings for the knights of chivalry, but Galahad now wore a Frenchman's face, Launcelot wore dandy's dress as he pressed his lips on his lady's wrist.

Her heart was light—and for no reason. Her neighbours and tenants agreed that the young Countess had never been so lovely, with such a bloom. The kind old ladies thought she was *enceinte;* the less kind murmured behind their fans that surely the young lady had taken a lover.

Soon it was time for Damaris's autumn visit to Great Heron, sanctioned by the Earl. She went, still with her strange new light-heartedness, and for once the sight of the gloomy Forest of Heron did not send her into despondence. She played with the children, who treated her as a pleasant visitor, a half-remembered friend, but even the pain of this did not stop the pleasures of her dreams.

Her meeting with Lord Malfrey, stiff and formal as always, the long evenings at dinner with the endless parade of dishes before them, her inward sigh of relief at the appearance of the port and her escape to the drawing-room, gave her feelings of another sort.

His brief, cool salutation, his cold kiss of her hand, was oddly repellent to her in a way it had not been before. She looked at this stern, impassive man—the repugnance she had felt for him since the scene she had observed at Greystones, faded with time, now came back in force. His touch on her hand made her want to shy away like a frightened mare, and the remembrance of their close embrace made her clench her teeth in horror. Worst of all, she fancied something new in his manner. Perhaps it was her own inner excitement which roused it, but sometimes she caught a side-long glance that suggested desire.

It was a relief when they left for Town, for there she would rarely see her husband alone. She warned herself that she must be careful about the young Marquis. The delight coursing through her blood when she remembered him must not presage something more. Many women in Society had lovers—but the Earl's disposition was so strange! He wouldn't want to dishonour his house and his children by divorcing his Countess, but she knew he was not always rational—his strange aversion to her closeness with her own children was proof enough of that. She must be prudent, and if she was attracted to d'Egremont, she must avoid him.

When she returned to Town, she found all her resolution unnecessary. D'Egremont was in Paris with King Louis and not expected to return for several months. The depths of her disappointment, her loss of good spirits, should have been a warning. But she still dreamed her dreams, and when her husband sometimes, in the intervals of his work concerning the peace treaties, seemed to want to unbend, to address her in a manner slightly less formal, almost affectionate, she drew back—she became, clearly, the Cool Countess and their relation returned to what it had been.

It was the next spring before d'Egremont returned. He left his calling card at Malfrey House, and a day or two later an invitation arrived for a *bal masqué* at his London mansion. Damaris, shaken by her sudden excitement, intended to send her excuses, but Lady Gratton exclaimed at the idea.

'Refuse! But it will be the great affair of the Season. Your refusing will be so marked! And I have heard'—Lady Gratton gave her a piercing look—'that d'Egremont had done you some service, in Brighton.'

Damaris blushed. 'Yes, Aunt. But I am so weary of balls—really one cannot go everywhere.'

'At your age, indeed! However, there is no need for you to go to the Carroways this week. Lady Jersey and Mrs Drummond Burrell are not to appear—there is too much scandal attached to that house. But it would be ill bred to decline d'Egremont. His cousin, the Duchesse de Langcourt et Montrevet, is receiving for him. They are related by blood to the Bourbons, you know. The whole of French society will be offended if you refuse her.'

Certainly, it would not do to seem particular in her avoidance of the Marquis. And Damaris found herself humming happily as the day approached, and then suddenly indulging in a burst of bad temper that surprised Mrs Chambers when the seamstress failed to deliver her dress for the ball. Messengers were sent, the seamstress was harried, the dress borne back in triumph. Damaris felt soothed and ashamed. She had never been the kind of Society woman to bully those who served her or to become hysterical over a gown or an ornament. What did it matter whether the Marquis was impressed by her appearance? He had seen her in some hardly flattering circumstances, and besides, she was not going to become his mistress. The Countess of Malfrey was going to keep her head!

On the day of the ball, she was being dressed in an elaborately rich costume as Madame de Montespan, the favourite of Louis XIV. Her gown was of silver brocade, and her slippers had diamond heels. Chambers was assisting the hairdresser in piling her hair up in the old style, when Damaris, to her own surprise and horror, in an unexpected fit of nerves, snapped at her maid like any bad-tempered, spoiled rich woman. Had she but known it, Chambers rather approved of this display. Her mistress was no longer acting like a country miss; she now had the manners of a true woman of fashion.

The style of the ancien régime of France suited her mistress well. The dignity, the grandeur, could be carried off by the young Lady Malfrey. She would be by far the most striking figure in the beautiful ballroom of the d'Egremont house—it was a pity she had to wear the tiny velvet mask. The servants lined up to see her go, and as her carriage rolled along the street the eyes of the passers-by were drawn to the beauty inside.

The scene at the d'Egremont house was one of the greatest splendour. The line of carriages before the door brought the cream of London society. The glitter of jewels, the sweep of the ladies' gowns, took the breath of the spectators even at a time when gorgeousness was the order of the day and brilliant gatherings a nightly occurrence.

The d'Egremont house was one of the loveliest in London, and when Damaris entered, to see d'Egremont and the Duchess at the head of the twin staircase before the six regal columns, she knew she had seen no such elegance before, not even at Carlton House, where the Prince Regent always hovered between the gorgeous and the absurd.

The Regent himself, dressed, it was claimed, to represent Charles I and looking, in his bottle-green velvet coat, more like the Frog Prince, entered right after Damaris, and the ball began. The Regent, who had forgotten the contretemps of the previous summer, demanded the first dance; then she was claimed by her host.

'But you are not masked, M'sieur le Marquis,' she murmured as he took her hand for the waltz, the coolness of her tones belying the sudden, inexpressible delight she felt in his touch.

The Marquis was too experienced a lover to miss the sudden

blaze in the blue eyes behind the mask. The gentle, calm voice added a piquancy that he had never known before.

'My guests must know their host, Madame,' he said. 'It is for me to be bewildered by all these masked charmers—it is Madame la Comtesse, is it not? And not perhaps a certain Miss Marianne—'

'Hush, you rogue,' she said nervously. 'Is your promise to be broken so quickly?'

He grinned. '*En effet,* Madame, I am a dreadful rogue indeed. To buy my silence,' he whispered, 'you must give me two more dances and allow me to take you in to supper. And perhaps you will allow me to show you the garden? Alas'—he made a moue—'it is a very small garden. I am afraid we cannot lose ourselves.'

She laughed. The orchestra began to play a waltz. As he put his arm about her waist she felt a pounding excitement that she could not believe. They whirled, outwardly decorous, round the room, but Damaris's heart as well as her feet seemed to be flying. Lord Hallbury, who was standing with the Beau, looked at him ruefully.

'And we thought we had defeated the French.'

The Beau put up his quizzing-glass.

'I do believe we have,' he murmured. 'I rather think that young wretch d'Egremont has met his match at last!'

CHAPTER

21

Most of the young men in Town were to agree with the Beau. The young Marquis was known as a great lover of women, but never before had he been so slavishly at a woman's feet. It was obvious to all his friends that he was in love at last, and that state, so unlike his usual happy lechery, caused them much amusement. Wagers were offered as to his success, but with remarkably few takers—the Countess was a citadel not to be stormed by the French after everything that English gallantry could do had failed.

D'Egremont laughed and did not trouble to deny his passion—he was enjoying the quite new sensation of love. He had been drawn to the lovely, cool Englishwoman when he first saw her in the Regent's salon at Brighton—so much so that he had no intention of allowing his host to seduce the guest he had obviously drugged. 'Marianne Midnight' had intrigued him—that kind of recklessness matched his own—and the long delay before they could meet again had whetted his appetite further. Yet much as he admired her, it was her appearance at his house that made the final, irrevocable touch at his heart.

He had been a young child when he and his father had escaped from France, yet his memories of the great days were still surprisingly bright and clear, much polished from the habits of the lonely youth who would comfort himself in a foreign land by recalling his old home and reliving each night a life gone forever.

It was too painful to think of his mother, who had been torn apart before his eyes. Instead Marie Antoinette, who had caught his fancy as a little boy, haunted his mind: elegant beyond words, pale, unapproachable, that lady whom all the vaunted chivalry of France had not been able to save—she had left an image that caused his flesh-and-blood loves always to seem lacking in an unknown, essential quality.

His ball had been splendid, with all the women elegant and many of them lovely, but when the young Countess of Malfrey had glided in with the smooth little steps of the ladies of Versailles, dressed like the greatest ladies of the old régime, her incomparable air of breeding made piquant with the beauty that would have entranced the Bourbon kings, his wayward fancy was caught, fixed; and from that time the pale image of the dead Queen was replaced in his ardent heart.

In spite of Lady Malfrey's reputation, he was well aware that his desire was reciprocated. As they waltzed, the blaze in her eyes, the rise and fall of her lovely bosom, the blood coursing swiftly through her hand as it lay in his told their own tale. All that remained was for him to ply his suit—but everything must be *convenable,* discreet; the lady must not be embarrassed. Lord Malfrey, that monument to dullness, with his political life and his well-known cold amours, might not be as complaisant a husband as good manners demanded. The Marquis shrewdly suspected an ocean of jealousy under that calm exterior. Yes, discretion was the order of the day.

The Marquis smiled to himself, for he had other ventures where dissembling was necessary, and he had developed a taste for it. He found he was absurdly happy, yet his life just then was tangled in the extreme, and when he thought of it, he knew that it was not going well.

Damaris was not analyzing her feelings; she had decided firmly against love, but she dreamed at night of the Marquis. She determined not to see him; yet every time she heard his voice or saw his figure at a dinner, rout, or ball, her heart beat wildly and the day took on an exhilaration that made the time without him hopelessly dull and tame. He had taken on the attitude of one of her many respectful admirers and did nothing that they did not do. He came to her box at the opera; he visited her while she took supper at Vauxhall; he wrote verses to her beauty, sending them to her with flowers. Yet when their eyes met in rooms crowded with a hundred people, it was as though they were alone; he saw her colour mount and a tell-tale pulse beat in her throat.

For the time he attempted no seduction. One day Damaris saw the Marquis escorting Miss Hawksworth-Lane, the most beautiful and eligible debutante on the marriage market that season. The Countess felt a sudden gloom, with tears prickling her eyes and a choking sensation in her throat. For the first time she felt a dislike of Lady Gratton when she heard her remark to Mrs Farthingale that all in all the match would be a good thing for d'Egremont. It was time he settled, and if Louis was not going to return his estates, then the Hawksworth-Lane fortune and the seat in Sussex, good, unentailed property with no male heir, would be a handsome addition to his wealth.

The tears she shed that night were turned to sunshine in the morning when the Marquis appeared in company with the Beau, who complained bitterly of being dragged out betimes by his impetuous friend. While the men chatted agreeably in the pleasant morning-room at Malfrey House, chiefly concerning the fit of the Beau's boots, Damaris and the Marquis gazed at each other as though the space between them must collapse leaving them at the end of the world in each other's arms.

Damaris was in a fever when they went. She no longer knew what she wanted. Her mind was clear that she must not take d'Egremont as lover, yet she yearned for his presence, the touch of his hand, as she had desired nothing else in her life. Her emotions, with their dizzying transports from the peak of joy to the depths of mortification, were so new to her, so unexpected that she knew not what to think. She did not think but lived from day to day in expectation of something—something longed for but not ever defined.

Her dreams changed. She saw herself in France, the Earl magically vanished, as the Marquise d'Egremont. Napoleon had broken out from Elba—but all *that* was ignored. She imagined herself on the Marquis's estates in Burgundy, strolling in the vineyards in the hot sun that brought the grapes to ripeness and filled them both with languor. They sank upon a bench; she leaned upon his breast; in her light summer dress she could feel him close against her body, which seemed to melt in some new warm sweetness for which she knew no name. His hand would touch her bare arms; his lips would come down upon her own; her eyes would close as she received his kiss. Trembling with this new, insistent sweetness, she moaned and pressed her face into her pillow, longing for the next day to come; longing just to see his face or even hear his name.

One evening, at a ball at Almack's, when the Marquis brought her a glass of lemonade, they found themselves a little apart from the rest, though under the eye of Mrs Drummond Burrell. He bowed deeply, then leaned towards her, his eyes snapping with mischief, and whispered.

'Madame, pity! I am devoured, I am dead. Pray say that you will come and see me tomorrow. My cousin is gone, my house will be empty, we can talk—in private. There is so much that I must say.'

In the stiff formality of Almack's rooms, the citadel of proper behaviour, from which such ladies as Mrs Carroway found themselves excluded, his invitation struck a jarring note. She did not realize that the Marquis was prevented in her case from his usual habit. He could not call upon her at Malfrey House and rely upon her husband's discretion; nor could he carry off a lady of her position, in the middle of the Season, to some country retreat and feel her safe from gossip.

She was, for a moment, repelled by his impudence; her passion cooled. He saw it, and the reproof that it implied, and although he was touched with a flick of anger and chagrin, yet he found himself at the same time curiously pleased. Yes, the English beaux had told the truth: the wayward Countess was virtuous and haughty as well as, he was sure, passionate. What a woman—for the first time he wished he could marry. What a marquise she would be if only she were not married to the Earl! If only—he went home to consider more carefully how they could come together. Damaris, feeling cold, downcast, and unhappy, went back to Malfrey House with the idea that the Season was impossible, that she did not feel well, that she would like to go back to Great Heron. Failing that, if the Earl was disagreeable she would go to Angelhurst. She was tired of Society. Perhaps Lady Gratton would go with her. If not, perhaps she could take Betty down. It would be as it had been years ago, when they were both children. They would go to the cottages and eat berries and cream . . . and with those soothing thoughts she fell asleep. But her dreams, fragmented and troubled, such as she had never had before—the Earl, her honeymoon—came strange and distorted in her wandering mind. Her husband in his passion took on her own face—she was horrified, disgusted at she knew not whom.

But when Chambers brought her breakfast, there was a heap of notes upon her tray, and Damaris's gaze fastened, almost before her eyes were wide open, on a square missive with the d'Egremont seal. Under her maid's grim look she sipped her coffee but soon put the little flowered cup down and tore open the Marquis's letter. Not that she cared what he had to say, she thought; but she ripped it open in such haste that the contents were ripped too. But it was merely an invitation. His cousin, the Duchesse, apparently had returned, for she had sent invitations for a musicale—just a little music after dinner, the Duchesse wrote, but Mr Cramer was in Town and perhaps might amuse her friends.

The musicale was quite a popular entertainment, especially in such a house as d'Egremont's, with its fine salon built especially for the purpose and with the garden, unusual in Town houses, where the guests could stroll on pleasant nights after the confinement of the evening, before they returned to the house for supper.

Damaris didn't think she would go. Her mind was not changed, she told herself. When Chambers returned, she would tell her to pack for Angelhurst. But when her maid came, carrying a new gown brought over from France, of severely plain but dashingly fashionable cut, in her favourite blue, the words were not spoken. Chambers, for once, wore a wintry smile.

'Such a beautiful day, my lady. The whole world will be in the Park this afternoon. I thought you might like to wear the new gown—you will be taking the barouche, of course.'

The gown, and the new straw hat that went with it, would certainly cause a stir as she dashed along in the open carriage. And certainly, all the world would be there. The fragrance of the coffee was delicious, and as Chambers pulled the curtains back a sunbeam danced on her bed.

'Yes,' Damaris said dreamily, 'I will wear the blue gown. And Chambers—the new slippers with the blue heels.'

She lay back upon her pillows, smiling. The dreams of the night before faded into nothing; the shock of the Marquis's words at Almack's was dismissed from her mind. Certainly she need not leave today. Now that she remembered, she had a dinner engagement that evening, and she had promised the Beau and Alvanley most faithfully that she would be there, for they had declared that otherwise nothing would induce them to attend.

'But the Sedgwick-Darnleys do so long to see you, George,' she had said.

'Yes, but do I long to see them?' he had replied plaintively. 'What have they done to deserve it? Never mind, dear lady, if you attend, I will oblige you.'

Yes, she was bound to stay.

Chambers looked over the invitations.

'Why, the musicale at the French house is just two days away! What will you wear, my lady? The thin blue silk with the violet trim would be well, but you wore it last night and—'

'Perhaps we could get something new. The Duchesse after all is always the height of elegance. . . .'

Damaris sprang out of bed. With such urgent business her journey to Angelhurst was quite forgotten. It was the first warm day of spring, and all the beau monde was taking the air in the Park. As Damaris bowled along in her spanking new high-perched chaise drawn by a pair of white horses, she was the focus of every eye. Her blue promenade gown certainly became her, and she felt a new joy in her own good looks and in the beauty of the day.

She enjoyed, with a new relish, every admiring glance—and looked about discreetly for one more admiring gentleman. He did not appear, and the day was dimmed a little with disappointment, but she laughed and chatted with Alvanley and Lord Hallbury, who rode along beside her for a time, telling her that the Beau was to have ridden out with them, but he had already tied on fifty cravats and pronounced himself unsatisfied with any of them.

Her laughter struck the ears of her listeners agreeably, and none more than d'Egremont, who had been watching from the bridle-path. He cantered forward; their eyes met, and suddenly Damaris's pleasure in the day was complete. Her blood seemed to sing in her veins, and a delicious excitement stroked her skin down to the very soles of her feet. He greeted her and her friends with debonair ease and glances that belied this manner, and begged the Countess to save his weary mount by taking him up for a turn round the Park.

'For the day is so exhilarating,' he observed, 'that I have broken all the rules and have been galloping *ventre à terre*.'

He gave the reins to his groom while Damaris, laughing, took him up; Alvanley and Hallbury rode on, and the two glided round the Park in view of all the beau monde, in perfect propriety yet just a few inches apart, with every nerve in both their bodies quiveringly aware of each other and those few inches—hardly a barrier and yet a chasm of teasing frustration. Her coachman was in front; two grooms were up behind; the Marquis and the Countess chatted idly of the people in the Park and gossiped a little of the ball. Society saw the elegant young nobleman lounging dandy-fashion at the side of the lady, who looked as cool as ever in her severe blue gown and the modish hat that shielded her face from her admirer unless she turned directly towards him, and gave her an air of great indifference.

The grooms, closer to the pair and from their place in life less impressed with outer appearances than the gentry, felt something in the air almost sparkling between the two and saw the sudden glances, no different between a lord and lady from those between man and maid. As they drove through a quiet narrow path out of the sight of other carriages, they waited for the armorous Marquis to put an arm round the waist of the Countess, to steal a kiss before they came out once again into broad view. The boughs of the trees, heavy with the young and spreading leaf, dipped confidingly over the carriage; the air was sweet with all the scents of spring. The Marquis turned to speak, their lady held her face up to listen —but the grooms were disappointed. The two were silent once again; nothing had occurred. After all, as the younger of the two remarked later when they took a pint of ale, the Marquis was a dandy, 'not a man with sperrit in 'im. My God, if I 'ad such a woman as her ladyship set right up agin' me—' But the coachman, also taking some refreshment, heard and reproved him sharply for talking about his betters. 'And if you want to keep your place, you

don't go talking about what goes on with a lady in her carriage,'
he said darkly.

The young groom said nothing but waited until the coachman
was gone to swear at an old man's folly. Half the grooms in London were talking of Mrs Carroway, and it was said one of them
might be asked to go to court if there was a divorce. 'Which goes
to show,' the elder groom remarked, 'that coachman, he knows
what he says. For what will become of the Carroway's groom
after? Ten to one the family will dismiss him—*they* won't want to
see his face again. And what house would hire a groom that spies
upon his mistress? Answer me that.'

The grooms were not the only ones to leave the Park with a
slight sense of disappointment. The Marquis had his own plans,
but none of them included bringing disgrace upon Lady Malfrey
by making love in the Park as if she were one of the pretty young
prostitutes who rode there on splendid mounts to find buyers for
their patrons' horses and gallants for themselves. Damaris had set
him down when they came back to the place where his grooms
were waiting with his mount, perfectly fit and restless, and the
Marquis had left her with a cheerful '*à bientôt*, Madame.'

Damaris's eyes were glowing. She had not known exactly what
she had expected; she would not admit that there was anything she
wanted. But yet . . . ! When the Marquis had spoken in the
shaded path and she had turned towards him, his gesturing hand
had, perhaps accidentally, touched her breast. The leaping sensation of most exquisite, thrilling joy had been something never
known, never imagined. She had gasped and then, somehow collecting herself, made some trifling answer; he had looked down on
her, half-smiling, his eyes snapping in mischief, and they had gone
their decorous way.

She had returned home in a dream, a daze, feeling at once
gloriously happy and yet in a delicious, tantalized state where she
could neither think nor act. Chambers took her dress off as though
she were a doll. She looked thoughtfully at her young mistress,
who was usually too helpful to her maids—that dragon of propriety considered such helpfulness not quite the thing. Now she
put her in a light morning-gown of white muslin to rest in before
she changed for dinner. There were letters Damaris had to write,
but instead she sat in her little chair, kicked her slippers off, and
gazed at her feet pensively, half admiring their slim elegance and
half dreaming of—she knew not what.

A maid came to the door with a message from Mrs Sedgwick-Darnley. There was illness in the servants' hall and some fear of a contagion—Mrs Sedgwick-Darnley regretted that her dinner must be cancelled. The sheet of paper fell from Damaris's fingers. She had no interest in whether she went or not—d'Egremont had said he would not be there.

While she sat, Chambers asked her mistress for her plans that evening and what she should lay out for her to wear. Damaris, unable to decide on anything, told her she would give instructions later. Lord Malfrey was dining out. She could not really care about dinner—though she supposed she could hardly sit in her chair all evening looking out of the window over her little garden, reliving again that flash of pure delight, wondering where the Marquis had gone.

The light was only beginning to fade when another letter was brought up. Her heart pounded. Even before she saw the d'Egremont seal, she knew without doubt who had sent it. The bold and spiky script proclaimed the Marquis.

'I learn that your dinner has been cancelled. I, too, am deserted by my cousin, Madame la Duchesse. May I take you for a drive to enjoy the splendid air? We could have supper or not, as you wish.'

She clutched the note, once again flooded with a warm and tingling elation. Of course, she would not have supper alone with the Marquis, but—

'The Marquis is waiting downstairs, my lady,' Chambers said in her perfect servant's voice, without expression.

Damaris caught her breath.

'Send word I will be down immediately,' she said with great calm. 'Chambers, get me my hat and cloak.'

'You are going driving in your white muslin, my lady?' Chambers looked affronted.

'I will lose the light if I stop to change,' Damaris said. 'I go merely for half an hour, and my cloak will cover all.'

It was not long since ladies of fashion had gone driving—and everywhere else—in a lot less than the modest muslin being worn by her mistress, without a cloak to cover their shoulders even in winter weather, so Chambers attired her mistress without further demur.

When she descended, the Marquis, dressed in breeches and top-boots, came towards her smiling. 'You are kind indeed. As you see, I was ready to go and fetch Madame la Duchesse from her friends in Greenwich, but she sends me word she is staying another day. A matter of a picnic, *au Petit Trianon,* no doubt, that cannot be missed. And here I am longing for the spring breezes and the open air.'

Laughing, they went out to his carriage. For all his desire for open air, Damaris saw with a certain relief that he had brought a closed coach; he handed her in, away from the stares of the curious. They drove sedately along the crowded streets, but when they came to the edge of populated London, he dismissed his groom and took the reins himself, with Damaris up on the box beside him.

They drove at spanking pace. She had hardly ridden outside since she had left Angelhurst, and she loved the feeling of the wind on her face. The air was still deliciously warm and fragrant. Sunlight turned to twilight, and still they drove on through the country lanes. The half-hour she had spoken of was already gone, but with the vital, dashing, debonair yet very masculine d'Egremont at her side, somehow she forbore to question their destination.

They were really in the country now. The twilight had dwindled to almost nothing; the moon was rising.

'If Madame la Duchesse can have a picnic,' the Marquis said gaily, 'why can we not do the same?'

He tethered the horses by a grassy bank under a huge chestnut tree in candle. Taking a basket from inside the carriage, he set it on the grass and then spread his great-coat for Damaris. He took her hand to help her down and it trembled in his own.

The air was swooningly sweet from the chestnut blossom. They drank the wine and crumbled the delicate food between their fingers. Their talk became less and less and dwindled into silence. There was no wind. Damaris, warm from the wine, stifled in her voluminous cloak; d'Egremont slipped it from her shoulders. The moon rose high to shine through the silvered blossoms, and Damaris's arms and shoulders gleamed silver, too. Her eyes looked dark and fathoms deep; d'Egremont was a figure black above her as he took her in his arms. Her eyes closed; his lips came down upon her own, bringing swift joy and new torment; and at his touch that slid along the tender hidden places, her whole woman's strength and sweetness rose in a curve of passion to meet his own.

22

Damaris woke up next morning to another lovely day, in the full knowledge that she had taken herself a lover, and there was no regret to mar the beauty of the morning. She felt in turn happy, joyous, shy, surprised. There was no question in her mind as to whether the relationship should continue; it was already the dearest part of her existence.

She lay in bed in a delicious lassitude, incredulous of her own happiness, hardly understanding her joy. She was elated by the knowledge that she could love and be loved, amazed by the pleasures of passion that still trembled and tingled along her nerves until she shivered in delight. How strange it was, she thought, yawning, raising her arms to rumple her hair, then shaking her head and laughing. How strange that it could be—and she had never known it.

She turned and rested her chin upon her hands and thought mischievously that now at last she could understand *some* part of her husband's feelings. But with her lover there had been no ugliness of shame, nor the rancour of remorse. D'Egremont's tenderness had not vanished with his first outpouring of passion; he had cradled her in his arms and spoken of love—they had been two enchanted creatures under a magic moon.

And he had not forgotten his care for her. It had been d'Egremont who remembered when they must leave, d'Egremont who met his groom at a place previously arranged so that they could drive back quietly and privately through the town; it was d'Egremont who had smoothed her hair and gown, with little laughing compliments, and wrapped her carefully in her cloak and hat. The Countess, if she arrived at her home rather late, nevertheless returned with every look of propriety.

No, she had no thought of dismissing her lover. The danger she had feared before she now dismissed as nothing. She, the Countess of Malfrey, knew how to behave. There could be no damage to her position or her family. But d'Egremont she must have. She was not, she realized with a strange sweetness, the woman she had been the day before. In learning love, in receiving this most exquisite of pleasures, her body had become less her own—it was bound by invisible bonds to that of the Marquis. Now, in his absence, she felt curiously incomplete. She wondered when she would see him again—at the musicale, of course. In company with a hundred others and under the eye of Madame la Duchesse. Her spirits plummeted, and then she remembered with a little smile that the Marquis was a young man of resource. She need not concern herself. He would manage all.

She had teased him the night before, asking if he had long planned his sudden abduction, but he had sworn that any plans he had made had been of quite a different sort and that he had been inspired that night by the illness at the Sedgwick-Darnleys and the stirring of the spring. 'Moon madness,' he said.

'And the Duchesse's defection?'

He looked ashamed, but not very much.

'I had known before she was not coming—that was a tale for the servants. She had written of her picnic—it seemed an excellent idea!'

He had laughed and she had laughed with him at the small deception, and in the morning she smiled again. Jean-Philippe was a rogue—but a delightful rogue. At last she jumped up, smiling and impatient. Suddenly the two days until the musicale seemed endless. Her spirits soared again when she went down to find a great bouquet come from the Marquis—the freshest of spring flowers, pale jonquils and dark blue forget-me-nots, purple moonwort and, cleverly woven among green leaves, the spikes of creamy chestnut blossom with their sweet and memory-provoking fragrance.

'Chestnut flowers in the house! I never saw such a thing,' one of the maids exclaimed to the manservant who brought them. 'I wonder,' she frowned, 'is it lucky?' She scuttled away when she saw her mistress, who was charmed at the attention. The chestnut flowers soon faded, and she longed to ask the Marquis if his love would prove as transient—happy in her own certainty that it would not.

In the bustle of the matter of the new gown, the two days went at last, and Damaris once again was driven to the d'Egremont house. To her dismay there had been talk of the Earl accompanying her—he was fond of music. It was the only relaxation that brought peace and warmth to that stern man. But at the last moment he had been called away for a conference. She had thought him busy about the Congress at Vienna during the peace, but now that wretched Napoleon was back in France warring on the King he was busier than ever. She felt a pang of pity for Jean-Philippe—it must be hard for him to see his King in such straits, whatever disagreements there had been between them. Like so many of the émigrés, of course, d'Egremont was an 'Ultra,' resisting all compromise. But the armies would soon put all right again—no one doubted that. And she entered the rich and famous house with her heart beating wildly but the outward calm of a nun.

Inside she was amused to see that the elaborate court costume she had worn at the *bal masqué* in such triumph had started a fashion. Many of the ladies present had taken what they thought was a lead from her in colour, jewels, and rich fabrics, and they dazzled from every side. Damaris herself that night wore a deceptively simple-seeming gown, a column of plain white silk fastened on one shoulder, with no jewels and merely a plain silver fillet in her hair. The other ladies at once looked overdressed and had an air of struggling to impress. Damaris's young beauty shone proud and clear. It captivated the viewer, and she rejoiced as she saw the delight in the eyes of her lover as he bowed formally and led her to the great salon which was the music room at the d'Egremonts.

Cramer was already seated at the pianoforte. He was an artist of consummate skill. Damaris listened with pleasure, though her attention—but not her gaze!—was bound to the Marquis. Some of the younger women chatted, to the displeasure of the Duchesse, who called them to order with a tap of her fan. When the recital was over she was heard to remark that the young Countess should be the model of behaviour for the girls in their first Season—it was such as she who proved that England was not a nation of barbarians.

A light supper was served. Damaris went to the performer and thanked him knowledgeably for his performance and the pleasure it had given her. She treated him as a social equal; the other guests, at first surprised, followed her lead, and the old man with his disgracefully snuff-stained fingers found himself lionized by the ladies and even some of the gentlemen of the *ton* and enjoyed his hour of glory.

The guests, carrying glasses of wine or orangeade, strolled in the garden. The Marquis paused beneath a flowering chestnut tree and smiled at Damaris; her heart turned over, and then they moved on. Lady Malfrey strolled with Madame la Duchesse. The two great ladies talked of the difficulties of Society and the necessity of having the Regent as a guest; the Marquis, hearing them, agreed but allowed that it was essential. To all the world nothing could have seemed further from storms of passion, yet Damaris was in a high fever of excitement until she could learn what the Marquis planned.

Cramer played once more, and then the guests began to leave. Carriage after carriage came to the front door. Damaris, who always arranged for her coachman to be one of the first to arrive, was surprised that he did not appear, and yet she found she was not surprised when word came that there had been a small accident with her carriage wheel; it was being attended to, and she would only be detained a very short time.

The other guests had all departed. The Duchesse gave a little sigh and admitted she was *very* tired. Would Madame la Comtesse like to accompany her to her boudoir for a tisane until her carriage readied itself?

'In a few moments, my dear Marie,' d'Egremont said smoothly. 'Pray rest yourself. I will bring Madame la Comtesse to you if her carriage does not arrive in a moment. But first I would like to play for her—not, alas, with the expertness of Cramer, but a simple French song or two that I think she would enjoy.'

The Duchesse nodded, swayed her elegant form upstairs, and disappeared from view. The Marquis, decorous, took his seat at the pianoforte, ran his hands over the keys, and began to play and sing softly. His playing, of course, was not of the quality of the master's, yet he had ease and charm and his voice was pleasant, pleasant to Damaris as he sang songs of love.

The servants had vanished. Some of the lights in the great salon had been extinguished, leaving deep pools of shadow. D'Egremont rose and took Damaris's hand. She looked up at him breathlessly. He led her to the darkest, furthest corner of the room. Once again her heart was beating hard; she was puzzled and watched his every movement with all her nerves on the *qui vive*. His hand was touching the wall. His fingers slid along the twisting gold ornament of the panel; he found something, pressed—the panel swung open.

And Damaris saw for the first time, lit by one tall candle, the secret room. Her eyes were wide and dark. D'Egremont led her inside gently, and the door, heavy, silent, closed behind them.

There had never been such a Season. The country was excited with the thought of the coming and, they hoped, final battle with the Emperor; Damaris's excitement was of another sort. Every day was a delight, knowing that at any ball, rout, fête, dinner, or concert the Marquis might be met—urbane, witty, the cynosure of every female eye, while she had the secret knowledge that his love was hers and that somehow, soon, they would find their way to the enchantment of the hidden room.

The hidden room. Damaris thought of it and smiled. Their first love, their first joy in the moonlight, had seemed to her all that any woman could desire, but as day followed day and in the long, sweet, stolen afternoons she lay in the Marquis's arms, she learned all the many pleasures of leisurely love, love as practiced by a man who was a master of the art, who liked nothing better than to spend his time in giving happiness and receive it back tenfold. He discovered to her all the many hidden stores of delight with the delicacy and skill of a master, in the sweet, loving intimacy that only such a man could create, a man who truly enjoyed women and all and everything about them.

Now she understood the hints, the things half-said, of ladies in Society, complaining of their husbands and their lovers; she understood their desire for d'Egremont—knowing, with a pang of jealousy, that he had been lover to most of them, though he swore to her that he had never before been in love.

'Dandies,' one great lady complained, 'have their minds, after all, on their costumes. When they fling off a coat to make love, they worry through the whole as to whether the wretched object will take a crease.'

A younger woman had giggled. 'Or worse, call for a valet before the breath is hardly back in one's body'—but she had received cold looks; she was far too new a wife to be so bold.

'And the young bucks with their minds on their sport and their horses,' the first lady had gone on. 'How can a man make love while he is thinking of the new pair of greys he wants at Tattersalls or that he has an appointment at Jackson's Boxing Saloon?'

'In France, they say, it is managed better,' the young wife had said dreamily, and at those sad words the ladies had fallen into regretful silence. Later, two of them had written notes to the Marquis.

'But Jean-Philippe,' Damaris asked as she lay beside him, admiring the ripple of muscle of his strong brown arms, 'if you were not in love then how—'

'How? How what?' He laughed to see her blush. 'Little English prude. I could love them, because I did love them. All. For a man like myself—I love women. I love the whole sex. It is real; it is true, and I can demonstrate that love. Now that I have you, Madame, I am indeed blessed, for I love your charming self as well as the female sex that you represent so delightfully.'

He looked down upon her, amused but for once telling the truth. Certainly he had been a dreadful rogue and liar with women —it was part of the game of love—but now he was sincere. The woman beside him gleamed, pearl-like, in the half-light from the window. She lay on her side, her arms above her head, one slender foot drawn up to her knee, unconsciously assuming the most graceful, provocative shape of love.

Here at last was everything he had ever wanted—beauty, passion, nobility, and something even more. He could not name it, but her quick smile was an enchantment and her blue gaze drew him—further certainly than he had ever meant to go! There had been a marriage proposed by Louis, to the young Giselle de Harcourt-Fleury. He had not refused, but now—besides, what did he care for that monarch turned bourgeois sitting in Ghent? He had other games to play. Damaris stirred, sighing; her lovely breast rose and fell, and he caught her to him once again, politics and France all forgotten.

Jean-Philippe spoke to her only of love, but as Napoleon grew in strength and Damaris heard from the Earl that a million men would be needed to take the field against him, she marvelled a little at d'Egremont's coolness. He had been trained as a soldier, and she wondered that he was not with Wellington preparing to march —though she was very glad that he was not.

They never talked of the war in the stolen hours, but one evening when they were with a large party in the gardens at Vauxhall, some turned off here and some there, and they had a moment to talk of things not too private to be overheard.

The lanterns were lit and the music played charmingly, but as they strolled up a leafy walk, Damaris noticed that the Marquis was quieter than usual.

'You are somewhat distrait, M'sieur,' she said softly. 'Is all the talk of battle disturbing you?'

Lady Rise and Mrs Farthingale, together with a young Hussar in their party, had been indulging in great invective against Bonaparte and the French army which had rallied to his flag.

D'Egremont shrugged. 'The gossip of old women and a boy who has never seen battle except on the sands of Brighton? No, they may talk if they wish.'

Lady Gratton, who had joined the evening party, came up and asked Damaris if she was going to the concert in the rotunda. Her niece hoped for better things than sitting demurely in silence for the next few hours and declined. After Lady Gratton had gone, taking with her Mrs Farthingale and the young Hussar, who looked somewhat dismayed, Damaris inquired again.

'Would you be with the Duke of Wellington, perhaps?'

Her heart beat a little faster at the thought that perhaps it was for her that the Marquis had stayed.

For once his answer was not dictated by gallantry.

'To fight for England?'

'For France, for your king,' Damaris answered, surprised.

'Ah, the English. I am not sure. Your countrymen are far more interested in owning the former French colonies than in really restoring the old régime. It was the English who persuaded Louis to grant that infamous constitution and accept the concordat that left his own supporters in ruin—those who were not killed in Brittany in '95.'

His voice had a note of seriousness, indeed of bitterness, that surprised her.

'We were deceived then, the flower of our young men sent in with not a trace of English help when it was needed. Your Pitt refused to recognize little Louis XVII, so that the traitors saw fit to murder him—a boy of ten years. When the naval base of Toulon surrendered to the royal fleet, Pitt refused them soldiers, so that Toulon was retaken and the people massacred. To the English government all French are enemies—they play us one against the other.'

Damaris was shocked to hear him speak so. It was assumed by all of English society, which had taken d'Egremont to its heart, that he, like all the émigrés, was as strongly opposed to the Emperor as they themselves—more so, in fact, for the Frenchmen's hatred of the Revolution and all its works was a plant whose roots had sprung from their own blood. But she had a delicacy of feeling as well as a special sensitivity towards the Marquis—he was a Frenchman after all; the Emperor's army was of Frenchmen; she could understand his pain. Suppose there had been a revolution in England. Could she, hiding in Scotland or America, be happy to see an English army beaten by foreigners, to know that the young men of Angelhurst and Little Heron were being maimed and killed?

She touched his arm, a butterfly's touch, there in the public gardens to give him comfort, and he turned and smiled, once more the gallant beau as he whispered in her ear a plan for a meeting—a rendezvous at Richmond. She agreed as she always agreed with d'Egremont's plans, although she had to fail a hostess at a dinner arranged long since, a piece of bad manners that Lady Malfrey had never indulged in before. She felt herself wrong, but the idea of spending a day alone in his company was too sweet to her; she could not resist it.

But once the pleasures of that long, languorous day on the river were behind them, she found their stolen meetings much too short and far between. Her visits to the d'Egremont house could not be too frequent, and the Duchesse had to stay to lend her countenance, though she longed to go to Belgium with some other ladies to offer civilized comfort to the allied armies as they gathered for battle. Or in lieu of that, she complained at last, she must go to Brighton, where many members of the *ton* had already gone, leaving Town thin as the warm weather came.

The Marquis had told Damaris he could not go to Brighton for some time, and so she delayed her own departure. It would be difficult. The Earl would stay in Town, of course—he was busier than ever—but soon all of Society would be gone. There would be no houses where she and the Marquis could 'happen' to meet. A solitary lady and gentleman of fashion were far too conspicuous for safety.

She wondered why the Marquis could not leave. As far as she knew, he had no occupation of any kind to bind him. Of course, he had the handling of his fortune and that of other members of his family; he was the chief of the d'Egremonts since his father had died, but it seemed unlikely that such business could keep him in Town in the unfashionable time of year. But, she reminded herself, she knew little about such things. If there was something the Marquis wished to tell her, doubtless he would.

The danger, which should have made them cautious, made them both more reckless. The Marquis, whose passion grew stronger with the passing days and with some new and feverish urgency, forgot his early protection of her reputation and urged her ever closer to the edge of scandal and disaster. Lady Gratton, before she went to Brighton with Mrs Farthingale, looked at her niece as though she would speak but then, it seemed, decided against it.

Lady Gratton had observed the affair from its inception. At first she had not disapproved. It was inevitable that Damaris would take a lover, and the young d'Egremont was perfectly suitable. His fondness was only for women of the *bon ton;* he was well skilled in avoiding the jealousies of husbands. She had become concerned when it was apparent that love, with all its attendant folly, claimed them both, yet still she had faith in her niece's good sense. The fires would burn themselves out. D'Egremont had never been a faithful lover; soon his restlessness would be at work again. Even now, her calm eyes had noted, his demeanour was not entirely that of a happy lover: he was nervous, too reckless, unnaturally gay. Lady Gratton liked the young nobleman, but now she perceived him as too mercurial, not steady. And all the time, she was aware, Lord Malfrey's eyes were on the lovers.

Society, too, was taking notice. Hostesses who cared nothing about the private love affairs of their friends became offended by the sudden cancellations that spoiled their tables. And Lady Gratton heard that some of the beaux not of Damaris's set were beginning to call her niece, not the Cool Countess, but—most dangerous —the Careless Countess.

So perturbed was she that after her farewell visit to Damaris, Lady Gratton did something she had never done before. Her carriage was already proceeding in stately fashion down the street when she ordered her coachman to turn round and drive back through the gate, where her niece still stood, straight and tall against the portico of Malfrey House.

Lady Gratton leaned over the glass of her chaise, her red hair, grey-sprinkled, framing her face under her bonnet, her sharp face

intent and thoughtful, as Damaris was to recall it for many years
to come.

'Remember, Damaris,' she said in her measured, calm voice,
'life is long, very long. It is well in what you do to remember that.'

And then she drove away.

Damaris did consider her aunt's words. She knew how much it
cost her to utter them. Lady Gratton's dislike of intimacy, necessarily overcome to some extent by her position as guardian to a
child, had returned in force when her niece became Countess of
Malfrey and she herself had regained her freedom of movement.
Lady Gratton did not speak lightly. Her meaning was very clear.
She had observed her niece's behaviour; she was warning her that
any more folly could bring her to ruin, a ruin that would be very
painful and, considering her youth, very long.

Yet all her respect for Lady Gratton, all her own good sense,
melted in the passion and the need she had for d'Egremont.
Added to her need was a certain fear she had of refusing him anything. His temper was ragged. He needed her love as she needed
his, but his need was different. At times it seemed as though he
would drown himself in love, like a man seeking oblivion. Damaris believed it was the impending battle, with nearly all of
Europe now arrayed to meet the Emperor in the field, that was
causing his deeply buried grief, and she tried to show added tenderness in her love to give him what comfort she could, and she
acceded to all his demands, no matter how outrageous.

Now that the Duchesse had gone, she learned to take a hackney
carriage to his door so that no one could report the Malfrey carriage with the arms blazoned on the panel waiting outside the
d'Egremont mansion. They met outside the town and used false

names at modest inns. Marianne Midnight, with her lover, appeared again at her old rooms, but these experiences were not successful; the Marquis shuddered at the second-rate, the plainness that to him was sordid, and he vowed he would not use his lady so.

He took to coming to Malfrey House, unannounced, when he knew the Earl was absent, and they would lie abed, with Damaris enthralled yet cursing her own folly, while the birds outside her window sang the joyous notes of summer. Her need of him was still intense yet hardly satisfied, with fear leaping up at the sound of a step during the very peak of her passion.

One day as he dressed, leaving her in a nervous exhaustion, she voiced her thoughts and asked what oblivion he was seeking.

He smiled, the mocking, familiar smile that she loved.

'The good oblivion. What else?' he said lightly. After his one outburst in the gardens of Vauxhall he had never spoken seriously again.

She sighed. 'You must hurry,' she said. 'I sent Chambers off, all the way to the bank. I said I would need the Malfrey diamonds— she must think me mad; there is not a ball in Town tonight. But even so she will be back within the hour.'

Her hair fell dark and shining across the whiteness of her back. He played with it idly, turning it to ringlets, softly caressing the nape of her neck. From the warmth of the afternoon a light veil of sweat lay over her skin and settled in the hollow of her throat. He bent down and licked it softly, persistently, with his swift, cat-like tongue; she tried to draw away; he held her closer, her resistance increasing his desire, gripping her arms so tightly that she could not escape, and made love again with an urgent intensity that seemed to want to give pain as much as pleasure.

She was startled, terrified; then in the rich deep rush of longing slowly sated, her terror faded. Himself again, he laughed at her delight, scolding her for timidity and telling tales of the daring ladies of France: royal ladies who had taken lovers under the very noses of their kings; the mistresses of the Bourbons who had braved the jealousy of that amorous tribe to disport themselves with gay young aristocrats for their pleasure. He told her of the famous Duchesse de Chevreuse, who swam to meet her lovers. 'And whether she was as good a lover as she was a swimmer we will never know, though rumour gives her the accolade,' he said, grinning as he left.

For a time he was more careful, more *convenable,* as he said. He came only rarely to Malfrey House, and he found an old aunt to be chaperon at his mansion. She felt safe again and had all her former joy in the secret room, thankful that the Marquis had recovered his good sense—but the Marquis was incomprehensible. It was only two weeks after her fright at Malfrey House that he spoke of her portrait, and when she had reluctantly agreed, he had surprised her by bringing Claude Baptiste into the secret room while she had still been breathless with love. She had known, even at that moment, with the painter's eyes gazing at her naked flesh, that she should refuse, rise up, and leave her importunate lover no matter what he said.

But Jean-Philippe had been at his most charming, most soothing, the painter a very model of discretion, slipping into the shadow with his charcoal and canvas, impersonal as a valet de chambre. And perhaps she had been a little afraid; afraid of Jean-Philippe's mocking laughter if she behaved, as he would say, like a Bath miss; afraid of losing his love if she could not match the great ladies of France in all the courage of passion.

The painting was completed. The lovers toasted the artist with champagne and then made love again in the secret room, warm from the artist's candles and the glow of the afternoon sun. But all the time Damaris could see, propped on the stool where the artist had left it, the portrait of herself abandoned to love. And she wondered how she had allowed herself to come so far and what was yet to be.

Book Two

THE FLIGHT,
1815

The brilliance faded; the candles guttered, and the little room was pervaded by a grey-blue light that presaged dusk.

'*L'heure bleue,*' d'Egremont whispered, and held her to him closely.

This had been their favourite time for love-making, but that evening Damaris felt a faint chill in the air. She shivered again.

'It is late,' she murmured. 'I must go. The Earl dines at home this evening.'

D'Egremont gave a mock pout.

'Does he not realize that his presence is a gross inconvenience? To dine at home the third time in a week—it is hardly *comme il faut*. One would expect better manners!'

Damaris tore herself from his arms, jumped up, and dressed hurriedly and carelessly, afraid that d'Egremont might tempt her to stay. She knew she was late even now, and the Earl would think her discourteous. Not that he would reproach her, but his usually cool manner would become cold, and his always measured conversation lapse into stretches of silence.

D'Egremont snatched her hand and kissed it, pressing his lips into her palm and ending with a bite. 'At least for the first time, when you leave, I am not desolate. I have the portrait to keep me company. I am half inclined to have my dinner served in here so that I stay in this charming bed and pretend that you are with me.'

He grinned at her impudently.

'Oh, you must not!' Damaris said, in fear that her indiscretion would become known in spite of all the Marquis's assurances.

He laughed. He had merely been jesting. The Marquis liked his food and liked it well served—the tiny room would hardly do. And besides, he had an important visitor coming that night. D'Egremont's heart beat fast as he imagined the result of this meeting. In the meantime, there was the pleasure of the moment. He loved to see Damaris agitated—she, who was known in Society as the Cool Countess!

'But I am so proud and happy to have the portrait,' he insisted. 'You know how I have wanted your likeness since first I saw your portrait at Malfrey House.'

He had seen it often enough when he had visited her there. Damaris thought of them taking their pleasure in her room—foolhardy as she was. Quickly she turned her mind from the folly that was beginning to be hateful.

'I have always loathed that portrait,' she said.

'But it is an acknowledged masterpiece,' d'Egremont said, surprised.

'It was an advertisement,' Damaris said bitterly, 'by means of which I was sold. Malfrey saw it in old Mansart's studio and asked for the introduction. He made an offer to my aunt before he met me. We could not afford to buy that portrait, my aunt and I, but certainly the result of my sitting exceeded even her expectations.'

Her mind flooded with recollections—all the reasons she had for loathing the Mansart portrait—but she kept her silence. Family loyalty was strong in Damaris; she had not sacrificed it in the confidences of love.

D'Egremont raised an eyebrow at her unusual vehemence. The Cool Countess was agitated indeed! He laughed again.

'Certainly I am glad you do not love your husband,' he said, 'for if you did, Madame, I would of course have to shoot him. Yet your distaste for the noble Earl surprises me. After all,' he said, shrugging, 'his mistresses find him charming.'

Damaris said nothing in reply but asked him to call her carriage. She would not discuss her husband; such behaviour was outside her code. D'Egremont knew this and, although he missed the pleasure of gossip, admired her more for her breeding. He stirred himself, as she wished, and dressed, wishing that he could decently call his servants. His coat, cut in the English style, really took two men to help him into it gracefully.

While he struggled, he thought about the Earl, his curiosity aroused.

The Marquis preferred the charms of *les dames du monde,* but at times he succumbed to an opera dancer. The room in the back of the opera house where the scantily-dressed girls practiced before long mirrors was an attraction to many men in Town, and there was always a group of beaux lounging in wait for the obliging beauties. From these girls the Marquis had heard strange tales of Lord Malfrey. Such tales were scoffed at by most people in Society. Who paid heed to the talk of opera dancers? But the Marquis had not found them worse liars than the beau monde—a few tales to glorify themselves, perhaps, but there was little glory in what they said of the Earl.

He stopped teasing Damaris and helped her to leave his house discreetly. It would be good, he thought, to take her from Malfrey House and the Earl. In the circumstances, an annulment of her marriage might be arranged. His excitement mounted almost unbearably as he thought of his secret dream on the eve of fulfilment.

CHAPTER

26

Malfrey House was not far away. Damaris, with little time to dress for dinner, was impatient, yet her coachman, skilled as he was, could move but slowly. The streets and squares were full of carriages bearing ladies returning from their afternoon excursions, and many elegant equipages were clashing in their haste.

Damaris recognized some of these ladies, and they were not the flower of the *ton*. Women of fashion took their rides in the Park at the correct hour, never later than five, and had been at home long since. The women rattling along now, who had come from goodness knows where, were for the most part the high-flyers, the saucy young chippers whose position was precarious, and not all of whom would receive cards for Almack's in the coming Season. Lady Lade was driving her own high-perch phaeton with her usual air of vulgarity; the young Mrs Carroway was bounding along in a barouche, stuck up in the back all alone, the flaming red hair that escaped from her bonnet catching the eye of the curious and the malicious. It was common knowledge now that she was on the verge of ruin—the rumours of divorce were growing. Damaris shivered.

The blue shadows in the streets, the slight chill of the air, increased the uneasiness she had felt before leaving the Marquis. Even if she cared nothing for her own position—and in her heart she was not sure she would keep the Marquis's love if she were disgraced, for he was a man who enjoyed the pleasures of society above all things—there were her two children to consider.

She did not consider them often enough, she told herself with a deepening sense of guilt. Now she remembered that before she had met d'Egremont, she had longed to become a real mother to her children and had planned to mend her broken marriage. Then she had been cruelly snubbed by the Earl, and she had withdrawn in hopeless anger. She had soon stopped trying to break the barriers he put between her and the children and resigned herself to the brief formal visits he approved. On these visits the children would be brought to her, beautifully dressed, tongue-tied with shyness, for fifteen minutes before dinner. She would look at the two little strangers and try to remember the babies she had loved.

Only sometimes at night in her sleep, alone in her room in Malfrey House, could she picture them—her baby Griselda, the new-born Christopher—and she would wake suddenly with a sharp feeling that she had lost more than she would ever have again; and d'Egremont seemed merely a foolish girl's dream. But in the morning her love for him always came flooding back, with all the excitement of her day's engagements, all the thrilling possibilities of public meetings and secret love, while the children receded in her memory like little ghosts. Yet as her carriage drew further from the d'Egremont mansion she knew herself to be a bad mother, a woman reckless beyond the limits imposed by Society and beyond the bounds of sense.

She was still nervous and unhappy when she entered the plain wooden gate to her own house. For the first time the high wall that kept Malfrey House from public view seemed not a gloomy, old-fashioned barrier designed to suit the solitary temper of the Earls of Malfrey, an expression of their wish to immure their wives, but a welcome privacy. She was conscious of her *déshabillé* —she had made a poor job of dressing herself, and the light gown she had put on that morning was unsuitable now that the lamps were being lit.

That portrait was a wretched piece of folly! She wondered miserably why d'Egremont urged her on to the brink of disaster, why she had obeyed his wish. He did love her; she knew that. So many of the young beaux had been at her feet, and d'Egremont was as adoring as the rest—yet she never felt quite certain of him.

Jean-Philippe, whom she had admitted to a closeness no one else had ever known, was still in many ways a stranger to her. He was very much a Frenchman, of course—but she knew many young Frenchmen, and there was nothing strange about them. But there was much about Jean-Philippe of which she was ignorant: what it was that sent his spirits soaring, or sometimes plunging to the depths. Really she knew him as little as she knew her husband, she thought in a moment of perception, forgotten as the steps of her carriage were let down and her front door opened. She ran in quickly, intending to go straight to her room, but she was stopped short.

Standing in the large, square hall, illumined by the light of the chandelier that blended with the cold blue haze coming from the fan-light over the door, was Lord Malfrey, already dressed for the evening, a servant holding his hat and stick. Cold, calm, beautifully turned out as always, he was a figure to fill the eye. Damaris remembered the Marquis's words: 'his mistresses find him attractive.' Yet it was hard for her to repress a shiver of revulsion as he lightly touched her hand and asked her to join him for a moment in the drawing room.

The quiet elegance of that room usually pleased the young Countess: the fine but seemingly simple furniture and the subdued decoration appealed to her taste more than the sumptuously rich French household of the Marquis, who had bought many of the pre-Revolutionary pieces that came on the market and a few things of Empire fashion he could not resist. That evening, however, she would have been happier almost anywhere else. She was uneasily convinced she cut a most unimposing figure.

Lord Malfrey of course was impeccable in a dark blue coat the cut of which the Beau himself could have envied, snowy white waistcoat, black trousers, and silk stockings. He looked what he was, master of his house. His manner as usual was urbane but distant.

'I beg your pardon, my dear. You must forgive me, but I find I am unable to dine. An urgent message came from the secretary, and I must attend him.'

Damaris did not fully understand why, but she had never been

interested enough to inquire. Lord Malfrey, who had held a port-
folio under a previous government, was out of office. Still, she
knew he was often consulted on foreign affairs and matters to do
with the war. D'Egremont often teased her by saying that the
Earl's political commitments were an excellent excuse for a husband who wanted to slip off to his mistresses. Damaris had accepted this—though with the Malfreys' domestic arrangements the
Earl had little need to lie. But even Damaris was aware now of the
crisis in the campaign on the Continent. Bonaparte was indeed a
menace winning battle after battle.

Lord Malfrey was murmuring of Wellington and Blücher, his
carefully controlled voice sounding, as always, slightly bored. His
pale grey prominent eyes were half-hidden by his drooping eyelids, but Damaris suspected that he noticed her *déshabillé,* and she
feared that the very texture of her skin and the quickness of her
breath were proclaiming her adultery.

She was right. She revealed more than she knew. Lord Malfrey,
knowing his marriage was a disaster, and knowing that he alone
bore the responsibility for it, was prepared to countenance his
young wife's taking lovers according to the custom of people of
his rank. She must be discreet, she must not parade her infidelities
in his face, and certainly he would prefer that she did not fall in
love.

But Damaris had become indiscreet; it was obvious that she
loved the Marquis; the signs were plain before him. She had never
looked so beautiful. He had thought his wife cold, a proper Bath
miss, very suited to be Countess of Malfrey. Now her delicate
complexion glowed as though it were lit from within; her blue eyes
were enormous, and a pulse beat in her throat. The Earl burned
with jealousy, anger, and something like despair—his wife had no
idea of the love he bore her, this strange, unhappy, and complicated man.

He spoke the truth about the appointment. Although officially
part of the opposition, his knowledge was such that he was often
consulted by the present government. Unlike his wife's playmates,
the social butterflies of the *ton,* Lord Malfrey understood the desperate nature of the coming battle against Napoleon. The former
Emperor's genius still lived. He had returned from his defeat and
imprisonment to take France from Louis as easily as a girl plucking a ripe apple from a tree. Even now, with all the might of the
allies ranged against him, he could yet snatch victory. And almost

on the eve of this decisive battle, matters had just come to light so disquieting that they must be settled at once.

Lord Malfrey knew he should hurry, but he could not move. He gazed on his wife, still ruffled and trembling in the aftermath of love, longing to say something to bridge the gap between them, to explain—but that was forever impossible. Certainly he had no wish to know about her and d'Egremont, yet scenes painted themselves before his mental view. His instinct bade him go and hunt his wife's seducer down; his intelligence told him he must go about his business. Proof had come that there was a spy in high places. This spy must be rooted out before Wellington's final plans could be made. The Earl's personal life must wait.

Yet he had to speak. His Countess's folly would not only destroy their lives but would cast a shadow on their children. A public scandal, for the woman at least, would not be tolerated, even in the lax days of the Regency. Lord Malfrey, who could speak without preparation on almost any subject in the House of Lords, now hunted desperately for some words to say to his wife that would point out her danger without going beyond the formality that had always been the tone of their relations.

His Countess was murmuring that his absence would not at all upset her arrangements. No guests were invited; she was tired and would have a tray in her room.

Lord Malfrey inclined his head.

'Very good. Perhaps it is better so. You look, if not exactly tired, my dear,'—his gaze flickered up and down her body—'not quite the thing. Perhaps you should get a new maid.'

He dipped into a small, rich snuff-box and sniffed delicately. He meant to go no further, but the blush rising from Damaris's bosom to suffuse her cheeks goaded him on.

'Your country days are over, after all.' His voice was still cool. 'It does not do for the Countess of Malfrey to look as though she had been chased through the fields by a ploughman—and perhaps overtaken?'

Lord Malfrey was known among his colleagues for his sharp tongue. In this case he did not mean to wound, only to warn, but his jealousy, disappointed love, and torment of guilt made him cruel. When he left, Damaris was scarlet, and she stood in her own drawing-room in an agony of humiliation. Her eyes were so moist that she could hardly see; she dashed her hand before her eyes as a child would, and there before her gaze, above the chimney-piece, was the portrait, painted when she was fifteen. She saw it clear: the young Damaris St Cloud about to begin life, her gaze candid, her lips eager, wondering about love, hopeful, expectant, and yet shy.

She ran to her room to escape but saw herself immediately in her long looking-glass and blushed painfully once more, seeing herself as her husband had seen her: her hair tumbled, her gauze gown too revealing; for in her haste to dress, unable to manage alone, she had abandoned her tight-fitting chemise. I must have been drunk from the champagne, she thought in misery. The fragile gown was torn, too—she saw the tell-tale ragged edge where d'Egremont, impatient, had tugged it from her. Why, with her gilded nails she looked like a woman of pleasure.

Her eyes filled with tears, and she felt weariness and disgust. She could not blame d'Egremont for all this. She had been bad enough, she thought, before they met. Unwilling, she recalled the episode she had tried hard to forget, when in her folly she had almost fallen a victim to the Prince Regent. Then, as now, her dress had been torn. Remembering the girl of the portrait, Damaris flung herself down on her bed and wept as if she would never stop.

CHAPTER

27

Damaris lay long upon her bed, feeling as if she could face no one and only wanting to hide. But after a time she roused herself. The Countess of Malfrey did not cower in her room while the servants gossiped; she would appear as usual and eat her dinner in state in the great dining-room. She called for her bath and had Chambers, with grim approval, lay out a dress of great formality: white silk, with an overskirt patterned in crimson roses and a dark red ruffle sweeping round the hem to form a train behind her. She had never worn the colour before, and as she saw herself in her long glass she thought that she disliked it, but its newness, its high fashion, gave her a look of the unapproachable Countess of Malfrey—it would do.

While she finished dressing, to her surprise she heard Lord Malfrey return. He went to his room and left again, very quickly. Chambers told her he had left the house. Damaris wondered if he had come to see her and found himself unable to do so. It would be like the Earl. She decided, as she put on a pair of diamond ear-rings, that she would wait up, however late it might be when he re-turned. Let him not believe that she was ashamed to face him. She thought of the scene that had passed between them, and her anger rose. He could keep her from her children; the law was on his side —yet how dare he upbraid her for her fault! At least her sin was natural. She had kept silence about his sin that was far greater than her own.

Anger restored her courage and her pride. She descended the stairs with her head held high, and so stately was she, so full of hauteur, the very picture of great aristocratic breeding, that she caught the eye and the approving attention of d'Egremont, who had rushed into the house, brushing aside the hall-porter, with his mind full of very different matters.

She was shocked almost beyond the power of speech to see him there at that moment, bursting into the hall, strange and dis-traught, not dressed for the evening, his cravat awry, his blue coat oddly dark in spots—soiled, in fact. Her head began to spin.

'M'sieur—' Her voice was hardly above a whisper.

Firmly he took her arm and led her away from the eyes of the gaping servants to a small reception room that Damaris hardly knew, a formal little room with a long bench where callers not favoured enough to be shown into one of the more pleasant sit-ting-rooms were kept while their names were sent up to the master or mistress. This room, strange in her own house, added to Da-maris's feeling of bewilderment, of her world turning upside down.

'Pack your trunks,' the Marquis said with no preamble. 'There is not a moment to lose. I have a coach and six waiting. We must get to the coast and catch the first tide.'

She looked at him as if he were mad, and yet she had a dreadful feeling that his words were not mad. It was as though she had played in an enchanted circle, thinking it so wide, yet now it was closing about her.

Impatient, he gave her a little shake.

'Come, Madame! You have no choice. Everything is known. Your ruin here is complete but—trust me. We must leave now.'

She did not doubt him, yet she hardly heard what he was saying. Where his arms had touched her there were crimson smears on the white silk of her gown. It was the pattern, she told herself. She had never liked it—she should not have bought the silk. Horrible red splotches quite the colour of blood—but her bare arm, too, was reddened, sticky. She raised her eyes to his.

'The Earl—we fought,' he said briefly. 'The blood is not mine. I lifted him to see—he is not dead, or was not when I left. But make haste—I will help you.'

She stood, unable to move.

'You may be shot if you linger,' he told her grimly.

'The Earl?'

'The King,' he replied.

She could not understand. What did the poor mad King have to do with her?

'Your husband did not come to me merely for vengeance against his wife's seducer,' he said.

He wondered how much of the scene that he had left he should describe.

'The War Office had word that I have been spying for Bonaparte. Your husband had the proof.'

The Marquis looked at her with narrowed eyes, dark and secret. 'There was a paper I had borrowed from his bedroom on my last visit. I had not yet been able to return it.'

The room turned about her. She could understand nothing, she told herself—yet, awfully, she understood everything. That was why the Earl had returned; he was searching. But Jean-Philippe? She looked at the man before her. Spying—for Bonaparte? He, always *plus royaliste que le roi?*

'I will explain later,' he said impatiently. 'But the army will be searching for me—and you, too, are implicated. On the very eve of battle—our lives will not be worth a pin. Be of courage!' he adjured her. 'The Emperor will win the battle, and you will come and live with me on my estates. I am to have Egremont and much more. If the Earl is dead, you can be the Marquise d'Egremont at once.'

He laughed suddenly, his dark eyes snapping with all the joy of adventure. But for once her eagerness could not match his own.

Though she had dreamed sometimes of a better future life where she could become Jean-Philippe's Marquise, their love could be fulfiled and she could take her children off to France—her children.

The faces and forms appeared before her, not ghostlike but in their rosy flesh, damp curls on their foreheads, little fingers clutching—she saw them as babies still, not the toddlers, formally dressed and remote, that she had last seen on her short, circumscribed visits to Great Heron under the jealous eye of the Earl. But her children were lost to her in all events, a disgraced mother, perhaps a convicted spy—she shuddered. She could not take it all in, but she knew this projected flight was no gay and rash elopement; the emotion that filled her heart was horror.

'The general will win, I tell you,' d'Egremont said feverishly, misunderstanding her reluctance. 'He cannot fail. He never has.' His voice had the note of a fanatic. 'He was only betrayed.'

He entirely mistook her, Damaris thought. Yet she stood, simply unable to move, unable to think, to decide what she should do.

D'Egremont looked down at her, and all his knowledge of women came to his aid.

'You must come,' he said slowly, and took her gently in his arms. 'I need you. I love you, Damaris.'

He had spoken of love before, many times, but this simple declaration, with no laughter, no fever of passion, using simply her own Christian name, touched her as nothing else could have done. His sincerity was clear. He used the truth, yet it was true.

She found refuge in his embrace.

'I must go, my love,' he murmured. 'Will you not come with me?'

All her love and longing flowed back into her. She felt as weak as water, unable to resist. Her power to think faded. No, she could not let him go; she must follow, wherever it was he led.

Shock had followed shock that night. When she had run upstairs to pack—she had to have Chambers help her and muttered that she must go to her aunt—d'Egremont had ordered her to bring all the money in her possession and all her jewels.

'But I can't take the Malfrey family jewels,' she said, aghast. They were still in the house, after her sending Chambers for them on her fool's errand so short a time before.

'Bring what you can,' d'Egremont said shortly. 'I cannot wait to draw upon my bankers in the morning. It will take time before matters can be settled.'

He had spoken truth about his belief in Bonaparte's victory, but even in his most sanguine moments he knew that the war might not be won with the next battle—though it could be lost. Time must pass before the Emperor could devote himself to d'Egremont's affairs.

Damaris could not do it. She, who had been Damaris St Cloud, seemed to have become a traitor, but she was not a thief. Foolishly, from sentiment, brushing her tears aside, she took the small pieces of no value that had belonged to her mother; left the massive, old-fashioned jewels of the Heron family, worn only on state occasions; and, hesitating, took the sapphire and diamond collection that the Earl had given to her on their first Christmas at Great Heron, and some other personal gifts. Perhaps later she could send them back, she thought, trying to avoid despair. They would be for her daughter, little Griselda, when she came of age.

Griselda—if the Earl lived, what would become of her? The heir would be protected, but her daughter? Lady Gratton, she told herself—Lady Gratton would contrive. But before she could think any more, the Marquis himself burst into her room, declaring he would wait no longer and was ready to carry her down bodily. Damaris, who had put on a travelling cloak and a close bonnet, left her house with her trunks being carried down before her, feeling, even without the Heron jewels, like a thief in the night.

As they made their way, d'Egremont told her a little of what had occurred. It did nothing to raise her spirits. Her husband had left Malfrey House certain in his mind of what the ministers had suspected—that d'Egremont was indeed the spy. A few weeks before, a courier had been arrested trying to cross the Channel on a smuggler's craft. When he was searched for contraband, his dispatches had been found. That there was a spy in high places was certain, and at last, to save himself, the courier revealed the name of d'Egremont. This much d'Egremont had learned from Lord Malfrey's accusations; what had followed he surmised.

There had been doubt in the inner conclaves. All of these men knew the young Marquis and could not believe him treacherous; his cousin the Duchesse de Langcourt et Montrevet was at that very moment with Louis—the courier could have lied. Yet word had come from Wellington: the enemy possessed information from a memorandum known only to themselves. Lord Malfrey was one of those who had had a copy; Lord Malfrey had been called to account. He had gone home and found his copy of the memorandum missing fron his bedroom. His wife's room was next door, and she was the Marquis's mistress.

He had rushed to the d'Egremont house, whether to confront the traitor or to kill the lover the Marquis himself could not know. Certainly, Lord Malfrey had found incontrovertible proof that the Marquis was the spy. He had gone straight away to the secret room, which was no secret from him, flung the door open, and surprised the Marquis and his guest.

The carriage bumped and jolted as the guilty pair sped recklessly through the dark, moonless night.

'You had company, Jean-Philippe?' Damaris cried, unable to believe her ears.

He grinned; his face, half-lit, half-shadowed by the carriage lamp, looked demonic.

'Not a lady, Madame. I had to receive a messenger from the Emperor—a man too well known, alas, to come to the front door. He was also known to your husband. The game, it was clear, was up.'

Damaris looked at him in horror.

'The portrait! The Earl saw the portrait!'

He looked at her, stifling a laugh. It was like a woman to trouble herself about a trifle with her very life in danger. She seemed hardly to realize how desperate her situation was. He could easily have saved himself by getting off at once, but he could not leave her behind to face ruin, trial, imprisonment, or death. No one would believe her innocent—and then there was the matter of the Earl. If he should die—there was no witness to prove there had been a duel. Murdered by the French spy—and his mistress, it would be said. That wretched portrait would tell its own tale.

The portrait—as Lord Malfrey had burst into the room it was almost the first thing he had seen. It had maddened him more than the appearance of Etienne Giscard, Bonaparte's most brilliant spy, for whom all Europe had been searching. Lord Malfrey, very calm, had killed Giscard with one shot. Then he saw the portrait. Wildly furious, his face heavily empurpled, he had lifted it down and made as if to take the full-size canvas with him, yet not forgetting to keep his pistol trained on d'Egremont. The Marquis had challenged him sharply. The Earl had paused. As a spy, the Marquis was not entitled to challenge his discoverer, but he was also the seducer of the Countess.

The husband, the gentleman, won over the adviser to the Crown. The Earl had accepted the challenge; the portrait was flung to the floor; the Marquis took Giscard's pistol, and the two men faced each other in the long, elegant music-room where only a few months before 'Glorious John' Cramer had played Sebastian Bach to the polite applause of the ladies.

The Earl was an excellent shot, but so was the Marquis, and he was the younger man. Danger invigorated him; he was not wild with misery and fury like the Earl. The Earl's shot had grazed the Marquis's arm; his own had struck the Earl's breast just a few inches from the heart. The Earl lay in a pool of blood. With the idea of causing enough confusion to make delay, the Marquis had dragged the body of Giscard to lie ten paces from the Earl and put the pistol into Giscard's dead hand.

Then he had taken the portrait, flung it down in the secret room, closed the panel, and left his house—until he could return, he told himself, riding through London with the Emperor. Yes, with the Emperor, no longer an émigré—petted, it was true, but powerless in the land. He would be a man who could have half the counties of England at his disposal. Now his imagination went further. The Emperor was fond of making his family kings and queens. He, d'Egremont, through his mother was related to the Hapsburgs, and therefore to the Empress Marie Louise and the Emperor's son, the King of Rome. Perhaps d'Egremont would be king of England and Damaris his queen. But he did not tempt her with the prospect. She was too much an Englishwoman—as yet—to contemplate the future with equanimity. Still, the claim of the stupid Hanoverians to the English throne was, in his mind, worthless, and England had had French kings before. There was time for her education in such matters.

'But how could he have entered the secret room, Jean-Philippe?'

He chuckled. She heard the real amusement in his voice with a sense of shock. The Marquis was *happy* with the turn of events. His previous nervousness—now she understood all. The strain he had undergone was the strain of a man playing a masquerade, a masquerade more and more dangerous and quickly nearing its close.

'Obviously he knew the little trick of the panel. You forget that while I was with Louis the Faithless I had let the house to Lord Ramage. Perhaps you did not know that Lady Ramage was your husband's mistress? I am afraid he knew that room as well as his wife, my dear.'

The joke appealed to him, and he laughed heartily. Damaris sat back, appalled. No, she had not known. There had been so much she had not known. She thought wearily that when she had married the Earl against all her natural feelings, her new life had seemed to stretch before her like a grey and misty path along which she would have to grope her way. But now all her life, past and future, had collapsed into something unknown, chill, ashen; she knew not where she had been, where she was, or where she was going. She turned to d'Egremont for comfort, but his gaiety and laughter, which always before had won her heart, now made a barrier between them. Still laughing, he urged the coachman on ever faster. As they plunged deeper into the darkness, she had a sudden, wretched longing to find herself once more a girl, dreaming in her room at Angelhurst.

If wishes were horses, beggars would ride. Lady Gratton's often repeated words came to her mind when at first light she was boarding a small fishing vessel off the coast of Kent and knew herself to be a fugitive indeed.

'Where are we?' she whispered.

'Near Ramsgate,' d'Egremont replied. 'We had to avoid the estuary and any barges that might still be coming down from

Chatham carrying troops. I don't believe they could have word as yet, but—'

On that dark morning, the small, smelly boat was very different from a pleasure craft on a sunny day at Brighton. All the passengers were ill from the choppy waves and very thankful when they reached Ostend. D'Egremont was anxious to proceed, but Damaris, weary and dishevelled, longed to bathe and change, at least. Even to her tired eyes and overwrought nerves, Ostend was a civilized port. The streets were full of well-dressed women and uniformed men, many of them English. Her conflicting emotions, flaring up and being suppressed in turn, had left her bewildered and passive, but the scarlet coats provoked an automatic response. While d'Egremont saw them as danger, Damaris was jolted back into acting as Lady Malfrey—she could not appear like this.

Resigned, d'Egremont took her to an inn.

'But we will have to kill off the Countess of Malfrey,' he said with his characteristic mischievous grin. 'Long live Madame la Marquise!'

But the Countess was to live a little longer. The inn was crowded beyond belief. In the entrance-hall, watching their belongings being carried up the stairs, was a small knot of English people—two menservants, an elderly maid, and a grey-haired lady of fashion. The lady turned, and Mrs Farthingale effusively greeted her dear friend the Countess, as well as the Marquis, her eyes, small and dark between plump wrinkles, shining with all the pleasant delight of scandal.

The Marquis was nothing if not quick-witted. He bowed low over Mrs Farthingale's hand and smiled with a great air of relief.

'Chère Madame Farthingale! What good fortune! You can give the Countess your assistance. She was on her way to join my cousin, Madame la Duchesse, at Brussels with Lady Gratton, when poor Lady Gratton became indisposed. She left the Countess in my care, but I must make haste—I join the King. I am, as it were, his minister to the Duke. Lady Malfrey is too weary to travel at such a pace. I imagine you travel by barge?'

'Certainly. I understand it is the only possible way,' Mrs Farthingale said, disappointed of her scandal but very willing to have the Countess's company. 'My dear Lady Malfrey, I am travelling with Lady Rise and Mrs Sedgwick-Darnley. Mrs Sedgwick-Darnley is joining her husband in Brussels. We will be flattered if you would join us, and certainly you will be far more comfortable travelling by water than on the roads.'

Damaris had been taken aback by the Marquis's sudden change. The man who had abandoned England, and Society, the night before, now sounded like a dandy keeping up the prized appearance of convention. Nevertheless, she remained outwardly composed. She had played the role of a lady of fashion so long that it was simpler for her to continue it than to do anything else.

She replied to Mrs Farthingale languidly that nothing would suit her more than to join that lady's party. The venture would not have tempted her, she went on, had she known the journey would be so devilish uncomfortable. It had been Aunt Gratton's notion— 'for she felt, you know, as we all did, that with the excitement in Brussels, to stay tamely in the country was not to be endured.'

Mrs Farthingale, who had come to visit a nephew she had never troubled herself with before, agreed fervently. Then she followed her trunks upstairs, and Damaris went with her after the Marquis had bade them an elaborate farewell and whispered to Damaris that he would see her very soon.

The only room available was a small one at the back of the inn. Damaris took it without demur and sent for hot water. Her mind seemed too tired and confused to think, but her body at least enjoyed the luxury of the hip-bath, and she leaned back in her first moment of repose since Jean-Philippe had appeared—was it only the night before?—and bathed away the soil and weariness of travel.

Jean-Philippe—she *must* think, now that she was quiet. But then there was a tap at her open window and the Marquis himself appeared, smiling and impudent.

'Jean-Philippe, what—?' she whispered, half in joy to see him, half in fear at his terrible rashness.

He caught her up just as she was, naked, wet, and covered with bubbles of soap, and bore her to the bed. Just as though, Damaris thought between admiration and despair, they were not fleeing for their lives, pursued possibly by the Earl and almost certainly by men sent from London with orders for their arrest. He made love as though they had all the time in the world to spend in idleness and pleasure, and in his arms, for a little while, Damaris forgot her fears.

'But why keep up the masquerade?' she asked at last. 'Should I not come with you?'

'It is better this way,' he answered, for once sober. 'I have had a few words with the commanding officer of the latest contingent to arrive—in my character as emissary to the Duke. The officer is an old friend of mine,' he said, and grimaced at his own treachery. 'He tells me they are the last of the troops in the draught. The battle will be very soon. He obviously had heard nothing of our trouble; there has as yet been no hue and cry. It is better that you travel with the ladies. If the military are following, they will be looking for me on the swiftest route; they won't search a slow barge full of sensation-seeking Englishwomen. I will join my General faster alone, and we'll meet in Brussels after the battle. Go to my cousin the Duchesse so that I can find you. By the way,' he added with a grin, 'she knows nothing. You need not acquaint her, yet, with my affairs. When we are victorious, she will be pleased enough to return in triumph to her estates. And in the meantime, French troops will respect her house.'

Damaris was not so bemused that she could not see a hundred things going wrong with this plan, but she could think of nothing better. Love-making over, her gallant, up and dressed in a trice, was eager to be on his way, unencumbered, ready for new adventure. She might be shot as a French spy by the English in Brussels or killed as an English prisoner if the victorious legions of the Emperor reached Brussels before the Marquis himself—he seemed over-confident of the temper of an army after battle. Yet she could hardly join Napoleon's camp. . . .

'Are you going to fight in the battle?' she asked, knowing the answer in sudden anguish.

'Chérie, do not be frightened. I am indestructible,' he murmured. 'And perhaps, if there is time, I might visit you in Brussels before it takes place. Don't be surprised.'

He laughed again and looked out of the window to the stable-yard below. Apparently satisfied that all was clear, he departed the way that he had come, leaving Damaris to shiver in her damp bed, staring up at the ceiling of the room that was suddenly strange, lonely, terrifying.

29

She had little time for her lonely terrors. Very soon after the Marquis had departed, Mrs Farthingale was tapping at her door.

'My dear, seeing that you have no maid with you, I wonder if you would like to borrow Mitchin? Oh, I see you are resting. I hope I didn't disturb you. Mitchin is inclined to pull the hair—I cannot cure her of it—but she is a genius with the damp sponge and flat-irons.'

'You didn't disturb me,' Damaris said, suddenly demure, lying with the sheet to her neck to cover her nakedness. 'I would be obliged for Mitchin. Chambers cannot travel; she is the most dreadful nuisance out of Town. I assume there will be maids enough in Brussels.'

Her voice was normal enough, she thought. She played her part as well as Marianne Midnight had played hers in Cuckfield Street.

'Oh certainly,' Mrs Farthingale said, beaming. 'I understand it is *most* pleasant, and the entertainments dazzling.'

She sat on Damaris's bed and retailed all the gossip of Brussels, which, it appeared, was bidding fair to outdo in English festivities the past Season in England's capital. Damaris had to invent a headache to get her to leave so that she herself could rise, and then she had to endure the ministrations of her maid. Mitchin did pull her hair, and Damaris thought she should be glad of it, for the small pains distracted her from the greater one in her mind.

Gradually her terrors receded. Her husband—was he dead or alive? What was happening at d'Egremont's mansion? Had the army sent men to drag her back to England? All the things that had caused her to quiver with fear on the dark road, and on the sea in its strangeness, slowly began to seem less real, less pressing now she was in the company of English friends, still the Countess of Malfrey, stylish, fashionable, a sought-after member of the *bon ton*.

The maid Mitchin looked as though she might be cousin to Chambers herself, but she talked as much as her mistress. She prattled of a ball to be given in Brussels that same week and of all the ladies who were trying desperately to get cards.

'Mrs Farthingale sent a message in the army pouch to make sure it got through quickly, informing the Duchess that she was on her way. It would not be at all the thing not to be there. But I am sure a card will be sent to *you,* my lady, as soon as you arrive.'

This invaluable Mitchin did put Damaris's travelling clothes to rights, and she made a creditable figure when she took her place in the barge with the other ladies of the *ton.* Some of them had heard of the appearance of the Marquis, but they could not do more than raise their brows when the Countess appeared in the company of Mrs Farthingale. Mitchin had sniffed at the close bonnet as Chambers would have done, and she had taken out a smart hat of finest straw trimmed with blue ribbons, so that Damaris, seeing herself in the glass, had a dreamlike feeling that nothing had really occurred; and she floated down the canal on one of its famous barges in all the elegance and comfort that could be provided, regarding the rich and pleasant countryside in the first glowing warmth of summer.

Brussels was full of English and full of fashion. Madame la Duchesse, who had become bored with the provincial court of Louis at Ghent, had taken one of the most impressive mansions in Brussels to be close to all the excitement. She had had notice of the arrival of the Countess, and she received her with no hint of surprise but only smiling pleasure. Her only anxiety was whether Damaris would be rested enough to go to the great ball that night, for which a card had already been procured. Damaris, partly reassured by the Duchesse that so far, at least, d'Egremont was safe, in her character as a woman of fashion declared that she would go to the ball if she were dying, an attitude that brought a smile of real sympathy to the Duchesse's lips.

She urged her guest to rest, but Damaris was far too nervous to lie down and instead asked to be driven about the famous gardens, in full flower, that she had passed on her way. The Duchesse, thinking that some air might benefit her complexion, agreed to go for a short drive; the two ladies politely called for Mrs Farthingale, and the fashionable English were further enlivened by the sight of those three members of the *ton,* two of them the most fashionable women in England, displaying themselves in the Duchesse's elegant barouche.

Damaris did not, as she had at Ostend, shiver at every red coat she saw, expecting its wearer to approach with an order for her arrest. Her knowledge of her crimes was pushed back in her mind, obscured by some desperately held notion of their impossibility and her helplessness before the truth. After their drive, the Duchesse let Mrs Farthingale down at her hotel; the noblewomen returned to the Duchesse's mansion, and Damaris was sent to rest in her room, which looked out over a fragrant garden. She might for all the world have been in Malfrey House, except that the servants spoke French, not English, and she had a pretty little Celeste to attend her instead of the grey and wintry Chambers. It seemed that the world had turned upside down; London was in Brussels, and if her fate trembled with the blowing of the wind—why, so did the fate of all Europe. Yet no one worried, and for the moment neither did she.

She was overjoyed, though not really surprised, when her door opened and there was the Marquis, his eyes full of mischief, wearing a red coat and a braided cap.

'You see how easily I get through the lines,' he boasted. 'I half wish the battle would never take place—never in a long life will I enjoy myself as much!'

He leapt onto the bed, laughing.

'I have little time, Madame,' he said. 'Pray forgive me—I could not bring my valet—may I have the honour while still in my boots?'

She laughed helplessly, against her will.

'Sometimes I think we are both mad, Jean-Philippe,' she said. 'We were almost caught *in flagrante delicto* by Mrs Farthingale in Ostend.'

'No one will trouble us in *this* house,' he said comfortably, pulling off her light robe and kissing her arms and shoulders. 'The Duchesse has her household well-trained. . . .'

As the sun dipped he told her he must leave, and laughter deserted them. She held him close, realizing with a frantic fear that it might be for the last time. 'My darling,' she whispered, and for once even Jean-Philippe was serious.

'Whatever happens, you will be cared for,' he told her. 'I have made my will; it is in the hands of the General's staff. Everything I have is yours, and whether I am alive or dead you will be treated with all the honour due to my wife.'

The possibility of his General's defeat did not seem to enter his mind. To Damaris, surrounded as she had been by English and the supporters of King Louis, who were so supremely confident of victory as to hardly find it worth discussing, his attitude was strange, yet she knew from her gambling friends of the blindness that overtakes a man who has staked everything on the fall of the card. She would say nothing to add to his troubles; though if he died, she thought in despair, she didn't see how she could live.

'But don't worry,' he said, raising his head from her bosom, where she had cradled him as though he were her child, 'I will come for you here—perhaps tomorrow or the next day.'

'Tomorrow?' she said in disbelief. 'You mean the battle—but it cannot be so soon. Why, tonight is the ball—'

'The ball!' He laughed derisively. 'You are a silly little English miss. Go to your ball, Madame. Enjoy it. That ball will be the last English festivity for some time to come.'

Once again when he was gone she was assailed by fears and hopes in impossible opposition. She could not wish for a French victory, yet without it she was ruined; if d'Egremont was killed nothing mattered, and she might as well die herself—then the maid Celeste entered to dress her for the ball. Damaris laughed; the absurdity struck her in force. Nevertheless, she had accepted; she would be looked for—better to go than to stay in her room trembling. She wore a gown of tissue silk of blue and silver, with sapphires in her hair and studded in the heels of her silver slippers.

Her coldly flashing beauty among the scarlet coats was the sensation of the ball. She danced all night long, only pausing to drink glass after glass of iced champagne. Mrs Farthingale looked on with complacency and told her friends that whatever the Duke of Wellington might do, the Countess had certainly won the battle of Brussels.

The great, brilliantly-lit ballroom, the uniformed men, the dazzle of the ladies' gowns and jewels whirled about Damaris as though she were in fever. The scent of the banked flowers and of the ladies' lotions grew stronger and stronger in the warm room until it turned rank in her nostrils like the halitus of blood. And before the ball was over she saw the men, as a whisper went round the room, bid the ladies adieu and take their leave. It was as d'Egremont had foretold. The armies were on the march.

30

It seemed as though the confidence of the Marquis had not been misplaced after all. The first news that came was that the *Armée du Nord* had passed the Sambre. That night no one slept in Brussels. The bugle call to arms, the roll of drums that took every gallant from his lady, brought sobriety at last, and though victory was still assumed to be the outcome, the danger to each man was felt and the town was full of weeping women as the columns marched away.

Despite the late hour of the ball, Damaris could not sleep and soon rang for Celeste to come and dress her. The little Belgian girl was full of excitement and stopped to chatter with a manservant at Damaris's very door, not realizing perhaps that the English lady understood French so well, or possibly not caring. The allies, Celeste was saying, had been surprised; Marshal Ney was bearing down at Quatre Bras; soon the Emperor would be in Brussels, victorious. The manservant was voluble in agreement, and Damaris realized that the Belgians had never shared the confidence of the English but had been expecting daily the arrival of Bonaparte.

Even the Duchesse, for once, was up early, and the two ladies breakfasted together in some state but with little appetite. The Duchesse, who still believed her cousin, the head of her family, to be serving Wellington, was concerned as to his whereabouts, hoping he was not putting himself into too much danger—'That young man is too brave, too reckless,' she said, and sighed. 'It is in the d'Egremont blood.'

There were dark shadows under her eyes that her carefully applied maquillage could not hide, and for the first time Damaris's heart warmed to the *grande dame*—they were both in terror for the life of one man. She said nothing to the Duchesse of her cousin's treachery—despite all her love for Jean-Philippe, Damaris still thought his actions treacherous—for his life was in danger no matter which side of the battle he fought. If he was still alive at its end, there would be time enough for elucidation . . . if they survived themselves. Celeste's lively description to the manservant of what she expected the fate of English ladies to be when the victorious French arrived was hardly cheering.

Too restless to stay indoors, the ladies took the barouche and drove about the town, seeing nothing but gloom and depression everywhere. By the time they returned to their dinner, which neither of them wanted, the cannon began to roar. The servants shrieked and dropped the dishes; the noblewomen did not stir but spoke perseveringly of fashionable trifles. The whole of the household staff longed to run from the town, but they were abashed by the demeanour of their mistress and went on with their duties. Still their ears were trained on the noises from the streets.

People were running, shouting, calling out scraps of news that were quickly contradicted. The Prince of Orange was holding his line; his force was scattered. The Duchesse sent a servant to the Namur gate for news; he returned at last, having pushed through the frantic crowds—Reille's divisions were overcoming Picton, who had seemed to stop the French advance. The messenger advised his mistress of what was already obvious by the noise of horses and carriages in the streets: most of the visitors were leaving Brussels. Mrs Farthingale sent word to Damaris that she had a carriage and horses and was leaving for Bruges within the hour. She begged that Lady Malfrey join her. Lady Malfrey wrote in reply that she was remaining with Madame la Duchesse, upon which that lady, nodding in approval, announced her intention of going to church and asked Damaris to attend her. The Duchesse, of course, went to the Catholic church, but Damaris felt then she could pray in any church. The manner of worship could hardly matter if the Lord would hear her prayers—the prayers of a runaway wife, a woman who had brought her husband disgrace and perhaps death, who had abandoned her children and even now was not in a state of repentance: she remembered the time she had spent in the arms of the Marquis even after she had learned the whole truth. She sighed for her sins and prayed. She prayed like the Duchesse beside her, for all the men in battle. If she could not find peace in the belief in divine forgiveness, at least she had rest from her own torments in compassion for the black-garbed lady at her side, for though the Duchesse must wish for victory for the English and her King, still she was a Frenchwoman, and half a million Frenchmen were engaged in this battle to the death.

They returned to the house calmly to wait for news. The town had half emptied; many people who had served the English had run off. The Duchesse's servants stayed; a French duchess, they believed, would bring them protection.

The ladies drank tisane and worked on petit point with which the Duchesse proposed to cover her chairs in her house at Richmond. That night lights shone in every house that was still occupied; knots of people still gathered in the streets, talking excitedly. Rumour came that Wellington's army was utterly crushed, and the Duke himself killed; later rumour had it that he held his ground.

Just as the ladies were about to retire to their rooms, if not to sleep, a message came from King Louis's court. The presence of Madame la Duchesse so near the scene of battle was causing anxiety: she was commanded to return without delay. The Duchesse was an obedient courtier; at once she ordered her trunks prepared. She begged Damaris to join her. After their long vigil polite pretence was at an end: 'Jean-Philippe will find us there with the King.'

Damaris looked at the older woman with her fine-boned face, her look of perfect breeding, and an understanding as kind as it was complete. The Cool Countess of Malfrey took the Duchesse's hands and pressed them, but she had to refuse. If d'Egremont was alive, he would come for her here. If the Emperor had won, they both could go to Ghent; if the Emperor had lost, then she and Jean-Philippe were fugitives. She must stay.

The Duchesse gave her a blessing and withdrew. Within an hour the ducal carriage, with the trunks strapped up behind, was on its way. One by one the servants crept from the house taking the wages paid them by the Duchesse and any small and valuable trifles they could put their hands on. Damaris's jewels would have gone with them, but on the Duchesse's advice Damaris had changed into travel dress, had her own trunks brought down, and kept her jewel case beside her.

As the noise of battle seemed to thunder ever closer, Damaris stood at the window of the palatial house in Brussels, quite alone, staring out into the street, with only one clear longing in her heart: to see the figure of Jean-Philippe. But he did not come that night.

Damaris dozed a little in her chair. In the morning she woke to the empty household and ran out into the street for news. Blücher's army had been defeated; Wellington was at bay. She got the news from a wounded British soldier brought back on a cart, pale from loss of blood, a soiled, bandaged stump where his leg should have been.

Shaken, Damaris went back into the house and for the first time went down into the kitchen quarters, which had been left in much disarray. She gave thanks for her familiarity with the kitchen and scullery of Angelhurst, which saved her from the helplessness of most ladies of fashion, and collected what she needed to make coffee, though there was no milk or cream. Suddenly thirsty, she drank cup after cup; then, feeling queasy, she resumed her station at the window. Unable to stand still, she soon went back into the streets. Wellington was retreating, the wounded reported; Napoleon was in hot pursuit.

Damaris returned to the little church to pray again but could think of no prayer to make, except to repeat over and over the words 'Save him, save him.' When she came out the skies were dark. Lightning flashed; thunder rolled; a rainstorm, tropical in intensity, flooded the area. Damaris returned to the house, found a little cold food, ate though the food stuck in her throat, and waited. The storm continued, and all through the long dark day the only news was that the French were somewhere between Rossome and Genappe, bivouacking in the sodden fields.

The next day the roar of cannon sounded. The armies were locked in combat at Waterloo. Real news for a time was impossible to get; rumour brought news of victory and defeat first for one side, then the other. People had been to church, for it was Sunday; returning home they heard the dreadful sound, far worse than anything that they had heard before. As evening came the carts of wounded spoke of the long red line of dead that they had left behind. The whole of the Twenty-Seventh was lying dead in square. Others claimed the French had lost all their artillery and spoke with awe of Frenchmen dead in tens of thousands on the field.

Damaris sat by her window. However Jean-Philippe might return, she would be there to greet him. She was surprised soon by sounds in the house coming from below. Celeste had returned, her face streaked with tears, and working soberly at her side were two more of the Duchesse's servants, as though they had never run away.

A supper was prepared ready to be brought upstairs. Sheepishly the servants explained that they had had to go about their affairs but were now returned to the service of Madame la Comtesse, as the Duchesse had ordered, for as long as she needed them. The brother of Celeste, she learned, had been killed on the first day of battle.

Damaris commiserated with the bereaved sister but could not help speculating on what had brought about this sudden return. When Celeste had received the news of her brother, she must have learned some news of the outcome of the battle. Could the tide have turned? The cannon still roared without respite; the day was not yet done. Might the Duke be victorious after all? And if he was, what of Jean-Philippe? Was he alive or dead?

She pressed her hands to her aching temples, hardly able to touch the dainty food set before her. Afterwards, she realized that she had fallen asleep in her chair, because she woke quite suddenly with a jump. The sound of the cannon had stopped.

The silence, after so long, was eerie. Damaris stirred. The battle must be over. Who had won? Who had lost? Where was Jean-Philippe? She saw the servants run out into the street—was it to be French or English troops who soon would march in glory through the town?

By morning she would know, she told herself. By then all would be made clear. She could not even tell what she wished: her feelings, her mind were numb, except for the one great craving to see Jean-Philippe alive. Yet when he suddenly appeared before her fatigue-dimmed eyes—surprisingly, for he had crept into the house like a thief in the darkness—her relief from the worst of terrors was short-lived and soon overlaid by anxieties of another sort.

Jean-Philippe was dressed in the uniform of an officer of the Imperial Guard, tattered, filthy, and covered with blood and dirt. He hobbled up to her, and she saw to her horror that his trouser leg was cut away, his leg in splints and bandages from hip to ankle, and that he moved with the aid of a stout stick. His face was grey and only his red-rimmed eyes still looked alive, with an expression she recognized at once, though only later realizing why —it was the reckless stare of the gambler who had staked everything and lost.

'My darling, you are hurt—' She moved to take him in her arms, but he brusquely evaded her embrace.

'No time for that. Help me up the stairs.'

'Rest here on the sofa. I will fetch a doctor—'

'Fool!' he said roughly. 'I will be shot on discovery. Don't you understand? We are done. The Emperor was betrayed.'

'It is over, then?' she whispered.

'Grouchy might still be fighting, wherever he might be,' d'Egremont said bitterly. 'He deserted the Emperor when he needed him. The guard fought until we were cut to pieces; the grenadiers held to the last. But Grouchy never brought the reinforcements, while the Prussians poured in without end. I would rather have died on the field,' he said, acid with rage, 'but I had to come for you, Madame. When the excitement is over, someone will remember to look for the traitors. We must fly. But first I must change. For the sake of *le bon Dieu,* help me up those stairs.'

She tried to help him, but short of being carried there was no way he could mount even the shallow, graceful stairs of that house. Leaving him on the sofa, she ran upstairs and found him a change of clothes and, with great difficulty, brought down a trunk that he had left in readiness. The servants were either asleep or about the town, looking for news. There was no sound belowstairs, and for that, at least, she was grateful.

When Jean-Philippe had finished dressing, he looked half-dead with pain. 'How can you travel so?' she cried, but he gave her his hard, bright grin. 'The devil drives,' he said. 'Come. There is hardly a horse to be had, but I have stolen a waggon and pair—let us be off before the owner finds them missing.'

'Help me up,' he said irritably, when she stood by the waggon, gazing almost in stupor. 'I am now a thief' came to her mind. Then she ran back to close the door of the Duchesse's house. D'Egremont grimaced with impatience. 'You will have to drive. I will rest in back. Call out if anyone tries to stop you.'

She couldn't possibly have loaded their luggage—she had hardly been able to drag the trunks outside the door of the house—but a roughly-dressed loiterer in the street had come to her aid. Her helper had looked at the fine lady, the rude conveyance, the man in civilian dress at her side who was so obviously wounded, but he held his tongue. There would be others like that in Brussels on such a day, he thought cynically, and the Countess rewarded him well for his pains.

'Not so lavish,' the Marquis protested irritably. 'We have a long way to go, and I have come somewhat unprepared, my dear.'

Damaris took up the reins.

'Where are we going, Jean-Philippe?'

'Make your way to the coast. It is easy enough. Follow the road to Ghent and then to Bruges and on to Ostend.'

A thought struck him. 'If we could find my cousin at Ghent— she might be able to supply us with funds—' But he sank back dispirited. 'No, that coward Louis, who declined to show his face near the field of battle, is probably in Ostend already, taking ship for England. If not, one of his minions will probably have me arrested. So much for the King of France!'

He winced with pain as they moved off.

'And from Ostend?'

'We will take the first vessel to leave—anywhere except for England,' he said with a grimace. 'We must go far away. Martinique, perhaps. Mexico.'

To Damaris's amazement he managed a laugh.

'Our lives are as precarious as any chance of the dice, Madame. Let us arrive at the coast, and then we will see how our dice have fallen.'

He gave a sudden groan as the waggon bumped over the road. Damaris understood now why the passage by canal barge was so much preferred by travellers. D'Egremont took a flask of brandy from a store he had supplied himself with from the house in Brussels. He drank long and thirstily until he fell back in the cart, almost unconscious. Damaris thought it better so; he would feel the pain less, but how he could continue she didn't know. He had asked her to drive to the coast, and that she would do. She remembered her leisurely, luxurious progress when she had arrived. How long would this journey take, and what could she do for d'Egremont's wound?

When she reached Ghent, weary to the bone, she paused to make inquiry for the Duchesse. But Ghent was in disarray; too many conflicting tales had come; the whereabouts of king and court were not certain. Damaris didn't dare linger to make a search. She found a physician and brought him to care for d'Egremont's wound. If the physician wondered about a man with battle wounds who wore civilian clothes and travelled with a fine lady in a rough waggon, he said no more than the street idler in Brussels had done. The physician was a Belgian, and the victory of one army or the other meant little to him. He was being well paid, but he protested that the patient should not travel.

'Madame,' he said bluntly, 'this man has been injured badly in the thigh. A field surgeon has attended him, but roughly. He should be taken somewhere where he could be treated properly and given rest.'

D'Egremont opened his eyes and swore.

'Please do your best, M'sieur,' Damaris said, her low voice and lovely, tired face striking the doctor with all the force of her charm. 'We must go on at once.'

He did his best. Damaris procured some small refreshment for herself and fed the complaining Marquis before she took the reins again. When they reached Bruges he seemed to have benefited from the doctor's ministrations and sat up and looked about him, but urged her on after a brief stop. Damaris had paused at an inn and persuaded an ostler to take the two tired horses with a handful of gold for two fresh ones, and the speed at which they made their way brought them to Ostend before definite news had arrived there of the outcome of the battle.

The Marquis, concerned for Damaris even more than for himself, insisted that they take the first ship no matter where it went. They went to an inn by the docks, where Damaris sold her horses for a poor price, and there she left the Marquis while she went about the port looking for a ship. Most vessels were plying the route from Ostend to London. Some went up and down the coast, some were leaving for more distant ports in Europe—but the Marquis had refused to stay in Europe.

'We will be hunted down, my dear. The English, they do not give up.'

He did not tell her of the nightmare image haunting his mind. Time after time he had taken his column up the hill of Saint Jean, which the English had so stubbornly held entrenched with their artillery. Wave after wave of men had he sacrificed to those guns until at last he had reached the height—only, under the onrush of the English, to see the sad remnant of his command break and run. The English had held Saint Jean; the flower of France had fallen. Even now, any man left alive was being pursued by the accursed Prussians. He, Jean-Philippe d'Egremont, by going forward instead of back, by taking his audacious route right through the allied lines to save his lady, had very likely saved his own skin. The idea did not please him.

At last Damaris found a vessel that was crossing the Atlantic, though it was not heading for any port where they wished to go. It had brought in cotton from Charleston and was now taking on a mixed cargo for ports on the east coast of the United States; its first destination was far north, and then it was to call at port after port on a southward route until it reached Charleston again.

The captain of this ship, the *Bonne Chance,* a big, dark, sullen-looking man called Bosquet, was willing to give them passage, for a price. The price was more than Damaris had left in guineas, but they had come to a bargain. His eyes had glittered with interest when he saw the diamond and sapphire bracelet the lady was willing to exchange for a cabin. His ship was not fitted up with luxuries for a lady, he told Damaris, but it was clean, and he thought he could make her and her husband, M'sieur le Marquis, comfortable.

D'Egremont had already explained to Damaris that now she must use his name. 'At sea, among rough sailing men, you would be in danger if you were thought to be—not my wife, let us say. After all, we are merely a little premature. Either you are a widow, or else you soon will be divorced.'

When she returned to the inn and explained about the voyage of the *Bonne Chance,* he laughed.

'The name, at least, is apt,' he said. 'But where exactly is it going?'

She explained the ship's route and he frowned.

'From Charleston we can get a conveyance to New Orleans. That would suit me well enough. In any case, we have little choice. We dare not linger here another day. We will take the *Bonne Chance,* Madame. And *la bonne chance,* let us hope,' he said with his sudden grim laughter, 'it will turn out to be.'

32

Remembering her illness when she had crossed to Ostend, Damaris had boarded the ship, with all its familiar smells of tar, hemp, and salt water, expecting the voyage to be miserable. Her spirits were low as she left the port, still bustling with her own people, for life in an unknown land.

D'Egremont had shown no interest in the ship when they boarded, only complaining of the accommodation, which was clean enough but simple and confined. Damaris found later that Captain Bosquet had given them his own cabin, and she was grateful, but the Marquis was impatient with her gratitude. 'Churlish dogs—they are honoured by our company. It is more than they deserve.'

Damaris stood on deck for a time and watched the anchor being hauled and the coast-line slipping backward. She had felt a confused sensation of relief and regret, in which regret played the larger part. When she returned to her cabin, a young sailor brought them bowls of hot soup and she was grateful for the attention which calmed a mind even more weary than her body.

The Marquis took but a mouthful, threw the spoon down, and swore.

'We have boarded a ship without a cook,' he said in great disgust. 'Your friend the captain did not warn us. This is going to be a most damnable voyage; that is plain already.'

Damaris helped him to his berth and took her own, glad that exhaustion quickly brought her sleep.

In the morning, she woke to see the same young sailor. He was a pleasant-looking fellow, now she really saw him, with merry brown eyes and cheeks as rosy as the bright red jersey he wore. He held a tray with hot rolls and delicious-smelling coffee.

'Madame la Marquise,' he said respectfully. '*Votre petit dejeuner.*'

Damaris, seeing the Marquis still sleeping fairly peacefully, smiled at the young man and motioned him to silence. Over his arm were her travelling cloak and gown. Someone had taken her things while she slept, and the sailor displayed them to her proudly, with all the evidence of her weary walk about the docks removed, restored to cleanliness and smooth enough for the Beau himself to approve.

She had heard of the clever housekeeping of seafaring men, and she knew that on the regular packets across the Atlantic much in the way of comfort and attention could be expected, but on this ship she had looked for little. For all of the Marquis's strictures, the food was good. The bread was freshly baked, the butter obviously had just been taken on, and the coffee tasted as delicious as it smelled. Surprisingly, she had a good appetite—the salt air, perhaps. The cabin she was in, though not luxurious, looked cheerful that morning with the sun shining brightly through the port-hole.

When she finished her breakfast the obliging young man brought her hot water; she bathed and had a tussle getting into a morning-dress—but she would not rouse the Marquis to ask for help. She was hardly provided with suitable garments for a voyage, she reflected. The trunks which had been so hastily packed in London contained garments for a lady of fashion on a visit to Brighton, and the Pavilion had figured largely in Chambers's calculations. She took out a crisp white silk promenade dress with blue ribbons, looked at it doubtfully, and added a light blue pelisse. None of her slippers looked at all suitable for tarry decks, but she picked a pair of the plainest—she was not going to spend the whole voyage shut up for lack of a pair of stout shoes! A hat was also a problem. Impatient, she tied her hair firmly with a twisted ribbon, put on her close bonnet, and leaving the Marquis in what looked like a healthy sleep, made her way on deck.

A fine breeze was blowing; the ship was in full sail. Although this old merchantman was not kept navy-style, like the ships Damaris had inspected under the beaming eye of the Duke of Gloucester, nevertheless she made a brave sight. They were still in the Channel, but for once it was reasonably calm, the fresh air, the sunshine, the motion of the ship, and the sight of the grinning seamen, busy about their work but with a bold admiring gaze for their passenger, all made a cheerful scene.

The chief mate, whom she had seen the night before, came over and spoke to her civilly, introducing himself. His name was Étienne Luce. He was a short, square Fleming with a full beard and a cheerful, capable look. He explained that he was to look after the passengers as the captain was kept to his cabin. Damaris remembered that she hadn't seen him the night before, even with all the work of disembarkation, and wondered if he was one of the captains she had heard of whose affection for the bottle was greater than that for their ships. Fortunately, the chief mate inspired confidence, and she had no worry for the ship's safety.

Luce then apologized for the lack of passenger comforts and asked if she had been served well by young Jacques Durand, whom he had given the duty of her service. Damaris praised him and his cleaning of her cloak—'My own maid in London couldn't have done it better.' Luce was gratified by this praise, as well as relieved at Damaris's command of his language, as he had little English.

He told her of the capabilities of young seamen, who had to learn all the household arts in order to serve the officers, and the particular skill of Jacques, a young Breton—'Good seamen, the Bretons,' he said smiling. 'They prefer sailing to the Emperor and his eternal wars.' He shrugged. Damaris had heard from the Duchesse how many young Frenchmen had fled to avoid the hated conscription. She thought with a pang of the Marquis, lying below, weak from his wounds and disappointed hopes. It had been as she had feared. Not all of France had rallied to the returned Bonaparte, however the army had welcomed him. She wondered what had happened to the shattered remnants of that army, falling back to Paris before the Prussians. When she had reached Ostend the news of Waterloo was not yet widely circulated, and when she left, rumour was piling upon rumour as to the fate of the once *Grande Armée*.

The mate questioned her closely as to the outcome of the battle. His interest was obviously greater than that of the ordinary man. Although the *Bonne Chance* was of an English build, it now carried the new flag of the Netherlands—safe at sea from the English since their occupation of the Low Countries. Damaris wondered how the ship had fared when Napoleon controlled the ports and England's blockade had stopped commerce from the west to the Continent. Later on in the long voyage, the mate, deciding that this English Marquise was to be trusted, showed her, grinning, the flag of the United States that they had run up, years before, 'when necessary.' This practice, he had said, laughing, had led to the small dispute between England and the United States—but that was all settled now.

'We have had our awkward moments,' he said, dryly.

Damaris remembered that there had been trouble with the former colony. British troops had been sent and had burned their capital, the city of Washington. She remembered the Earl speaking of it with some satisfaction. But with all the talk of the war with France, it had been only one item of news among so many. She remembered it chiefly from the jest of a young dandy who had amused the assembled company at Almack's by saying plaintively, between two pinches of snuff, 'But of course our troops had to retreat. That barbarian Jackson led them into a *swamp*. Consider the state of their coats and boots!' He had shuddered. 'They could hardly have gone into town like *that*—even an American town.'

And another young dandy had remarked that it was a great good the war was over before we ruined everything by complete victory—'For then, you know, we might have had to take the colonies back!'

And in the general laughter, it had been forgotten.

War. Standing up on the bridge beside the mate in the sparkling light, with a new-found bodily strength, Damaris yet trembled. War had seemed a concern of old dull people like her husband, a matter almost never discussed by the *ton*—except perhaps by some of the émigrés who were allowed to have a pressing interest. It had seemed a matter of well-dressed men taking counsel in clubs and drawing-rooms, utterly prosaic: columns, supplies, money—all figures, one total matched against another. Nothing like the realities of Brussels, of Waterloo: the bugle call to arms, the pounding of cannon, the terrors of the people, the line of carts dragging the dismembered and the dying, the smell of men's life-blood in the street under her windows.

Thank God, at least it's over, she thought, and then felt guilty for her failure in loyalty to Jean-Philippe. For she could not wish the battle would go on; nor, although it meant her banishment, could she wish the outcome any different. She had given up her person, her life, to the Marquis, but now she realized that something had been kept in reserve. He had gambled and failed, and sorrowful as she was for him, for them both, she was still an Englishwoman and she was content that he had failed.

But such thoughts, which had been so tormenting while the battle raged, she determined to put behind her. With the blue sky overhead, the sparkling waves before her, a change had come. She was leaving one life irrevocably behind; a new one was before her. And if her heart was not light, at least she was not crushed; she could think and act. As she strolled about the deck, making herself familiar with its light artillery, the mysteries of its masts and rigging, she vowed to herself that she would not look back. What was done was done; what was past was past. A new life was before her and Jean-Philippe; they must make the most of it.

Then she went down to arrange that he receive his breakfast when he woke, hoping that he, like herself, would be in better spirits. She was disappointed. The Marquis was already awake, fretful, and in pain. The pain, he assured her, he cared about very little.

'A wound is expected to be painful. It is nothing. But this accursed ship with these clumsy berths—how could one sleep, even without pain? I have not closed an eye all night.'

Damaris had watched him sleeping well but said nothing. She knew about the fretfulness of illness—though only from her children when they had been infants. Lady Gratton, if she was ill, retired to her room and did not speak of it; she thought talk of ailments to be a weakness and a bore. If the Earl had ever known an ache or pain, it was revealed only to his physician. But neither of them had suffered from wounds—then reality came flooding back. There in the cabin, dark because d'Egremont had ordered the port-hole covered—the light, he claimed, hurt his eyes—she remembered the Earl. Was he still lying wounded? Was he dead? Deliberately she once again closed her mind to the crowding thoughts and inquired if there was anyone on board who could treat d'Egremont's wound.

D'Egremont, petulant, said that he could hardly wait for her interest. He had already sent for the second mate, who acted as physician to the ship. The second mate soon bustled in, a cheerful little man, round as a tub of butter, but his pudgy hands were deft, and Damaris thought his eyes looked kind. Later, she and Jean-Philippe were to laugh at the aptness of his name, Barelle, but for the moment the patient was bad-tempered.

'A clumsy fool,' he said, almost before Barelle was out of the door. 'But I suppose he has the knowledge of an apothecary. I will try his pills and potions.'

Damaris learned later that these were merely drugs to ease the pain. The Marquis refused food, but she patiently urged him to take a little coffee and a morsel of bread. His appetite failed to improve as day followed day and week followed week. Damaris's strength and spirits returned; his did not.

The weather on the Atlantic was fair and warm, with only the wind they needed to send them westward. Damaris, to her surprise, found herself to be a good sailor. Her young body responded to the fresh air, the exercise on deck, and the sound sleep she had at night except when the Marquis, still suffering, woke her with his groans and she would sit by him, holding his hands and bathing his brow.

Barelle shook his head and looked grave about the wounded thigh. He told Damaris plainly that M'sieur le Marquis should not be travelling; his wound was not healing as it should; far more expert attention was needed than he could provide.

She could only ask him to do his best. When they reached New Orleans there would be good doctors, from what Jean-Philippe had told her of that once French city. Then all would be well. At least he had no fever; he would heal at last. But in the meantime his weakness and chagrin kept him despondent. He had not yet left the cabin, and he grew thin and wan, lying on his berth hour after hour, his face to the wall.

Up on deck Damaris could tell herself she was more fortunate than she deserved. Since the day when she had first met and loved Jean-Philippe her wildest dream had been that they could be together always, not just at stolen moments; that she could become his wife, the mother of his children. In regard to that, a thought crossed her mind. At first, in England, she had taken due care— not for her the freedom of some of the ladies of the *ton*. As her husband no longer visited her room, she could hardly present him with another child. But at last she had grown careless. She wondered now: her sickness and faintness during the battle—were they caused only by the sights and sounds of war? Her body felt young and full of life. A strange, strong happiness sprang from some glowing centre deep within her body, coiling slowly from the loins to rise, unaffected by the shallow surface perturbations of her mind, and bring secret delight.

The weather grew warmer, and on her morning strolls about the deck she discarded the enveloping pelisse and close bonnet, relying on a shady hat and a light shawl over her muslins. Her spirits rose as d'Egremont became well enough to move about the cabin and to eat, though he claimed he could not enjoy his food. One day the captain, at last recovering from his long bout with the bottle, appeared, and Damaris thought him in a particularly churlish and unpleasant mood. His nose was red; his face was pale; he cursed his men—as evil as d'Egremont at his worst, Damaris thought wryly. She heard him swearing at his first mate before he spoke to her, and then his manner seemed hardly to improve.

'*Bonjour*, Madame,' he said abruptly. He eyed her up and down. Damaris, since she had fled London, was slightly thinner than usual, but her breasts were full and firm under the thin muslin dress—his gaze, she thought, was insolent. 'I hope you are comfortable in my cabin?'

It was hardly a question. Damaris, putting aside her annoyance at his too frank appraisal, thanked him in her soft, gentle voice and hoped that he was not too disturbed by the change he had made.

He waved his hand. 'It is nothing. I only asked, Madame, because I must tell you that you had better confine yourself to your cabin and not show yourself about the decks.'

She protested that she could hardly spend several weeks penned up below.

'Your husband is there, Madame,' he said coldly. 'I must be plain, I see. I speak for your protection. This crew is but a mangy pack of dogs, the scum of the seas. Half of them are deserters from Napoleon's armies, the other half God knows what. My chief mate is the only decent seaman on board, the only one I trust out of my sight.'

Damaris was indignant. 'But they have been kind, very kind. I have received nothing but courtesy since the day I boarded.'

He looked at her, his dark stubble of beard sombre against the redness of his eyes. She gathered from his expression that he wanted to call her a fool but hesitated to so address a marquise.

'The day you boarded was one thing, Madame,' he said, and spat over the rail of the ship. 'Now these dogs have been a few weeks at sea, they will undergo the usual change. You are the only woman on board, and you are young and pretty. Very pretty. Your husband is kept in the cabin below. The best course is for you to stay at his side and let those wretches go their way with their minds on their work. They are a lewd, bawdy lot, and they are beginning to talk in the fo'c'sle in a way you would not like to hear. If you must take exercise, take a turn outside your cabin while the men are at their meal. It is cooler at that hour, and you will be able to cover yourself.'

He slouched off, after a muttered '*bonjour*,' and stood talking for a moment to the chief mate, who had been observing them.

She saw rather than heard Étienne Luce's protest, but she had no difficulty in hearing the captain's reply, borne clearly on the breeze.

'Parbleu! It is all very well for these dames of the *haut monde* to show themselves off naked before their men in Paris and London! They have soldiers there to protect them from the rabble. I have none on this ship. The sight of the lady in her chemise gives me no pain—it is her welfare I am concerned with.'

Damaris blushed scarlet but could only submit. She thought his speech exaggerated by his fit of temper, brought on by all the miserable effects of a bout of drinking, but there might be something in what he said. His words were rough, but the captain of a merchantman was not expected to be a gentleman. The men *were* long at sea and would be that much longer. Now she recalled rather unwillingly that there had been one huge, dark, red-eyed man—looking rather like the captain, but a lower rate—who had been following her with his eyes and something of a leer about his countenance whenever she happened to pass. She had ignored what she had not wished to see, but . . .

Still, she regretted having to give up her vigorous exercise in the sparkling daylight; she had come to love the expanse of sea and had even, with the first mate's guidance, helped unfurl the mainsail and taken the wheel. But it would be better perhaps. The Marquis was mending, and he would enjoy her company. Soon they could take their walks together. The thought cheered her; the sting of the captain's words faded, and she went below full of sober and sensible plans and hopes; the girl brought up to Lady Gratton's dry strictures could take reproof with chagrin and yet without resentment.

Her Breton sailor, seeing her confined, discreetly applauded the captain's wisdom. He brought her extra dainties, took her clothes from her trunk and aired them—but just outside her cabin door. The Marquis complained about the boy coming in and out with the garments and told him to take them away and bring them back altogether, but young Jacques whispered to Damaris that he would not take them down below.

'There are a lot of rough fellows in the crew that have never seen fine ladies' garments. It is better I do it here,' he whispered. 'I will try not to bother M'sieur le Marquis.'

Jean-Philippe still had difficulty walking and refused to stir outside the cabin. He was weak and weary, and rested most of the day in his berth. He liked her to sit beside him, and through the long days and nights he told her a little of what had driven him to take up Napoleon's cause, though even to Damaris he could not speak of the days of battle, with the hope of France destroyed, his Emperor and idol forced to flee, this time never to return.

It had begun long ago, perhaps before he himself knew. He had loathed the men of the Terror and had been brought up to hate the Revolution and all its works. Yet he was very conscious of his family's position in England. His father, embittered by the loss of his wife, his estates, his power and position, had found the kindness of the English, and the wealth he had managed to spirit abroad, no substitute for what he had lost, no satisfaction for a man too old to look forward to much future change. The kindness was much tainted in his eyes by the pusillanimity of the English in failing to crush the Revolution at once and forever. The wealth without power brought him no pleasure—and was far less than his friends believed. The Marquis d'Egremont maintained his standards, and this he had done by living on his gold and not the interest he could have had by investing in the funds. The huge fortune he had left his son by will proved to be the dream of a dying man. Most of the money was gone long since.

Jean-Philippe as a youth had not known about the money, but he understood his father's rage. Unconsciously he began to dislike the people of the nation that sheltered him; their ease, their calm confidence, their seeming indifference to the fate of the nobility of France aroused the resentment of a youth hot-tempered behind his pose of easy nonchalance. As Napoleon brought victory after victory to France, d'Egremont could not help but be impressed; he liked to see all Europe quaking in its boots. The imperial bees of Bonaparte masked the bloodstains on the *Tricolore,* and the Bourbon lilies looked faded and wan as King Louis sat placidly at Hartwell.

If the English were not observant, there were those French who became aware of the fires of rebellion in young d'Egremont; men, traitors themselves to Louis, swore to the young man that Louis could never reign in France; Napoleon was invincible, but he could be generous to those who aided him. The d'Egremont estates, they said knowingly, would be returned more quickly by the triumphant Emperor than they ever would by the timid King, who was already murmuring that not all the effects of the Revolution could be turned back.

'A strong emperor can deal with the hoi polloi; a weak king never will,' his seducers had told him. Jean-Philippe had come to believe what he wished to believe: the glorious Emperor was his emperor. His orders were to attach himself to Louis, to be known, as he already was because of his position, as the most royalist of the émigrés, to keep his eyes and ears open in the company of English friends, those men so calm and sure, who talked far more than they should in the presence of the French dandy.

Napoleon had rewarded him with large sums in gold—a considerable benefit to a man on the verge of ruin.

'In fact,' he told Damaris, 'after the Emperor went to Elba and my source of income vanished I was in considerable difficulty—living on my creditors like your friend the Beau.' He laughed, without much mirth. 'Even if I had not been discovered, I might have had to fly from England to escape them—I don't think Louis would have stepped in to prevent my ruin.'

Damaris listened, trying to understand.

'But did you not—when you were among your friends—' She hesitated, not wishing to say, 'How could you betray the people who trusted you?' But he heard the question in the unspoken words.

'You wonder that I betrayed those closest to me? Well, my dear'—he laughed with some amusement—'one can hardly betray people one doesn't know.' He caught her glance and shrugged. 'I enjoyed it vastly. It was a great game, greater than cards, more exciting than a duel. It was my brains, one man, against England. And the stakes were high.'

In the little cabin, under the alternating light and shadow of a swinging lamp, she saw once again the gambler's light in his eye and the reckless smile on his lips. For a moment he was once again the d'Egremont who had caught her eye and heart. He, responding to her thought and look, reached out and caught her forearm.

'You are beautiful, Madame,' he whispered, 'even with no maid to do your hair.' He drew her to him not as a fretful patient but as a lover, for the first time since they had left Brussels. His hand caressed her body. The quiet of the cabin was suddenly intimate, sensual. The ship rolled; the timbers creaked; the light swung again and shadowed the Marquis's face, giving him a look demonic, mad, possessive. Damaris hesitated, drawing back. Then another roll and toss sent him bouncing in his berth and made him groan and turn away.

'Curse it,' he said, and bit his lip with pain. 'Get me the brandy, Madame. I'm afraid I'm useless as a lover to you this night.'

All that night the sea was rough; the ship rolled and tossed. Damaris, whose healthy body had accustomed itself to the movement of the vessel, slept on; the Marquis, irritable, rose to get his pills and brandy himself. As squalling winds hit the sails, the cabin rocked and the Marquis slid and tumbled to the floor, striking his injured leg against the wooden rail of the berth as he fell.

Damaris jumped up to attend him, calling for Barelle. The rest of the night was wretched. In the morning the second mate told Damaris what she had already guessed: pus had formed in the wound, and the Marquis now had fever. Her morning promenades were all forgotten as she spent days and nights in attending her patient, bathing him, feeding him broth, cooling his forehead, and holding his hand. Sometimes she sang French songs to please him; sometimes she remained silent; but when his fever broke and he began very slowly to mend, she was worn down by the care and confinement. The little cabin had become a prison, and she longed for land even though it were a wilderness populated by savages.

Luce came to her and said bluntly that she must get some air and exercise, and Barelle supported him. Remembering the captain's words, Damaris agreed to accompany the first mate and young Durand while Barelle attended the Marquis. Well wrapped in her cloak, she walked the deck sedately, invigorated by the fresh breeze and marvelling at the constellations revealed in the cloudless night.

These sailors knew their stars. Damaris found new pleasure in her nightly walks, making out Cassiopeia, the Swan, and Sagittarius the Archer with his arrow trained on the Scorpion, gazing at all the splendour of a star-bright ocean and sky. When she returned to her cabin she tried to share with d'Egremont what she had seen and her excitement, her new sense of all that nature and life contained, the lifting of the heart at seeing that endless sky. But he was weaker and more peevish than before his accident and begged her to spare him her enthusiasm.

'For if you can find pleasure in talking with this canaille and burbling of sea and sky, pray do not bore me with it, Madame.' His words were biting. 'Had you seen the palace of Versailles, with its gilded ceilings and marble floors, you could speak of it. *There* is a work of art. I care nothing for these accidents of nature.'

She never spoke of such things again but resumed her ministrations. When the knock came at the cabin door at nightfall and she left with her two escorts despite d'Egremont's sharp and irritable comment she found she was happy at the short respite. She remembered with a pang of guilt the days when all she looked forward to in life was the chance to be alone, for just an hour, with Jean-Philippe d'Egremont. Love was strange, she thought, and had its own ways. Yet she loved him still, and if his demands were those of a child and his torments those of an imp, she believed that to be the result of his illness and thrust the thoughts from her mind—as she had learned to do with many thoughts. And for a week or two all went on with seeming smoothness, and the captain talked of sighting land within the fortnight. Then the winds changed and soon dropped altogether. The ship sat helpless in the ocean. They were becalmed.

CHAPTER

33

The sun shone down from a sky like brass. The cabin felt like an oven. Damaris spent weary hours fanning the Marquis, but he tossed, fretted, mumbled, and swore. His pain was worse, the pills helping him less and less. Barelle, sweating from every pore, looking, as the Marquis said, like a dish of butter melting over a candle-flame, did what he could, but he was busy, for if he had few duties up on deck, he had plenty below. Supplies were growing short; fruit and vegetables were almost at an end; there was an outbreak of scurvy—and the captain, Barelle told Damaris, was at his bottle again.

'He and that brother of his,' he said, shaking his head.

'His brother?'

'Yes, Jules Dessin—the one the men call Le Gros. The rogue is the captain's brother—but Madame would not have observed. The same mother,' he murmured, his eyes rolling, his hand waving expressively. 'Usually the captain ignores him, a mere seaman, not fit for the captain's table, but when he drinks, Le Gros is a drinking companion worthy of him. They consume—how much they consume! And Le Gros has the better head of the two—not so much trouble with his liver. But then, he is much the younger man.'

So, Damaris reflected, the huge, red-eyed seaman who had followed her with his eyes—he was the captain's brother. No wonder that the captain had spoken the way he did. He must have heard his brother's thoughts expressed freely before he himself slid under the table. She grimaced. It was Le Gros she had to thank for her imprisonment—she liked him less than ever.

Luce was busy with his duties on the ship in the captain's absence and doing what he could for the stricken men. One of them was the cook, and his helper was an inexperienced boy. Luce, as he told Damaris later, had to watch the food being prepared, 'so as not to sicken us all.' He found time late one afternoon to escort

Damaris up on deck and advised that she take her parasol. Young Durand was not with him—nor had he appeared to bring her meals for two days past. His place had been taken by a burly seaman who had spilled the coffee on the Marquis and brought on a roar of anguish and complaint.

Durand had come down with a bout of scurvy, but not as badly as some of the others, Luce told her. Barelle was pleased with his progress. Luce apologized that her exercise must be cut short, but in any case the glare of the deck was not refreshing. As Damaris made her way along—no sea legs were needed now, for the ocean was as flat as the ponds of Heron—she had a feeling of being observed, yet she saw no one watching her. The look-out had his eyes trained ahead; the man at the wheel was standing listlessly, as though he half slept in the sun; a few of the seamen off watch had rigged a tarpaulin to shade themselves, and they lay beneath it, not finding much more comfort there than in the fo'c'sle.

Some small sound made her turn. She had just passed a cabin—she thought she saw a glimmer of a face, dark and red-eyed, at the door. Luce saw her backward glance. 'My cabin,' he remarked. 'Cap'n has it this voyage. He and Le Gros are drinking themselves silly.'

Was it Le Gros who watched? The captain must be insensible. Not wishing to dwell on the thought of the lascivious Dessin, she made some remark about the captain's proclivities, though really she felt no shock. There were too many men of the English nobility who had to keep a servant to attend them at dinner and loosen their cravats when they slipped under the table for her to find drunkenness in itself strange, but it did seem irresponsible in a ship's captain.

Luce was loyal to his master.

'The captain, he would be up and round if he were needed,' he said. 'He always is. The captain's not a bad man, but it's a hard life. He once had a fine ship for the India run—but the English put a stop to that. And they take the cream of the Atlantic trade; poor pickings left for anyone else. Captain Bosquet was a wealthy man, but when he was under French flag he was taken by the English and lost his ship and cargo though he cared nothing for Napoleon, or the English either. Now he's poor and sails on. The *Bonne Chance* is all he has, but it's a slow old tub, and with the war over there'll be newer, faster ships taking up the trade.'

Damaris could understand why the captain was not fond of a French marquise who spoke with an English accent. Yes, a disappointed man could take to drink—she thought of d'Egremont and his brandy bottle and sighed.

It was strange and rather frightening to see the big, solid, heavy-bottomed ship with all sails drooping, floating like a fat duck on the water.

'How long can it last?' she asked Luce.

The solid Fleming shrugged. 'A day, a few days, a week—no one ever really knows the winds or the seas,' he told her. 'I have been at sea for nearly forty years, and what I know best is that I don't know. The sea, she keeps her secrets. The winds blow as God wills and not as man expects.'

Despite the glare she was reluctant to go below to the closeness, the cramped quarters, the grumbling of Jean-Philippe. The next day passed, and the next, with no wind, no break in the torrid heat. Jean-Philippe's constant cursing at the food was unendurable, yet she had to admit that it grew worse and worse. The cook was still a sick man; supplies were low, and the desperate youth in the galley had no idea of what to do with them. Damaris would have liked to visit the galley herself, but Luce politely but firmly refused.

'But if the men are ill?'

'They are not all ill, Madame. It would not do. It would not do, indeed.'

The only cheerful thing that happened was the return of young Jacques Durand, pale, thin and weak, but smiling. He had found some tea and brought it to her, as the coffee was not fit to drink. She had been glad of the attention and smiled at him, in a way she had not smiled since she had boarded ship.

He blushed; she was sorry she had smiled so—he was no young dandy to enjoy her smiles and then forget them in the tying of a cravat.

That was the end of pleasure for the day. Luce, who was much engaged, could not come to walk with her. Durand was busy helping in the galley and nursing his comrades. As the sun went down and there was still no remission of the stifling heat inside her cabin, Damaris, staring at her face dead white in the captain's looking-glass, thought she must have air or she would faint. She pressed her hands against her breasts, her womb—almost certainly she was pregnant. Sometimes the rigours of travel could deceive, but her body told its own story. For the sake of this child as well as herself, she must have some relief. Le Gros was locked up with the captain; at this hour every man except the deck watch would be at the evening meal.

She slipped out and walked quietly along by the deck rail, fancying it cooler. Was there, perhaps, a suggestion of a breeze? The light was almost gone. She peered out at the ocean and thought she saw a ripple floating lazily across the water. Wearily she leaned on the rail. It was still so warm her muslin clung to her skin. She could feel sweat on the nape of her neck under her hair and between her heavy breasts. Unbidden, the thought came of Jean-Philippe's kisses, his cat-like tongue licking the sweat away to her wild delight—Malfrey House. It seemed not only another place but another world. It was her pregnancy, she thought, that made desire so remote. A woman, pregnant, wanted no man's touch—certainly she had not when she was pregnant with Lady Griselda and the heir! She grimaced at the remembrance of the heavy touch of the Earl—and jumped, startled and confused at the touch of a heavy hand upon her back.

She had heard no one. The man had crept up behind her silently as only a seaman could move. The light was grey, but she had no trouble recognizing Le Gros, who stood beside her grinning, red-eyed, unkempt, with matted hair and wine stains on his blouse.

'Waiting for me?' he said with a leer. 'I thought I'd find you; I saw the way you looked back at me the other day, flirting your parasol to catch my eye.'

'M'sieur, you are mad,' Damaris said sharply. 'I must return to my husband at once.'

She felt little fear. The Countess of Malfrey was too strong in Damaris for her to tremble before an inferior.

But Le Gros laughed. As she made to go, a strong and powerful arm held her back against the rail.

'Husband?' He leaned forward, and she caught the sour smell of wine upon his breath. 'The cripple? If he is your husband, Englishwoman.'

He laughed again at her discomfiture.

'You think we humble seamen are such fools? A marquis, after a victory for his king, would not be taking his marquise, his little English marquise, like a thief in the night, on the oldest tub on the seven seas with the family jewels for passage money. What husband did he steal you from, my pretty bird, who gave him the wound before the two of you ran off? Well'—his gaze took in her figure, plain to see in her damp gown—'perhaps you were worth a wound or two, after all.'

Her peril became real to her. She was alone on this deserted corner of the deck. The men who normally would have been returning to scrape chain or to perform other non-urgent duties had been given permission by Luce to rest themselves. If she screamed, who was there to hear?

Panic-stricken, she tried to pull away. But her movement excited him; he held her closer and crushed her mouth under his. The rank odour of his body and his foul breath almost overcame her. Now she tried to scream but could not free herself—if only she had called out at once. She moved her head sharply and called 'Help! help!' but no one came. Le Gros caught her head with one hand and with the other tore the gauze of her gown. He gazed at her breasts and fondled them roughly. She began to scream again, but as she twisted and turned, almost tearing the hair from her head, she was struck with another horror—if the men should hear her screams and come upon them, seeing her as she was, unless it should be her friends, her state then might be worse than this.

Silenced, she fought desperately. Le Gros's hands were ripping the shreds of her gown and chemise from her body. He pushed her back against the rail, sucking on her breasts, his male member rising stiff against her. Still she fought, feeling her strength nothing against his, terrified, disgusted. A wave of anger swept over her at his contemptuous use of her body, and she sank her teeth into his neck until she tasted blood.

He started back, his eyes wild.

'Vixen,' he said, grunting, and raising his great hand, he slapped her hard across the face so that her teeth chattered and tears sprang to her eyes. He looked pleased at her pain and grasped her hips, squeezing her flesh until she cried. He looked about and in the dim light of the deck saw the tarpaulin cover left by the crewmen when they went below. Deciding it would serve, he dragged her roughly towards its shelter.

Now she was consumed with terror and screamed and shrieked without regard for what might befall. He cuffed her once again and dragged her faster; her slippers clattered to the deck as he held her aloft, his hands enjoying the freedom of her nearly-naked body as he strode along.

They were all too few paces from the tarpaulin; surely, she thought in agony, someone had heard her cry? She believed she heard a sound somewhere, but no one came. Le Gros thrust her, still screaming, to the deck and muffled her cries with kisses while his hands ripped and tore and found the smoothness of her naked thighs, forcing them apart. His tongue thrust deep into her throat. She felt his body urgent at the entrance to her own—when suddenly he swore and spat and turned, grinding her body into pain while she choked with sudden relief. There was a form above him, pulling, tugging, raining blows, a slight figure, his fists hammering on the larger, stronger man whom he had caught unawares.

Le Gros jumped up and caught the youth—now she saw young Jacques Durand, his face glimmering pale. The men wrestled, grasped, exchanged blows, Jacques weak and desperate, Le Gros maddened and enraged. Damaris was frozen in fear, unable to move. Jacques's blow landed, Le Gros swore, and a knife-blade gleamed in the dusk. Damaris found her voice and screamed again, scrambling up; there was a thud as Jacques slipped in his own blood.

Le Gros turned towards her, knife in hand, smiling, the blood on his hands not calming but inflaming his desire.

Jacques gave a choked, sudden moan. Damaris's consciousness wavered; dark clouds gathered in her mind. Le Gros picked her up as she fell, his great hands clasping her waist as if she were a doll, the blood from his palms dripping down her body.

'Sauce to the meat,' he muttered, and knelt over her.

His words struck through her faintness, and she raised her hands to ward him off; he grasped her wrists, and then a voice, so like his own, said with a calm, stern certainty, 'Loose the woman.'

She looked up with drowning eyes. There, as the first mate had told her he always was when needed, stood Captain Bosquet, unshaven, dishevelled, but with all his authority plain upon him.

Le Gros loosed her.

There was a scampering on the deck as other seamen came up from below. The captain stood before Damaris, blocking her from view.

'Put him in irons.' He pushed Le Gros towards them. 'And take the corpse away.'

CHAPTER

34

The horrors of that night and what followed were shot through in Damaris's mind by the strange chances of a ship at sea and a new, personal sorrow. While she was in anguish and disbelief at the death of young Jacques Durand the captain covered her with a cloak, and led her to his cabin so that she could right herself before she returned to the Marquis. Hardly had they reached his cabin door when the cry from the look-out came.

'Wind ho!'

Before the cursing Le Gros was stowed safely in the brig, the ship's complement was running to the main-deck. The wind arrived, no small breeze but a wind of great power. All sail was up, and men were running, calling, crying to each other in relief at the end of their miseries and in the press and urgency of work.

Before leaving Damaris, the captain said little.

'I will have to hold an inquiry,' he said. 'A man is dead. You had better return to your husband as soon as possible, Madame.'

He sent for a fresh gown, and he threw it before her, watching her with eyes that were worldly but not, Damaris thought, without a hint of kindness.

'The Marquis is sleeping. You can return without fear. Better to say nothing, Madame. The inquiry and the story of the fight must become part of the ship's record—the cause need not. Le Gros will receive the punishment. My men will be silent.'

She returned to the cabin to find the Marquis fast asleep. The breeze had brought coolness; for once he was enjoying his rest. In the tragedy that had befallen, the horror of her encounter with Le Gros faded. The man was disgusting; she had been abused, but he had not succeeded in overcoming her. His punishment would be severe, but she wept for young, merry Jacques Durand, whose life she had sacrificed, she thought sorrowfully, for a breath of fresh air.

Her body was bruised and scratched. She had to hide herself from the Marquis, but by the time he woke she had good reason for that. Over and over she had told herself that she was not truly injured by the attempted rape, but her body was not governed by the decision of her mind. During the night she was assailed by a well-remembered pain, not as severe as the pain of childbirth but that nevertheless made her sweat, grit her teeth, and clutch the board along her berth rather than cry out.

The child that was to have been died the same night as young Durand. When d'Egremont awoke next morning, much refreshed by the good sleep, cheerful as he saw the ship scudding before brisk breezes, Damaris told him gently of her loss. He had not known she was with child, and so the knowledge of what had occurred hardly damped his spirits.

He was kind and held her hand, more thoughtful than he had been since his fever had begun, but he hurt her more than he knew when he said with a sanguine air that perhaps it was for the best. Their new life would be difficult enough at first without a fixed abode, familiar attendants, or good friends. Perhaps it was as well that the birth of their first child should await a more propitious occasion.

Damaris, now she felt ill herself, longed for some privacy, but there was none to be had. Barelle could do little to ease her suffering—pregnant passengers were not part of his experience. She kept her pain and grief silently, but to d'Egremont the sight of his lady lying pale and still on her berth was not as pleasant as Damaris, faithful companion and nurse. In a day or two he decided he was well enough to take a turn on deck and see the ship in action, and he called for two stout seamen to assist him.

He returned in an hour much refreshed in body and in mind. He told Damaris exuberantly that he thought at last his wound was mending. His pain was less and his fever had not returned for several days. As yet he would not put any weight upon his leg, but even Barelle—'that old woman,' the Marquis said scornfully—admitted reluctantly that the leg seemed to heal.

'I will go on deck again; there is to be an entertainment,' he went on, 'now that the crew have adjusted themselves to the idea that the winds can blow—*mon Dieu*, how it took them by surprise! The lazy swine were probably all lying drunk in the scuppers.'

'Entertainment?' Damaris asked faintly.

She did not care to think of the crew during the calm. Now she was trying to blot out the memory of that night, as she had put behind her so many other memories. In tormented dozing, with her body still weak from her loss, she would feel again the touch of Le Gros upon her body, swirling in her consciousness with buried memories of the hateful embraces of the Earl; shuddering, she would turn her head upon her pillow, and then she would be swept with sorrow for the child, who sometimes resembled her son Christopher and sometimes Jacques Durand. Barelle had given her a potion for her pain, a drug that made her sleepy, though not always bringing sleep.

'There was a fight among the canaille during the calm,' the Marquis said cheerfully. 'One stabbed the other and he died. Alas, the murderer is not to be hanged from the yard-arm—that would have been a sight to see—but I understand from the whispers of the rogues who attend me that the man is the bastard brother of our dear captain. So—he gives him his chance. The man is to be spread-eagled and flogged. He gets fifty lashes. If he survives, he is free of his crime. It should be almost as amusing as the hanging. I will certainly be on deck for the treat.'

Damaris shuddered and did not speak. She was, she thought, a poor Christian; she wanted Le Gros to die. His violation of her person, his murder of the sweet and smiling Jacques, a young man who hardly knew as yet the pleasures of his God-given life—it seemed fitting he should be put to death. Yet flogging, though no doubt a custom of the sea, seemed barbarous. But to a man, she knew, it was useless to speak. With their sports of cock-fighting, watching prize-fighters batter each other near to death bare-fisted, men were not nice in such matters.

The next morning she awoke reluctantly. Barelle came to see how she fared, bringing her some withered apples.

'You must eat them, Madame,' he said. 'You need their goodness now.'

'But what of the sick men?' she said. 'They need the fruit more.'

'Have it,' Barelle insisted. 'You have lost much blood.'

He didn't tell her that the seamen who had had the scurvy very badly had already died—the poor lady was troubled enough.

The Marquis spoke to him jovially about the 'entertainment.' After he had been assisted from the cabin, Barelle returned. He had observed the trouble on the lady's face, as d'Egremont had not.

'Do not fear, Madame,' he said gently. 'The punishment will take place aft, up in the shrouds. You should hear nothing. It will soon be over.'

Damaris thanked him for his kindness, with some relief, but buried her face in the pillows to be sure. She was unlucky. The breeze that carried them so quickly westward brought the man's shrieks of pain, muted by distance but clear enough, to her ears. Shriek after shriek; she shuddered, twisted her hands, and pushed the pillows closer against her ears—how long could it go on? How could the man live? Hanging would have been more merciful. As his voice lifted in agony, Damaris thought she felt the lash of the rope. This was no solace for the insult and the injury to herself; the red-cheeked Breton Jacques would not have wanted this torment as revenge.

And then there was silence that had nothing of relief in it.

The Marquis, half-supported by the burly seamen, came in laughing as he had not laughed in many weeks.

'Great sport,' he said, tossing his hat into a corner. 'Parbleu, it makes one wish for a ship and crew! At sea, at least, a captain is master as a noble used to be on his own land. No weak-kneed liberals here; the captain's word is law—and life! Fifty lashes he declared the punishment was to be; fifty lashes it was. The man hung there like a flayed beast and screamed for Jesus. After the fortieth stroke Barelle told the captain he thought the rogue was nearly done for, but Bosquet—more of a man than I took him for—stood like a stone, the mills of God, in fact. What a sight, and all those wretches looking, shivering, wondering if their turn might be next! Not a murmur did they make for their own comrade. Fifty lashes he had, and when they cut him down he was dead. And you can be glad, Madame, because I learned the man he murdered was the pretty boy who had caught your eye.'

He smiled down at her. 'Perhaps I should have been jealous— while I was ill did you amuse yourself with this fine young Breton lad?'

His voice was teasing. She had always loved his teasing; she could not enjoy it now. Engrossed in his own recrudescence of health and spirits, he failed to observe her distaste and weariness. For the first time since they had left Brussels, his eyes sparkled.

'I was weak and feverish too long,' he murmured. 'A mere crack of the thigh-bone—a nuisance, but mending well. Soon I can do without the splint and stick. Already I feel a new man—you look lovely, lying there so quiet, my chill English beauty. Do you still have warmth for me?'

He turned the linen back and ran his hand down her body to her waist, where Le Gros had held her, where young Jacques's blood had trickled down her skin. Now, as then, she felt faint but managed to murmur softly, 'Jean-Philippe!' and reminded him of her condition.

He rose and shrugged.

'*Mon Dieu,* I had forgotten—the mysteries of Lucina! The dullest goddess in the Pantheon. Well, there will be time enough, Madame! In one week,' he said gaily, 'we will be ashore. And start our new life. New Orleans! I begin to long for it.'

Damaris smiled wanly to see him restored. As he chatted he grew restless and called for help to go on deck again. She closed her eyes, telling herself it was her condition with its attendant weakness and her exhaustion after the events of the last few days that had brought about her coldness, her lack of pleasure in her lover's touch. Rest and time would renew everything, she thought. The words that had struck so callously upon her ears were those of a nobleman, a Frenchman who had suffered much at the hands of the people. He was no different from what he had been. It was her own nerves and emotions that were strained.

There seemed to be no one to heed his call. The quiet that had come after the flogging was gone. Men were racing about busily, calling to each other in words she failed to recognize; her French was not equal to the working language of the ship. But she could feel that the wind, already brisk, had risen; and though it was early the sky was growing dark.

'The dogs are deaf,' d'Egremont said, 'but I will go myself. With this stick I can manage well.'

'Don't go, Jean-Philippe,' Damaris said, alarmed. 'Indeed, without help you must not. The wind is high, the ship may toss, and if the decks are wet you can slip and fall—'

D'Egremont scowled. 'I may have failed against the Iron Duke,' he said, 'but I am still fit enough to hobble a few feet. Allow me to leave you to your mysteries, Madame. I might take a glass of wine with our friend the captain; he has shown himself to be a man of parts.'

Damaris shuddered but, feeling the force of the snub, had to let him go. She should get up and go with him, she thought. Yet she was sensible enough to know that if she did herself an injury now, there might be no children ever for her and d'Egremont.

No one came to light the lamp. As the sky grew darker it seemed that the ship was driven on a gale. The timbers groaned and creaked; a lashing rain came down. D'Egremont didn't return —he had taken the place of Le Gros at the captain's side. She wondered how the captain felt, having executed his own brother by torture. The discipline of his ship apparently meant more to him than his blood kin.

Would he gossip, Bosquet, in his wine? She believed he would not. Then she wondered why she hadn't told the Marquis of Le Gros's attack; she had not been at fault, except in going out against the captain's orders. But she had been at fault; her imprudence cost young Jacques his life. And she had no wish to speak. The captain had been right. No good could have come of her confession. The Marquis would have been furious, depressed at his own helplessness, and would have despised her just a little, however innocent she was—she had felt the touch of a ruffian.

She wondered now what rumours were flying round the ship. There had been no previous quarrel between Jacques Durand and Le Gros. Had any of the men seen her as she lay there, helpless in the shadow of the tarpaulin? What were they saying and thinking, all those men huddled there below? She stirred uneasily. Now she wished she were not alone, wished the Marquis would return—his presence was protection, and she had lost all sense of security even here in her own cabin. The captain was probably drunk again. Luce was busy about the deck—but almost all the men were busy now, she comforted herself. They were not idle and restless as they had been during that wretched calm. The swell of the sea tossed the heavy old ship as though it were a cockleshell; she could see nothing in the dark and driving rain.

Carefully she rose from her berth to light the lamp. She would lock the door as well, she thought; when the Marquis returned she would still be awake. Then there came a tap on the door, and she froze in sudden fear.

'It is Barelle.'

She gasped in quick relief.

'Alone?' he said, peering round, 'and in the dark?'

He lit her lamp and complained that she had left her berth. She was relieved to have the illumination though the lamp was swinging wildly from the beam. Barelle was soaked from head to foot, the water running from his beard despite his sou'wester.

'I wondered who was with the captain in his cabin,' he said glumly. 'M'sieur le Marquis should not be out this night. The decks are awash; there is hardly sound footing for a sailor. And you should not be alone, Madame.'

Damaris shivered. Barelle, who had heard certain rumours and observed the bruises about the lady's person as he attended her and tried to ease her pain, looked grim.

'All hands are aloft now, Madame,' he told her, partly to ease her mind. 'This wind blows like a hurricane. The mainsail has been ripped in two, and the topsail is gaping open from earing to earing. The main-royal is loose and flapping like washing on a line.'

'Is the ship in danger?' Damaris asked.

'No, Madame, have no fear. But there is much work for the men. I will go to the captain's cabin myself and fetch the Marquis to you.'

He saw the doubt on her face and smiled.

'We sailors know how to walk and hold onto the ropes. I will have my arm about the Marquis, never fear. The worst of it is the captain.'

His fat face looked comic in a grimace.

'He won't relish having his party broken up by a lower rate. Mr Luce should go, but he has his hands full. The yard-arm broke like a twig, and he is all over the deck at once.'

Damaris looked up, feeling she should prevent him from angering his captain and doing himself harm, but her fear was still coiled within her and she couldn't say the words.

Barelle smiled cheerfully. 'Have no fear,' he repeated, and left.

Damaris felt nervous when he had gone. She wanted the Marquis to return, yet if he was enjoying his wine with the captain, he wouldn't be eager to leave: he might come back in foul humour. Outside the wind howled at screaming pitch, and the great waves were slapping against the side with a force terrifying to a landsman. Still, the captain's cabin was only a few yards away. Barelle would bring Jean-Philippe back safe—but she reckoned without the obstinacy of her lover.

When Barelle, hesitant, apologetic, had appeared at the captain's door, the party was already breaking up. Bosquet, though usually willing to leave the work of the ship to Luce, was aware enough of the conditions to decide to take the bridge. The Marquis understood the nature of Barelle's mission before he had spoken, and the Marquis was displeased. To be sent for by a woman to act as lady's maid was hardly becoming a d'Egremont. He half blamed Damaris and looked with disfavour on the now subservient Barelle. The man had become too familiar for his good, fussing over Damaris as though he were her physician instead of a mere dog of a sailor.

The Marquis was weaker than he knew, and the bottle after bottle of wine and the strong brandy of northern France that the captain had produced had had their effect. The Marquis was not fuddled but ugly-tempered, dangerous—once before in such a mood he had killed a man. He had been aware of the storm but hardly conscious of its force in his enjoyment; Bosquet had proved an amusing companion and was not a nobody like his crew. Bosquet's father had served the Bourbons and had a slight connection with one of the great families of France. D'Egremont had felt full of strength, restored to all his manhood.

When he threw open the cabin door, he peremptorily refused the arm of the fat little man. He forgot his stick; he would not go back. In truth he was surprised as he was hit with the force of the gale wind and intimidated by the rolling lurch of the ship. But there was too much wine in his head for judgement, and Barelle's repeated pleadings to assist him sounded in his ears like the barking of a little dog.

'Be off,' he said tersely. For all his bravado, his hands clutched the ropes. The door to his cabin was just a few feet now in front of him. The wind struck again, with a force to lift a man from his feet, but he held on grimly.

'M'sieur le Marquis, permit me—' The words were carried off by the wind.

D'Egremont cursed and went forward. Almost there. The ship shook; his sound leg came down on a slippery spot and flew outward. He tried to save himself, holding onto a rope, but the hawser itself was wrenched from the deck. The rope slackened; he slid forward, and as the smaller man tried to catch him d'Egremont fell heavily upon the deck, his splinted leg twisted under him.

CHAPTER

35

Barelle was a faithful friend. The gale raged for two whole days, and though he told her the ship was as full of broken bones as whole ones, he attended the Marquis punctiliously. Damaris, recovering from her indisposition, wearily went back to nurse.

The Marquis had cracked his thigh-bone again, in a place close to the wound. The attentions of Barelle saved him from further infection and fever, but his spirits were lower than they had ever been. The sudden surge of vitality had quite gone. He lay on his berth, uninterested in anything, even the news that the gale had driven them off course, so that the end of their voyage was still not in sight.

'What does it matter?' he said bitterly. 'It is better so—I will not be able to walk on land. I will be carried into this wretched country like a babe in arms.'

His talk went back to what it had been before his recovery. He thought endlessly of King Louis, of his return to Paris, of the possible fortunes of the émigrés who had gone in his train.

'Madame la Duchesse will be in her glory,' he said in great

gloom. It was important to him to be the head of his family in fact as well as in position. 'Ah, I might have been there had Louis been a man as well as a king.'

If the thought crossed Damaris's mind that he might have been there were it not for his own reckless folly, she pushed it away unacknowledged. His helplessness made her tender. His words, she thought, were like the fretting of a child.

With the gale over, though the winds remained high, Luce returned and told her the news of the ship.

'We are landing first in Boston. It is a civilized city; perhaps the Marquis would like to disembark. He will find doctors, and you will be able to rest before continuing your journey. We call at many ports; it will be long before we reach Charleston again.'

But d'Egremont laughed bitterly.

'Boston? I have heard they are ready to hang aristocrats from trees. I am in no hurry to disembark. I might stay here and die.'

When the Marquis slept, the friendly, plain-spoken Luce took Damaris aside.

'It is better, Madame, that you disembark as soon as possible. Barelle tells me the Marquis needs better attention than he can give him. This new break in his bone could cause much trouble. And the men are restless from the long voyage. We are overdue, and the captain will not give them shore leave until we reach our final port. You will talk to M'sieur.'

The captain also spoke to d'Egremont. What he said Damaris didn't know, but d'Egremont, sulky, agreed to disembark at New York, the third port of call.

'I will have to mend before we travel on to New Orleans,' he said, dejected. 'But what does it matter? One barbarous place is much like another.'

Still in high seas, strong winds, and dark weather when they arrived at Boston, Damaris gazed at the new land and did not find it welcoming. She was almost relieved to be staying on board, even with all her problems. There was something bleak and terrifying about that wind-swept coast.

But then a new trouble came upon them. Perhaps from long confinement, perhaps from the turbulence of the coastal waters, the Marquis was overcome by a bout of sea-sickness. It was sea-sickness of a most fearsome kind.

Barelle was perplexed.

'It happens,' he said with a shrug, 'but usually the first few days at sea or the first storm, the first high-tossing seas.'

He surmised, but did not say, that perhaps it was the sight of land, the reality of a new life, that had brought on the Marquis's sickness. That was not his business, and he tried to find some potion to give the man sleep, if not ease.

The Marquis was in such torment that, groaning, he insisted on being put off at the next port of call.

The captain himself came to see them and spoke to Damaris courteously. He had never made reference to her flouting of his command that had ended so grievously. Neither by word nor by look had he hinted that it was her fault young Durand had died, that his brother was dead and he himself had been forced to bring about his execution. He was a strange, complicated man, she thought, but she felt a certain respect for him as a gentleman and as a man.

'He seems ill indeed,' the captain said, looking at d'Egremont, who had lost far too much weight on the voyage and was weak, sallow, and wan. 'Otherwise—this port of Newfield is a small place, hardly suitable for such travellers as yourselves. We only stop there to unload a few stores of goods. But doubtless you will find a vehicle to take you on elsewhere. Barelle is fearful for your husband's life if he stays on board. I have seen a man die from such weakness, though such a thing is rare,' he added reflectively.

The man who had seemed to her the merest churl at Ostend now appeared to Damaris to be gallant. Although his men were busy with the ship in the foul weather and were endlessly shifting and hauling cargo, he spared two men to help with her and the Marquis's possessions, packing trunks and getting all ready to go ashore. She remembered, with a pang at her heart and a curse for her own folly, how young Durand had unpacked for her, careful as her own maid, rosy of cheek and bright of eye as her Betty had been before her troubles came. Betty—the thought of Great Heron came to mind, unbidden, and was as quickly pushed away.

She had one more interview with the captain, in the cabin he now occupied and that soon would be returned to Luce. Bosquet had asked her to come to him. He had some advice to give her before they parted. She looked at the man, tall and dark, with red-rimmed eyes so like those of Le Gros but with the redeeming spark of intelligence behind them.

She thanked him again for all that he had done and paused,

feeling she should say something about Durand and Le Gros, not knowing what to say.

'I'm sorry—' she began in her low voice, but he cut her short.

'Please say no more. What happened was not your fault, Madame. Rather blame *le bon Dieu*. Beauty such as yours will always inflame—has it not lit fires among the men of the nobility, with all that their rank and wealth can buy them? My poor sea-dogs, what chance had they? Even I—' he said steadily, 'I have been moved by your loveliness, your great *gentillesse*—'

He broke off and drew back—he had said more than he intended.

Damaris was surprised. In all the weary troubles of the voyage, she had hardly thought of herself as a young woman in the flower of her beauty. She had been a nurse and a patient. The lust of Le Gros had seemed to her only a response to her sex, having little to do with any individual charm she might possess. But she had been courted enough to recognize the light of attachment in the captain's gaze. His words to her were brief and to the point.

'The people of New England are not savages—though doubtless the Marquis will think so. They make scant ceremony of rank, but courtesy to them will procure you good treatment more easily than gold. And as for gold—do not, Madame, exchange your jewels for necessaries by the way. Go to one of the larger towns and find a jeweller of repute who will give you a fair price.'

She was to be surprised again.

'While the Marquis and I played cards, he lost an emerald ring to me.'

Damaris caught her breath. She had not seen the ring since leaving Belgium. It was a valued family heirloom of the d'Egremonts, with their crest carved into the emerald, but the Marquis seldom wore it—the dandies of London, under the tutelage of the Beau, wore only rings of the plainest gold.

'It was too valuable a possession to take from a man well in his cups,' the captain said dryly, 'and it more than pays for your passage.'

Turning to his locker, he took out her diamond and sapphire bracelet and clasped it on her arm. The moment of intimacy, she believed, pleased him, but he made no attempt to prolong it. 'You will need all you have, Madame,' he said. 'And—' He hesitated. 'The people of New England are also still Puritans at heart. I might suggest, to save confusion—the *M* on your belongings perhaps should be changed to an *E.*'

He smiled. She didn't remember seeing him smile before. It became him well. 'Good-bye, Madame. We will not meet again, but my thoughts go with you.'

When they parted, she felt a sense of loss. Once, as a girl, she had dreamed of a man, tall, strong, chivalrous, heroic. Bosquet, with his weakness for drink, was not that man but . . . On her last, sleepless night aboard the *Bonne Chance* the foolish, romantic thought came to her mind—was there such a man? Could he exist?

Book Three

THE NEW WORLD,
1815-1816

On the next day, when Damaris and the Marquis were on deck ready to disembark at Newfield, there was no thought of romance. It was a day of dark skies, scudding wind, and heavy rain. They could see little of the harbour that was to give them shelter; they knew themselves to be in port from the high, wild screaming of the gulls. Damaris could hardly make out the dock even after they had anchored and tow-ropes were being thrown to some dim shape that was the shore.

Knowing the hard labour of coming into port, Damaris had already said her farewells to her good friends, the sturdy Luce and the kind Barelle. She had left her cabin, now stripped and bare, feeling a strange sense of loss. She had longed with all her heart to escape from its confinement, but seeing the place that had been her refuge swept clean of all her belongings, with every trace of her presence cleared away, it seemed a little death; already, though her body was still present, it was as if she were gone, the life of the ship going on busily without her.

With the rain full in their faces, Damaris and the silent, grim d'Egremont were taken ashore by two men whom she didn't recognize. D'Egremont had to be half-carried; he could only move by dragging his injured leg while he stood on two crutches. He stared into the driving rain as though he would spit back at the country now before him.

Standing on the wharf, feeling strangely abandoned, Damaris looked about. She could make out nothing but the dark outline of sheds and bales of goods being carried about by some rough and loutish men. She shrank from approaching them and, giving d'Egremont as much help as she could, made for the shelter of an open wooden structure at the dock-side. If he took cold, she thought desperately, she had no idea what might happen in his weakened state. They waited helplessly, watching what d'Egremont called the wharf rats unloading goods from the *Bonne Chance*.

'Surely we will see some conveyance,' Damaris said, trying to sound cheerful. She had not been able to move her trunks from where the *Bonne Chance* sailors, apparently in some great hurry, had left them, and she was concerned for all that was left of her possessions—like a servant with her boxes, she thought ruefully.

'I don't see why,' the Marquis replied. 'Obviously, passengers are not expected off the *Bonne Chance*. An ill chance it appears to have been for us,' he added, as if determined not to lighten their troubles by any display of good humour.

As the pile of goods from the *Bonne Chance* grew high upon the wharf some vehicles did in fact appear, rough carts come to take the goods to their destination. There was discussion and argument among the new-comers, the sailors, and some men who might have been officials of the port. Then the work of loading began. Damaris picked the least rough-looking of the carters and begged for a ride for herself and the Marquis to any inn, anywhere.

But she found difficulty in procuring even such a rude conveyance. The men were working swiftly; they had come in a hurry from their business, and all were anxious to get back to their own concerns. At last a man who was directing the loading of a team of waggons heard of a lady stranded in the rain and paused to see this strange sight.

Damaris looked up at the burly fellow, roughly dressed, the rain running down his face as it was her own. She smiled suddenly at their shared predicament; he looked and then asked if he could assist her. Damaris had received but brief replies from the other men and now had a moment of thankfulness that he understood her and spoke recognizably. She had known that the language of the country was English, yet the mumbling carters had made her afraid that she could not be understood. Pointing to the Marquis and their trunks, she asked if he could convey her to the nearest inn.

He was thoughtful. Instead of answering, he rubbed his chin slowly.

'Them waggons be going over to slit-steel mill. And them be going to button manufactory down-river. This one here goes over to paper-mill—a lady like yourself has no call to go there, I reckon.'

'Anywhere that we might find shelter,' she begged.

'Ain't no room in any of they waggons,' he said, shifting his weight from one leg to another as he considered.

'Please—' she said, almost frantic for Jean-Philippe.

One of the carters came up and mumbled something to him.

'. . . for the Booth house, Mr. Cox?'

Without answering, Cox nodded. Then he looked about.

'In the waggon I drove in,' he said, and then ordered some men to help Damaris and the Marquis up into his waggon with their trunks. The Marquis refused to be carried, and the rough assistance caused him pain.

'*Sacrés paysans!*' he swore.

Cox, who might be slow in manner but apparently was quick enough in mind, turned and gazed at him with a downward pull at the corners of his mouth.

'I would be most grateful, Mr. Cox,' Damaris said swiftly.

'I can take you,' he said, mollified. 'These goods are for my master's house over to Litchfield. There is a good inn just outside. You'll be comfortable enough there.'

'Put him in the back,' he told his men, jerking his head towards the Marquis, who was bundled into the waggon while Damaris was lifted up beside Cox, who took the reins. They drove off from the wharf at what seemed to Damaris a snail's pace.

At last, the force of the rain diminished. They travelled through country lanes; the road was covered with sodden leaves. Although Damaris was wet through, it occurred to her she was not chill; the temperature at least was mild. Perhaps the Marquis would not take cold after all. His temper, she thought ruefully, should help keep him warm, if not dry. Her spirits rose just a little, and she looked about with curiosity.

There were orchards, heavy with fruit; many windfalls lay on the ground from the gale. Cows grazed in the fields—there was some look of the country-side at Angelhurst, but there were no hedgerows here and patches of grass were dun colour. 'It were a hot summer,' Cox told her, seeing the direction of her glance. 'Not much rain until this gale. Rivers flooding and the lake at Bantam washing over the road like all get-out.'

Such houses as they passed were made of wood, mostly painted white. There seemed to be no great house among them, no structure of stone or brick, and no cottages either. Some were larger, some smaller, all had their barns—but there was an absence of the familiar pattern: a cluster of cottages round a church with a spire, and one great house to a parish.

The journey was longer than she had expected. They drove for mile after mile, the road following the curves and bends of a river that Cox told her was the Housatonic, and then one called the Naugatuck. Strange names, she had said, but Cox shrugged. Indian names—there had been Indians thereabouts, but they were not much seen any more.

The rain stopped at last. As the sun rose high, Cox stopped to eat some food he had in a basket; meat, bread, and some cider made in that part of the country, he told her. He offered to share his food with the travellers; the Marquis refused with no pleasant look—the Marquis d'Egremont did not break bread with peasants.

Damaris saw that the man understood his refusal, and hastened to accept some bread and cider. She knew country people. It wouldn't do for all the villagers in these parts to bear them rancour before they had even settled at the inn. And besides, the man had given help; she had no wish to give him hurt. Already she could see what Captain Bosquet had tried to prepare her for—that in this New England arrogant manners were offensive even to lowly people.

The bread was good, coarse, and wholesome. Damaris liked its country taste, and the cider, which she drank thirstily, was extremely strong. She felt a surge of vitality and, to turn the thoughts of the now sullen driver from the Marquis, inquired about his master. As he spoke she listened half to his words, half to the voice itself. Cox looked like an English countryman, and his voice was similar, slower of speech than a townsman's, much like the slow talk of the Angelhurst farmers but without the distinctive Somerset burr.

He answered her in the indirect way she was to become accustomed to with the Yankees.

'Most land you see about here belongs to Booth. Guess they own more'n any other folks in the state. Mighty warm. And old Mrs Booth, she came from a warm family herself. Old John Booth, now, he was a sharp one. He set up manufactories all up and down the valleys. Everything from ladies' corsets to all manner of tools and contrivances is made by Booth's.'

'This tradesman, he is squire of this land?' d'Egremont asked. It was the first remark he had addressed to the waggoner.

'We have no squires in this land,' Cox said, dour. 'All born free and equal. Mr Booth, he's a gentleman, I reckon.' And he lapsed into a silence that lasted the rest of the journey.

It had not been lost upon the Marquis that the man addressed neither himself nor Damaris by their titles, and the air between the two men was not friendly. Damaris sighed a little for the future of herself and Jean-Philippe. Certainly they must leave this place as quickly as possible. The republican temper of the North would never suit the head of the house of Egremont. She had heard him talk often enough of his contempt for the men of the new United States—their wretched Revolution was the inspiration for all the fools of France, he had told her.

When they drew up at the inn, the path was awash in mud. Silently Cox carried down their trunks, with the help of a rough-looking red-haired youth, who also assisted the Marquis. Damaris thanked the driver again, addressing him punctiliously as Mr Cox, and paid him with her last golden guinea; he gazed at it with some suspicion, bit on it hard, regarded his tooth marks, and then seemed satisfied.

Their arrival at the inn brought no joy to d'Egremont. It was a plain wooden building, like the houses they had seen but a little larger than most, the entrance cramped and low, and no one to greet them. But the noise of their arrival brought a stout country-woman in a mob-cap and apron. She peered at Damaris and ex-claimed loudly.

'Glory be! What a pretty lady, and all soaking wet! Flora,'—her voice rang out clear and strong—'hot up some cider for these folks —drownded they be in the waggons. Such rainin'—we ain't seen nothing like it since spring thaw.'

The departing Cox muttered that he had brought the lady—he said nothing of the Marquis—off the *Bonne Chance*.

'The *Bonny Chant?*' the landlady said jovially. 'And a bonny young woman you've brought. A merrymaid from the sea.'

The Marquis, hanging on his crutches, looked murderous, but Damaris began to laugh. She learned later that Mrs Duckworth— for such was the landlady's name—was famous for her jumbled words. Just then the portly person, rosy-faced and direct of speech, made her feel safe and welcome.

Mrs Duckworth's eyes were wide as the Marquis gave his title and demanded rooms for himself and his wife. Less prickly than the waggoner, the landlady seemed somewhat impressed. Ordering the rough lad to follow with the Marquis, she took Damaris upstairs to the bedrooms.

'Lucky our best rooms do be empty,' she said cheerfully. 'Full we are on market day and when the stage comes by; lots of folks stop here on their way to Hartford.'

She showed Damaris two rooms in the front of the house that looked small, plain, and bare enough, but the words 'best rooms' made her hesitate. She had not one guinea left in her purse, and she had yet to arrange to sell her jewels.

'Perhaps we don't need your *best* rooms,' she said. The inn seemed clean, at least; that was a comfort.

'Oh, I couldn't put a lady like yourself up two pair of stairs where we have the ostlers sleeping. Besides, the poor gentleman could never get there.'

So the trunks were brought; the Marquis was helped into the larger of the two rooms and sat down on the bed. Mrs Duckworth bustled off and returned with her daughter, who bore two steaming mugs of cider. Flora, a big, strapping girl of about eighteen, looked as Mrs Duckworth must have looked at her age—brighteyed, rosy, and buxom.

'My Flora do be very popular with the young men,' Mrs Duckworth confided. Damaris thought that was very likely so. Flora had a saucy air, and the kerchief she wore across the front of her gown was loose and dishevelled, with a large portion of healthy brown bosom spilling over it. 'They come around with their geetars, and she do be assassinated almost every night.'

Damaris could hardly keep her countenance, and when the busy pair had gone for hot water, she allowed her laughter free rein.

'Whatever can she mean?' she said.

The Marquis grunted. He had looked with acute distaste at his room, bare except for the bed, a wooden chair, and a chest of drawers. No wardrobe was visible, and the only cover on the floor-boards was a hideous object, oval, about three feet long, which should have been a small carpet but wasn't. It seemed to have been put together from bits of rag. The only decoration was a square of canvas on the wall, with crudely embroidered words— 'A fat wife and a big barn never did any man harm.' D'Egremont looked, shuddering in disbelief.

He sighed. 'Assassinated or serenaded—I imagine there is little difference in it. The one might be preferable to the other. Madame, I seem to have brought you to an abominable hole. I apologize. Desperation will heal this wound quickly, and we will be on our way.'

Damaris bathed and changed and saw the eyes of Flora Duckworth, who was helping her, wide with admiration as she viewed her gown. Her blue *gros de Naples* was hardly suitable for such a place, but she had nothing that was really fitting, and she hoped that the sight of an elegant gown would be pleasing to the Marquis. Mrs Duckworth, practical as well as kindly, had promised to send for a physician the next day. Damaris was thankful that despite the long, jostling ride in the waggon, the dreadful pangs of sickness had not returned; the Marquis was weak and fretful, but the nausea had subsided.

Yet though she was relieved to find herself safely bestowed, she was anxious about the future. There would be bills to pay very soon, and until she sold her jewels she was penniless. But Bosquet had been right; she must wait until she could get a good price. A home would have to be purchased in New Orleans, and d'Egremont would not be satisfied with a small establishment. As to what they would do for income—she wouldn't think about that. She would do what she had done for so long now, take each trouble as it came.

Dinner was to be served in the Marquis's room—she was sure it wouldn't please him. She had better go at once and try to conciliate his wrath. Fortunately, he had had several glasses of the hot cider while complaining bitterly of the injury to his palate, and might be somewhat soothed.

And in fact when she reached his room the atmosphere was not distressing. Flora Duckworth was assisting him to sit up in bed, and Damaris heard her address him as 'my lord,' which pleased him. He was smiling when Damaris entered, with a look of mischief glimmering on his face, and for a moment he once more resembled her lover, the dashing, irresistible young Marquis d'Egremont.

37

This happy state of affairs, of course, did not last. The next morning Damaris woke, more cheerful, hopeful. She looked out of her window at clear skies, strong sunlight—she thought she had never seen a sun so bright—a green country-side, and all the lively clatter of a stage at the door. The mud was certainly deep: the ginger-haired lad was running back and forth with armfuls of straw to ease the path of the passengers.

Mrs Duckworth and Flora were busy with their influx of guests, and for a time Damaris and the Marquis were not attended. The Marquis, who had after all taken a chill from his wet ride, was fretful, miserable, and scornful in turn. He complained that she had allowed the carter to bring them to a wilderness.

When their breakfast was served at last, it was a huge meal such as farm workers might eat served with mugs of ale: thick slices of ham, parsnips, turnips, horseradish, and pickled mushrooms, which last, Mrs Duckworth told them, was 'a real delinquency in these parts.' As the food was brought, not on serving dishes but on heaped plates, d'Egremont took one look, turned his face to the wall, and groaned. He called for wine, and the boy brought a bottle of bright yellow liquid. Damaris poured it doubtfully; the Marquis took one swallow, choked, and spat.

'That be Missus's dandelion wine,' the boy said, wide-eyed. 'Made it herself fresh this summer.'

The Marquis moaned.

'*Mon Dieu,* Madame,' he said. 'We have indeed landed among barbarians. I think I would prefer to be scalped than endure this savagery.'

Damaris was hungry and she ate. The food, though not dainty, was good enough. As a child at Angelhurst she had been used to plain fare and simple service, and though the roughness here could not please, she was not mortified by it, though she did long for tea or coffee.

'Come, Jean-Philippe,' she urged. 'Try some of the meat. Imagine, please, that you are on campaign.'

This brought a grin.

'Madame, if my body-servant had ever brought me such a mess as that, he would have been first flogged and then shot. Not even an Englishman could eat this mess, and I am doubtful of a French pig.'

The doctor arrived, looking enough unlike a physician to raise d'Egremont's suspicions at once. The husky man with a weather-beaten face and rough dress might have been a small farmer. Mrs Duckworth had introduced him as 'Dr Brewster from Litchfield—rare good with brukken bones. He was army doctor over to Canada, and we be rare pleased to have him back—a reg'lar sojer of fortune,' she said, beaming, and Damaris could only hope that her judgement was clear even if her speech was muddled. The man looked sensible, and an army doctor would understand the complications of a wound.

She left the room while he made his examination. Mrs Duckworth, her stage passengers having moved on, gave Damaris the use of a small parlour on the ground floor with a cheerful fire burning. It was a room much like the one above: plain, white-washed, low-ceilinged, with simple wooden chairs and a high settle and another of the oval rugs made from twisted rag before the hearth.

Damaris stood at the window, longing to escape outside into the mild air under the sparkling sun, but she must wait for the doctor and then—how was she to make her way through the thick mud that she saw splattering the hens and geese in the farm-yard?

Dr Brewster came down looking grave and spoke plainly.

'Well, Ma'am,'—she was inwardly amused at this form of address, ignoring her title but making some gesture of respect—'I've left your husband comfortable, if not best-tempered. He's weak, he tells me from sea-sickness. That'll soon mend. But his leg, now —that last crack he made in the bone is healing. It was properly set from what I can see and tended well.'

Damaris had a moment of thankfulness for the smiling, pains-taking Barelle. 'But the wound he got on the field—'

Jean-Philippe had told the truth to this doctor, Damaris noticed. Doubtless it was safe enough to do so here.

'I don't like the look of it. It was not well attended at the beginning.'

'The field doctor,' Damaris murmured, 'and then, on the road, a physician at Ghent—they did what they could. But my husband had fever on the ship.'

'The travelling didn't help,' Dr Brewster said. 'There was putrefaction. Don't concern yourself with it too much, Ma'am; the wound has healed, but I fear the bone set badly. When your husband starts to walk he will find his leg is short—but he *will* walk,' he added, seeing her dismay, 'well enough, when he is used to it. But he will limp; yes, Ma'am, he will limp.'

Damaris was aghast. She knew Jean-Philippe well enough to know that for him to be crippled would be intolerable. The doctor saw her sudden pallor.

'Be of good cheer, Ma'am,' he said. Underneath his gruffness she saw that he was kind. 'There's many a man never risen from the battlefield, and many of those that have would be glad to have the use of their legs, never mind the loss of an inch or two. We have Jack Steel farming with the use of one arm since Plattsburgh, and Tom Butler cleared his land before you were born after losing an eye and a foot up in Quebec with Benedict Arnold on that wild goose chase.'

Benedict Arnold and Quebec meant little to Damaris, but she understood the doctor. Her heart was not much lightened; she could not see d'Egremont turning farmer—at that moment she could not see any future for her once gay lover. He never spoke of the future himself, except to wonder if any lands and monies would be restored to certain émigrés by Louis *l'Impossible,* or to predict that 'the English puppet' would not keep his throne. Sometimes he spoke wildly of Napoleon returning once again, but in his sober moments he knew that dream was gone forever.

'I have not told your husband,' the doctor added. 'It is better to wait until his general health is restored. Be sure he keeps his weight off the injured leg, give him Mrs Duckworth's good food, and let him rest.'

Damaris felt a quick, great relief that d'Egremont had not yet learned his fate, and then abused herself for cowardice. But just now she had much to do to arrange for their new life. In spite of Captain Bosquet's warning, some jewel must be sold at once.

'Thank you, Doctor,' she said gently. 'You—you will send your account to me here at this inn, if you please.'

He looked at her keenly from under his grey, shaggy eyebrows.

'It is not the custom here to send in accounts. But I understand you have just arrived and must settle your affairs. I will come this day week to see the patient, and you can pay me then.'

He was gone, leaving Damaris to wonder how she would do that. When this accursed mud had dried, she could walk into the village. There might be some tradesmen there to take some of her trinkets, enough to get some money for her immediate needs and to hire horses to travel to some larger town.

She was about to return to the Marquis when Mrs Duckworth entered in a great state of bustle.

'Doctor, he do say your husband will do well,' she said, beaming. 'And Lord, the ladies of Litchfield have come to call on you. Cox the carter, he must have told over by Booth's that you was come, and word be spread like greasy lightning all over village. Bless me if everyone of the ladies ain't come; couldn't wait for meetin' Sunday. Mrs Hatch and her daughter, Mrs Buell, Mrs Wadsworth, Mrs Welch, and Mrs Lord—even the temperance ladies that have never set foot across my threshing-hold.'

She had the look of a farm wife who had won first prize at the fair for a fat goose, Damaris thought, amused, and then wondered about these ladies. She did not need to wonder long, however. Apparently not used to waiting, they followed hard on Mrs Duckworth's heels. Suddenly the room seemed tiny, filled with their bulky forms and strong voices as they advanced with determination on the foreign lady.

Damaris had only time to whisper to Mrs Duckworth, 'But M'sieur le Marquis—' and Mrs Duckworth to assure her, 'Now don't worrit, my Flora she be doing for the gentleman,' before she found herself addressed, in clumsy but recognizable French, by a deep-voiced matron.

The republican fervour of the men of New England, Damaris had already observed, didn't apply equally to the women. This stern and terrifying dame, black of brow, sallow-skinned, with dark whiskers above thin lips, referred to 'M'sieur le Marquis' and addressed Damaris as Madame. She introduced herself as Mrs Hatch, apparently thinking Mrs Duckworth an improper person to make the introduction, and her daughter, who looked very much like her but without the whiskers, as Verity. The other ladies, ranging from stout to buxom, some of whom were also tall and broad, were introduced, and as Mrs Duckworth had failed to persuade the ladies to move into the larger tap-room, the muddy-footed, red-haired boy was sent scurrying for chairs.

Damaris was diverted by the scrutiny with which she was being studied. For lack of anything more suited to her simple surroundings, she had that morning put on a dress that had been in the forefront of fashion when she had run off from Town, a promenade gown in light blue crêped gauze, with gathered sleeves and a high-arched collar. Her hair was simply done, for on the ship she had tired of the front curls considered so essential by the fashionables and had let her hair grow. Now she wore it smoothly brushed with the ends turned up in a Psyche knot. Her little low-heeled slippers were of Denmark satin, and though she wore no jewels, all unknowing she presented the assembled ladies with a vision of another world.

The black-browed lady was persevering in her attempts at French, when Mrs Duckworth, who had been collecting their cloaks, much amused, informed her loudly that 'Madam Markiss' was English.

'You don't need to trouble your tongue, Beulah. Don't pervert yourself on this lady's account.' And she banged the door behind her.

The room looked as though a flock of pigeons had descended on it. The ladies were nearly all in grey, or light brown, and white; their rather old-fashioned gowns were of silk too heavy for the style in which they were cut, close to the body and high in the waist, with large starched muslin fronts. The dark and glowering Beulah Hatch stood out as the leader of the flock, for she dressed in deep puce, much hung about with jet, and wore a large hair-brooch on her bosom—the hair of her dear departed, Damaris guessed. No one would have thought that the dignified, cool, and composed young Marquise, who had even the redoubtable Mrs Hatch stumbling over her words, was repressing a quite insane and totally reprehensible desire to giggle.

The daughter, Verity, who was dutifully arranging a light shaw about her mother's shoulders, looked different from the rest in a white gown that was too young for her—a gingham that Betty might have worn at Angelhurst. Surely she was well over twenty, Damaris thought. The ladies were asking questions about her journey, obviously longing to know what chance had brought the noble couple to this quiet country place but holding back from asking directly.

Between their muslin-puffed bosoms and their suppressed curiosity, Damaris had the feeling that these good ladies were about to burst. Accidentally her gaze met that of Verity, still standing over her mother, and for a moment she thought she saw in Verity's dull, tired-looking brown eyes a glimmer of sympathetic understanding—but then it was gone.

'Verity, you are tumbling me,' Mrs Hatch complained. 'Light, child, somewhere, for goodness' sakes.'

There were no more chairs. Verity, thus dismissed, retreated to the window. In her twenties and on the shelf, Damaris thought; such a state seemed as uncomfortable here as it was in England. Poor Verity. But she had to find answers for the ladies and wondered what taradiddle she was to serve up. The truth, she decided, would probably do as well as anything—these Americans, after all, were no lovers of England. The truth—except, of course, for the Countess of Malfrey. She was dead and would have to remain buried. Suddenly she had a wrenching recollection of little Griselda, but she put it firmly from her mind. Lady Griselda would be cared for by her great-aunt. She, Damaris, had lost the right to think of her—a disgraced mother was no inheritance.

'And your husband, I hear, is ill,' Mrs Hatch said, persevering.

'He was wounded at Waterloo,' Damaris replied in her low, clear voice, and watched the ladies thrill with excitement. 'He was fighting for the Emperor, and so we had to leave when the battle was lost.'

'We have only just heard the news,' Mrs Hatch said, nodding portentously.

'We are on our way to New Orleans,' Damaris continued, 'but my husband needs rest before we can go on.'

This caused a buzzing among her visitors, with little cries of sympathy and expressions of sorrow. The sympathy, she was to learn later, was real. New Englanders understood the position of a wife with a husband on one side of a battle and her own kin on the other; not *all* Americans had favoured the Revolutionary War, and in the war against England just ended, Connecticut had stood out sturdily. 'Madison's war' they called it, and there had been guarded talk of a separate peace.

If Damaris didn't yet know their reasons, she felt the warmth of the sympathy. Looking beyond their costumes and their curiosity, she saw a group of women, sensible, practical, mostly kind, genuinely desirous of welcoming a stranger. Then the boy came in, staggering under a pile of goods he had brought from the ladies' various conveyances.

The ladies must have been afraid that Mrs Duckworth would starve her, Damaris thought, because they had brought gifts of fruit and jams, honey from their own bees, cakes, and bottles of home-made wine. She thanked them warmly, hoping that Mrs Duckworth would not be roused to fury by these slurs upon her larder, and promised to visit them all as soon as the Marquis was well enough to be left alone. They offered her the use of their conveyances, and she also got the useful information that there was a light waggon for hire in the village when necessary.

Mrs Hatch announced firmly that she would send her carriage for Damaris to go to meeting on Sunday—unless, she added with elephantine delicacy, the Marquise was of the Romish persuasion. Damaris informed them gravely that of course her husband was a Catholic but she herself was a Protestant. The ladies beamed. Damaris felt she had been taken into the fold.

As the visitors were leaving, Verity slipped out ahead of them and came back when the room was clear. Rather shyly, she presented Damaris with a neatly-wrapped parcel. She opened it at once, over Verity's protests, and found two cushions with tapestry covers neatly embroidered in petit-point in a pattern of birds and flowers.

She thanked her with genuine pleasure.

'Oh, please,' Verity said, not exactly shy, Damaris thought, but with a certain modesty. The girl's colour rose, and it occurred to Damaris that though Verity looked so much like her mother that side by side they both looked plain, seen alone her face was not unhandsome.

'I was making these for Christmas,' Verity explained, 'and I had some extra ones by me. I thought they might be welcome—the settles and chairs here are not too comfortable for a lady.'

It was an attention truly thoughtful, and Damaris was touched. Verity slipped away quietly, and Damaris, surrounded by her gifts, for the first time thought she might find real friends in this place. It was not just a stop on her way to a future home, a stage-coach inn to be forgotten before the next, but a complete if small society, as real as that of Angelhurst or Heron and much more friendly to strangers.

Mrs Duckworth came bustling back, her face alight with all the pleasure of unusual incident and cheerful gossip.

'Lands, poor Miss Verity got her hem in the mud, and how Beulah is scolding!'

She picked up the jars and parcels of food with composure, not at all annoyed, to Damaris's relief.

'Dora Buell has brought you her apple butter—I'll send that up with your breakfast. A good receipt—but never can I get it out of her. And Mrs Lord's blackberry wine; that will be a nice change for your good man, my dear, when he gets tired of my dandelion—though I do say it's the best dandelion wine that ever was drunk at the congregation's roast-beef supper.'

Damaris, who had drunk some of the wine so that Mrs Duckworth's feelings might not be hurt, voiced her appreciation gravely, visualizing for a fleeting moment the face of her friend the Beau if he could have watched and heard her.

Mrs Duckworth was gratified.

'Beulah Hatch would like my receipt, but she'll never have it. She is too high and mighty and fond of running everything and everybody. Her husband left her rich and mine left me poor; hers died and mine ran off, a poor thing as ever was, so she thinks herself too fine for me, for all we were girls together and I was a sight more handsome, as anyone can tell you. Like my girl Flora, I had all the swines after me.'

Damaris was exceedingly diverted.

'And Mrs Hatch has Verity.'

'Poor girl,' Mrs Duckworth said, and shrugged. 'Beulah can't forgive her for not marrying, and that's the truth. It's no credit to a mother to have an old-maid daughter, but Verity, such a good girl in everything, she turned rare obstinate. When she refused Dr Brewster—he has a good farm besides his doctoring—oh, just a year or two ago, I thought Beulah fit to be tied.'

This was a new light on Verity.

'Miss Hatch had offers?' she said, thinking at the same time that gossip in this foreign place was not so different from that of London and Brighton.

'My, yes,' Mrs Duckworth replied, poking the fire vigorously. 'She looks right plain now, but when she had her bloom she was a fine girl. And as good a housekeeper as you'd find. Beulah don't need to keep a servant with her in the house but for the Hatch pride. And, of course, all the land and money goes to Verity when Beulah dies, so the men had their eye on her when she got her growth. But if you ask me,' she went on confidentially, 'I think she always had her eye on Howard Booth, and if she can't have him she'll take no one.'

Damaris smiled at the familiar tale, though in her experience girls did take someone. Their families saw to that, even if the families had to be severe and very stern to get their consent—just like Mrs Hatch, in fact.

'Is that the Mr Booth who owned the waggon I came in?' she asked.

'Oh, yes, he owns that and most everything around here you can think of—save only what the Hatches own. The Booths is clever, hard-working folk, and they be the biggest people in these parts. In your country, I dessay, they would be lords of the manner born. Though Mr Howard, he be not much like a Booth—leastways when he was young. Beulah Hatch thought little of him then, I can tell you.'

'Was he wild?' Damaris asked.

She placed one of her cushions on her seat and the other at her side and found them comforting. After all her troubles, she reflected—indeed, while she was still engrossed in them—she would not have expected that she would be enjoying a cheerful gossip.

Mrs Duckworth swept all the parcels into her capacious apron and prepared to depart.

'Well, Madam Markiss, I wouldn't say wild exactly.' Her tone had become guarded, and Damaris fancied her reluctant to speak further. 'But I will say, whatever the Hatches thought, it wasn't them that stopped a marriage. Mr Howard, he never looked to Miss Verity either before or since.'

Before or since what, Damaris wondered, intrigued by this rural romance. But Mrs Duckworth was not prepared to say and left the little parlour with a clatter of parcels and the thump of her heavy-soled shoes on the wooden floor.

'Rufe, Rufe.' Damaris heard her call the ginger-topped boy and smiled, and then she went up to d'Egremont. Fretfully he asked where she had been for half the day, leaving him to the tender mercies of knaves and fools. Soon Flora came, bringing their dinner, which was a salted cod. D'Egremont cursed and flung his plate aside; then, to Damaris's dismay, he produced a bottle of brandy, a local drink made from apple cider, that he had had Flora bring to him. He swore it was foul and filthy stuff, fit only for the peasants of the district, but he drank the bottle, and the rest of the day he spent half-sleeping, half-waking, cursing the fate that let him live after the battle, until darkness fell and Damaris went away to her bed, though not to sleep.

Damaris's little pleasure in her new surroundings was quickly swallowed up in her anxiety about d'Egremont. She had begun to enjoy the fine weather that had dried up the mud and allowed her to walk into the village; she was charmed by the houses of Litchfield, unexpectedly gracious and dignified in their white weatherboard, many of them what she still thought of as gentlemen's residences, though pigs and geese ran free in the road.

She had expected that once Jean-Philippe had recovered from the effects of his sea-sickness he would begin to improve, and that soon they would move on. Not that she was in a hurry to leave this place, but New Orleans would certainly be a more suitable haven for the Marquis d'Egremont. He had never lived in the country and had always claimed that English country life was intolerable—and to him the country had meant Oatlands, where his hostess was the Duchess of York and the Beau himself found elegance sufficient for his taste.

But he hardly ate or left his room, even when the doctor told him it was safe enough for him to walk as long as his leg was splinted and he used his crutch.

'I will not appear before these wretches hobbling,' he said with a scowl, but Damaris had to forgive him when she saw the pain and misery etched on his brow and round his mouth, where so short a time before there had been only the creases of an impudent smile.

Sometimes her heart ached for that Jean-Philippe as though he were a different man, someone left behind with her children, Lady Gratton, Betty—all that she had loved. Then she would scold herself. It was a poor love that could not survive the fretfulness of illness. She had given up so much for this love—could she really be so shallow? Of course her love was still there, she told herself, but of necessity the love of a mistress had had to turn to that of a fond nurse. When Jean-Philippe was strong again, they would be as they had been. Yet one late afternoon when, warmed by brandy, he drew her to him, murmuring with a faint smile, '*L'heure bleue,* Madame,' his hands possessive on her body, she drew back instinctively, without thought, and was glad to have her confusion covered by the loud knock and entrance of Flora Duckworth, bearing two more platefuls of the hated cod.

She hoped, she believed, that Jean-Philippe had thought her drawing back the result of Flora's approach. It would be intolerable to hurt him. Fortunately, he had been so furious at the girl's ill-timed arrival and the crudity of the meal that he seemed to forget the incident itself. Weary from his continued ill-temper, she could still understand it.

She had a sudden recollection of their last dinner together in Town before their world had ended. It had been at Carlton House, where the Regent had been entertaining some of the dignitaries from the stalemated congress at Vienna. She saw again the elegance of the great dining-room at Carlton House, the light of a hundred candles gleaming on vermeil, the footmen in their powdered wigs serving a dinner that she, herself a noted hostess, must admire.

The gold and silver tureens held eighteen different kinds of soup; there were ten different varieties of fish and what seemed to be fifty different sorts of entremets. Then had followed roast larded plover, *poulets à la reine,* stuffed red partridges, pullets with water-cress, pheasant garnished with ortolan, woodcock, a dozen or more roasts, a dozen dishes of sweet soufflés filled with different fruits and chocolate, Parmesan fondue, jellied fruits, and a dessert that was a great architectural triumph—the Prater of Vienna in pastry with trees of marzipan and angelica. The champagne had flowed, Jean-Philippe had remarked, like the fountains of Versailles. How happy he had been that night! Now she understood. His wild, mad dream was at the point, he thought, of being realized, all his rainbow-coloured fantasies were taking on a solidity and strength—but only the solidity of the pastry Prater, so soon to be shattered to bits like the dessert on its dish.

She could understand so well the depths of his disappointment, aggravated by his wound and weakness, but as week followed week, it was terrifying to see no improvement, no interest in his present life, no concern for the future. New Orleans had become so distant a goal that he no longer cared to reach it. His life was bounded by his bed, his room, and his bottle—good French brandy, once he had found he could make arrangements with Mrs Duckworth to get it. He was reliving his life on the ship.

Damaris had obtained dollars by selling a few of her trinkets in the village, though it hurt her to part with some—a locket of gold and seed pearls left to her by her mother, ruby earrings that had belonged to her Mayne grandmother. Bosquet was right; she had received terrifying little, only enough to pay her bills at the inn for a few weeks and the fees to Dr Brewster, who still attended the Marquis although his face grew long at the lack of progress in his patient. She knew she must go to Hartford, the nearest town of some size, and sell one of her big pieces, but while d'Egremont was confined to his room he begged her not to leave him for more than a few hours at a time.

'*Mon Dieu,* but I am bored,' he grumbled. 'I think it will kill me at last—I beg your pardon, Madame,' he said, and grimaced. 'It is no reflection on your charm—but how I loathe this America!'

Damaris tried to point out that as yet he had seen nothing of it, but he retorted that he had no wish to see it. Perhaps he was right, she thought at times. He was a man of the old world; he would never accept the new. Yet all her youthful courage protested that he was not giving it a fair chance.

'New Orleans will be so much more to your taste,' she said persuasively. 'Marie de Langcourt knows people there, and she told me the life was very gay and civilized.'

Madame la Duchesse had added that it was more fashionable than Paris under the parvenu Bonaparte, but Damaris kept that to herself.

'Set in a swamp—a paradise for mosquitoes,' d'Egremont said with a grimace. 'Oh, we will go there. What else?' He shrugged. 'When this accursed leg heals.'

Damaris said nothing more that day. Dr Brewster had told her that the crack in the bone was healed, and he had explained that to the Marquis. He could walk now—as well as he would ever be able to walk—and the prolonged stay in his room could only weaken him. She must get her husband up and out, the doctor said bluntly, or he would ruin his health with drink. Damaris knew Jean-Philippe well enough to suspect that he had already tried to stand without his crutches and knew himself to be crippled. Perhaps he had suspected all along; he had walked to Bosquet's cabin that night on the ship—it was not only the wet and slimy deck that had caused his tumble. He would not wish her, nor anyone else, to see him as a cripple.

She sat in her own room that night and by the light of her single candle tried to take stock of their position. If d'Egremont was well enough to travel, they should move on. If they were to begin a new life in Louisiana, it was better to do it sooner than later. Once she sold her jewels, the money must go to the purchase of their house and a plantation. Yet she understood too well the pride that made him unable, for a time, to face this future. And in truth, she herself had a reluctance to leave this place. She felt fear of travelling through this unknown land with only a sick man at her side. Her experience at the hands of the brutal Le Gros had left her feeling weak and vulnerable in a way that the protected English-woman had never known. Here she felt safe, and the thought of safety brought a grateful warmth.

D'Egremont could never understand, but Damaris, who had been so rudely torn away from her home and everything familiar, had already begun to put down roots, tiny and fragile as yet, in this new place. The ladies had been kind. She had gone with them to church, which was hardly a church at all but a plain white wooden building like the rest, very neat and clean, with Verity Hatch at the organ, a service curiously informal—much like the Methodists at home, she thought, with a sigh and a smile for poor Betty and her Methodist lover Jem. The Litchfield minister thundered of hell-fire and torment but after the service joined the ladies in a sort of picnic in an adjoining room—each lady brought a dish, and Damaris was invited, if she could get a house of her own, to contribute also.

She had paid calls upon the ladies in their homes, so like English country houses and yet curiously unlike. The furniture was much like English country furniture, but there were no rugs, few heavy curtains, no comfort of a stuffed sofa. It was as though they had taken English rooms and stripped them almost bare. Here one saw clearly that these people were descended from the Puritans; the Regency, with all its follies and splendour, had no touch of influence in Litchfield.

The ladies had been prepared to extend their kindness to Jean-Philippe. Damaris had wondered how these fiercely Protestant people would accept a Catholic, but she found that now a certain tolerance existed, at least to French Catholics—French regiments had come to help here in the Revolution, and the suspicious folk of New England had found that they did not, after all, have hooves and horns.

Jean-Philippe would have none of them. One day Verity Hatch had brought a bouquet to brighten their rooms, a few of the last rare autumn flowers, yellow and gold, with twisted leaves and stalks dried and carefully preserved. Damaris, pleased, had taken her to Jean-Philippe's room so that he could thank their benefactor, but he had been surly and afterwards begged her not to bring him any more women who looked like that.

'It is bad enough to be here at all, in this place where the women look as if they could draw the plough instead of the horses. Pray do not remind me of it, Madame.'

Somehow she must coax Jean-Philippe from his room and secure some return of his health and spirits before they moved again. Perhaps, she thought, she should look for a little house—it would be cheaper than living at the inn. If only she could do something to earn a little money, she thought, so that she could husband their resources. But what could she do? Mrs Duckworth and Flora, as well as young Rufe, often were run off their feet. Perhaps she could help. As Damaris St Cloud, although she had not worked about the house, she had been familiar enough with what the servants had done. The next day she asked Mrs Duckworth if she could work to pay part of their bill for lodging, but that lady only laughed.

'Glory be, Madam Markiss, I can't see you a clearin' up of the spittoons or muckin' out the pigs. Tain't fittin' for a lady of your quantity,' she said, beaming. 'Don't 'ee fret, your man, he'll soon be up and doing. My Flora tells me he has been standing on his legs when you weren't by. He be a little lame-like, and poor man is shy for you to see it. But he'll get over that, don't bother your pretty little head.'

So her guess had been right. D'Egremont knew his condition—it would take him time to accept it. Mrs Duckworth saw that clearly enough. But she was wrong, Damaris thought rebelliously, to say that she, Damaris, could do nothing. She was no fine lady here. It would not injure her pride to be useful. Her mind was made up; she would show Mrs Duckworth what she could do. She would need to. D'Egremont might leave his room, but as for what he would do, Damaris could not imagine. It would not be anything that would pay their reckoning, of that she was sure.

The next morning she was up while the sky was yet dark. Her

fire had not been lit, nor did she have hot water, but she somehow made her toilet and looked through her gowns—they were kept in a cupboard, for there was no wardrobe here—to find something for her purpose. Of course, there was nothing. The plainest-looking gown that came to hand was of the finest Indian mull muslin, a fragile, delicate garment that was worn over a flesh-coloured chemise. The little satin slippers that completed the costume were absurd for her purpose—she must buy some of the stout shoes, in leather and prunella, that these Litchfield matrons wore. But this would have to do for now.

She crept down the back stairs, unwilling to be discovered before she had completed the task she set herself. Someone was already stirring in the kitchen; she must make haste. Very quietly she left through the back door into the farm-yard, the air striking disagreeably chill. She should have brought a shawl—but there was no going back now. Besides, the barn would be warm enough.

Thank heavens it had been dry and there was no mud. She pushed open the barn door and entered, almost reeling back again at the close and fetid air. The cows moaned restlessly, awaiting the attention of Rufe or Flora Duckworth. She had often been woken by their bellowing in the morning—the young people enjoyed a few extra stolen moments in their warm beds. Leaving the door a little ajar to clear the air, she found the lamp and lit it and discovered the milking pail. Then she regarded with trepidation the large beasts moaning in their stalls.

As a girl she had milked the cows at Angelhurst with the help of Jem the cowman. She did not remember this—what she could only call stink—in the Angelhurst barn, and the cows that she recalled had a cleaner, smoother, more gentle look, not like these large rough-coated animals with tails aswitch about their none-too-clean hindquarters. Perhaps it was the enchanting distance of memory that made the Angelhurst dairy so neat and shining in her mind, or perhaps cow-keeping was different in the colonies. Whatever the difference was, she had decided to do the milking that morning, and she would do it. Mrs Duckworth must be made to see that 'Madam Markiss' could be a useful woman.

Taking the milking stool, she went grimly about her work. If she had forgotten exactly how to perform the task, her hands remembered, and the large clumsy cow, the first in the row, was pleased with her labour, giving a rich flood of milk and trying to lick her with its enormous tongue.

Damaris moved on to the next with a renewal of confidence, but there were flies in the barn; the cow's tail flicked suddenly at a specially irritating insect, caught Damaris across her cheek, and she almost dropped the pail.

'Oh, bother,' she said crossly, and after the sound of her English voice, so gently bred, strange in that crude and draughty barn, there came a laugh: deep, male, and very much amused. She looked up to see a man in the doorway, with the glimmer of pre-dawn light just behind him. He was leaning casually against the door-jamb, a tall, spare figure with his hands in his breeches pockets, regarding her casually as though he had all the time in the world. The light of the lamp glimmered on the face under the broad-brimmed hat, a lean, craggy face with the eyes narrowed and the lips twisted up in laughter.

'Morning, Ma'am,' he said. 'I heard a noise and I thought there must be thieves in the barn. But I see Mrs Duckworth has a new milkmaid.'

The cow, impatient at the pause in Damaris's work, flicked her tail in the milk pail, sending a shower over her dress, and the man laughed again.

'Might I suggest, Ma'am, that that there rig you're wearing don't do for the Duckworth barn.'

Damaris's chin went up, but her hands resumed their work deftly. A restless cow might be a problem to her, but a quizzing man was not. This man, although he was dressed soberly like the other gentlemen of Litchfield, was very different from those stout husbands and fathers. He had an air that would have pleased the Beau—but there was a strong masculinity about his person that no dandy ever achieved. She fancied that his eyes were grey—and was very conscious of his gaze on her bare arms and throat.

Well, she had been quizzed by the greatest teasers of the *ton;* she would not be overcome by a countryman in the wilderness. She went on composedly, pleased at her neatness, with the steady stream of milk making a respectable quantity in her milking pail.

'La, sir,' she replied as she might have done at Almack's, 'the modes have changed vastly in the last year—no gentleman *now* can be an authority on female dress.'

His shoulders shook with laughter.

'I would've guessed that we were being honoured by the Queen Marie Antoinette if that poor lady had not lost her head from her pretty shoulders,' he said with mock gravity. 'Well, since the stock is safe and you need no help, I will be off about my business. Your servant, Ma'am.'

He removed his hat and clasped it to his breast, bowed low, and departed.

Damaris, in spite of the foul air and rough beasts, found herself suddenly light-hearted. She was milking well; the laughing stranger had seen and admired her skill—and it had been fun, after so many weary months, to indulge in a little raillery. She was humming to herself when Mrs Duckworth, red and sweating from her fire, burst in through the door.

'Lands, Madam Markiss, you here a-milking! If that don't beat all. I've been shaking and shaking Flora, thinking the animals fit to bust. Flora, she was up late again last night with her swines, and it don't do for an innkeeper's daughter. Better she be married than courting and lying abed all morning, I say. But when I heard you was here and milking fit to beat the band I could've jumped in the pan and fried myself. Think of your fine dress! But Lord, you do right well!' she said admiringly.

Damaris was more pleased than she had been since—when? she wondered. Her success on her first Season had been a more diffuse, less sharp delight. Suddenly she remembered her joy when she was fourteen and her masters had gone to Lady Gratton with great praise of her accomplishments, saying that few young women of twenty could match her in knowledge and deportment. Lady Gratton had given her a word or two of praise, very rare. 'Well done, Niece.'

She had to laugh at herself. What would her friends think, she conjectured, if they knew the Cool Countess of Malfrey was flushed with delight at being praised by an innkeeper as she sat at the side of a cow? Yet she was delighted, and she thought Mrs Duckworth's praise well worth obtaining.

'Do come out of the muck, Madam Markiss,' Mrs Duckworth said. 'I'll finish with they beasts.'

'I'm almost done,' Damaris said. 'Mrs Duckworth, please call me Damaris. I am in the United States now, and you have no titles here.'

In the first light she could see Mrs Duckworth's flushed face grow even redder with pleasure.

'That's right friendly,' she said. 'Well, wait till Beulah Hatch hears me call a lady markiss by her given name. She will turn pea-green.' She sighed in happiness. 'But you don't need to do farm chores to earn your keep, Madam Damaris.' Her tongue shied at the use of the Christian name alone. 'There's things more fittin' for a lady like you. Mr Howard, he was just a-saying so.'

'Mr Howard?'

'Mr Booth. Mr Howard, I always thinks of him; I knowed his father well. He just come back from meetin' over to Hartford. Lord, he had heard about you all the way over there, and he just said to me he thought to find a lady much too fine for Litchfield, and just look how he did find 'ee. And you with milk all over that good gown.'

She chuckled and chattered on, her good-natured voice prattling endlessly, but Damaris's attention was caught by her last words. So that smiling, lounging, attractive stranger with appreciation in his glance and a joke on his lips—that was Howard Booth, the great gentleman of these parts. She found she thought more of this place than ever before, since it had produced such a man. He seemed very much a man, she thought, this Howard Booth.

CHAPTER

39

Despite her success, the milking was not resumed. Mrs Duckworth had confided in her favourite, Howard Booth, about the problems of the young and beautiful Marquise. Booth called on Damaris formally, soon after their first meeting, in the small parlour, his tall, bony person dominating the room though his head had to bob down to miss the beams.

Damaris knew without much thought that he found her attractive, without realizing how greatly he was struck by her cool, poised, blue-eyed English beauty. He had heard of the elegant Marquise while he was in Hartford, but nothing had prepared him for the young, fragile-looking girl with the courage of a pioneer and a dignity that could put away the formal trappings of honour while keeping all its substance.

A plain-spoken man, he came at once to the point. Mrs Duckworth had told him that the Marquise needed to sell some jewels. He was often in Hartford on business and political matters—and would be willing to undertake the errand for her. Damaris looked at the steady eyes in his lean, tanned face and there and then gave him her lasting trust and confidence. She fetched her jewel case, and together they looked over the gifts from the Earl of Malfrey to see what might be most suitably sold in the capital of the New England state.

Booth stroked his chin reflectively.

'These pieces are a set and should be kept together, Ma'am. And I don't reckon,' he said wryly, 'there will be much call in Hartford for this.'

He was looking at her diamond and sapphire tiara.

'Don't think our Hartford ladies have much chance to be wearing crowns. Not that some of 'em wouldn't like to, I'll be bound.'

He gave her his easy grin that made their differences nothing, and Damaris was struck afresh by the kindness of these people to an English noblewoman, with whose country they had been at war only a year ago.

'Suppose I take these ear-bobs,' he suggested, taking the huge dark sapphires surrounded by diamonds that had provided so pretty a sparkle in Damaris's ears at many a great ball. 'They'll be easy to sell. With the peace there are a lot of well-to-do folk in the capital, and the women like to fix themselves up.'

Damaris had a pang of very feminine regret at the thought of her favourite earrings on a sturdy Connecticut matron, but she bade herself firmly not to be foolish. Booth folded them up carefully and put them in his watch-pocket; she felt certain, rather abashed, that he had noticed her regret. He was smiling, but the smile was tender, and he stroked his chin thoughtfully, his gaze lingering upon her, before he took his leave.

She followed him to the door of the inn and watched him walk away with his long, loping stride, mount his horse lightly, and then turn back, waving his hand in farewell. The sun was behind him, and he rode off in a blaze of light in that clear Connecticut autumn weather. The sky was high, without a cloud, azure; the air invigorating, winy. She felt a certain lightness of spirit, almost happiness, but then she had to turn from the door to go and tell the Marquis what she had arranged.

It might cheer him to know that they had some money forthcoming. He had learned from the loose-tongued Flora about her attempt in the barn, and she had had to listen to much sarcasm as a result—Madame Milkmaid, and *la belle du Petit Trianon,* referring to the late queen's game *au Petit Trianon,* where she had pretended to be a dairymaid. Howard Booth had also teased her about poor Marie Antoinette—but with a difference! Jean-Philippe's taunts were meant to sting. He had also learned that Mrs Duckworth had offered to pay Damaris for some trouble she had taken with Flora.

'You are to be a governess, Madame?' he asked with contempt.

Damaris had felt sorry for the girl. She was pretty in a coarse way, good-natured, but obviously too brash, uneducated, and vulgar, giving the impression of being a little simple-minded. She would never, as she was, make a good match for herself in the prudent, sober society of Litchfield. Her 'swines' were apt to be too gallant, and Damaris had, in the time when she was confined to the inn, endeavoured to teach a little deportment and had given some lessons in speech and writing to the girl, whom she found to be slow but willing enough to learn. The Marquis had scoffed at her efforts and spoken of silk purses and sows' ears, but she had not been deflected from her purpose.

'Madame de Maintenon was a governess,' she said mildly. 'Yet she became wife to Louis XIV.'

D'Egremont smiled, mollified for a moment.

'A blue-stocking,' he said, teasing with more lightness. 'My own dear lady a *bas bleu.*'

D' Egremont was sitting in a chair by the window, his injured leg stretched out in front of him. She knew he had been walking, and she knew he was aware of his limp, but it was never mentioned between them. He never allowed her to see him walk, and when he wanted to be up and about she left his room. It occurred to her that it was just as well she had come to tell him of her meeting with Booth: he had been watching, obviously, from his window.

She explained the business and added that she thought Booth both kind and fair.

'We can only trust you are right,' d'Egremont said, scowling. 'You are very free, Madame, with your jewels. I hope that this country fellow, who rides a horse too good for him, has some idea of the value of such gems and that he proves honest. As for kindness—it was not kindness that I saw in his gaze at you. He should be flogged for that look, as that wretch Le Gros was flogged.'

She shuddered at the recollection. For Jean-Philippe, she was sure, the propinquity of the two ideas—the admiring look and the flogging of Le Gros—was fortuitous. He could not know that the crimes for which Le Gros had been punished had begun with an assault upon her person. But she loathed the reminder and felt an unreasonable impatience with his ideas of Howard Booth.

D'Egremont, she believed, had been shut up too long. He was well enough to move about, strong enough to resume some kind of life. But he did nothing. She noticed uneasily that he had made no more advances to her. He was a proud man; her withdrawal had not passed unnoticed. And there was another problem. Flora Duckworth had been taking an unconscionably long time in her attendance on the Marquis.

It was far from unknown in the society in which she had lived for gentlemen to look upon female servants as persons existing for their comfort and convenience. The Earl was not such a man, she thought now with respect. At Heron and at Malfrey House the maidservants had worked unmolested. To be fondled and caressed was considered no part of their domestic duties, and no male guest had the right of admission to their rooms. The Marquis, pursued all his life by the most beautiful women of French and English society, would have had no dealings with servant girls, but that was a matter of taste and not because of any moral restraint. He had told her one afternoon in the secret room at the d'Egremont house while they were resting from their mutual passion that neither Louis XIV nor Louis XV thought it amiss to jump into bed with one of their mistress's attendants, should the mistress not be immediately available.

'But of course, even the maids were women of some fashion, if not of blood,' he had said, grinning, and had asked her with a serious face if she could spare him the grim-faced Chambers. It had been a great joke then, but now she wondered what was happening between him and Flora. She had seen the girl coming from his room adjusting the muslin top of her dress. It was then she had begun instructing Flora in the female arts—she hoped it would serve to keep her out of the Marquis's way—and from then on, whenever she could, she took his meals up herself.

'I could have taken the jewels for you,' the Marquis said abruptly. 'I have arranged to hire some ancient and no doubt decrepit carriage together with two nags so that I can go about this wilderness. If you will excuse me, chère Madame, I will leave you now, for I see it below in readiness.'

D'Egremont took his stick and crutch and left the room as quickly as he could, but the polished floors were treacherous, and he slipped and nearly fell. Damaris, before she could think, had reached out to steady him, and when she saw his face, it was stone-like. He looked at her with an aversion that took her back in time to her honeymoon at Great Heron. After he had banged his way out and clattered down the steps, shouting for Rufe to attend him, she sat on the one chair in the room with her hands covering her face, shivering uncontrollably. She knew that it meant nothing —nothing, that is, to do with his real feeling for herself—but his pride was too strong for him to be easy about a woman seeing him, Jean-Philippe, Marquis d'Egremont, brought low.

From that day on, she saw little of Jean-Philippe. He would rise late, sometimes take breakfast but often not, and then go out in the hired carriage, which looked like a battered, crudely-made curricle or whisky, now reserved for his use. Where he went she did not know, but he would return late at night or the next day, often drunk, sometimes penniless, sometimes with his pockets full of dollars.

Dr Brewster told her plainly that if the Marquis continued these habits he would never fully recover his health. It was Mrs Duckworth who discovered that d'Egremont was going to inns in nearby villages, spending his days drinking and gambling with any companion he could find.

'Poor gentleman, he do feel it,' she said to Damaris, but whether she meant the crippling injury to his leg or the loss of his possessions and country, Damaris was not sure. 'Dick, the ostler over to the inn in Bradleyville, he says the gentleman do like to talk of wars and politics and such. Not about the convention that was over to Hartford and the shipping laws and such-like, but he likes to hear of the old times—how Aaron Burr from these parts killed Mr Hamilton in that there jewel and how he tried to start a war down with New Spain and was taken up on charges of trea-

son. Your man, he can talk for hour by hour about that Bonaparte
and how he was the best sojer ever was to live. Though Lord,
Madam Damaris'—Mrs Duckworth had never managed to call
her 'Damaris' without a title, though some of the Litchfield ladies
were calling her Mrs Egremont—'we all know for all the world
that that Boney lost, and just as well to my mind. But gentlemen
do like to talk. Why, Duckworth, before he ran off and drank himself to death, he would talk about what he did in the calvary in the
Revolution as if General Washington just followed his orders,
though Duckworth got the measles in camp and was sent home.
But there, poor gentleman, it passes the time for him, I don't
doubt.'

Damaris silently agreed. If only d'Egremont would think about
going on to New Orleans—but he seemed quite unable to face the
thought of a new life; he preferred his drunken dreams. Sometimes
she wondered in despair what had happened to the dashing, daring
man she had loved, and then again counselled herself to have patience.

She had one bit of good luck. Howard Booth had returned from
Hartford and brought her a very good price for her earrings, far
more than she had expected, close to their real value. She calculated that in English money it was a sum well over a thousand
guineas. That would take care of her and the Marquis for some
time to come. It could pay their way to New Orleans and there
would be enough left over so that they could take their time before disposing of the rest of the jewels. Or it would if Jean-
Philippe did not spend so much on his drink and gambling.

Gambling was a vice with so many young men—she had known
that he gambled before, but even at Watier's, where the play was
always deep, he had not been among the most profligate. That was
left to her unfortunate friend the Beau. She wondered how her
rash dandy friend was faring. Now she realized that d'Egremont's
whole life had been the stake that he had played—more profligate
than the Beau after all, he had gambled his life and her own. Yes,
Jean-Philippe had played and lost, and there was no amusement
left for him except the bottle and the cards.

Howard Booth came again to visit her in the small parlour. To
her delight he brought her coffee and tea. He assured her it was
easily available, and she would find that she would be served
coffee by the Litchfield ladies, though the country people kept to
their ale and cider. Mrs Duckworth had said he was the busiest

man in the county, perhaps the state, but he had time to sit with her before the fire, his long legs stretched out, and talk of small matters, nothing that anyone could not have heard.

He did not have the habit that Damaris had come to think of as almost a national curse—the chewing of tobacco, and the consequent spitting, not only an evil in itself but resulting in the yellow stains that disfigured Mrs Duckworth's tap-room no matter how hard she and Flora scrubbed. Nor did he take snuff, but instead, with Damaris's permission he smoked his tobacco in a pipe. After he departed the smell of the tobacco smoke he left in the room had a curious excitement for her, a reminder of masculinity. It was the sense of protection that made her welcome him, she told herself, and knew already that she lied.

Yet he was certainly protective. He saw her anxiety about d'Egremont and his extravagance—the whole village and everyone round about knew of it. Booth did not discuss the Marquis but instead offered them the use of a house.

'It's not a great place, Ma'am,' he said, 'but it's sound. It keeps the winter out, and you'll find that's important in these parts. It can be mighty cold, come December. It's not in the town, but it's not too far outside, in the woods, over to Bantam Lake.'

He saw her interest and went on.

'And it has enough rooms so you could have your school there right away.'

She had talked with Booth about a plan to teach a few girls besides Flora. There was a seminary in Litchfield, a very good one, but many girls could not be spared by their parents for so much of their time as the seminary required. They were needed about their homes. There were few servants here, and girls of prosperous families would spend their days in baking, washing clothes, and cleaning, while their brothers became educated men. For these girls Damaris thought she could offer informal classes that they could attend when their mothers could spare them; the duties of kitchen and farm need not leave them quite unlettered and unpolished in manner.

Booth had applauded the idea. Unlike many men, she noticed, both here and in England, he approved the idea of female education. Damaris had been somewhat hesitant, for if she was going to leave soon for New Orleans it would be unfair to begin something that could have no future or real fulfilment, and they had both agreed that the inn was not a suitable place to bring young girls.

The night before he offered her the house there had been a celebration downstairs ending in a drunken battle in which the chief
weapon had been handfuls of salted cod. Neither the Marquis nor
Damaris had been able to sleep, and the Marquis was now getting
ready to go off, after telling her that he probably would not return
that night.

'Mrs Wadsworth's been over to Beecher's,' Booth told Damaris
with his slow grin. 'Lyman will be favouring us with six more sermons on intemperance.'

Damaris laughed. It was a joke between them that the deacon,
who regularly preached sermons written by the stalwart temperance advocate Lyman Beecher, himself kept a still, providing
some of the best spirits in the county. The deacon's sister, the ardent Mrs Wadsworth, could make the deacon preach, but she
could not make him practice, and as his slurred periods denounc-
ing drink wafted over his congregation, Damaris would sometimes
catch Booth's eye, and it was all she could do to keep her countenance. She had become a regular 'goer to meeting,' like the other
ladies, mostly from a desire to meet her neighbours and enjoy
some society.

The bright, white meeting hall, kept fresh by the ladies of the
congregation, decorated with autumn leaves, seemed very little
like a church and a world away from the Gothic gloom of the
church at Little Heron; and the deacon's impassioned if somewhat
jumbled sermons had little to do with the dry, learned, repetitious
mumblings of her old friend Mr Poyntz. Damaris had been accepted by the ladies as part of their normal life. 'Mrs Egremont,'
Mrs Buell had said with satisfaction, 'is just like reg'lar folks,' and
Mrs Wadsworth had nodded her approval.

If Damaris had been present at the Hatch house, where that
conversation had taken place, she might have noticed that Mrs
Hatch had not joined in the chorus of praise, though Mrs Hatch
was usually first and others followed. And to Mrs Hatch Damaris
was still 'Madam Marquise.' The ladies noticed, but as yet not
much was said.

Damaris thanked Booth for his offer. There was nothing she
would like so much as a house of her own—but she doubted that
the Marquis would be willing to take it. She had brought up the
idea before, but to him a house would be an earnest that they were
not merely travellers but residents, and though he could not bring
himself to move on, neither could he admit the truth that time was

passing and they must take root somewhere. Booth had warned her that winter could come swiftly and that travelling would be very hard for a lady and a man not in good health.

'If you stay much longer,' he told her, 'better you stay till spring.'

But d'Egremont refused to think further than the day. She went upstairs and found him dressing with the help of the boy Rufe. He dressed here as he would dress at Oatlands, in pale buckskin breeches, top-boots, an exquisitely-cut blue coat, and cravat that the Beau might have worn—Damaris, observing the deficiencies of the Duckworth's, washed them herself, making use of the secret that the Beau had confided in no one but her: starch.

As soon as she entered, the Marquis sat in his chair and the boy withdrew. Damaris sighed inwardly, wondering when Jean-Philippe would accept his lameness and her knowledge of it. She had noticed that he seemed to prefer the rougher society of the neighbourhood—he claimed he preferred peasants to the bourgeois society of Litchfield. She knew that to be true, but it was also true that he felt no injury to his pride in being observed as he was by the humble, but to be seen by people with any pretension to gentility was gall and wormwood to him.

She told him of Booth's generous offer and was not surprised when he instantly rejected it, but she was somewhat taken aback at his vehemence.

'A house in the woods by the lake, Madame?' he said, sneering. 'How convenient—especially if the husband is away. I fancy I have heard of that house. Your horseshoe-nail maker kept his mistress there, I understand, until she ran away. It is indeed an honour, this gift he wishes to bestow on you.'

The Marquis always referred to Booth as the horseshoe-nail maker. One of the manufactories on the river with the strange name, the Naugatuck, made horseshoe nails and other small useful goods. But it was new for him to talk about Booth having had a mistress. Of course, Jean-Philippe heard all the gossip of the taverns. Damaris felt an odd jumble of emotions that she did not care to examine too closely. In the meantime, she had to reply. D'Egremont was looking at her with a particularly black scowl, and it came to her for the first time that he was jealous of her friendship with Booth.

There had been so little love, or even possessiveness, in Jean-Philippe's manner to her recently—he was content to lie on his bed

or carouse and leave her to cope with all the business of their lives
—that she had come at last to believe, despite her own protestations to the contrary, that his love for her had died. He had loved
the Countess of Malfrey, and when the great Society beauty had
vanished forever after Waterloo, his love, she thought, had
vanished with it. She could not find it in her heart to blame him,
for she herself felt nothing like that woman, spoiled, petted, admired, and adored, though she still perforce wore her clothes and
lived on the proceeds of her jewels—as a thieving servant might
have done, she thought sometimes, ironically.

'I think he meant to be kind,' she said in her gentle voice. 'But
of course, it must be as you say, Jean-Philippe.'

The carousing of the night before had ended, and the bustle of
the work about the place now subsided until the dinner preparation began. The Marquis's room was very quiet. Suddenly d'Egremont took her by the wrist and drew her down and kissed her
roughly. She was taken by surprise and could not follow his sudden swing from anger into a long-forgotten passion. Her mind
worked fast enough to warn her not to pull back, but it was too
full of thoughts of houses, horseshoe nails, mistresses, and Malfrey—together with doing sums in her head on how many of the
dollars Booth had brought her still remained, and how much Jean-
Philippe would spend that very night—to be able to feel a surge of
love and desire. Her acceptance of his kiss was more endurance
than response, and Jean-Philippe, that lover of women, could not
be deceived.

He thrust her from him and gazed out at the landscape, which
was beginning to turn bleak with the sky dark and threatening.
Damaris felt a sudden pain, a sorrow for something dear and
dead, and anguish for a failure. In her own mind she had praised
herself for her endurance, for her ability to act in this strange land
with all that was familiar left behind, and she had tried not to condemn Jean-Philippe for his unwillingness to change. But now it
seemed to her that so much of the failure of their love was her
failure. Her change no longer seemed an act of virtue. Their love
that had cost them both so much—she remembered his making his
way, still in the uniform of the Imperial Guard, through the allied
lines from Waterloo to Brussels, wounded, faint, to carry her off
to safety. The words of a song she had heard old troopers singing
came, for some reason, to her mind. 'The world turned upside
down.'

She knelt beside him, put her arms about him, the tears running down her cheeks. He regarded her with an expression she could not fathom.

'This accursed sky looks about to fall, Madame,' he said with a return to his usual manner. 'If you will excuse me, I must finish my toilette or I will be late for my appointment in the famous inn of Bradleyville.'

He made a comic face of disgust, and she left him slowly. There could be no apologies to Jean-Philippe, but she saw her fault. The storm soon broke and lasted the best part of three days. The river flooded and roads were washed out; Jean-Philippe did not return. Damaris kept to the inn and stayed in her room, in tears and repentance. She had never thought herself a light-skirt—she had taken a lover, but he had been the only man she had ever loved. Now she felt like the despised Mrs Carroway—a woman whose ungoverned passion moved her as the wind blew, careless of her own dignity, her family's honour—indeed she was worse than Mrs Carroway, who at least had had no children to abandon and ruin.

She wept for herself, for her children, even for the Earl, to whom, she now thought wretchedly, she had not given his due. They had made a bargain; he had kept his part, but she had been more than grudging in her own. Since then she had learned so much: her own wild passion for Jean-Philippe, the brutal, death-bringing lust of Le Gros, the sudden hatred on the face of Jean-Philippe when she saw him crippled, her own cold inability to respond to the man she had once so greatly loved—all these things had taught her that love and passion were not simple. Perhaps she might have helped her husband—as she never could help Jean-Philippe. The Marquis d'Egremont wanted neither tenderness nor compassion, only respect and ardour.

But she could change again, she promised herself silently on her wet pillow. If Jean-Philippe could still love her, she could so discipline her mind and thought to love him again; she did love him still, in a fashion, and her warmth and desire would return. They must leave this place, winter or no. Jean-Philippe, among people of his own sort, would relish life again, and in his happiness her own would live again.

So she told herself, and she determined to have no more private meetings with Howard Booth—Mrs Duckworth could be an intermediary if such was needed. It was natural for Jean-Philippe to be jealous; Booth was whole, while he was crippled; Booth was in all but name a lord in this territory, while d'Egremont was a penniless adventurer. He believed her smiles at Booth meant more than they did, and she assured herself they were merely smiles of friendship.

On the third day, Sunday, the rain abated, and she went with Mrs Buell to the meeting. Mrs Hatch had stopped sending her carriage. Damaris had thought little about it, considering it a matter of that lady's convenience, but now, when she entered again with Mrs Buell, she noticed little nods and looks among the ladies. She felt tired and depressed—her good resolutions had not raised her spirits.

So low did she feel that the whispers and nods towards 'Mrs Egremont' or 'Madam Marquise' troubled her for once. When the kindly Mrs Buell commented that she looked poorly, she took the excuse, pleading a headache to avoid the social gathering after the service. It meant an uncomfortable ride back to the inn on a farmer's cart, where she shared a seat with a sack of potatoes that did no good to her cloak of best English superfine, and when she arrived, to make her way through a party of rough, obstreperous travellers, she wondered why she had been in so much haste to leave the only society open to her.

Jean-Philippe would not return before nightfall, but she had an impulse to serve him in some way. She could collect his linen—he had no idea, but she did all such work for him and brushed his garments, as neither of the Duckworths had any knowledge of the degree of care the Marquis expected. She smiled, feeling a surge of warmth—the high standards of her lover, that he refused to compromise even in this semi-wilderness, seemed to her now to be admirable, a refusal to sink no matter what the difficulties, a holding on to the dignity of the station to which he was born, with all the exquisite demands of taste that the Beau would have shown in his place and that the nobility of France had demonstrated in prison and on the very steps of the guillotine.

She wrinkled her nose. Outside Jean-Philippe's door were several chamber-pots—Flora Duckworth was making a belated collection. It was fortunate that Jean-Philippe was absent; already he referred to Flora Duckworth as 'Mademoiselle the slattern'—if he did not call her something worse. Treading cautiously round the offending receptacles, she opened the bedroom door.

Before her were Jean-Philippe's clothes in a muddy heap on the floor. Female garments, coarse and much soiled, lay beside them.

The window was shut against the drizzling rain, and the room was full of the fumes of brandy.

A man's shape, naked, lay on the bed, and kneeling over him, straddling him with her knees, was a large, naked woman. No lamp was lit against the darkness of the day, but Damaris could see clearly enough the huge pink haunches rising and falling, and there was no mistaking the grunts and cries and groans of pleasure from Flora Duckworth. Damaris wished to withdraw, but she was trembling too much to move. The man, who was lying back idly, fondling the huge pink breasts, caught sight of Damaris over the girl's shoulder and gave her a long, insolent grin. Jean-Philippe caressed the girl's body, his fingers plunging deep into the mound of Venus, playing lightly, knowingly, until Flora squealed like a barn-yard fowl and flung herself down, satisfied for the moment. D'Egremont had closed his eyes for an instant at the peak of his own pleasure but opened them again at once, regarding Damaris with an expression cynical and old, while Flora Duckworth, moaning, rubbed her sticky sweating body up against him in an attempt to renew her pleasure.

Damaris, still shaking, reached for the door and turned away, sickened, as d'Egremont resumed his caresses of the girl, turning her willing body about, stroking her inner thighs, and then licking and sucking from her breasts to her navel and deep into her body's cleft, Damaris's presence forgotten or ignored.

CHAPTER

40

Damaris went to her room, not feeling anger or even hurt. She was only cold, cold with a chill that penetrated deep. Her bed, under its goose-down quilt, looked like a haven, and she crawled in and huddled in its comfort, pausing only to remove her gown. She lay quiet, not thinking, gazing up at Flora Duckworth's handiwork, which she had learned was called a sampler. 'A fat wife and a big barn never did any man harm.'

How Jean-Philippe had shuddered when he first saw it and insisted on its removal! It had made her laugh. She buried her face in the pillow. No use to remember anything, or to think at all. The rain was coming down hard again and beat steadily against the window. The scuffling sounds in the next room ceased. The bed grew warm. Very gradually, the tautness left her limbs, her eyes closed, and soon she was in the blessed relief of sleep until the dreams came, grey, frightening.

She was alone, lost in the great Forest of Heron. She had been pursued by someone, perhaps the Earl, perhaps Le Gros—the form twisted and changed. She was lost, faint and chilled, her feet wet from the pond near Greystones; she was pregnant but she lost her child—the child that was to have been hers and Jean-Philippe's. Sick with despair, she yet knew that somewhere there was hope. If only she could get so far; near the forest's edge there was something, someone—a form that was still formless, a name unnamed, a beacon of hope, steady, safe, on the unseen horizon. Her despair receded; she would run to that distant place—and then, peremptorily, came the sound of a knock. Her door was flung open, and she jumped up in her bed, completely awake, to see Jean-Philippe, booted, cloaked, dressed for travel.

The room was quite dark. She must have slept all the afternoon away. He lit her lamp, looking down on her composedly.

'A thousand pardons, Madame, for disturbing you. But I must bid you farewell. I am off to try our fortunes in New Orleans.'

Of course he would not apologize or explain, but this sudden flight—

'Jean-Philippe,' she said slowly, trying to collect herself, 'are we not going together?'

'You are safe here. It is better that you stay until I have made a future possible for us in Louisiana.'

For once he was grave, neither mocking nor morose.

'I go into the unknown. I have taken you once into a dark future; this time I will go alone. When I am ready to receive Madame la Marquise, I will send for you.'

She was bewildered and could not think what to say.

'Can't you at least wait for tomorrow's stage? We could talk—'

'There is no need for talk, Damaris.' He so rarely called her by her name that it struck her with a certain tenderness. Was it, she wondered, grief at parting—perhaps a final parting?

'I have known for some time what I would do. Yesterday I won enough at cards to take me to New Orleans—if I go alone. And I ride tonight with some men of these parts who travel to New York.'

It became real to her. He was going. She looked into his face; his expression was guarded, distant, as though he had already gone. Whatever he had done, he was still Jean-Philippe. She jumped up with a little cry, found her jewel box, and opened it with feverish haste, tossing her large pieces—bracelets, necklaces, her tiara—all in a glittering heap upon the quilt.

'Take them, Jean-Philippe, you will need them,' she said. 'They are to buy our plantation, our home.'

He smiled, the guarded, distant look quite gone. Leaning down, he clasped the bracelet on her wrist, the necklace about her throat; smoothing her hair, he placed the tiara on her head.

'I have not seen you attired so for some time, Madame. The sight is a pleasure I will carry with me.'

The mockery of his tone was meant to hide the truth—that to his gaze she was at that moment infinitely desirable, with the patrician elegance of her fine bones, the delicate curves of her slender body, and the blue eyes shining up like the sapphires in the lamplight.

'Your jewels will buy a home if that is necessary. But I will fend for myself until you come.'

Perhaps he was afraid he would gamble them away, she thought. It was that—or the accursed d'Egremont pride. Despite his look of resolution he still was very thin and pale.

'Take these, at any rate, Jean-Philippe.'

She took the rope of pearls that the Earl had given her to wear on their wedding day and put them in his pocket.

'You are still not strong, and you may need something for a little while.'

He kissed her hand formally, and then in a gesture of intimacy rare for him outside the time of love, he touched her forehead, his hand resting there for a moment as if he were loath to leave.

'My blessing,' he said lightly, 'the blessing of the d'Egremonts— I hope it keeps you safe, Madame. *Au 'voir.*'

And in a moment he was gone.

She stood at the window and saw him mount his hired conveyance by the light of a lamp that Rufe was holding for him. He gave the boy something, the red head was raised in parting, and Damaris, surprised, saw a glitter of tears on the boy's cheeks. D'Egremont had not made himself generally liked in Litchfield, but oddly, unaccountably, in the way of boys, young Rufe had come to be his admirer—almost a courtier in his clumsy way.

Strange, she reflected, feeling very tired, and then her mind went to Flora. She dismissed that thought. It could be considered later, when her mind was clear. D'Egremont was gone; she was alone. She was quite alone—abandoned, perhaps, she did not know. A sense of emptiness pervaded her, but the fretful melancholy of the afternoon had gone. She returned to her bed and though she felt she would not sleep, slept soundly.

The next morning the skies had cleared. The sun shone bright and woke her early, or perhaps it was the singing of the birds. Birds would come from miles around to eat the leftover bread and scraps that Rufe threw out every morning. They made a rare sight, Damaris thought, leaning at her window-sill—birds of colours never seen in England, bright to match the brightness of these woods: the brilliant blue of the jays, who made the most noise with their squawking; the scarlet of the cardinals; the bright orange-red breasts of the robins, so different from the small, rosy English birds that bore the same name; the flashing gold of the finches.

She was hungry. The day before she had eaten only breakfast. When Flora, noisy as the jay and red as the cardinals, brought her a dish of the inevitable salt cod and fried potatoes, she ate a good part of the dish. Blessing Howard Booth, she drank a cup of coffee that Mrs Duckworth had been kind enough to make.

As Flora prattled on about the departure of 'the Markiss' Damaris felt sure she had no notion that she had been discovered—her attention had been directed at the time in quite another way. Damaris felt no anger against the girl, only a sense of responsibility enhanced by anxious fear. A healthy country girl like Flora, with an amorous disposition and a little slowness in the wits, would have had no chance at all against the charms of d'Egremont. Even his sickliness and pallor might have had charm for a girl used to her bronzed and husky swains. His very hauteur and contempt had probably increased his desirability in her eyes as a badge of his superior state—Damaris had noticed that the doctrine of equality, so vigorously espoused in words in this New England, seemed to leave certain longings unfulfiled.

As she drank her coffee—wishing she could have had the brewing of it herself—she felt she should have managed matters better. Mrs Duckworth had been kind; her daughter should have been kept safe from seduction. How long the affair had been going on Damaris could not know—certainly the two had had the ease of familiarity. If Flora should be pregnant—Damaris sighed. She had no idea how the mothers of bastards were treated in this still puritanical land.

To listen to the ladies, the idea of virginity in brides was as important as it was to the families of the *ton*. Indeed, it was exaggerated to a point of such false modesty that girls were not allowed to mention certain articles of male apparel. Though Flora Duckworth did all the washing for the inn, when one day shortly after her arrival Damaris had asked her for the Marquis's shirts, Flora had blushed, fallen into a paroxysm of giggles, dropped her basket of clean wash in the mud, and run away. Mrs Duckworth had told Damaris very seriously that it was 'not fittin' for young girls to hear such talk,' and though she didn't blame a lady from foreign parts who would know no better, she begged Damaris to remember that 'my Flora be a good and decent girl even if she be a bit overgrowed.'

Damaris had promised gravely to respect this virtue. She had most signally failed and felt a certain discomfort at facing the ladies of the inn. It was as well, she realized, that she had adopted the name and title of d'Egremont. What these people thought of adulterous wives she did not know, but certainly they would have a view very different from the easy circle of the Regent.

Certain whispers she had heard from the ladies of the congregation suggested that a man might sometimes fall by the wayside. The penalties could be severe—ostracism, a harsh punishment in a small country place, might be one. A woman in such a case was not discussed. She shuddered a little to think what would happen to their respect for 'Madam Marquise' and 'Mrs Egremont' if the truth were known. The thought of the black-browed Mrs Hatch came uneasily to mind.

And now what? she wondered. How long would it be before the ladies thought of her as an abandoned wife? What would happen now to Jean-Philippe? She forced herself to put these thoughts from her—there was her immediate future to be decided on.

Before the day was over, she had decided to accept Booth's offer of a house. There she could start her school and occupy her time and mind until something was settled and she rejoined Jean-Philippe. It would be pleasant to have the arranging of her own quarters and to be away from the sight of those execrable spittoons. Charmed with the idea, she hummed happily as she sat with her small writing-desk on her lap—a dainty affair of polished woods inlaid with gold and mother of pearl. The Earl had presented it to her on the first anniversary of their marriage, but it was not of the Earl she was thinking.

She gave her note to Rufe and bade him take it to the Booth house and give it to the housekeeper. Most likely Booth would not be there; he travelled about the state on his political affairs, and up and down the river valleys on his varied business interests—he was rarely at home. Mrs Duckworth had hinted once that he was not overly fond of his big house, but then, tantalizingly, she had said no more.

Certainly, Damaris told herself, she did not have to consider Jean-Philippe's jealous suspicion. A house was a much more suitable shelter for a woman than a public inn. Whatever had been true of Booth's past—and she could hardly imagine a gentleman of Litchfield daring to keep a mistress openly, flaunting her in the face of all the worthy wives—his manner towards herself was one of great courtesy and nothing more.

The answer came promptly the next day. Damaris did not know that the faithful Rufe, though it had meant great scolding from his legitimate employer, had not left the note at Litchfield but had taken it down to the village of Naugatuck, where Booth had been staying. The house was hers as soon as she was ready to move in; it had already been prepared for occupation. Booth added that he could be at the inn whenever he was sent for and would bring a waggon to move her things.

Damaris went to find Mrs Duckworth to inform her of her plans. She found that lady, her face still streaked with pastry flour, taking the reckoning from some departing guests, eager to hustle them off, as she was bursting with talk.

'And so your good man, he do be gone at last, and leaving his pretty lady here.' She beamed as though she was pleased at this turn of events. 'Lord, how quick a man do move when once he makes up his mind to travel. Duckworth went off in the middle of the night, I do remember, drunk as he could be, and with every dollar we had in his pockets and nothing left to pay chandler or ostlers and only his old boots left on bedroom floor. But it's all to one a better thing that you don't travel in winter weather. . . .'

Damaris saw Mrs Duckworth eyeing her figure, wondering if Madam Markiss was pregnant. She told her she would be moving into a house owned by Mr Booth, the better to conduct her school until she went south to join her husband. She pressed payment on her from the store of money she had left. D'Egremont's gambling had made a sad hole in the money she had received from the sale of the earrings—when the stakes had become dull to him in such places as Litchfield, Bradleyville, and Naugatuck, he had gone as far as New Haven, a prosperous port town, to gratify his thirst for deeper play.

Mrs Duckworth protested that she owed nothing more than she had paid already and that her services to Flora had been worth the price of her room. Knowing what she did, Damaris could not accept that, and the two ladies battled the matter amicably back and forth until Mrs Duckworth conceded. Damaris also gave her a seed-pearl brooch to wear on her Sunday hat, which struck the countrywoman into such delight that she was silent for quite two minutes.

Then, very gravely, she asked Damaris to accompany her to the small parlour, and called for Flora to bring hot cider. She thanked Damaris for her gift and fell silent again while Damaris speculated unhappily as to whether the mother did, after all, know of the injury to her daughter. What could be done to repair it Damaris did not know—although she realized, with almost a desire to giggle, that of course the Marquis could marry Flora Duckworth; he was certainly not married to anyone else. But she kept her thoughts to herself until Mrs Duckworth should come to what she was determined, if reluctant, to say.

They drank their cider; the large clock on the chimney-piece ticked on, but still Mrs Duckworth had not come to her purpose. At last, after a few remarks as to the 'danged noise of they birds' in the morning and the laziness of Rufe, who disappeared when he was needed, she made the leap.

'You knows, Madam Markiss'—'Damaris' had proved awkward for her to say and had been given up—'I would be proud to keep you here as long as you fixed to stay. But if you wants a house of your own, why, I say, good and nat'ral. Nat'ral—any woman wants her home, and if I had my druthers, I'd be in a house and not an inn with all sorts coming in and out; but that was Duckworth's wish and now it's, as they say, my cap over the mill.'

Damaris choked as she covered a laugh with a cough. Water over the dam, the good lady doubtless meant, but where she had got the expression she used Damaris couldn't think. If she had known what she said, the virtuous relict of the departed Duckworth would doubtless have fallen in a faint on the parlour floor, on her own rag rug. She wondered when she would get to the point, but Mrs Duckworth was a Yankee and must go at it sideways, as it were, in true Yankee fashion.

'No better man than Howard Booth,' Mrs Duckworth said firmly. 'His father was a good man, but Mr Howard's better. Even if he do call me Mrs Cluckworth to my very face and still pulls my apron strings same as he did when he was a boy. But people in the village up at Litchfield, they do talk. Powerful religious they are in Litchfield, and no one, be he man or woman, can step out of the way. Like to brand 'em with a scarlet letter, some folks would, like in the old days, and they might as well, for do a body make a mistake, why that scarlet letter sits on 'em just same as if it were burned into their flesh.'

Damaris's head was spinning with thoughts of Booth—she gathered that there must have been some truth in Jean-Philippe's assertions—and of poor Flora. She shuddered to think of a branding of that capacious chest—and there was her own to be considered.

'Wild they said he was,' Mrs Duckworth went on, her mind running in the past, her voice muted. 'Not that he was wild, only nat'ral and kindly, but he stood up tall and didn't hide his doings like some I could mention. Men in these parts ain't no more angels than any other,' Mrs Duckworth sniffed. 'Ask any innkeeper. But they go off if they mean to do wrong and do it quiet where they don't be known. Mr Howard, he's straight as all get-out, and folks—some folks—take it hard. Oh, it's an old story, most forgotten now, Madam Markiss. Mr Howard, he took over everything when his father died and did real well, and folks respect him. He's first selectman now and could be governor, to my thinkin', if he had a mind. His young days do be forgotten, even by such as Beulah Hatch, who was most strong against him. Why,' she said, her voice lighter, 'she'd swallow her teeth now for Mr Howard to marry her Verity, who's more an old maid every day, but I don't think he'll do it, for all he likes the girl.'

She looked at Damaris with her kind brown eyes, which held wisdom despite her comic manner.

'It would be a different kind of lady, I'm thinking, to catch the

eye of Mr Howard. It's rare hard'—she rose, speaking abruptly—
'for a lady with her husband gone. I live here all my days, yet
there was those that turned their noses up at me when Duckworth
ran off. Beulah Hatch, as was Beulah Wadsworth when we were
both girls, she never asked me up to Hatch's since. And no good
to complain, for if Beulah do take a spite, she can make a deal o'
trouble, talking to the deacon and to the ladies here.'

Having been led around the cart, Damaris now saw the horse.

'I am going to be an ordinary tenant,' she assured the kindly
innkeeper. 'I will pay a good rent, because I will have my school.
The girls will be by me most of the time, and if I prosper, I will
take a servant—if one can be found in these parts.'

'Oh,' Mrs Duckworth said, relieved to be off the difficult subject
and on to her favourite complaint. 'If so be you find a girl to help
—but Lord! They'd rather be down to manufactories, standing
about like men with they machines—all devil's work, to my mind—
and none wanting to do a hand's turn in someone else's kitchen.'

She grumbled her way off, rubbing at her brooch with her
apron, gazing down with an expression of immense gratification.
Damaris could not help wondering exactly what Booth had done
to bring down upon him the wrath of Mrs Hatch. She must keep
to her plan of taking Booth's house; she knew of no other that was
available. As the houses of Connecticut were built of wood, if
people moved from one place to another they usually took their
houses with them, leaving merely a hole in the ground. Nevertheless, she would be circumspect and not cause problems for herself or Booth. She called young Rufe and asked him to make arrangements for the transporting of her goods—it would be better
for her to leave in the hired waggon and go through Litchfield
under her own auspices. She knew that Booth would understand.
There was something about the quiet man with the humorous eyes
that made her feel he would always understand.

41

She took possession of her new home on one of those bright, clear days, cool and fresh, that she had already come to love. The autumn seemed to stretch on endlessly here, though she had been warned that winter could arrive with sharp severity. As she rode through the town in the waggon, with all her wordly goods piled behind her, she bowed to the ladies who greeted her from their porches, enjoying all the friendly smiles, conscious of the sweetness of the air and the blue sky that arched so high overhead. She had a feeling of lightness and buoyancy. This land was so like England and yet so unlike, without the low-lying cloud that made the homeland intimate and close. Here men could stretch themselves as they gazed on far horizons—horizons, though so distant, that they were free to reach. The very woods she drove through were like and yet different from the Forest of Heron—here conifers grew, spreading dark green up the mountains, while the maples shed their last leaves of scarlet and of yellow to the earth beneath.

Her house was at the edge of a clearing in the woods. A lane went by from Litchfield to Hartford, and beyond the lane was a canal. On the other side was Bantam Lake, sparkling like her sapphires in the sun. The wooden house was unpainted, weathered, and dark on the outside, but there were many windows full of tiny panes. It was in no style of building that she could name, yet it had a certain dignity and charm.

She entered happily—there were signs of recent visits, and someone had taken thought for her occupancy. The furnishings for the most part were old and simple, but someone had added a pianoforte and a harp, shining and new. A fire burned in the hearth and—the ladies of Litchfield had certainly been there before her—there were vases of the maple leaves and dark marsh grass on the tables and window-sills.

Rufe and Dan the carter carried down her trunks, smiling, and Verity Hatch came in with her arms full of packages. In recent weeks, Damaris had seen Verity only in church. Although all the Litchfield ladies had called upon her at the inn, and she sometimes returned a short visit in the afternoons, she had not accepted their invitations to dinner, as d'Egremont most certainly would not accompany her. Once he was known to be up and about, his refusal to meet the local society had caused a certain tension.

Damaris had always pleaded the same excuse for her own failure—she could not leave the Marquis for long—but gossip travelled as fast here as it did anywhere else, and it was talked about that the Marquis spent his days drinking in the taverns. Although she did not know it, this did not cause Damaris any lessening in popularity. Hard-drinking and useless husbands were not unknown even in this country, and she received the sympathy while d'Egremont had the censure. The only exception was at the table of Mrs Hatch, who gave it as her opinion that if a man went to drink, the conduct and character of his wife might be called into question.

'A man who is happy in his home does not run to the taverns,' she had said, awful in her best purple silk at Sunday dinner.

Her sister-in-law, Mrs Wadsworth, another pillar of the church, nodded in agreement, but Mrs Buell protested mildly. 'But the poor Marquis does not have a home. And it can't be very comfortable over to the inn, where the poor things have to eat in their bedroom so that they won't be spat upon by the stage-drivers in the tap.'

'A man's home is where his wife is,' Mrs Hatch pronounced, and the ladies remembered respectfully the late Mr Hatch, stalwart, portly, sober—certainly he had always been at home for Sunday dinner, though his business, which had consisted of many stores and an interest in the cotton and wool trade, as well as his farm, had taken him often from the side of his wife and family and had necessitated his staying in one or another of the villages in the river valleys, sometimes the better part of the week.

Damaris looked at the shyly smiling Verity, who had brought her all manner of supplies to make her first days in her new home easy: fresh-baked bread, butter, jam and honey, a ham—and a sharp knife to cut it with. She felt herself warm to the girl who showed such real kindness to a foreigner. It was Verity, she suspected, who had arranged the vases, and she thanked her heartily.

'Mrs Buell sent the preserves,' Verity explained, 'and Mrs Wadsworth the butter—her dairy is the best in Litchfield. It was

Flora Duckworth who sent the knife. She wanted to make you a fine present,' Verity said, smiling, 'but I told her a good sharp knife would be more handy than all the fancy goods that caught her eye on the peddlers' waggons.'

Verity was sensible as well as kind. Damaris noticed, as Mrs Duckworth had done, that she had put off the trappings of a young girl. Certainly she must be twenty-four or twenty-five—strange to think that Verity was years older than she herself—and she wore the dress of a matron, a gown of garnet-red silk partly covered at the moment by a black silk apron, and a close, plain bonnet, quite out of the fashion. Damaris thought this manner of dress suited the young woman with the sallow skin, strongly-marked features, and large, strong frame, but she also knew its significance to all who saw it. Verity had taken herself deliberately from the marriage market. Mrs Duckworth's words came back to her. Verity was suspected of a *tendresse* for Howard Booth, and Damaris felt pity for the girl as well as warmth.

Verity was taking off her apron and preparing to go. Someone had left her at the little house, and she had already made her arrangements to go back with Dan. Damaris was seized with a desire to show hospitality in her new home and brought out a bottle of cidar, a gift from Mrs Duckworth. Verity helped her find the glasses that, well-washed, were already waiting for her use in the little dining-parlour, and the ladies, the carter, and the speechless young Rufe drank a toast to the new establishment.

'Towpath Farm,' Dan said. 'And may you be happy here, Ma'am.'

Damaris felt a pleasure in this entertainment that she could not remember being equalled by her first dinner party at Malfrey House, where she had been attended by a dozen footmen in powdered wigs for the benefit of the most illustrious members of the *ton*. The blue of the lake sparkled through the windows and at that moment seemed no bad substitute for the gloom-bringing great wall outside the London mansion.

As she walked with Verity out to the waggon, Verity explained that this had once been a farm but most of the land had gone back to the woods. Its name came from the path that ran alongside the canal where barges still sometimes were drawn by horses, though most goods now went by the roads. The young women stood in the bright day looking about them. Between the house and the canal was a half-acre or so of land that looked as if it had been a vegetable garden, now sadly overgrown, though someone had, Damaris noticed, made some recent attempts at clearing. Beyond the canal the ground rose to a majestic hill, part of a noble line of hills, covered with dark green and bronze, that formed the horizon. Under the great vault of pellucid sky, reflected from the sparkling lake, the place was matchless in its beauty.

Verity felt it too. She looked about her with a smile that softened her features and that had something a little sad in it.

'This place belonged to Mrs Booth's family, the Marshes,' she said. 'The Marsh brothers were both killed at Bunker Hill, and it came to her. Rare fond of it she was, and kept it for a summer cottage. The Booth boys loved it, and I used to play with them when Mamma came over to visit—though she was in fits lest I see them go a-swimming in the lake.'

'And did you?' Damaris asked, mischievous.

Verity looked at her, laughing.

'Mrs Egremont, not only did I see but I tried it. I hid myself until everyone was out of the way and then plunged in. But first I floated on my petticoats and then I sank, so I never tried again. And if you should tell any of the Litchfield ladies or my mamma, she might turn me from the door this day.'

Verity went off with Rufe and Dan, and Damaris waved to them as they went. The more she saw of Verity, the more she liked her. Certainly she would make a good and suitable wife for Howard Booth—Damaris wondered why he had never married. In such a strict society, she thought, it must be easier to marry than to face the certain condemnation that went with bachelorhood. Had Booth really kept a mistress in this house? It could not have been easy for the lady. What had become of her?

She put such thoughts aside as she explored her house. It was a strange little dwelling, with low ceilings and doors and windows in unexpected places, with many rooms having a step or two down to a different level. Obviously the house had been built at different times; a small central house had been added to, a room here and a room there as it was needed. There were two parlours, both quite small, and a large kitchen with a strange contraption made of iron beside the fireplace. A pile of logs, cut up small, stood beside it; puzzled, she decided she would examine that another time. A scullery was built out from the kitchen, and there was a good-sized pantry in which she put away her supplies. At the back of the house was another small room with no fireplace. A box held reels of cotton and needles and a pair of scissors—this had been the sewing-room of the mistress of the house once but, by its looks, not used in many a long year.

Upstairs were the bedrooms. A room looking out over the garden had been made ready for her, the simple furniture polished, the wooden floors shining, the linen on the bed fresh and sweet. A bright, very new rag rug had been placed at the bedside, its crude jumble of colours not unpleasing to Damaris's eyes as she thought of the kindness it represented.

She found herself humming as she looked over her small domain, and it did not strike her as strange that the Countess of Malfrey should feel such pleasure in finding an old milk churn when she had no cow, but she did feel a pang that the 'Marquise d'Egremont' should be so blithe about setting up a household in which the Marquis would never have a part. But she dismissed the thought. It was needful that she remain here while Jean-Philippe . . . established himself. She phrased it that way in her mind after searching for words, without considering how that was to come about.

Since she found herself well situated, she might as well be happy if she could. It was perhaps Damaris St Cloud who looked out at the garden plot and wondered if she could grow fresh vegetables; and after she had eaten a meal of bread and ham, with the added luxury of coffee, she looked again at the small sewing-room and wondered whether she could turn her talent for fine embroidery into simple sewing. She could buy a few yards of plain dimity very cheaply and make herself some gowns more suitable for her present life than the confections which had won the delighted approval of all the beaux of St James's.

It took some time and effort to carry hot water upstairs for her bath. Afterwards, she sank gratefully between the sheets—pleasantly scented with dried lilac flowers—her mind still running on seams and dimity and the possibility of a cow. Certainly she would want a plain gown for milking; she had not forgotten the amusement in Booth's eyes for her elegantly-trimmed mull muslin, made, did he but know it, by Madame Mathilde.

It was quiet in the little house, very different from the noise and bustle of the inn. She fell quickly into a sound sleep, forgetting even to lower her lamp. Some time in the night she was awakened by the sound of a horse's hooves and realized that there must be a traveller on the tow-path. The sound stopped; the traveller had paused. Suddenly she felt how much she was alone, and her body trembled in a swift rush of fear. Dimming the lamp, she went to the window, standing to one side so she could not be seen.

A man was dismounting from a horse on the path. His broad-brimmed hat, his coat and riding breeches were like those of any gentleman of these parts; his easy gait, his air, was all his own. He walked towards the house and stood a few yards back, gazing upwards at her windows. His eyes were shadowed, but the moonlight struck clear upon the lower part of his face, the chin firm and strong, the mouth curiously tender. He watched for a moment and then made a circle of the house, pausing at doors and windows to see that all was secure. Then he turned, remounted his horse, and rode away. And Damaris felt no more fear that night.

CHAPTER

42

Damaris saw little of Howard Booth now she was installed in Towpath Farm. He was too much aware, she believed, of the difficulties of her position to cause embarrassment to his tenant. Sometimes she heard him riding by, taking the tow-path when he left the village of Avon on his way from Hartford, but he never came again to stand beneath her window. She learned from the ladies of Litchfield that he was busier than ever with trade and politics—an important convention at Hartford had been officially adjourned almost a year before, but gentlemen still met informally, not content with the dealings of the men in the nation's capital concerning European trade.

Damaris knew even less of what was taking place in politics here than she had known in London of the affairs between England and her enemies. The ladies spoke of their household matters and guardedly of their daughters' admirers—the word 'lover' could never be spoken; even a cock must be called a rooster, and a bull was known as a 'cow-brute.' She went now to the Litchfield houses to dinner and heard the gentlemen talk, grumbling about 'Madison's war' and the subsequent treaty, some of them speaking with great heat. A courteous, erudite old man called Tapping Reeve, if he was present calmed the hotheads but most agreed that new treaties should be made and that Connecticut should be represented at the making of those treaties. Sometimes they spoke of the old days, and of the wicked Aaron Burr, who had come from these parts and studied at Mr Reeve's law school. But the men left the ladies early to their glasses of elderberry or dandelion wine; they retired to another parlour where they could smoke and chew tobacco and drink whisky—a strong, cheap drink to which American men seemed much addicted—and the ladies' talk reverted once again to housekeeping.

Fortunately housekeeping was of great interest to Damaris at this time; she was busy from morning till night. She was now the proud possessor of two cows that got her up before dawn. Booth had sent his man Cox to repair the barn, and Damaris watched the work closely. Cox, who had become her friend, was amused at her ideas.

'Mrs Egremont,' he told his friends in the tavern, 'she want a barn finer than most folks' houses—not one crack for a draught of air to blow upon they cows. That lady, she fuss over they beasts like they was prize stock goin' up to the fair, instead of Flora Duckworth's old Ayrshires with not much more milk left in 'em.'

She hoed the ground in her garden. It was hard labour and gave her pains in muscles she had never known she had, but she went on and carefully spread the ground with dung as the cottagers of Angelhurst did to prepare the ground for the next year's sowing. In the afternoons she had her classes and taught the country girls a little music, embroidery, and more gentle speech to those whose parents wished it, who were few enough. National pride forbade the notion of any deficiencies in American speech. The parents requested Damaris to use the *Compendious Dictionary* in instructing their daughters, a work compiled by a New England gentleman, one Noah Webster. Damaris looked at this work and saw that the proper pronunciation of *ask* was *ax* and *deaf* was *deef*, but as the girls had already learned this, she felt she was not required to go further. The harsh, nasal voices that seemed to Damaris properly belonging to Miss Hoydens remained secure to the daughters of the local farmers. She gave instruction in Latin and

Greek to a few pupils, though classical learning was not too much favoured by the country people; the most eminent families, of course, sent their daughters to the select academy of Miss Pierce. Most of her girls were already full-grown, and she did not try to do more than give them a little polish and interest them in reading something other than the newspaper.

She was to have only one failure, a girl called Jenny Brandywine. Mrs Brandywine, inspired by Flora Duckworth's progress, begged Damaris to take her daughter Jenny, though she was as big as Flora and very much more backward. A rampaging, boisterous girl, not only could she not learn herself, but she disturbed the other pupils. Damaris was concerned, particularly as the mother pleaded with her to keep the girl to learn anything she could. On fine days Damaris could set her to simple outdoor tasks, but when she had to be inside, discipline was impossible. Regretfully Damaris had to dismiss her from the school.

There were other problems. One day she was visited by the pastor of the Congregational Church, Mr Lyman Beecher. He was deeply shocked at finding on her shelves the letters of Madame de Sevigné, a gift from the Duchesse de Langcourt et Montrevet, and was warned solemnly of its evils. Mr Beecher suggested she would be well advised to keep to Bible reading in her classes. The visit of the rather awesome Mr Beecher would have been dreadful indeed had he not brought with him his four-year-old daughter Harriet, a playful little girl who fortunately took reproaches from Damaris to herself by stealing cake from a dish—the very cake sent with her husband by Mrs Beecher as a friendly gift. The look of sanctity had perforce to fade in Mr Beecher's glance while he wiped the crumbs from the young offender's lips, and in laughingly refusing his apologies for his unsaintly child, Damaris escaped more scolding.

After, she hid the work of Madame de Sevigné in her bedroom and tried to use books of a sort that would not raise a blush on the dourest matron of Litchfield, but she found it difficult— Shakespeare himself was considered improper by many matrons, and there was hardly a writer in the English language who did not use words considered unfit for the young ladies to read. It would sully their innocence, their mothers believed, even though such young ladies assisted at the birth of foals and calves and every day saw all the life of the barn-yard and the fields about them.

There was no one to share her laughter, with Jean-Philippe

gone—and his laughter she had thought unkind. He called America a nation of servants. She understood: in England such open piety was for servants and simple people, only expressed by Methodists, to be laughed at by fashionable folk. But many of those simple people had been those closest to her as a girl at Angelhurst, and the warmth she had felt for them was reflected in her response to the people of Litchfield. She wondered what had happened to Betty—surely the Earl had left her to watch over the Lady Griselda and the Viscount. But even Betty and the village people had been able to mention breeches without blushing—she laughed alone and wished suddenly for Howard Booth. There was one who would see the joke of a dairymaid who could not pronounce the forbidden word *teat*.

Prudently she restricted most of her efforts to the unexceptionable fields of music and embroidery, and she prospered. She now had a young girl 'come in to help'—the word 'maidservant,' she found, was disliked among the Yankee girls—and was able to return the hospitality of the Litchfield ladies in her own dining-room —the ladies only, for she had been advised by Mrs Buell that it might be thought indelicate for her to ask the husbands while the Marquis was away. From Jean-Philippe himself she had no word.

For the occasion of Thanksgiving, which came near the end of November, a celebration was planned. This holiday, she learned, was partly a memorial to the Pilgrims and partly a harvest festival. She was to be busy, she found, for she must attend not only the Congregational Church, or meeting house, but also the New Episcopal Church. She had been visited by the Episcopal ladies, and her duty as an Englishwoman and a member of the Church of England had been indicated. The service at the Episcopal Church was at least familiar, but religion was complicated here, with the schism in the Episcopal Church and the talk of Old Lights and New Lights among the Congregationalists. Of one thing she was certain—she was going to contribute to the feast which was part of the festival. She would bake her own apple pies of the sort she had eaten at Angelhurst, and she would serve with them the clotted cream of the West Country, which was not known in Litchfield at all.

Kate, Damaris's 'help,' was beside herself with excitement at the thought of the holiday and became rather useless in consequence. Damaris smiled at her eagerness, for usually the very young girl was brisk in her duties. She came from a farm family near Bradleyville. The father had cleared a few acres in the woods, and he and his wife had set to work with that fierce devotion to labour that seemed so common among Americans. Their farm was self-sufficient: they grew their own corn, long ears of golden maize, and ground it to bake their bread; meat and vegetables came from their own land; the wife and the daughters carded the wool from their own sheep, spun it, and wove it into cloth to make their clothes. Their furniture was made from their own trees, and even the candles were dipped from tallow in their kitchen. They bought almost nothing from the shop in the village known as the 'general store,' where everyone went; having no money, they merely exchanged from time to time for salt and a few lengths of cotton to make shirts and summer dresses. So busy were they from morning till night that rarely, even on Sunday, could they walk to the nearest village to go to church—their one horse was too valuable to be ridden for such a purpose.

Damaris had visited them, having to applaud in her own mind their great industry and self-sufficiency, and yet sighing a little for the girls, brought up in a social isolation that seemed brutish. Yet she remembered the fears of the people of Angelhurst when the Duke of Camberly was selling the estate. A new owner might have enclosed the common and left them all to poverty and ruin—that could never happen to Kate's independent family. These people had fought a war for freedom, and she saw it was a great thing—great that common folk owned their own land, tenants to no man, living without fear or favour from any lord.

While she was thinking, she worked quickly. She set her cream in pans like any farm wife of Angelhurst, scalded it until it set in thick clots. Her apples were already sliced, and while she and Kate fed the stove with firewood she rolled her pastry as she had seen it done so often—layer after layer spread with butter and rolled lightly, full seven times, until it went into the hot oven to rise, she hoped, in all the glory of delicate puff-paste. It would be something new in this place where the pastry was like the leather, only thicker. She wondered if Booth would be at the meeting to sample her contributions and swept up with a certain vainglory, she burned her finger on the hot stove.

'Damme!' she swore in great vexation, for her hands were a trouble—her skin bruised and cut so easily from her labours, and here she could not even obtain Denmark lotion with which to soothe them. Kate had taken pity on her and brought some grease used by her sisters after they peeled, or as they said, 'shucked,' the corn—dark unpleasant stuff, but it served.

'Such language, Ma'am,'—a drawling voice came from the door —'ain't considered fittin' for ladies hereabouts.'

Howard Booth sauntered in and pulled Kate's hair until she collapsed in a gale of giggles; he helped himself to some of the sliced apple, propped his long body against the table, and regarded Damaris's attempts with some amusement. Since Kate had arrived to serve as chaperon, Booth had taken to stopping at Towpath Farm if he passed it during the day—and he passed there often.

He presented parcels—tea, coffee, and to her joy, a bottle of Denmark lotion. 'And not before time, I see,' he remarked, looking at the rapidly-forming blister on her hand.

Pleased as she was, Damaris also felt a certain regret that she should be seen blistered, floury, and with her face warm from the stove by Howard Booth. Still, she thought with some pride, she must look a very proper New England dame.

To Booth, the delicate lady who appeared to be made of porcelain, with her jewel-like starry blue eyes, dressed in her white dimity gown, still looked like Marie Antoinette playing at being a milkmaid; but he knew now she had more sense than that unfortunate lady, and a courage that, if it was not tested by the prospect of imminent death, was perhaps of an even higher nature—the courage to live.

He gravely admired her pastry confection when it was withdrawn from the oven, and offered to drive her into the village. She explained hastily that she had hired the waggon and driver, and he nodded in acquiescence—Mrs Egremont must not seem too friendly with Mr Booth.

Just the same, she could be hospitable now she had Kate by her, and she brewed some coffee and set a tray with the pretty French china that she had found in the house and that had been sent there for her use, though she did not know it, by Howard Booth the day before her arrival. She added some tarts that she had made from a flaky pastry receipt and Mrs Duckworth's blackberry jam, and she had Kate take this feast into her sitting-room. Booth followed her obediently, hiding a grin—the customary offering to a male visitor was the hard cider of the region, beer or whisky, or Madeira in the houses of the rich, but he had to admit to himself that if the coffee were always as good as this he would be happy to take it more often.

He stretched his legs out and looked round the little parlour, bright and more shining than he could remember having seen it; tall vases had appeared from somewhere, filled with the last of the autumn leaves, framing the windows that looked out over the lake. There was a gleam of richness—Damaris's writing-desk on the side table, a likeness of a lady, painted in miniature, in a frame of gold set with seed pearls. He scrutinized the face, with its look of Damaris, the eyes grey instead of blue.

'Your mother?' he asked.

'Yes,' Damaris replied simply. She had hesitated before she put that picture on display, but no one here could know of the Maynes and the grand-daughter who had married the Earl of Malfrey, and it gave her a feeling of some attachment to her past.

To change the subject she thanked Booth again for bringing her the very welcome supplies.

'No trouble, Ma'am,' he said. 'Years back you could have bought such goods right down in Litchfield—it was that pesky embargo got folks out of the habit of relying on foreign comestibles.'

Damaris had heard about the embargo or embargoes—the world, it appeared, had conspired to stop the New England trade. England had had her Order in Council, Napoleon his embargo, and a former president of the United States, the Mr Jefferson who was so much disliked here, had made an embargo of his own, keeping all the American ships in dock. No wonder these New Englanders were resentful—even at the height of the war, in England there had been no shortage of goods, even French goods for those who wanted them; the smugglers who plied their trade in peace had continued much as usual in the war.

She regarded Booth with some suspicion. He had drawn out that word 'comestibles' in a very meaning way—he must have heard of her struggles with her pupils' families on the matter of pronunciation.

'I see you've come to tease the schoolmistress, Mr Booth,' she said. 'I'm glad you have the time to spare for such frivolity—you American gentlemen are always so very busy.'

'Not today,' Booth said reflectively. 'Not a man works on Thanksgiving—the mills shut down, the factories close—even over to Hartford they stop calculating the insurance and reckoning up their profit. Today's a day only ladies work, seems to me.'

The ladies, Damaris reflected, were always working; there were no fine ladies here. But the men did work hard too. The Countess of Malfrey had not known the merchants of London, but she could not imagine an Englishman always about his business like the gentlemen of Litchfield, from early until late, and even after a late dinner talking over business yet again.

She said as much and Booth grinned.

'Looks like it comes upon us, Ma'am. When I was a lad I had different plans. Meant to be the laziest man in the country.'

He asked permission to smoke and she gave it, enjoying the sight of him drawing on his pipe.

'My father had a friend—Hartford man, he was—they were at Dartmouth together. How they came to be friends it's hard to say, except they were both young—no two men more different than John Booth and John Ledyard. But my father early on took to saying that Ledyard was a fool and would never come to anything.'

He smiled reminiscently through the light grey haze of smoke.

'I thought he was the greatest man in the world. When he was just a young feller he started out by boating down the Connecticut River in a canoe. Then he went off and took ship as a common seaman to Gibraltar, then off with Cap'n Cook—saw him murdered by savages on Sandwich Island.'

Booth sighed. 'How I would love to have met him—but he died when I was four years old. I used to listen to my father talk about him to the solid men of Litchfield. Wasting his time on foolishness, he always said. Ledyard went to northern Europe, marched himself through Siberia, and tried to cross to this continent through the Bering Strait. Ice stopped him, he turned back, and the Russkies, a friendly lot, arrested and then deported him. Said they'd execute him if he ever showed his face back there again. You'd think that might be enough for any man, but no. After he got himself to England, he took a notion to go exploring in Africa.'

'And did he?' Damaris said.

'Got as far as Cairo and died of a fever. Not a long life,' Booth said with a gleam in his eyes, 'but he saw a lot of the world. And to my mind then, it sure beat countin' up nails and bolts and planks o' wood and all the mess of goods we Booths get to contrivin'—even ladies' corsets, Ma'am—unmentionable though they be to the local ladies.'

He grinned.

'Not much to catch the fancy of a boy.'

'And what changed your mind?' Damaris asked. She knew well she should not be prolonging Booth's visit with such talk. It was bad for both of them to give cause for gossip, yet her interest in his early life was real and strong—and she was strangely reluctant to have that lean and lanky form, the keen eyes with the direct and humorous glance, withdraw from her presence.

'Yellow fever,' he said simply. 'Took my father and mother in a week, and my brother two weeks later. And so I had to leave my favourite occupation of nothing in partic'lar and look to all the business. Too many men and women up and down the river valleys waitin' on Booth's for wages. But I got my chance in the war.'

He laughed.

'I went on that damned fool expedition to Canada. Crazy notion—we've got more land than we can use in these United States for a long time to come. Folks round here don't favour all the new territories, and they didn't favour that war. Some of my neighbours are still right sore at me for goin'. But now I'm back, and all the ladies say I'm a real Booth after all—or almost.'

Damaris wondered about that 'almost'; why he had never married like nearly all the men of this country, and who the lady was who had caused all the scandal. Fearful that he would observe her curiosity, she turned the subject.

'It is amazing indeed that the wealthy families work so hard. It would be impossible for the London beaux—they take as much as four hours just to tie their cravats in the morning.'

Booth laughed. 'I daresay we might have gotten into such elegant ways, Ma'am, but you see, we couldn't wait quite that long to dress. Indians are well known to be early risers.'

'Indians!' she exclaimed, her eyes wide. She had seen no Indians since she landed and had heard little of them. 'There—there are no Indians about here?'

'Well, there were some, Ma'am,' he said, 'and we did have some trouble for a time. But it's nigh on a century since a white man was killed and scalped by Indians in these woods. Army set up a garrison in Litchfield after that. Twenty pounds each they paid for the scalps of enemy Indians, so we ain't seen too much of 'em since then.'

His expression was wry.

'A few wretched souls used to come round beggin' at the

kitchen door when I was a boy—but you won't be troubled now.'

He rose to take his leave. Damaris's spirits fell a little, and she hoped he would be at the meeting later. When the waggon arrived and she readied herself to go, she regarded her image in the glass critically. Calling Kate, she bade her give Dan, the waggon driver, a tankard of cider, and she took off the village-made gown of dimity, put on a flounced blue silk, and then took it off again. She shivered as she stood in her chemise—the day was chill though bright, and Towpath Farm was not Malfrey House. Her bedroom fire was not lit all through the day—young Kate had made a spirited refusal to do anything so unlikely and troublesome.

'My mother says it be more healthy to get used to cold,' she had pronounced, and Damaris, sighing a little for Betty yet admiring Kate's independence, had tactfully let the matter of the upstairs fire go.

If the dimity seemed too simple, her other gowns seemed too fine. Damaris longed for a dress that was different from anything she now possessed, something new, elegant, with a deceptive look of simplicity and faultless line. Recognizing the longing, she knew exactly what it meant. But she closed her mind to that knowledge —it was nonsense to think that way of Booth; they both knew there could never be anything between them.

She settled on a Brighton gown of white silk crêpe with a scalloped hem embroidered with blue forget-me-nots. Gazing in the glass, she looked at herself in a way she had not done since leaving Brussels—perhaps since leaving Town. Lately she had given her reflection merely the quick glance of a woman busy with other matters, only to see if her hair was tidy, or remarking the pallor of ill health.

Now what struck her with surprise was that she looked no different. The careful upbringing of Lady Gratton had ensured that she was well covered when working out of doors, so that her complexion was still white. Amazingly, there was no mark of care on her brow, and her cheeks had been restored to their translucent glow of health, never ruddy but with the hint of warmth beneath the skin. She was strangely shocked to see that she still looked like Damaris, Countess of Malfrey—and then she remembered that only half a year had passed since the night d'Egremont had come to her with her husband's blood on his hands.

She, who felt so different from that woman, regarded her own face, puzzled, pleased; pleased for reasons she would not examine.

A chilly wind was blowing across the lake, so she wrapped herself in a cloak of wool rather than one of her elaborate velvets; but the soft fur collar framed her face and caused Beulah Hatch to gaze at her grimly during the sermon, and to watch the eyes of Howard Booth, which strayed in the direction of the young Marquise far more often than they should.

Damaris's 'offerings' were placed with those of the other ladies in the adjacent room. But she found, to her surprise, that they had to eat them. Unlike the fruits of the English harvest festival they were not to be distributed to the poor—there were no poor, and the ladies and gentlemen had come prepared to devour them. The long table held puddings and pies and made-up dishes of various sorts, and cider and ale in barrels.

She had to slip away to attend the later, quieter service of the Episcopal Church, but found that many of those ladies, religious differences for once forgotten, were going with their own contributions to join in the festivities. The room was decorated now with hollowed pumpkins lit by candles and vases filled with dyed grass. Already the eating and drinking was well under way.

Damaris's pies received enthusiastic praise, from Mrs Duckworth to Lyman Beecher himself, and her clotted cream was received with surprise, consideration, and then warm approval. Howard Booth, who strolled in to join the celebration, partook of pie and cream and solemnly announced it to be an invention superior to the spinning-wheel, to the laughter of the men and the annoyance of Mrs Hatch, who was noted as the chief piebaker for the church and was not used to having her, or rather Verity's, efforts take second place.

The high Yankee voices exclaimed and grew louder yet when Mrs Buell began—or 'commenced,' as she said—to make her contribution in a huge pot larger than a milking pail over the roaring fire.

'One yard of flannel,' a rubicund, portly man said, smacking his lips appreciatively, and Damaris, fascinated, watched the matron heat a bucket of ale while she beat eggs and sugar with nutmeg and lemon peel into the contents of a bottle of rum and a bottle of brandy. When the ale was near the boiling point, she poured it in a great jug, mixed it with the rum and brandy, and tossed it from one jug to another until it was as smooth as cream. Then, to make sure it had lost none of its heat, she plunged in a red-hot poker and let it sizzle as she poured.

Her portions were generous, and the behaviour of the company underwent the usual change. The fellowship grew among the men, and growing bold together, they rallied the women; girls who had been allowed small glasses became more flirtatious than their usually prudish manners would allow, and even Verity Hatch had a blush on her cheeks as she talked to Howard Booth. After praising Damaris's pie, Booth had fallen into conversation with Verity. He seemed not to notice Damaris, even in her Brighton gown that had caught the Prince Regent's fancy. Verity was dignified in red silk. The two of them made quite a handsome pair, Damaris thought with a pang of pain for which there was no reason; she thought it a good thing that Booth should settle down to marry the kind and suitable Verity Hatch.

Mrs Hatch was affected in quite another way. Damaris, feeling suddenly that she had had enough of the entertainment, had persuaded the reluctant Dan to drive her home. A little later, Booth, telling Verity he had to get back to Hartford that night, left also. Seeing her leave early, Mrs Duckworth, whose mind still ran upon maternity, wondered to her old friend Beulah Hatch that 'maybe Madam Markiss was feeling poorly. Lord, it would be a fix for the lady if she were in fambly way, with the Markiss gone off wanderin' just like Duckworth left me with my Flora when my petticoats was fit to bust.'

Mrs Hatch, who had drunk two large glasses of the 'flannel,' sniffed and answered without bothering to lower her voice.

'Oh, Madam Marquise,' she said. 'Well, I would hardly know. A woman comes here with a man, and he goes off and leaves her. No letters come for Towpath Farm as ever I've made out.'

'Well, a woman can't help it if a man do go off,' Mrs Duckworth said angrily, but Mrs Hatch sniffed.

'I'm not talking about Duckworth, who was worthless from the day he was born,' she said, not mollifying her listener. 'But any decent woman knows that a man don't usually leave his wife without good cause.'

She looked as though she were about to say more, but one of the deacons intervened and pointed out to the company that the sky was growing dark.

'Storm's blowing up off Mount Tom,' he said. 'Looks like we'd all better be making our ways home.'

The party did begin to break up, though the ladies were longing to hear more of what Beulah Hatch had to say and some of the gentlemen were not willing to allow that any of the 'yard of flannel' be wasted.

They were not the only ones to regret the sudden break-up of the festivities. Even before the sky had darkened, Dan was gloomy at being taken off to work on Thanksgiving Day while his friends were still enjoying themselves. When they came to the lake-side and the tow-path, he stopped the waggon and looked at Damaris hopefully.

'Fine day for a walk, Ma'am.'

She smiled. It was still early; she would be home before dark if she walked briskly. Her cloak was warm—why shouldn't Dan enjoy this holiday? The clouds on the horizon were very far away. But after Dan had gone, grinning broadly, wondering if more 'flannel' was being prepared, she began to reconsider.

It was pleasant enough walking, despite a quite sharp wind, but she had forgotten how drastically the weather could change here, all in a moment. Clouds, thick and dark, now massed overhead in a threatening fashion. The storm broke before she was halfway down the path. In a moment she was drenched and buffeted by strong winds. There was no protection from their full force by the lake, and she fought her way into the shelter of the trees. For a moment she felt some relief but then was terrified to see the lightning strike into the trees further along the way. The woods were no protection; she was in worse danger there, and she turned to make for the lake-side again. The strong winds thrust her back, and hampered by her flying cloak, she could hardly move. In sudden fear she cried out, but of course no one was near, and her voice was borne away on the winds. She clung to a slender tree-trunk and to her horror felt the very trunk being torn up by its roots. In panic she ran, was caught by the plunging branches of the tree, and fell headlong to the ground.

There was a quick tread, and two strong arms closed round her.

'It's all right, Damaris.' The voice, firm and steady, spoke close to her. She was lifted up and placed upon a horse, and Booth was there beside her. They rode down the centre of the path at an even pace, and all her feeling of fear vanished. Even the pain across her back and shoulders where she had been whipped downward by the falling branch seemed merely a local ache, not truly distressing, and her heart most unaccountably felt light, happy—happier certainly than she had felt since she had seen Booth chatting amiably at Verity's side.

He carried her into the little house, set her down upon the parlour settle, and lit the fire that the exuberant Kate had omitted to build up against her return. He boiled water, took her cloak, and bathed her clean of mud.

'You must not—' she said faintly, but he bade her cease chattering.

'For lack of better, I did some doctoring when I was a soldier,' he said. 'If I can clean and bind a gun-shot wound, I guess I can take the mud off a lady's cuts and bruises. Time I rode back for Doc Brewster those cuts could get right nasty.'

His hands, certainly, were gentle as a woman's—gentler by far than young Kate's. But Kate, after the festivities, was going home for a day's holiday with her family. Without Booth she would have been still in the woods struggling against the wind.

'I was lucky that you were travelling after me,' she said.

'Saw that Dan was liquored up,' he replied briefly. 'Didn't trust him with the waggon—never thought he'd turn you out and leave you. I'll have something to say to him tomorrow.'

She protested that she had been agreeable to Dan's going, but Booth's mouth was set. He would not allow her to leave the fireside but brought her a light morning-gown and a large cashmere shawl from her room, and bade her change while he waited outside. Then he took her soaking dress and petticoat to hang in the kitchen near the stove—as if he were a lady's maid, she thought in amusement. Howard Booth had certainly lived with a woman and learned much more than Jean-Philippe had ever done.

When he returned she was clean, dry, and warm, leaning comfortably back on the cushions on the settle, feeling as well as she had ever felt in her life. The pain was nothing, nothing at all. It was rather agreeable to have a pain, an excuse to lie back and look into the fire with Booth at her side.

He brought her a glass of wine, not the dandelion wine beloved of the Litchfield ladies but good Madeira that he had sent to her from his own house.

She drank it but giggled.

'I drank that "yard of flannel,"' she said, 'and I am afraid I might be overset.'

'Some folks were,' Booth said with a shrug and a smile. 'Still, I doubt but that it ain't all washed out of you, Ma'am.'

He looked round with a frown.

'Maybe it was a mistake I set you here,' he said. 'This house is built strong and tight, and the wind and rain won't get in, but it is mighty lonely if you should get strayin' on the path.'

'The house is perfect,' she said quickly. 'It was stupid of me to be wandering about on foot so late in the year.'

They fell silent. Booth had offered her horses and a 'shay,' as they called a chaise here, but Damaris had refused. She could have sold more of her jewels and set up a stable, but that, in her mind, was treachery to Jean-Philippe—it was an admission that he had deserted her and that she had no thought of ever building the new life they had planned together. But just then she had no wish to think of Jean-Philippe.

She could only think of Booth and how he had stood with Verity Hatch, smiling, bringing the colour to her cheeks. Had something been settled between them after all? His care for herself, she was sure, betokened love, at least a little love, but like any other man somewhat *épris* of a married woman, he still must think of marriage, the begetting of his sons. She thought again of the lady of the scandal. Had he really lived with her here, in this very house? Had they shared embraces—perhaps before this very fire?

She was jealous, she realized, astounded. It was an emotion she had hardly known. Sometimes she had been suspicious of Jean-Philippe; with that rogue of love she could never be sure of his fidelity. Yet she was always certain in her heart that he loved no one but her. Jean-Philippe—once more she banished the thought from her mind.

She turned her head restlessly. Booth, believing her still nervous from her adventure, stroked her forehead gently.

'Why have you never married, Mr Booth?' With surprise she heard her own voice, low, gentle as always, asking the shockingly impudent question.

Booth appeared neither shocked nor even surprised. He rubbed his chin reflectively. 'The one question ladies always do like to ask. Well, it's true that most men in these parts marry, and right young. And if one wife dies they haul off and marry themselves another.'

He smiled. 'But Ma'am, you've been round the ladies for a fair piece now, and I would bet my boots you've heard all about my wicked ways. "The terrible scandal over to Booths." Some still say,' he said, 'that I'm not fittin' to be senator from this state, although that idea came to some Hartford gentlemen. But the wives have a long mem'ry—though Lord, it seems like a long time ago.'

He stared out at the rain, not seeing it, she thought, but looking at pictures in his mind.

'You know Miss Verity,' he said abruptly, and Damaris jumped. Surely no scandal could ever have touched the staid and proper daughter of the Hatches. 'She is right charitable, as good a woman as ever lived.'

Damaris felt a soreness at the heart that was much more painful than the soreness on her back and scolded herself for her folly.

'She started a Sunday school for some of the children down by the mills. And she has a temperance society down there—not that I'm for abstinence,' he said, grinning, 'but it helps the wives and families if a man's wages ain't spent on rot-gut whisky. Well, Miss Verity, she's working with Lyman Beecher to get together a Colonization Society as well.'

Damaris was puzzled. 'Colonization?'

'They reckon on collecting funds,' he explained, 'to buy Negroes from the South and give them their freedom. The plan is to send them back to Africa.'

It all seemed far away from Booth's youthful love affair—perhaps it was with a slave? She supposed that would be a scandal.

'Do they want to go?' she asked.

'I doubt it,' Booth said wryly. 'Leastways, most of 'em. You have to figure that by this time they'd feel as outlandish there as you or I. But the Society won't be ready to send them for a long time yet, and some at least will be freed. The point is, many people up here are rare interested in Negroes and the abolition, a good cause, I allow. But for all of that, there's hardly a soul to bother for the Indians hereabouts.'

'I have never seen an Indian,' Damaris said.

He nodded.

'Yes'm. That's just what I mean. Yet this place was once Indian land. A Booth bought his first acres from an Indian called Wonposet. Still have the paper at home with Wonposet's mark. Took off with his people to Mount Tom—the hunting was better there, but there was some argument with other tribes. Between wars, sicknesses, and some of them moving off to get away from the farming folk, there were precious few left, even when I was a boy. In the winter they would come around the village for food and blankets, and the housewives complained that if you fed and clothed one, the whole tribe would end up in your back-yard. True enough,' he said, and sighed.

'But they drifted off, family by family. And one winter morning my mother found a little girl sitting in the snow on the porch, ragged, like to freeze to death. Whether she was lost, or if her folks had just gone off and left her, we never did know. A little bit of a thing then she was, not more than four or five. Mother took her in and brought her up right in the house. She taught her to do chores about the place, and the girl grew up right handy. Some ladies thought Mother did real well, having no girls of her own to help her and outside help bein' so hard to find.'

Damaris, who could see the end now of his roundabout Yankee tale, found her imagination stirred. Her mind was full of John Smith and Pocahontas, the beautiful Indian princess, but that idea was soon dismissed.

'Right homely she was, but a good little thing. Never grew real tall, sort of squat-shaped, but mighty neat with her hands. Never did talk much, either, but I had to listen to all those ladies bawling at the spinning parties, and that quiet seemed just fine.'

He grinned again and then was silent.

'The folks reckoned my elder brother would marry Verity Hatch. The two families together would have owned about half of western Connecticut, and everything in it. We are all born equal, Ma'am,' he said with the humour glittering in his eyes, 'but some families like to think their sons will have a little relish on the good bread of equality. That left me free to do just as I pleased—which I would have done anyhow. I had no thought of marryin'—after Yale I planned to go off like Ledyard, to see the world.'

He shrugged. 'But nature is nature. I was rare fond of 'Becca— no one knew her name, and Mother had her christened Rebecca though it didn't suit her—and she was always fond of me. And though Mother brought her up real strict, 'Becca never took to all the ways of white women. Not that she had a chance to feel like one of them—there were those who saw to that.'

A log fell in the hearth, crackling and hissing, and Booth leaned over to push it safely back. For a moment or two Damaris could not see his face, but he went on talking evenly.

'Summers were the worst for 'Becca, penned up in the kitchen heat and her eyes always on the woods. We boys used to go down to the swimming hole out of sight of all the ladies, shuck off all our clothes, and swim all day, and Lord, if I didn't once come across 'Becca all alone, splashing about in a pond out of sight, she thought; run off from my mother and left her there with the bakin' in the August heat.

'That day we swam together. It was a secret between us. And sure enough, as we got bigger, we had more.'

'Did you love her?' Damaris asked.

Booth stared into the fire.

'Yes, I loved her. We had grown up together; she had tended to my needs almost all her born days. She was soft-footed, soft-voiced, and gentle, little 'Becca. She was my first woman instead of a prostitute from the ports, and as natural as if she'd never heard a preachin' of hell-fire. Never thought 'Becca really took to hell-fire,' he said meditatively, 'and she liked to laugh. Not from talk, as we might do, but in her way. Little things would set her off. She would watch two grackles on the window-sill quarreling for crumbs, and she would laugh, quiet as almost to make no sound, but jumping up and down from it. Or a rabbit with a fat rump loppeting over a field—'Becca would grin and hop and some-times clap her hands together.

'But the ladies of the town soon started talk. I was sent down to Hartford to work in a counting-house before I went to Yale,' he said, and grimaced. 'What happened at home I don't know, but when I went back on my first holiday I heard that 'Becca had run off. Never saw her again until after the folks died and I went home from New Haven. 'Becca turned up one night and offered to keep house for me. But it would have been cruel to have kept her there with all the Litchfield ladies calling her a squaw. So I sent her here. But she couldn't stand the loneliness and got the melancholy. And once when I came back from a long trip she had just gone off again. I never knew what happened to her, though some folk said she had gone to join up with some Mohegans north of here in Canada.'

'Were you very unhappy?' Damaris asked with quick sympathy.

'Unhappy? I worried about 'Becca. If she still felt an outsider, back with her own people after growing up with white folks. But unhappy—I don't know. I was a full-grown man. I'd known other women. I would have married 'Becca if she could have faced it, but I think I was not real sorry that she never would.'

He was silent. He had never spoken to anyone of 'Becca in her melancholy, sitting for hour after hour, her hands in her lap, while the house grew daily more neglected and forlorn and she grew thin, her bones jutting out like a starving cow's, her eyes glazed and vacant. The doctor he had brought her knew no cure; he shook his head and said he had seen such states before, but only in the old. Booth could not help her. Her warmth for him had turned to listlessness; there was no smile when he came or farewell when he left. In his heart he knew there had been some relief when she ran off—relief mingled with the fervent hope that she would be happy again with her own people, away from a life that perhaps to her was much like death.

'What was between us had been the love of boy and girl. Perhaps we were both happy when it ended. I did not love her as a man loves a woman—as I love you, Damaris.'

His voice was calm, almost matter-of-fact. There was silence between them, but it was a silence that said everything. Faced with this simple frankness, she felt the impossibility of mouthing the falsehoods of convention, of asserting fidelity to a marriage that did not exist or loyalty to her real marriage vows that she had broken long ago. The silence seemed to grow, charged with new meaning.

The little house was snug indeed. Now it was warm from the bright fire. Outside the rain still beat down; the wind howled, but it only served to make the little room feel more warm, the two people inside more close. Booth sat at Damaris's feet on the edge of the straight settle, smiling down at her. The logs burned crimson, sending showers of golden sparks up the chimney. The lamp cast a soft light shadowing half the room but glowing on Booth's face, which looked younger, more vulnerable, his grey eyes no longer bantering but filled with radiance.

She lay back, remembering the grasp of his hands about her in the woods, longing to feel them once again, not realizing the depths of invitation in her glance. He clasped her to him in a flood of passion that shook them both as the wind shook the trees in the forest all about them. His mouth came down hard on hers and sucked greedily in a line of kisses from her throat to her breast. Damaris gasped in an ecstasy of pain and pleasure; her body melted in a trembling surge of longing that no thought, no care could deny. She felt the hardness of his body close beside her, with all the relief of pretence and caution cast aside, and gloried in the outpouring of love that would engulf her.

So transported was she that she hardly heard the hoof-beats on the path outside—it was Booth who first drew back; the sound only forced itself on her consciousness at the moment when it ceased. Someone was descending from a carriage. Her door, country fashion, was locked only at night. A tread sounded in the entrance. Damaris had hardly wrapped herself in her long shawl, and Booth jumped up beside the hearth, when the door opened and Mrs Hatch, grim-faced, stood on the threshold.

'Some of us were afraid for your safety, Madam Marquise, when Dan Kenney came back so soon. But I see,' she said, her eyes taking in Booth, the wine glass, Damaris's light morning-gown under the cashmere shawl, 'I see I need not have been concerned. Good day to ye, Ma'am. Your horse outside is drenched, Mr Booth,' she added. 'I think the beast could use your attention.'

And she banged the door behind her.

Afterwards Damaris would believe that the intrusion of Beulah Hatch changed the course of all their lives. For the sake of her reputation, after a swift word Booth had left immediately, riding with Mrs Hatch to Litchfield. He returned later that night with a startling proposal.

The proposal was simple—that they leave New England and go west. They could make an entire break with the past, take a new name, and go where none would know them.

'We will be married in the eyes of God,' he said firmly. 'Pioneering folk don't ask too many questions. If you can bring yourself to forget about that shiftless husband of yours,' he said grimly, 'we can have a good life, Damaris. We can go to an established, prosperous settlement, and we will go with money. Verity's uncle, Simon Hatch, will buy some of my properties, and my cousin Wadsworth will run my mills. You'll be able to lead a lady's life soon enough in Ohio, or as far as we want to go.'

Damaris, now that she was sane again, knew that she must not do this. She had run away with one man and knew the bitter consequences. Booth was a very different man from d'Egremont; she was sure he could make a life for them in Ohio—or anywhere. But his roots were here more than he realized. His mills and manufactories, his ships at sea, the welfare of his state—his mind would be back on these things before they reached their destination. She knew that flight would be wrong, even while the memory of his kisses was burning in her breast.

Mrs Duckworth had told her that if Booth did make up his mind to marry Verity Hatch, he could be elected senator. For him, great affairs would satisfy his old longings for adventure. Damaris could not allow him to sacrifice so much. She had achieved a certain wry wisdom and knew it to be no good thing to be the recipient of sacrifice—she had thrown away her life as Countess of Malfrey for d'Egremont, and she felt sure that he rued the day.

Also, she well knew that Booth, although laughing at extravagance of zeal and prudery, was in his heart a religious man, as these New Englanders were. She wondered how long his self-esteem and his love for her would survive if they lived together in adultery. And adultery it would be. She was reluctant to confess the truth about herself and Jean-Philippe, afraid that it must lower her in his estimation. But if she did, what then? She had come to be almost certain that her husband still lived. The newspaper here had little news of Europe—little news of any kind, being filled with purely local events, receipts for favourite dishes, homilies, and mottoes. Yet the Earl of Malfrey had been a great man, not only in England but in the councils of Europe. If he had been violently done to death, surely the news would have been blazoned abroad to reach even this place—she had long feared that the gentlemen of Hartford, with all their foreign business, would some day hear the truth about Jean-Philippe.

Jean-Philippe. She had feelings about him that Booth could not understand. If her love for him had changed, it had not vanished. Until Jean-Philippe told her that he loved and needed her no more, she felt curiously bound to him, responsible for his well-being, with a duty to share his future—if he so desired. Whatever his behaviour had been, whether or not she would ever see him again, she was sure that Jean-Philippe had not intended to desert her, that in his wildly sanguine moments he believed that somehow his old life would be restored; and then—and then only—would he want her at his side.

Damaris gazed at Booth steadily across the hearth, now cold and sprinkled with grey ash. She had been certain that he would return, but sense had quieted her love, and firmness had controlled her longing. Carefully she had dressed again, to change the mood between them, in a gown of heavy silk, dark, with a stiff overdress in white—she would look cool, unapproachable, the nobleman's wife.

Booth himself, she thought, was changed. A heavy frown marked his brow, and his mouth looked hard. She fancied it a foretaste of regret for what he planned, not realizing that the face of Mrs Hatch, stern and scornful, had brought up memories, bitterness mingled with some fear that Damaris might share the fate of poor Indian 'Becca, and with no tribe of her own to turn to in time of need.

She loved him stern as she had loved him warm and tender; the sight of his figure at her hearth squeezed her heart and made what she had to do more painful. He in turn saw the difference in her appearance that she had intended him to see. It was the Marquise d'Egremont who stood before him, an unlikely immigrant to the crude new lands westward.

'We—we cannot, Mr Booth,' she said, her soft voice, for once not clear, almost stammering. 'The Marquis—I will hear from him soon, I trust. I—' Words failed her. Her hands reached out to touch his arm, but fearing the closeness, she let them fall again.

He saw her hands fall away from him and felt he was rejected.

'It must be as you say, Damaris,' he said slowly. 'I can't force you to run off. And I won't ask you to be my mistress in this place. You're d'Egremont's wife, and if you feel bound to him, why, no man can say you're wrong. I am as disappointed as a man can be, but I will bear it.'

He took his hat and made to go.

'I won't say that I'm sorry I troubled you, Ma'am,' he said with a return of something like his usual humour. 'Because I'm right glad I did.'

He was gone, and she was left with the ashes in the hearth. She was angry that he had left her, joking; sad and lost that he had accepted her decision. He should have taken her in his arms and let the whole world do what it would. At least they could have spent one night together—instead she lay in her bed alone and cried herself to sleep that night. And none of her tears were for Jean-Philippe.

CHAPTER

45

It was not long after that she did hear something of d'Egremont. As had been predicted, winter came swiftly, cold, with deep snowfalls, though still with many days of dazzling brightness. Damaris was glad of her furs and her Franklin stove. Some of her pupils had difficulty coming to class; the roads were often impassable. Damaris felt sorry for the ones who did come. The poorer girls were sent out to walk miles through the snow, their hands swollen with chilblains; for their mothers, having put them into red flannel petticoats and strong boots, believed that would suffice. She gave them hot cider before she began instruction and suggested they stay overnight when the weather threatened—but this offer was always declined. Their mammas would like them to come home.

She did not see Howard Booth. At the Litchfield dinner tables she learned he was in Hartford on political matters. The husbands, while praising Mr John Quincy Adams for his work on the treaty of commerce lately signed with England, were still not satisfied. But at least, they said before they departed to fortify themselves with whisky, American shipping was at sea—with the best ships in the world. As they spoke they looked at Damaris, smiling, expecting her to protest. It happened that she had heard a naval commander tell that to Lord Malfrey at her own dinner table, though she had paid little attention then. The courteous Mr Reeve looked reproachfully at the boasting gentlemen as he led them away.

She heard the news of the Marquis at Mrs Hatch's table. She was still invited by Mrs Hatch, who prided herself on having the best of the local society at her dinners, but Damaris felt uncomfortable in that lady's company; a certain hostility was not far from the surface. She felt sure that the night at Towpath Farm was not forgotten, the lady's suspicion not entirely done away with.

Verity was still her friend. Now that she had taken on the air and manner of a woman she looked quite handsome, and rumours were flying about the village that she was to marry Howard Booth after all. Damaris tried to close her mind to such talk—it could be of no concern to her. But her ears were treacherous and listened keenly to each word.

Her interest in the report of the Marquis was more sober. A traveller from Washington City told her he had made the Marquis's acquaintance on the road. Damaris, behind her civil manner, was surprised; the stout man wearing thick boots and a waistcoat embroidered with red roses did not seem at first sight to be one whom d'Egremont would accept as an acquaintance. Apparently they had travelled together on the stage and stayed at the stage-coach inn.

'A great fine inn,' the man said proudly. 'One of our best. You can find from fifty to a hundred people sitting down to the table and they serve French dishes with sauces good as you'd find in Paris any day, I've heard it from folk who've been there. But your husband,' he said, chuckling, 'why, he was hollerin' fit to bust. There was such a crowd that day that a lot of dishes were gone before he sat down—very fussy in his dress, the Marquis; he was the last man from the coach to the table. And he said all the other dishes were cold, and he said a lot more in French that I couldn't make out and I suspect was not fittin' for ladies' ears anyway.'

He sat chuckling to himself in reminiscence.

'In the tap-room he was cursing the spittoons and swearing at some folk that chanced to miss and spattered his boots and breeches. He flung off to bed, and I thought he would be quiet till morning. But your good man, Ma'am, had the room next to mine, and long before dawn he woke me up with his hollerin'. I was near startled into fits, and most of the folks around us besides. One lady had a fainting spell, and her daughter was running about in her night-gown and cap looking for hartshorn or a vinaigrette. And all because your good man found chiggers in his bed.'

The men grinned and the ladies tittered.

'Well, you know, Ma'am, there ain't hardly an inn on the road that don't have them pesky insects, and it ain't no use to take on so.'

Mrs Hatch looked grim. She did not care for such talk at her table, and her opinion of the manners of the man from Washington—invited at the request of her brother-in-law, Simon Hatch—was plain upon her countenance. It penetrated even the assurance of the usually self-satisfied man from the capital, in spite of the liberal amounts of whisky and water he had been drinking in preference to the Hatches' good Madeira.

'But the Marquis, he did say, Ma'am, that he had never seen such a-crawlin' in all his days, and up here at Duckworth's inn, which he had thought a poor place, bein' mostly just a small country tavern, there was not a chigger in the house. He did allow that the New England ladies were right smart housekeepers, and he said the food they cooked was better than the stuff at the stage inn that wasn't French or American, and not fit for man nor beast.'

The ladies were gratified, and Damaris was amused that the Marquis had found himself praising Mrs Duckworth—but then thought miserably of the straits to which he must have been reduced for that to come about. She sighed, fearing that d'Egremont would never accustom himself to this new country. Chiggers—she had never heard the name before, but she had a good idea of what they were. When she travelled herself she would take her own sheets; she could always sleep on the floor.

In the weeks that followed there were many heavy snowfalls. So many roads became impassable that her school was perforce abandoned, and she had much time to think of Jean-Philippe, herself, and Booth. She was glad, she told herself with no feeling of gladness, that she had estranged Howard Booth. It was better so. Better he think of her as a flirt, a noblewoman willing to play at love with an attractive man, yet willing to make no great sacrifice for love. If he knew the truth, the depth of her love for him, the quiet dying of her love for d'Egremont, the withering of her bonds to the Earl of Malfrey, Booth would find himself hopelessly ensnared. Such a man would not give her up because of her difficulties, but he would ruin himself for her sake.

Such a man. Once the tow-path road was cleared of snow she watched from her bedroom window. Sometimes she saw a horseman, but it was not he. As she did the work of the house, teaching young Kate to cook and serve in English style, she thought what pleasure it would be to do these tasks for such a man. A gentleman, strong, masculine—there was a quality about him that she could only describe as adult. Sometimes he seemed the only truly adult male that she had ever known.

She thought of her friends, the Beau and the dandies with their minds almost entirely on their dress, the bucks who lived for horses like their ostlers—now they seemed rather childish. Her husband, the Earl, had had adult concerns, and for that she gave him respect, but the loving side of his nature had been warped and twisted so that at his maturity he seemed half man, half monster. The Prince Regent, with his corpulence, lust, and gluttony, his fits and threats of suicide to any lady who refused his amorous advance, was also part of the world of folly.

Her pupils returned, and she was busy again, but then Christmas came and it was a sad time. The school was closed for a week; the girls were needed at home to prepare the Christmas treats. Damaris accepted an invitation from the kind Mrs Duckworth, who prepared a little private dinner in the small parlour. Damaris was happy to talk to her and Flora, somewhat quieter now under her instruction and, to Damaris's great though secret relief, showing no signs of any unfortunate results from the exuberant embraces she had shared with Jean-Philippe.

Christmas had been the time she spent with her children. The Great House of Heron now had its charms in her memory; her babies had been born there; little Griselda had taken her first steps in the nursery that had once been Cassandra's. Lady Gratton would be with them this year, the yule log burning in the Great Hall, the children, wide-eyed, receiving their presents from the stately Earl. She assumed he was alive and in good health. It was easier to do so. The servants would stand in a row, respectfully waiting their turn. She wondered if it would be Mrs Crump or Betty who would stand at the head of the women.

Mrs Egremont thought more about her children, she realized, than Lady Malfrey ever had. Sometimes at night she would wake with a stab of pain, a sudden piercing thought that she would never see them again. She would try to cheer herself—she would have a new life, another family—but the image of the father of her children yet to be was vague, indistinct. The face of d'Egremont would not come clear to her mind, and she would fall back to sleep at last, uncomforted.

Over the dinner table, augmented with offerings of her own—she had made Mrs Duckworth syllabubs, about which the innkeeper had been curious, and also flummery, an English country pudding which the New England women relished—she gave d'Egremont's compliments to Mrs Duckworth, who beamed happily.

'There now, I always said the Markiss was a rare gentleman. And I do give him the right of it,' she told Damaris severely, 'in what he said of they great inns. Travellers might bring in dirt, I don't deny, knowing better, but good boiling do clean up all, as I've told my Flora a dozen times a day since she was born. But down South they do be a dirty lot, for all they have black slaves to wait on 'em.'

Flora, at the mention of the Marquis, giggled and bounced in her chair.

'And you stop that fidgetin', Flora, every time we speak of gentlemen, or you will have no more Christmas pie.'

And when Flora was clearing the table, Mrs Duckworth grew confidential.

'I'll have to let her take a husband, for all I need her 'bout the place. She do be so a-heavin' and a-squirming, the men they be following after her like she was a Madam Pompimore.'

Damaris hid her amusement at the idea of Flora Duckworth as the elegant Marquise beloved of Louis XV, most spoiled of men, and gravely agreed.

'I'll ask Mr Howard who he do think best,' Mrs Duckworth confided. 'He knows all the young men hereabouts. He will know who be a good worker and who spends his money in the taverns and has nothing saved against his wedding day. I saw Mrs Ellsworth, the lady who keeps house for him, and she says he will be back after the New Year comes in. She was looking to buy one of my geese to fix a special dinner, since he had his Christmas far off, and Miss Verity has left her special pudding against his coming home.'

Damaris found she had not yet learned to hear Booth's name calmly. But with the coming of the New Year and her resumption of steady work with her girls, she found herself accepting what must be. So, it seemed, did Howard Booth. When he returned, he treated her with the same courtesy he had always shown, and as time passed the formal aspect of that courtesy melted once more into warmth. She was a guest at a dinner he gave at the Booth house—the handsomest of the many fine houses of Litchfield. It was set among gardens and an orchard; its exterior was graced by fluted columns, and inside it had dignity and charm.

All the finer houses of Litchfield had interiors such like those of the houses of the English gentry. Most of the furniture had come from England, imported by the more prosperous families, although furniture was made, in somewhat crude copies, in the country. In spite of their liking for the French there was nothing of French influence there, no glitter of gold, no sphinxes. These ladies polished their floors to a high gloss, and no carpets were seen—except for those rags that had horrified Jean-Philippe. Few cushions softened the chairs, and to an English eye the rooms were devoid of ornament. Yet the sparkling cleanliness, the gleam and colour of firelight reflected in the shining wood, would be, Damaris thought, attractive to the most discerning gaze.

But once inside the Booth house, she might have been in England itself. The Booth trading ships had brought home luxuries. Fine Oriental rugs glowed on the floors, vases from China caught the bright New England winter sun on the window-sills. It was rich and glistening, a house that any man or woman would be proud to own, and Damaris wondered a little why Booth was so rarely there—she had heard talk that 'Mr Howard' kept the house for memory's sake only. Then she remembered the boy who had wanted to follow the traveller Ledyard, and she smiled. And a house was not a home for a man without a wife.

Her attention wandered to Mrs Hatch, who, she thought, was now less hostile than she had been of late. Booth was walking in his gardens with Verity, pointing out some new plantings. Perhaps he was going to settle with Verity after all, as Mrs Duckworth had predicted.

That dinner brought her more pain than pleasure. But as the months went by, her relationship with Booth returned to much of what it had been before Thanksgiving night.

Unable to get about on foot through the New England winter, she had been forced to sell a set of black and gold South Sea pearls to the goldsmith in the village—the price she obtained seemed very poor compared with what Booth had got for her in Hartford on her previous sale—and set herself up with a vehicle much like a gig that was known as a one-horse shay. She did not know how often Booth's eyes were on her, watching her drive through ice and sleet with a gentle hand on the reins and her lovely head held high through the violent weather. His admiration for her courage in d'Egremont's long absence, her determination to meet each day as it came, conquered his resentment at her spurning of his love; and reason suggested that if the love he thought he had seen in the lady's eyes was real and true, she was only doing her duty to deny it and to quiet her own heart.

Little by little their friendship grew again, and he took her one Sunday morning, with Verity Hatch, to a manufactory and mill down on the Naugatuck river where Verity taught a Sunday school to his working girls.

The snow was deep on the ground but frozen hard, with many ruts and bumps. The roads in this country seemed at the best close to impassable to an Englishwoman. In many cases logs had just been thrown down and left there as they fell. When the new mills turned out smooth planks for these roads, it was hailed as an achievement of the first magnitude.

Booth had had runners placed beneath his coach, and the ladies reached their destination without too much bumping and jerking. Damaris had never seen a manufactory, but she had heard them spoken of, and in no pleasant way. People told of darkness and crowding, of pale-faced women and children who took to drinking gin as a relief from their sufferings, with many a young girl, tired of drudgery, coming to a worse end, to the sorrow of her family.

Here she saw a well-built structure, light and heated against the winter's cold. For the workers Booth had built churches, about fifty dwellings, and three shops, called stores in the local fashion. The houses all had gardens and looked pleasant and comfortable. About a hundred fifty people worked there. Damaris saw the looms on which broadcloth and cotton stuffs were made, and in the churches she saw the workers, many of them young girls, plump, bright-eyed, dressed neatly in good warm woollen.

'The girls flock here,' Verity told her. 'They make two dollars a week, and their board costs them little. They lay money aside in a bank for savings that was set up for working people, and when they have saved a good dowry they marry. 'Tis an excellent thing,' she said, and smiled, 'but of course, it makes servants very hard to get. And much hard labour for the ladies.'

Booth took Damaris round and showed her all the amenities of the place.

'My father built it,' he told her. 'It was a philanthropic plan. He insisted that the selectman of the district come and inspect the place regularly to make sure the workers were well taken care of. The girls are allowed to come and go as they will—if their families need them, there is no trouble about going home. But we always have a good supply, and the surprise was'—he rubbed his chin and smiled—'that the manufactory shows a profit. Trust a Booth,' he said, grinning. 'It's always paid us to have the Lord on our side.'

He joked, but she saw he was proud of the achievement, as he had a right to be, she thought. For a moment she remembered her own girlhood when she, not yet sixteen, had been presented with a choice of marrying one of three men, two of whom were actually repulsive, and at last had been handed over to the half-mad Earl. If she had had the chance of earning her own bread and choosing her own man in her own time—but that had never been possible.

She reflected that in this new country they spoke much of liberty, that every man had the right to life, liberty, and the pursuit of happiness. It seemed also that their women had liberty to love. The Countess of Malfrey, known as the Marquise d'Egremont, wrapped in her sapphire-blue cloak lined with sable, looked at the fresh-cheeked mill girls and envied them most heartily.

She nearly said as much to Verity but checked herself. For if the daughter of the Hatches had liberty to love, it only served her if the love were returned. *That* problem could not be solved by legislation; no revolution could help unrequited love. Still, even a stern parent like Mrs Hatch could not make her daughter marry against her will. Verity could have her class, her charities, her self-respect. Her person would not be given up against all her inclinations like the poor slaves she worked so hard to protect.

Then Damaris shook herself, despising self-pity. She had consented to marry Malfrey. There had seemed to be no other choice, but she had consented. She would pay now for that consent and dance at the wedding of Verity and Howard Booth. From now on, she thought, watching the smiling girls file out of church into the sunlight, she, too, could at least keep her person free. The Earl would never want her back, and d'Egremont had disappeared in this vast land. Her pain at her loss of Booth would fade as everything faded, she told herself. At one time she had thought her whole world would be ended if she lost d'Egremont. Now he seemed but a laughing boy, gay and courageous enough when all was well, sulking like a child when life was not to his fancy.

When she left Booth and Verity in Litchfield, taking her own humble shay home, she felt a sudden weariness, the clumsy horse straining at the reins tiring her beyond endurance. She felt, at least, thankful that d'Egremont had gone. No longer did she pretend that she wished to see him again, and she was glad he had not written.

But within a month he did write—such news that she could not have foreseen.

CHAPTER

46

It was in the late spring that the letter arrived from Jean-Philippe in New Orleans. Damaris had been tranquil. The success of her little school, full to bursting now that spring weather had cleared the roads, her new ease in managing all the details of her country life—though Kate did the milking, she herself had mastered the workings of the Franklin stove and with fine defiance of local opinion had put one in her bedroom—had brought her back to something like happiness. Very like happiness, but she did not examine her emotions deeply.

There had been an early thaw and, contrary to the usual pattern of weather in these parts, no spring freeze. The lake that had been a sheet of solid ice for months, its glittering surface only varied by men and boys who went out fishing in carefully-dug holes, was once more a ripple of water, grey, blue, and grey again, though much too cold for even the hardiest of boys to bathe in.

The fields that had looked so strangely dead and drab to the Englishwoman, with the grass itself withered dun and grey from frost, now bore young green shoots with varieties of spring blossoms that Damaris could not recognize. All winter she had kept a flock of brilliant birds round her house by putting out her scraps, marvelling at the dazzling red of the cardinals against the snow, and in the spring they were joined by migrants from the south that made her mornings loud with bird-song.

Well warned, Damaris was not perturbed by this New England spring's sudden slides back into winter, with days of cold succeeding treacherously mild weather. The buds were tightly folded on the trees, and all the promise waited until at last the backslidings were behind them, and then by May there were already days warm as an English August, and the green round her had turned to a lush splendour.

Only one thing had caused a rueful shake of Damaris's head at the strange and foreign happenings; so deep was the freezing of the ground here in the winter that in the spring the giant earth moved and stirred itself when the gripping frost first passed; 'heaving,' the New Englanders called this phenomenon, and Damaris had watched with dismay as the road to Towpath Farm, never too smooth, now heaved to make it impossible for her horse and shay to travel. But one morning she went out, to find men working with axes clearing the way. Sent there by the selectman they told her, but as she knew the first selectman was Howard Booth, she realized to whom she was indebted.

Not long after the southern birds had come and the first golden pheasant had strutted by her window, that other exotic, Jean-Philippe, caused a buzzing in the village by his first letter to Madame la Marquise d'Egremont. Damaris had two distinct emotions as she held the letter in her hand: surprise—she had felt a conviction that she would not hear from Jean-Philippe again—and something else that she could not pretend was pleasure.

Her surprise was even greater when she found the letter cheerful. Hardly did he mention the horrors of his journey. He was full of praise and great enthusiasm for Louisiana and the city of New Orleans. The *bon ton* there was French, and apparently of a Frenchness just suited to Jean-Philippe. He had been received with kindness and courtesy by the rich aristocratic planters of the region. Many of them were native-born and known as Creoles, but he found the polish of their manners unaffected by this—which only, she gathered, heightened the importance of a nobleman and was of consolation to his bruised self-esteem.

He even joked about her pearls, which he had sold the better to make his entrée into this society. 'Alas, *exquise Marquise,* how much I regret to tell you that I had to dispose of the pearls that so adorned your lovely neck, those pearls that had been a present to a wife on her wedding day.'

He had spent his time in visiting one great house after another and joined in the gambling, as much, it seemed, the chief occupation of the Creoles as of the Englishmen of St James's. He was happy indeed.

What a dreadful *bêtise* it was, Madame, that we did not make our way here immediately instead of burying ourselves in that Puritan mudhole in the North. The society here is as agreeable as any in Europe—more so, I fancy, than in France, for I hear that Louis *l'Impossible* is now so poor—his countrymen refusing to pay him any taxes—that he is living on the money extorted by gendarmes from the prostitutes of Paris. Europe is no longer a place for a man of energy— the future is here where everything is stirring; huge fortunes are to be made. There is no pestilent notion of equality, and an aristocrat can live as he did in the old days. I have great plans, Madame, and I would ask you to join me without delay except that I have one small plan I wish to complete before you arrive. I have seen a French doctor, very skilled in the mending of bullet-shattered bones. The custom of duelling is still pursued here to a degree long since forgotten in England and France—these young men are hot-heads, full of pride and courage. It gives the surgeons much experience. This doctor believes that my bone can be broken and set

again and by a system of his own brought back to its natural
length. There is some risk, of course, and so I do not ask you
to come at once, but as soon as this is accomplished, I will
want you by my side. I have plans that will make your
previous position seem paltry—my mind has been fired since
I left the northern gloom and the blight of your bourgeois
friends.

The virtues of New England housewives were already forgotten,
Damaris saw. But there was more.

Everything that I had hoped to shower at your feet after
the victory of Bonaparte (one should never trust a peasant!)
will be yours, and much besides. But speak to no one of this.
Your makers of horseshoe nails are timid and afraid of
change—have you yet learned that they were traitors in the
war just ended and lost the opportunity to take Canada
for their own? How I hate them, the men of the counting-houses
—there is not a real man among them since Aaron Burr
was tried. He was a man—but he is finished now. I stopped
to see him in New York about a plan I had, but he is old
past even dreaming. Not old so much in years but dead in
all ambition. But there are men here—

The letter went on with his new enthusiasms. Jean-Philippe had
found this mixture of French gloss and a new, rich country heady;
she knew how easy it was for him to be stirred. As for his talk of
politics and future grandeur, she paid little heed. She had heard
too much in his illness of his wild dreams. Louis *l'Impossible*
(now reduced in his mind, it seemed, to a Parisian pimp) would
forget his sins and recall him to glory once again in France. Napoleon would return, victorious, from St Helena. Louis would be put
aside, and the king of Rome become the new ruler of France, with
d'Egremont suddenly, mysteriously restored to power and prestige. Most fanciful of all was the notion that the Prince Regent,
remembered as d'Egremont's great friend, would bring them back
to London, restore them both to wealth and honour, contrive
Damaris's divorce without disgrace—for after all, Jean-Philippe
had argued, 'Did he not himself marry two wives, and is he not
sympathique? And he has always admired you, Madame.'
Damaris had felt then that the Prince's admiration was not the
kind required for such purposes, as d'Egremont himself might

remember, but she had not attempted to argue with a man feverish and weak. She was surprised that he had stopped to visit Aaron Burr, the old pupil of her kind friend Mr Reeve. She had not heard from Mr Reeve that Mr Burr was once more in the United States, returned from his exile. But she fancied it gave Mr Reeve pain to speak of him. Many people here said that Burr was a traitor, that he had raised an army not only to invade Mexico, but to war on the United States. Simon Hatch swore that General Jackson was part of the conspiracy and that at Burr's trial the chief justice of the United States had helped acquit him to buy his silence. But Mr Hatch was an intemperate man. Perhaps Jean-Philippe had fancied that Burr might be the Napoleon of the Americas and had seen himself once again in the uniform of an Imperial Guard, his limp forgotten, charging yet one more hill in one more cause.

His limp. She frowned. If her passion for d'Egremont was dead, she still worried about his welfare. This sounded like some new wild dream, some further piece of folly. Dr Brewster had told her that d'Egremont was lucky to have kept his leg at all.

'I fancy if the surgeons on the battlefield had not been so pressed,' he had said grimly, 'they would have amputated the limb. With a fracture of the sort he had, and all the evils of the wound, the chance of gangrene was very great. He was lucky he recovered, and very lucky in the excellent care he received on the *Bonne Chance*.'

Damaris had remembered poor Barelle and what little thanks he had received for all his pains. Certainly Dr Brewster would never advise the rebreaking of the leg—the dangers were too great. But it was like Jean-Philippe to prefer any risk to life as a cripple.

As for his requiring her at his side, she dismissed the idea without much thought. He had been idling this long in a rich and pleasant society; if he survived this operation on his leg, he would continue to do so. Perhaps, in his own mind, he believed that one day he would send for her; the belief was an earnest that he would make a future, but he would certainly enjoy himself day by day with such charmers as crossed his path, perhaps at last marrying some lady for the ease and comfort she could provide.

In which she was unfair to Jean-Philippe, who already could have had his pick of wives of good family, rich and some of undoubted charm, for on his arrival in New Orleans he had carelessly omitted to mention his 'Marquise.' He had been tempted indeed by one Eugénie d'Aubrecourt, a girl from a French family equal in blood to the d'Egremonts, sole heiress to a fortune and a great plantation and already rich with an inheritance from her long dead *maman*.

Eugénie was seventeen, fair with slightly tilted dark eyes, with a manner perfectly *comme il faut* and yet alluring. D'Egremont had found his limp did him no disservice with the ladies of Louisiana—if anything, they thought it made him more interesting—and he knew that he had only to reach out and this rich and most tempting prize would be his. All his problems would be over, and he could be a happy man. The great plantation with its hundreds of deferential slaves, the long white plantation house, the New Orleans mansion presided over by Eugénie—it was an inducement, indeed.

The young girls were closely guarded, but opportunities were made for the Marquis. One night in the drawing-room of the chateau as Eugénie was playing for him after dinner, with the candlelight glowing from the pianoforte onto her smooth young shoulders, he had almost spoken the final, binding words.

'Mam'zelle—' He had got as far as that.

Her head had turned. The candlelight now lit her face, creamy, oval, the doe-like eyes gentle, submissive, yet with an inner spark of young excitement and virginal desire. He saw it all, intrigued, amused, but the light had flickered, and suddenly he saw another face, another form: delicate and white as porcelain, full breasts against a slender body, the dark head upon the pillow, a profile of a chaste Greek maid, and the eyes, great blazing sapphires, now alight with laughter, now melting into love.

He had been claimed, d'Egremont thought. Damaris was as much his Marquise as if they had been married by all the priests in Christendom. Eugénie was disappointed when he merely asked her for another song; her father wondered testily what more this man could wish. But d'Egremont had left, rejoicing in his new freedom, his old chains. He cared nothing for one rich plantation; for himself and his Marquise there were great countries yet to conquer. And he had gone off to gamble with some new cronies and talk of schemes to stretch the eyes of these impressionable young men while he reflected that the lovely Eugénie might have proved insipid, after all.

47

Summer came, with all its heats. Damaris found it troubling. The high, clear sky she had admired turned to brass and made the houses stifling. The little house at Towpath Farm by the lake was one of the coolest in the county, but to a woman accustomed to the English summer it was often close and oppressive. To her annoyance her milk curdled although Kate kept it in local fashion, as she said, 'down cellar,' and Damaris took to cooling her churns in the lake water, toiling down among the rocks before the sun rose high to make the task much harder.

There were no more dinner parties, but the Litchfield ladies escaped to the woods and the lake, and the entertainments were picnics—large outdoor feasts that culminated in the great celebration of the Fourth of July.

On this occasion there were special services in both the churches, speeches were made, and the picnic was being held on a wooded, grassy slope not far from Towpath Farm.

Damaris had visited the Episcopal Church that day. Even there the sermon had been long, and she was pale and tired from the heat. Her horse had bruised a leg, and she was forced to walk. Now she thought of the long walk back to the picnic ground without enthusiasm. She could be taken up in the carriage of one of the ladies, but she hesitated. They all seemed uncomfortably crowded already. Worshippers were streaming from the Congregational Church, but the first and foremost, who paused to hold court among her neighbours for a time, was Mrs Hatch.

Mrs Hatch had resumed her coldness to Damaris—no betrothal had been announced between Verity and Booth. Damaris saw little of him; the small kindnesses he still bestowed on her—a store of ice, supplies of little luxuries from the larger towns, books for her school, wines for her table—were always brought by others. No scandal could arise—except from one who invented it.

Sometimes at night Damaris heard a rider on the tow-path road. When the moon was up she could see a figure on the familiar black stallion, straight and tall as the elms along the path. He would look up at her window and pause, holding his horse lightly in check, not moving. Damaris held her breath, wondering if he would approach, her mind bidding him stay away, her body longing for his, as she waited, tense, quivering, alive with desire in the summer's warmth and the long months of passion unfulfiled.

But always he rode on. A New England gentleman, she thought as she tried to return to sleep. She was proud that he would not tempt her to sin against her conscience even while she regretted that which caused her pride. Guiltily she knew she had no such conscience; her duty to Malfrey had been forgotten long ago; her weak bond to Jean-Philippe would have snapped the moment Booth crossed her threshold.

She could have given both love and loyalty to Booth: no demons, no thought of hell-fire would be needed to keep her faithful to the man who was her ultimate choice. But if she had little feeling of religion, she knew society, and she knew that he was right and she was wrong. They lived in the only way they could. But, contrarily, in the hot summer nights she wished Booth were as headstrong as Jean-Philippe; she wished she were as careless of consequences herself. She should have run off with Booth to Ohio—and she went to sleep at last, the next morning to shake her head over her own rashness.

Now, in the heat of the afternoon, Damaris looked about her. Mrs Buell, she knew, had gone to her daughter in the village of Naugatuck for the holiday and would not be present, and in the crowd pouring from the church she could pick out no one she knew well—all the country people had come to church this day. Many men, women, and children were already starting out on foot through the woods—the children, as soon as they escaped from maternal view, slipping off shoes and stockings to run barefoot in the grass.

She smiled to see them run, and her smile touched the heart of a quiet observer who had been on his way, very late, to the Congregational Church. Too late even to make his peace with the preacher, he decided quickly, and Howard Booth was at Damaris's side.

'You look tired out with this heat,' he remarked. 'Perhaps you will allow me to show you a pleasant path.'

He had come on foot after putting up his horses on his return from visiting one of his manufactories. He could have lifted and carried the poor lady, he thought—her face was as white as her summer dress—but that would hardly do. Instead he took her arm and, skirting the village green, took her round by the churchyard, passing the rows of old graves and pausing under the shade of a leafy elm a few yards from the holy ground.

The throngs of people were all hurrying to the lakeside, and there were no eyes upon them. Booth took his coat off and spread it on the grass in the shade.

'Sit down a little, Ma'am, and refresh yourself. Today's a holiday, and there ain't no need for you to be rushing off, heating yourself until you get a sickness.' He smiled at her as she sank down gratefully, rejoicing at the blowing up of a little breeze. 'I remember my mother saying that in the Revolution the English troops were killed as often by the summer sickness as they ever were by our brave men. And the Frenchmen who fought for us didn't fare much better.'

Damaris on this holiday felt a certain embarrassment. As a schoolmistress, she had been required to instruct her girls in patriotic sentiments, none of which were flattering to the mother country. Only the most educated and travelled people of New England had any idea of the attitude of the English to the American wars—how little enthusiasm there had been in prosecution, really how little interest. Often it seemed to her, after listening to the talk at the Litchfield dinner tables of the new settlements in the West, the venture up in Canada, the acquisition of Louisiana, and General Jackson's wars and raids into the Floridas, that the Americans were more eager colonizers than the English had ever been. But she kept these thoughts strictly to herself—excepting, sometimes, when she met the eyes of Howard Booth, whose grey gaze always held a hint of laughter as he perceived the vagaries of his countrymen, though with a certain affection. Nevertheless that afternoon she avoided his gaze—they were alone, and she must be guarded in her behaviour.

'Why are those graves there?' she asked, seeking a safe subject. Two graves, sunken, slanted, and overgrown with moss so that they were hardly noticeable, were close to where she sat, outside the cemetery wall.

'John and Mary Rogers,' he said. 'Born in the 1680s, died in the 1700s.'

Damaris saw he was not reading; he knew the history of those graves. She regarded them with more interest, but there was no further information to be seen; even the names and dates were obscured now by the lichen.

'They are not in the hallowed ground,' she said, the significance striking her.

'No,' he said, 'poor devils. Maybe the Lord took pity on them—they suffered enough right here. Brother and sister they were, the only ones left of a big family, time they were grown.'

Booth was not a man to mince words or to make a highly-flavoured dish of them, and he explained succinctly what the sin of the young people was. Not suicide—although they died by drowning, perhaps at their own wish.

'Reckon they paid for what they did,' Booth said wryly, 'many times, the measure full and running over. Life was hard in those days. Their folks had a place cleared way off, over where Bradleyville is now, miles away from the village. The parents died off young, and the other children one by one, and John and Mary only knew each other. They had no horse and waggon and hardly ever saw a living soul. My father said he knew some families almost as bad off when he was young, but since then we try to contrive so that every family can come to church and meet the neighbours. No good comes of folks being left alone out in the wilds—but that's another story.'

He pointed out another grave close by, so small, the headstone so obscured, that she had not seen it.

'John and Mary had a child. It died. They found they couldn't give it Christian burial, and there was none for John and Mary either. A lady like yourself couldn't understand, but loneliness then was worse than sickness. Those two children had lived through the dark and cold of winters, the fear of wild critters and the varmints and the Indians that came raidin' through the woods. I think the Lord forgave them. Though don't tell that to the deacon.' His eyes again were full of laughter. 'He's not sure that I'm saved myself, as yet.'

They walked through the woods path with the bronze-faced children running barefoot up and down—hooting, as Booth said resignedly, like the Indians that used the path before them. Damaris was contemplative. She had thought little enough of the Earl, even as to whether he was alive or dead. Now she thought of him, a young boy, in the gloomy Forest of Heron with Cassandra. Had those two unlucky children been like John and Mary Rogers? She remembered the portrait on the wall at Greystones, the young boy with the soft eyes and tender mouth, and for the first time her heart moved towards her husband in pity and understanding.

Watching the happy children, she could not blot out the memory of her own. What was happening to them, even now, in that same sad and gloomy place? Had Lady Gratton brought some light and cheerfulness there? Her decision to disappear for their own good seemed of doubtful soundness—but what could she have done? What could she do?

When at last they reached the clearing where the picnic had already been set out—Kate had taken the contributions from Towpath Farm—Mr Lyman Beecher had already finished saying grace and offering up a special prayer for the day. Old Mr Tapping Reeve had embarked on a patriotic speech, but not everyone was attending to his stirring words. Simon Hatch was muttering angrily that there was no need for Reeve to talk of Andrew Jackson. 'This is not the day for contention,' he declared. 'For one day, surely, the people of New England can be spared from hearing about that —that backwoodsman.' But his sister-in-law paid him no attention either. Her eyes were on Damaris coming through the woods, leaning on Booth's arm. Damaris had thought herself dressed suitably for the day in a plain white dimity gown of local make. But against the blistering sun she had added a wide hat of Leghorn straw, elegantly made and trimmed with ribbons of deep blue *gros de Naples* by French émigrés in London, and she had wrapped her arms and shoulders in shawls of Mechlin lace.

To the eyes of the countrywomen and the Litchfield matrons, as she emerged from the shadows of the trees she had a beauty ethereal, aristocratic, and alluring. Mrs Hatch felt a stab of jealousy and anger, seeing her beside Verity, who had approached the pair smiling: poor Verity, clad in calico, her sun-bronzed forehead sweating in the sun—for she had been among the first to labour at the picnic, ornamenting the banquet set out on the trestles with all the summer flowers and jugs of branches heavy with cool green leaves.

Mrs Hatch was not a bad woman. She tried in her heart to follow the dictates of her religion, but she had been too used to having her own way. When she had decided at last that Howard Booth was fitted to marry her daughter, she had expected an immediate response. The two had always been great friends, and many people had said that Howard favoured Miss Verity even more than his elder brother, her betrothed, had done.

When the proposal had not come, she had merely considered him a little laggard, respecting too much, perhaps, the memory of his brother, and believed that time would bring about the fulfilment of her wish. But then the d'Egremonts had come, and though the friendship between Verity and Booth was unabated, Beulah Hatch, like the other Litchfield matrons, had seen the eyes of Howard Booth as he watched the foreign lady.

When Damaris had not accompanied her husband to New Orleans, she had begun to suspect something wrong. Foreign women, she knew, were not as upright in their behaviour as the God-fearing citizens of New England. She had been furious when Booth had offered Towpath Farm, and all her suspicions had seemed justified the night she found them there together. Booth himself had quieted her then; as they rode back towards the village he had been so calm, so unemotional, talking of the Sunday schools, the temperance society, and the colonization mission, all Verity's favourite concerns—but it had not stopped her from writing to a lady in New Orleans. She had never met the lady, but she was the wife of a man who did business with Simon Hatch, and this was good enough. In a letter purporting to discuss a new branch of the temperance society, she inquired daringly about the d'Egremonts. A reply had come in due course. The cause of temperance was not favoured in New Orleans. The Marquis d'Egremont was a great favourite and had been welcomed into Creole society by Mr Bernard Marigny de Mandeville, its leader, himself. The writer also said that to her knowledge there was no Marquise d'Egremont, though there was a rumour that the Marquis favoured young Eugénie d'Aubrecourt.

Mrs Hatch had brooded over this, showing the letter to one or two close friends. They had pooh-poohed her suspicions. Mrs Buell had opined it was just like such a man as the Marquis to fail to tell the ladies that he had a wife—how many men, going to new territories, leaving their families behind them, did the same?

So Mrs Hatch watched that afternoon as Booth found a place in the shade for the Marquise, brought her food and drink, and lay stretched at her feet. They laughed a little together at the earnest eloquence of Simon Hatch, whose speech followed that of Reeve. Mrs Hatch's heart was filled nearly to bursting—she knew the jest that Booth was making to this foreigner. Her brother-in-law, like all the good men of New England, had set his face against Jackson and the frontiersmen—was it not Jackson who had caused the humiliation of the New England men when they had gone to Washington to demand a peace? Was it not Jackson, almost alone, who wanted to saddle the country with a thousand miles of wilderness full of wild men like himself, men who would take the government of the country away from the old and settled states and make it something new and barbarous? The men of Litchfield had been united in their disapprobation; only Booth had refused to utterly condemn the victor of New Orleans. And now she saw him grinning up at the Marquise—and in her rage Mrs Hatch blamed the Marquise for Booth's continued obstinacy, although in truth Damaris knew little of Federalists, Jeffersonians, or the supporters of General Jackson and had laughed merely because Mr Hatch had seemed more angry at the victorious general of his own nation than the Earl of Malfrey had ever been at Napoleon Bonaparte.

'Jackson!' Mr Hatch thundered—now in what was supposed to be private speech to a ring of attentive men. 'The friend of the traitor Burr!'

Damaris remembered d'Egremont's admiration for this Burr. Puzzled, she asked Booth to explain. Was Burr a traitor, and did the General defend him?

Booth told her some of the story.

'Whether Burr meant treachery—perhaps he's the only one that knows. And maybe he's not sure himself. He helped the thirteen colonies break away from England when they had a mind to do it. And not everyone in Louisiana was happy at the Purchase—they figured no one asked them if they wanted to be citizens of these here United States.'

He watched the blue sky through the leaves and chuckled.

'Daresay they figured they owed no loyalty to the government in Washington. But it's for sure that Jackson is a patriot, never was a greater. Too great, folks up here think. He'd take the whole continent for the United States if he could, and Cuba with it. He believed that Burr would help him—and I think he still believes that that was Burr's game. But if your husband is meeting Burr and his friends,' Booth went on, and stroked his chin—a habitual gesture with him when he was thoughtful—'then I would reckon he's fishin' in dangerous waters, Ma'am.'

A serious look passed between the two, quite misunderstood by Mrs Hatch. And that night, as soon as she arrived home, she went through letters and papers long since packed away in an old trunk kept in a small bedroom at the top of the house, stifling on that summer night. She searched carefully, not minding that her hands left sweaty imprints on her papers, until she found at last that for which she searched. Here were the letters to Captain Hatch from his comrade in arms of the Revolution, the young Lieutenant Beauregard, who had come with Lafayette. The correspondence between the families had lapsed after her husband's death, but Lieutenant Beauregard, who had become a lawyer and lived in the French capital, might be able to serve her. She sat at her writing-table and wrote a letter to his wife, and this time there was no pretence; her inquiry was simple and direct. Did the Marquis d'Egremont, of Burgundy, who had fought with Napoleon at Waterloo, have an English wife?

CHAPTER

48

All through the summer Beulah Hatch could hardly wait for a letter to come from France. Even before it arrived, she was sure in her mind there was something strange about the marriage of the so-called Marquise d'Egremont. Hate and jealousy sharpened her eyes. Damaris had forgotten the excellent advice of Captain Bosquet, and Mrs Hatch had noticed that her belongings were marked not with an *E* but with an *M*. The Marquise received no letters from France or England—excepting only the rare communications of the Marquis, she received no letter at all. And though she had been in Litchfield for almost a year, no lady of English or French extraction had found her way to pay this noblewoman a visit of respect. Why was the woman hiding there like a cast mistress? Mrs Hatch muttered in her bolder moments.

She spoke not so much to the Litchfield ladies, who knew Damaris well and would defend her, but to the countrywomen who lived all through the week on isolated farms and who enjoyed the gossip after the Sunday meeting at the house of Mrs Hatch—to which, previously, they had rarely been invited. Some of their fathers, a few of their husbands, had died in the wars against the English, and they were not averse to thinking ill of this unknown beauty from the hated island. And their egalitarian fervours were stirred against the frail aristocratic lady who shone jewel-like among the country wives as they sat in worship. Those whose daughters attended Damaris's school were her defenders, but Dorcas Brandywine, whose simple-minded, obstreperous Jenny had been dismissed, was easily roused against her. And Mrs Hatch's hints and warnings caused some anxious mothers to remove their girls from such a dangerous place.

Damaris was sorry to lose these pupils but did not suspect the cause. The country girls had always stayed at home when they were needed, and she merely supposed the summer must be busy for reasons unknown to herself. As she had had another letter from d'Egremont she did not think her own position was the cause of gossip and concern.

The letter was full of jubilation. His operation had been a great success. His leg was restored to what it had been—he now walked like a man and was fit for all a man's work. And a man's work was what he was engaged upon. He was about to lay a great empire at her feet. The Spanish were all but finished. She must come at once to New Orleans. Her gowns, he remarked, would be quite *démodées*—the fashions here were all from Paris, and luxury was taking the place of all-revealing simplicity. He had ordered everything new for her arrival.

Damaris for a moment had to laugh. It was so like Jean-Philippe to think nothing of asking her to change her life without speaking of a home—only of some vague, airy, impossibly magnificent plan—but to be most seriously concerned with the cut of her gowns. The Marquise must not be behind the fashion. The Marquise. He had gone on: 'When things are settled we must find out if Malfrey lived or died. If necessary a divorce can be arranged. How fortunate that you are a heathen, my dear; it will save trouble.'

Damaris shook her head. D'Egremont was so blithe about her problems! She wondered about her reception by the ladies of New Orleans if the truth became known. Uneasily she remembered all she had heard of the troubles of Mrs Jackson, the general's wife, whose indiscretions had been nothing compared with her own.

She could not have guessed that Jean-Philippe had told no one in New Orleans of her existence, that he had allowed himself to be known as an unmarried, unattached man. This worried him not at all. Amused by the idea of humbugging everyone, he considered announcing a wedding date or perhaps the arrival of a wife previously thought to have been lost at sea. In the meantime he did nothing, and neither did Damaris.

As the days passed she could not make up her mind to go. There were her girls, who needed her; there was the frail peace she had found in her country home; there was—but it was not for Booth she stayed, she told herself. They could not be more separated if she were in New Orleans—or in England.

The thought of England came to her more and more. Her young girls, of whom she had grown so fond, could not take the place in her dreams of little Griselda. Perhaps it was the strong family feeling which she saw all round her—even the sermons, she thought wryly, exhorting her week by week to remembrance of duty.

'Who can find a virtuous woman? for her price is far above rubies,' the deacon thundered, and certainly, she reflected, in this land it was true: these women, in work and devotion, were beyond price to their husbands, to their children. She longed to know what was happening to her family. Lady Gratton must know she had been in Brussels—but what then? Did they think her dead? And the Earl—she sighed. Certainly she could have written and learned all that had taken place—but perhaps it was better that she did not disturb whatever life her family had made after she was gone. The Earl might have divorced her—her mouth twisted; the idea was oddly bitter.

And a new trouble came. Perhaps it was merely the heats of summer, but her pallor had increased and she felt listless. She grew thin and sometimes was woken in the night by fits of coughing. She remembered Lady Gratton's constant care for her lungs and her fear of the complaint so disastrous to the Maynes. But there was little Dr Brewster could do. Kate did all of her rough jobs now, and August was a holiday from school. Booth sent her a sofa stuffed with horsehair, more comfortable than the wooden settle in the parlour, and she put this at the window by the lake and lay there and watched the children splashing in the cool blue waters.

She no longer watched the tow-path road. It was not for her

that the tall rider came along the path; it was not for her to expect him. The talk of the men of Litchfield was all of the coming election of a president, which they foresaw with great gloom. Booth, she knew, spent so much time in Hartford that his cousin Wadsworth had come from New Haven and was staying in Litchfield, the better to supervise the Booths' concerns. Verity Hatch had taken on much of the care for the working people of the valley. Her mother did not like this, Damaris saw, but Verity was now a person in her own right. Once more Damaris admired the freedom of the American girl.

When Damaris had seen Booth, rarely, after church, he was not talking of politics but was caught up in some great enthusiasm about steam-engines. He believed that steamships in time would take the place even of the new clipper ships on the Atlantic Ocean, though Mr Hatch had disagreed with loud emphasis.

'The New York-Liverpool packet is the fastest ship afloat. And no country can build ships as we can. Every captain on the ocean envies us the clipper.'

The men joined in argument. At least it was a change from politics, and Booth would grin over their heads at Damaris, reading her thoughts as he often did—uncomfortably enough for her times.

Damaris began to notice a change in the demeanour of some of the ladies towards her, a certain coolness. It was most marked among those she did not know well. And in the church, some rough countrywomen whom she did not know at all would give her hostile looks. She could think of no reason, except that the English marquise was no longer a novelty adding a little excitement to their quiet lives—and a lady without a husband with her, as she had been warned by Mrs Duckworth, was apt to be an object of suspicion.

Mrs Duckworth came to Towpath Farm with her after Sunday service. She had watched her friend grow thin and very pale and was concerned. She was also worried about the whispering campaign set afoot by Beulah Hatch. Wise in country ways, she knew there was nothing she could do to stop it. Gossip was a nasty thing, she thought. No one to come out and say something a body could prove to be false, and the more a friend would argue for a woman's decency, the more doubt there would be.

Mrs Duckworth had brought a rabbit pie and elderberry wine that she hoped would restore health to Damaris's wan looks. The two ladies dined cosily. Mrs Duckworth praised the little dining-parlour and all its comforts unreservedly and confessed it was a delightful thing to see a room not disfigured with the stains of tobacco juice.

'Men, they are plumb dirty critters, and there is no keeping a house decent with them around,' she said, and sighed.

Having praised and eaten, she still did not know how to get to her subject. She inquired how the Marquis was faring in New Orleans. Damaris told her what she had told no one else, that the Marquis now felt settled enough to have her join him there.

Mrs Duckworth looked at her with kind eyes.

'We will be rare sorry to see you go,' she said, 'but go I suppose you must. He is your husband, and your place is with him if he has a home for you. Which is more than Duckworth ever gave me, for a tavern is no home, but that is neither here nor there. *He* ran off with another woman before he drank himself to death—a philanthropist was Duckworth, if ever was,' she added, making Damaris smile, though she reflected that d'Egremont was certainly as much a philanderer as the departed Duckworth had been.

Yet she felt stung. She had been pulled up sharply. If Mrs Duckworth, certainly no admirer of Jean-Philippe, thought it her duty to go to him—of course, Mrs Duckworth could not know that Jean-Philippe was not her husband. But perhaps she had a duty to him just the same. She had taken him as husband when she left the Earl's house. The good New England woman perhaps saw plainer than she did herself. And she suspected Mrs Duckworth was warning her, warning against slipping into a love affair with Booth, an affair that must degrade him and cause misery to them both.

'But you are right peaked and mustn't go until the weather cools,' Mrs Duckworth advised. 'Up here in Bantam is about the coolest place in all of these United States, barring only New Hampshire and Vermont. If you feel the heats here, you will be right sickened down South with all the swamps and them nasty mosquitoes. Come October will be time to travel, and you can go and meet your good man.'

Staring out at the lake through the long days, Damaris came to the conclusion that Mrs Duckworth must be right. She wrote to d'Egremont and told him of her plans, wondering at the same time whether by October that restless, easily-stirred adventurer might be off acting on his dream of conquest anywhere a fire-fly of opportunity was glittering. Then she read her letter through, unsatisfied. It seemed lacking in tenderness or affection, even a proper concern. Yet she could think of nothing else to say and sent it, to have done.

Yet the relief of a decision made still eluded her. She grew more weak, and the faithful Kate fussed over her mistress through what she termed her 'summer complaint.' Damaris learned this name was given to everything from dysentery to malaria. She had the symptoms of neither, but only an increasing languor and very little relish for the long journey and the new life ahead of her.

An answer came in due time from d'Egremont, still happy, enthusiastic. He would come to meet her in New Orleans, he wrote, though by October he would not be living there. She would find herself received with much splendour.

Damaris wondered where he planned to be. By the beginning of September the heat had lessened, and some of her girls had returned. She thought she would ask Verity to take over her small school—Verity had shown her interest; the Sunday schools were not enough for that young woman's driving energy. And though Verity was not learned in the classics, Damaris knew it would be well within her powers to become so if she wished.

Her school was sadly reduced. Many girls had not returned after the summer. The coldness of some of the ladies had increased, to Damaris's puzzlement, and certain of the country-women—who attended the church rarely—when they did see her would get in a little knot outside the meeting house and mutter and glare. Damaris took to going to the Episcopal Church, where the ladies, if not as friendly as the Congregationalists had been, at least were quiet in their manner, and she met no hostile stares and caught no sounds of voices suddenly hushed at her presence.

Damaris, who had known the villagers of Angelhurst, was aware that country people easily resented an outsider; and she remembered the strange villagers of Lesser Heron who had considered all the world their enemy. And so she put it from her mind. She had much to think of: her journey to what was really another new country, though she had no curiosity to see it; marriage, perhaps, to a man she no longer loved. She supposed it would be marriage—certainly by now if she was not widowed she was divorced. The thought of her wedding to d'Egremont, once the great impossible dream of her life, now brought nothing but tears of weakness as she lay at night, restless on her pillows.

Her restlessness was exceeded by that of Mrs Hatch. When people spoke approvingly of her daughter and her good works and Lyman Beecher praised her as one of the most holy ladies of New England, Mrs Hatch was bitter, for her daughter's good works were those of an old maid. Good works were very well for matrons and widows, but for a young woman they were the outward sign of the settled virgin, and her heart rebelled.

She felt, not without some justice, that Booth was wrong to let her daughter be associated with him so closely in his model manufactories; in a frenzy of irritation, she complained to Simon Hatch that she thought Booth had compromised Verity. Mr Hatch was furious, in part with his sister-in-law because he believed no wrong of Booth or Verity, in part with Booth for not making the offer that was so clearly indicated, and in part with Verity herself for not finding a husband and sparing her family this embarrassment.

He was no more inclined to be silent in his anger than Mrs Hatch, and after a political meeting one night at the house of Tapping Reeve, where he had drunk a large quantity of whisky and water, he had taken Booth aside into the garden and told him frankly 'what the ladies said.'

Booth, who had drunk a little less and in any event had a stronger head than Mr Hatch, replied with great calm that no one could think ill of Miss Verity, whose reputation was the highest in the county. But if her mother thought it more fitting, he would ask some married lady to take over the Sunday schools of the river valley.

He was not as calm as he appeared, nor did he feel guiltless. Although he had never decided to marry Verity, he had never quite decided that it was out of the question either, except on the one evening that he had tried so hard to forget. He loved Damaris, but he knew that this love for a married woman faithful to her husband must be put aside. He was thirty years old: it was time he started a family. Perhaps if it had not been for poor 'Becca, he would have married Verity long ago and had thriving children round him. Now he felt as though he had been unfair to Verity and brought gossip to play round her name—even though he was certain that much of this came from Mrs Hatch herself. But he went home that night an unhappy man and was cross with his excellent housekeeper, which caused her to stretch her eyes, for Mr Howard was most equable in spirits, and a thoughtful master.

If he was unhappy, Simon Hatch was furious. Duelling was

frowned on now in New England, but for a time he considered it. After all, he stood to Verity in her father's place. But Booth certainly was a better shot. Irritated even more by that thought, Mr Hatch poured out all his rage on his sister-in-law, who turned an ugly red. She said little, but after he had gone she lay awake all night seething with frustration and resentment.

A September heat-wave was upon the country, and by morning the sticky heat lay upon her chest as though, she said bitterly, a full-sized bear had slept across her. Her rage at Booth for his insult to Verity and her family had turned in the night to a boiling fury against Damaris, who she knew instinctively was the real cause of poor Verity's loss. And it was that very day, thanks to the dispatch of the fine clipper ships, that she had her answer from Paris.

CHAPTER

49

The letter from the wife of Captain Hatch's old comrade was gracious. The former Lieutenant Beauregard, now a man of substance, remembered Captain Hatch as a man of substance himself, who had entertained the French gentlemen with an elegance not always found among the Patriots, and he suggested to his wife that she give Madame Hatch all the assistance in her power. This would have been little or none, for the Beauregards were not part of the society of returned exiles who knew d'Egremont, and Beauregard himself had to institute inquiries from friends who had some knowledge of the 'Ultras.'

When he received the necessary information he smiled and remarked to his wife that Monsieur le Marquis must be finding rare sport on that grim, puritanical soil. The information, plus her husband's speculations, was duly passed on by Madame Beauregard, and the letter was received by Mrs Hatch on the morning she woke feeling all the ravages of the autumn heat.

Madame Beauregard had sent her compliments. She was honoured to have the correspondence of the widow of the kind Captain Hatch. It was to be regretted that the two ladies could not meet. About Madame's inquiry, she, Madame Beauregard, did not know the noble family of d'Egremont, but information had been elicited from a friend of the Duchesse de Langcourt et Montrevet, his cousin, that the Marquis was never married. He had lived in England, Madame Beauregard added, and perhaps had had a little friend there—the ladies of the opera, it was understood, were most attractive. If Madame Hatch were ever to visit *la belle France,* the Beauregards would be most happy to return the debt of hospitality. She ended with gracious compliments, but Mrs Hatch never read that far.

All her blood was in her head. That woman, with her rare beauty—of course! Had it not always been obvious? Those were not the looks of a good wife. It was all so clear—she had been the pick of London's pretty harlots, brought to beguile a journey and then abandoned, now passing herself off as a noblewoman among people she no doubt thought were ignorant savages.

That Damaris was learned as well as elegant meant nothing. No doubt she had been educated by a wealthy lover; such things were known to happen. Perhaps the man with the initial *M,* she thought. Yes, the woman had been abandoned by the Marquis, and instead of going on to some city where she could take up her trade she had stayed on while her reputation lasted to try to catch some wealthy man in her net. She had almost inveigled Booth and made her daughter into a lifelong spinster—that evil wretch, the scum of Europe, Damaris the Damned! Beulah Hatch had always known it, and this day her suspicions had been proven and her judgement would be vindicated. The whore would be cast out.

Despite the heat she tied on her bonnet, called her carriage, and made her way to the house of every woman she had stirred up against Damaris, even old Sarah Kemble, whose husband was dead, her children gone off to Ohio, and who lived all alone in a tumbled-down house far less well kept than most barns, almost never went to church, and was thought to be mad. Nor did she neglect the most distant of the farm wives. Travelling with four horses to her carriage, she proceeded swiftly and aroused the women to righteous wrath with words and phrases hardly used within the century. The women saw the letter and took it as proof. Their daughters had been corrupted by an adulteress, a woman from the stews of London and Paris. This woman who had dared to sit in their own church, 'rotten with disease, no doubt,' said Beulah Hatch grimly, 'visited by who knows how many men—tempting all the husbands and fathers, drawing them in while she pretended to be a God-fearing wife.'

'Pretending to be better than we are,' said Mrs Henry Ruckle suddenly, sweating in her calico dress as she hung over the wash-tubs with a week's collection of her eight children's clothes, with the bitterness of near-poverty in a place where poverty was not respectable but pointed to shiftlessness on the part of the provider—and shiftless Henry Ruckle certainly was.

'Casting her finery in our faces,' Mrs John Carter added sullenly. She was not normally unkind, but the spring and summer had been hard. Her husband was not shiftless, but he had been ill of a fever all through the spring; one horse had died and the other had a sprained fetlock. John Carter had the grim New England pride and would not allow her to call on the neighbours for help. She had tried to pull the plough herself with the help of her two sons, and she had never felt right since. Something had gone amiss in her insides, and she had much pain, but she could not tell her suffering man. By the time July came she had determined to ask Howard Booth for help. She would wait, she had thought, for the Fourth of July picnic. It would be one friend talking to another, not a studied appeal for charity. Booth would always help if asked, and in a way that the proudest of folk could abide. She had trudged there in the hot sun, her feet raw and burning, for she lived full ten miles from Bantam Lake. She had waited without taking a morsel to eat or drink, nervous as she was, until Booth came, late, and on his arm the lady glimmering in clouds of lace with silk and jewels like something from another world. Booth had stayed at the lady's side, and Mrs John Carter had found her words stuck in her throat. The next day she heard that Booth had gone away, and she had had to apply to the Hatches like all the indigents and loafers, like a begging Indian. And that woman who had made her feel too soiled and muck-sweaty to approach her—she was a common whore. Prudence Carter's thin chest swelled in indignation.

'We will run her out of the village,' she said with bitter determination.

'They used to hang women for less than that,' Beulah Hatch added.

Dorcas Brandywine muttered something hardly articulated. Damaris could never know how much she had hurt her when she explained why her daughter Jenny must leave the school. She had tried to console her by speaking kindly, telling her about girls she had known, very much like Jenny, in English villages. Accepted for what they were, their lives were very tolerable, and they usually lived to a fine old age, helping in the simple tasks of cottage and garden, dairy, orchard, and field. But Dorcas Brandywine could never admit that Jenny was different.

She had come from a family where two of the sons were simple, and the young men from the farms about Litchfield had shied away from marrying Dorcas, although she was a very pretty girl. She had been considered lucky to get Brandywine, a widower with five children and a harsh, demanding man. All her life she had cringed, watching the neighbours tolerate her brothers; then she had to watch her husband and stepchildren eye her own brood to see if the curse would fall on them. Jenny was born the prettiest, and Dorcas fought herself and everyone else, refusing to admit that the girl grew and her mind did not. Dorcas had stubbornly blamed everyone for Jenny's troubles, from her husband and stepchildren to Miss Pierce's Academy, and then Damaris, for rejecting her. No one had ever dared to name Jenny's condition in her presence, and when the foreign lady had tried to explain, her bitterness against Damaris had become almost stronger than that of Mrs Hatch.

The women had been collected at Brandywine Farm, and now Mrs Hatch ushered them out. They were ready. On the inside of the kitchen door there was a big nail with a heavy leather belt dangling from it. Ezekiel Brandywine used this belt to chastise his children, and its blows had been felt often enough by his wife. On a sudden impulse that she could not have explained to herself, Dorcas snatched the belt from the nail as she left and clutched it tightly. Old mad Sarah Kemble saw her and laughed.

The women drove in Mrs Hatch's carriage, rough farm waggons, and one-horse shays. Mrs Hatch had not troubled with the likes of Mrs Buell, Mrs Wadsworth, Mrs Lord, or any of the prominent Litchfield matrons. If she had considered, she might have said the cultivated women were more suited to talk than the action that was so urgently needed.

With Mrs Carter and Mrs Ruckle beside her she led the procession of vehicles galloping through the village towards the towpath. Most of the people were resting after their midday meal, upstairs in back bedrooms, hoping for a breeze to blow down from the hills. Not even the sound of the cavalcade could rouse them from their torpor.

Verity Hatch was in the kitchen, still bending and sweating over the stove. Simon Hatch had come to dinner, and he, like many other gentlemen, liked a complete dinner with several hot dishes, though the milk was curdling in the coolest part of the cellar and the kitchen with the stove lit was like the fiery depths of hell. Dorothy, the maid, was groaning in her bed with the summer complaint. Verity had not seen her mother since morning but imagined that she was on her bed with her stays loosened, hopeful of a breeze.

The Hatch kitchen was built out on the back of the house, but the sound of hoof-beats in the road, so strange a sound on that hot day, took Verity from her tasks, through the alley beside the house, and out into the street. The last of the ill-assorted line of vehicles was passing at the corner. Dorcas Brandywine was laying on her rough and weary-looking horse with a whip, her hand careless on the reins, jerking to cause blood to tinge the foam at its mouth, when she saw Verity.

'Come along,' she screamed. 'Jump up—we're going out to flay the bitch!'

Then she looked ahead, saw the procession moving on without her, and forgetting Verity, flogged her horse on again.

Verity shaded her eyes and looked after them, uncomprehending. She went back into the house, up to her mother's room, but her mother was not there. Simon Hatch was in the parlour, sprawled in a big chair, sweating onto the cushion. Verity's entrance roused him from a light sleep, and he answered her question testily. He did not know where her mother was.

'A letter came for her this morning, all the way from France— some old friend of your father's. She ran off to show it to her friends. I don't know why you women can't stay peaceably at home on such a day as this,' he said, and shut his eyes again.

France. Those women—they had been going in the direction of Towpath Farm. Verity had no clear idea of what her mother planned, but she was well aware of her hatred of Damaris. And Dorcas Brandywine had looked half-mad. Verity's mind was swift to work, and she was swift to act. Hardly pausing to remove her apron, she half walked, half ran through the baking street, across the main road, and up the north road to the house of Howard Booth.

50

Before they left Brandywine Farm, the assembled women had refreshed themselves with copious draughts of cider and ale. The cider was new and raw, and the women were elated far past the bounds of temperance. They hollered and roared through the quiet woods, with words flying from cart to carriage, remembering old tales of punishment for evil women—from ducking in the lake to standing in the pillory on the village green, whipping, branding, even hanging—and their words fed their emotions as their emotions spun out words.

Only Mrs Hatch was almost silent, her mind working with cold clarity, interjecting a few comments here and there to keep the others at the boiling point. When they reached the secluded house they piled out of their vehicles, screaming for the harlot to come out. Some of them carried horsewhips, and Dorcas Brandywine held her thick leather strap.

'Let's duck her in the lake,' one of the women screamed, seeing the large body of water, sheltered from view by tall trees, so close to hand.

'No, let's drag her into the village and set up a pillory.'

'She should be flogged,' Dorcas Brandywine protested.

'A rope, that's what we need,' Joan Ruckle said, excited almost beyond endurance. They stood at the gate, agitated, feverish, and indecisive. Beulah Hatch walked up to the path, pushed the door, and found that contrary to custom it was closed. She put her shoulder to it, and the others quickly joined her, pushing and banging until the latch flew open.

Damaris was in the house alone. Kate had gone home to help her mother in a spate of family sicknesses. She, too, had been lying on her bed, thankful for the slight breeze that came down to the lake from the hills. Unlike the Litchfield ladies, she wore nothing at all, and she had hung her windows with gauze to try to keep out the pestilent mosquitoes.

Her sleep was broken into by the voices. She could not hear the words at first, but she knew instantly that the possessors of those voices meant her ill. She jumped up, instantly wide awake, thrust her feet into a pair of satin slippers that sat by her bed, and reached for the nearest gown to array herself in before she met this company. In a trice she had robed herself in a loose morning-gown of white tissue silk, smoothed her hair, and was at the head of the stairs when the women came bursting in.

The sight that met her eyes was not to be believed—and yet at once she was sure this was no nightmare. Her house was swarming with strange, wild-looking women, few of whom she recognized, drunk, dishevelled, their dresses heavy with sweat, grease, and all the soil of labour, screaming shrilly, brandishing weapons. And at their head was Beulah Hatch, dressed in her Sunday-best black silks, outwardly calm, her face curiously mottled.

'We know you for the harlot that you are,' she said, and her voice quieted the others. 'You came into this God-fearing community, ensnaring our men and our very babes in all your Devil-inspired deceits. We have come to give you punishment and to cast you out.'

So then, they knew. Damaris looked down at the eager mob, their vile weapons in their hands, ready to degrade and shame her. She was almost sick with fear that quickly grew to terror, and then she saw some old woman whom she was certain she had never met regarding her intently, her look growing into an almost lascivious sneer.

'Why, look at that whore,' she said, sniggering. 'She's half-nekked, ready for a whuppin' now.'

Her mouth was slack, her eyes glistening. She had begun to drool, saliva dripping from the corners of her mouth.

Suddenly Damaris felt courage flow back into her. Was she to be terrified by this flock of ignorant countrywomen, whipped up beyond their normal sense by a jealous matron like Beulah Hatch?

She, who had danced the whole night at the ball before Waterloo, danced with every officer from the assembled regiments when all the time she had known of the hue and cry following her and that at any moment the dancing partners who bowed so charmingly over her hand might take her out summarily before a firing squad and make an end of her—if she was spared the ignominy of a hanging. She had not trembled before all of Wellington's army then—she would not fear a handful of countrywomen now.

'I must ask your indulgence, ladies,' she said, her gentle voice calm and clear, 'but I had not the pleasure of expecting you.'

The women gazed up as she stood at the head of the stairs, as if seeing her for the first time. The lady who looked down upon them, her back so straight, her head so high, her voice so gently bred, seemed every inch a noblewoman. Some of these women had never been close to her before, had never heard her speak. A certain hesitation seized them, and even the women who had been ready to rush forward and strip the silk from that soft, naked body paused and fell back just a little. But Beulah Hatch did not fall back.

'It is no use to try to put on airs or fool us with your harlot's tricks,' she said grimly. 'I have a letter from a Parisian lady, and she tells me you are no wife to the Marquis but an English whore.'

If she had stopped there Damaris might have considered that she was, indeed, undone. An adulterous countess would be a whore to these farm women, and she could expect no mercy for her person. But Beulah Hatch went on.

'Coming among us with all your haughty ways, as a noblewoman born, and you nothing but an opera dancer that that Frenchman took up from the streets.'

To her surprise and shock Damaris laughed, a low ringing laugh that caused the women to withdraw a little as she came down the stairs and passed them composedly, advancing into her parlour that overlooked the lake.

'Won't you come in?' she said graciously. 'Pray be seated. The day is warm; you must refresh yourselves.'

Her invitation was more symbolic than real; there were certainly not seats enough for all the women, but it served. They stared about them, and their uneasiness grew. None of this was what they had imagined. This woman was not weeping, falling at their knees, and begging mercy. She was not cowering before their whips; she merely asked them to sit down, as any woman would with company in the parlour. One of them was confused enough to sit in a chair worked with Damaris's own petit-point and then was conscious of her grease-spotted gown and looked up bewildered into Beulah Hatch's grim, unyielding face.

Damaris faced the assembled women, regarding them as calmly as she did her pupils—her countenance, thought the infuriated Mrs Hatch, speaking more of easy tolerance to childish pranks than of a woman accused of adultery.

'Something seems to be troubling you,' Damaris said kindly.

'Do you deny,' Beulah Hatch said harshly, 'that you were that man's whore?'

She could hardly do that with much effectiveness, Damaris thought, since it was the truth. But Beulah Hatch had always talked too much, and she gave her some assistance.

'Do you deny you were a common prostitute?'

The women were staring round Damaris's drawing-room. Most of them had never seen a room of that kind. The silver ornaments and China vases provided by Howard Booth, the elegant trifles she had brought with her—they gazed at the miniature of Damaris's mother, the face resembling hers, framed in heavy gold, set with clusters of seed pearls. A gleaming box of tortoise-shells and silver set with ivory trays holding her embroidery silks stood open by the sofa; the writing-table of silver and gold studded with gems drew the eye—these did not seem like the possessions of a woman of the streets.

Beulah Hatch, familiar with fine things and Damaris's possessions, saw this falling away.

'Don't think we are impressed by the finery you have acquired in your sinful ways,' she said. 'We all know of the extravagances of gentlemen to loose women—often dearly paid for by their wives and children.'

The women stirred again. This was something they could believe.

'Look, ladies,' Beulah Hatch went on, pressing her advantage. 'The woman calls herself Egremont, but see for yourselves: her things bear the initial *M*. Some former lover, some doting old man, provided her with luxury, not young Egremont, who soon deserted her.'

Dorcas Brandywine muttered, still clutching the strap in her sweaty hand. Damaris caught her fanatic hostile gaze, the grim sour look of Joan Ruckle, the worn and haggard countenance of

Prudence Carter, the horsewhip curling slackly at her feet. Then she saw at the back of the room a Mrs Stayles of Litchfield, a woman she knew slightly and had met at spinning-bees and the roast-beef suppers at the church. Mrs Stayles was a merchant's wife, more gently bred than the women from the outlying farms. Always very much a follower of the great Mrs Hatch, she had been caught up in the general excitement, but her zeal had been the first to fade. She did not think yet that Beulah could have been quite mistaken, but the party, assembled first for an honourable purpose, had become too wild. Suddenly it seemed distasteful, and she wished she had stayed at home. It was not the sort of thing her husband would like her to be involved in, she thought belatedly, and tried to hide behind the others.

'Good evening to you, Mrs Stayles,' Damaris said. 'I believe that you have met M'sieur le Marquis. You will be glad to know, perhaps, that he prospers in New Orleans. He has seen a French physician for his leg wound, and he is quite recovered. He has written to me to join him there as soon as possible.'

She went to her writing-desk, took d'Egremont's letter addressed to Madame la Marquise d'Egremont, and brandished it carelessly.

Beulah Hatch waved it away as something of no consequence, which was much better, Damaris reflected, than if she had demanded to read that compromising epistle.

'We all know what the man calls you,' Mrs Hatch said with contempt. 'And who was he, this *M,* what did he call you?'

Damaris picked up her mother's miniature.

'I don't think you have visited me before, Mrs Stayles,' she said, 'so I have never shown you this likeness of my mother. She was a Mayne before she married my father, Captain St Cloud.'

Mrs Hatch stared. She did not believe a word Damaris said, but she saw the game was being lost. The women's passions were quickly cooling. The harlot might escape. In a fit of rage she seized the writing-desk off the table and scattered its contents on the sofa and rummaged through them desperately.

The desk was full of packets of letters, private papers that Damaris had kept there before she left England and that she had had no time to sort the wild night she ran away and had forgotten since. When Mrs Hatch seized the desk, Damaris had no idea what she might find.

'Who was this?' she roared in triumph. 'Who was the Duke of

Camberly who wrote you letters that you've saved—ready to demand money for them, no doubt.'

'I don't know whose letters you have there,' Damaris replied with great composure. 'They might be from my grandfather, who was the fifth Duke of Camberly, or they might be from my uncle, the sixth Duke, who wrote to me congratulating me on my marriage, I believe.'

Mrs Stayles collected herself and moved forward, the other women parting to let her pass.

'Beulah,' she said, her voice trembling. 'I think you go too far. To pry among a lady's papers—indeed, you might be wrong. Your French correspondent could be in error. I think—I think we should go home.'

It was a brave speech for one of Mrs Hatch's adherents to make; that lady understood all its significance, and her face became most ominously dark. She was not at all prepared, in spite of her setbacks, to give up her perusal of the documents that she felt shrewdly would uncover some misdemeanour, but she could see that the women, shocked into sobriety and sense, were anxious to depart. Nevertheless, she had her three lieutenants whom she was sure would still serve her, and as the others one by one began to drift away, she stood her ground.

'You were never that man's wife,' she said, grasping, as the other women had failed to do, that Damaris never claimed she was the wife of d'Egremont. 'Who your grandfather was means nothing to me. Dukes are no more to us than other men. Any good farmer's wife is better than a sluttish lady. You have sat in our church, and you are an adulteress, Damaris the Damned. You will leave the village tonight—if you have to go on foot.'

Dorcas Brandywine, who had been muttering, raised her voice a little. 'Strip her and whip her,' she said.

The four women stood before Damaris, holding their weapons, but under her steady gaze unable to move. Then one of the women who were leaving, old mad Sarah, who had so avidly watched Damaris on the stairs, turned back at Dorcas Brandywine's words. She saw them standing hesitant and laughed, moving forward swiftly to stand close to Damaris, grinning at her with her toothless gums.

Sickened, Damaris prepared to defend herself with icy calm. She could hold those four women with her gaze. Beulah Hatch was their leader, but she would not be the first to commit violence.

If only she could rid herself of this crone who looked quite mad and whose ale-soaked breath was foul in her nostrils. The old woman glanced round at the others; then, leering as someone muttered of 'fine ladies,' she reached out and pulled at the unexpectedly strong silk of the white gown.

Dorcas Brandywine, her eyes bright, flourished her strap. Damaris's heart sank, and she almost gave up. If she struggled, she knew she was lost—these women would lose all control. If she stood still—the madwoman's hands were sticky on her flesh. The first dread giddiness of a faint came upon her, and she was nearly swallowed up in darkness. She held on desperately, digging her nails into her palms to save her wits—she must not let go. But there was no air to breathe as the women, silent now, closed round her.

Then a voice came, breaking the silence—a deep, familiar voice that cut into the sweltering closeness like a chill wind.

'What in the name of hell is going on here!'

CHAPTER

51

A tall figure, his head scraping the lintel, stood in the doorway with Verity Hatch behind him. A woman who had hung back when the others left and watched from a corner to see what would happen took one look at the new-comers, made for the window, and bolted through like a rabbit. Sounds of other stragglers clattering down the woods road came into the parlour.

Booth's grey eyes were blazing.

'Whatever comedy has been played here this day,' he said, his voice as grim and cold as death, 'it is over. Verity, perhaps you had better take your mother home. This weather I think has overcome her.'

Joan Ruckle, Prudence Carter, and the ashy-faced Dorcas

Brandywine slunk away. Sarah Kemble laughed madly, and Booth pulled her away from Damaris none too gently and hustled her outside, telling the other farm women to see that she got home. Alone in the parlour with Damaris, Mrs Hatch was by no means finished. The coming of Booth had not changed her plan to cast Damaris out of the village—the arrival of her new lover, she thought grimly, might frighten the other women, but it would not deflect her. The woman might avoid public shame, but still she would have to go. She snatched up the letters from the sofa, ready to cast her proofs in the face of Booth himself.

Her gaze sharp with hatred, she soon saw the first letter from d'Egremont and tore it open, prepared to read aloud the incriminating words. But what leapt to her eye brought a wave of shock and disbelief. The spiky French handwriting of Jean-Philippe was not the easiest to read. She looked again but she had not been mistaken.

'*exquise Marquise* . . . , I regret to tell you that I had to dispose of the pearls that so adorned your lovely neck . . . a present to a wife on her wedding day.'

The letter fell from her hand. She looked up and saw Booth's eyes blazing with scorn and fury. The crushing blow, so utterly unexpected, defeated her, and she felt suddenly old. Verity, who had tried to stop her frantic scrambling, stood beside her. She had seen what her mother read, and she looked at her now with pity. The room was very quiet. Verity put an arm round her mother and with a murmured apology to Damaris led her away; for the first time, Mrs Hatch followed where her daughter led.

Booth looked at Damaris with anxiety. Her pallor was frightening. Without a word he poured a glass of wine and made her drink it, and put an arm about her waist.

'Are you better?' he asked. 'Would you like to lie down?'

The wine coursed through her body, giving her a sensation of new, swift life. His arm round her felt as strong as a tree. Placing her hand upon his shoulder, she rested her head there, just a moment.

'Are you ill?' he asked, his anxiety deepening, and he felt her body shake.

In great alarm he looked down but saw that she was laughing, not with the wild laughter of hysteria, but simply shaking with amusement. Her colour was coming back, glowing faintly in her cheeks, and her eyes were huge and starry. She laughed and laughed until she cried. She was unable to explain the utter absurdity, as it seemed to her, of the rout of Mrs Hatch. As she watched her read the letter and freeze with shock, Damaris had suddenly remembered Jean-Philippe's little joke, which had so taken in that humourless lady. Had Mrs Hatch read on—but the ways of fate and chance seemed suddenly too terribly comic, and Damaris laughed longer, helpless in the shelter of Booth's arms.

'Well!' he exclaimed, puzzled but relieved, caught up in an admiration of a new kind for his beleaguered lady. He had seen men caught in ambush by enemy troops; he had seen some beg for quarter and others face their hunters down with such a look as Damaris had given the women in her parlour; he had seen their joy when relief had brought them life and hope. But the gallantry of this laughing lady was something rare indeed.

'You are the damndest—' he said in the sudden lessening of tension.

'Damaris the Damned,' she said, wiping from her eyes the tears of laughter. 'Mrs Hatch said it, and doubtless it is as true of me as it was of my ancestress, a fierce old lady, Mr Booth, who refused to die.'

His embrace of his lady, now she was recovered, brought a sudden rush of a warmer tenderness, a glowing love. Aware of it, longing for that love to continue but knowing exactly what she risked, Damaris loosed herself.

'Beulah Hatch is a vile woman,' Booth said. 'I don't know what has gotten into her.'

Damaris, who knew quite well, avoided his gaze.

'She was right in her way,' she said. 'My presence here is—is disturbing. She could not have known that I was about to leave. Kate is with her family, but I will send to Flora Duckworth and have her come and help me pack my trunks. I will be giving up Towpath Farm, Mr Booth. I am about to join the Marquis in New Orleans.'

When she looked up, she saw he had received a blow.

'When are you leaving?' he asked quietly.

'By the stage tomorrow. Mr Booth, you will speak to Verity about the school. I think she will do well with it.'

He didn't try to argue but seemed lost in thought.

'I understand,' he said. 'You would not want to stay—after what has happened. Damaris, I don't think you should stay here tonight. Some of those women looked half-crazed. The heat has got them mad—heat and jealousy. Old Sarah Kemble could be dangerous. Verity has been wanting for the last year to put her in a home they have for sick old folk in Hartford, but she didn't want to go, and I told her to leave the woman be. But Verity was right, it seems. I'll send to Duckworth's for you, Damaris, but you come tonight to my house. My housekeeper, Mrs Ellsworth, will be your chaperon, and I'll bring Kate in. She can help Flora pack, and she can sleep in your room, all right and proper.'

Damaris assented after a little consideration. She had thought to spend the night at Mrs Duckworth's inn, but Booth's house would be even safer. She had no fancy to be set upon once more by the women of the backwoods, roused again, perhaps, by the miseries of another hot, sultry night. Her notes were dispatched, and with a certain feeling of cutting all her ties, she asked that her trunks, once packed, be placed in readiness for the stage.

Then she packed a bag with a few necessaries, and Booth drove her in her little shay through the woods for the last time. She felt a great sadness, as though the happy times of her life were gone forever. Strange, she thought; here she had suffered hardships; here her love for d'Egremont had died; and yet—her sadness almost overwhelmed her, her shock at the wildness of the women already fading into the past.

She entered Booth's house, so pleasing to her eye, with her throat constricted, holding back her sobs. Never would she see this house again, nor its owner, the man she so dearly loved. While she and Booth sat at dinner, a meal for which they had little appetite, Mrs Duckworth came in, bustling, furious.

'Aye, and I don't wonder at your going, Madam Markiss. This village has disgraced itself today, from what I hear. And all because Beulah Hatch for once found she couldn't have her way. But I tell you, Madam Egremont, that she has fair done for herself. She will end her days under Miss Verity's thumb, you mark my words. Even Simon Hatch, he is rare riled against her—first his dinner was spiled and then he hears she's dragging down the Hatch name, roistering around with such as Sarah Kemble. Mr Beecher, he be writing up a sermon on "the stranger within the gates." Beulah Hatch and all her charities! Why, she is a—a hippocras, that's what she is.'

Rufe looked sad at Damaris's imminent departure, and Kate cried. Booth promised to take Kate into his household; Mrs Ellsworth, he said, could use some extra help. Then she and Kate went to the room that had been prepared for them. Propriety demanded that they share a room in this bachelor house, even the large double bed. Exhausted from the day, Damaris, thinking she would never sleep, slept instantly, and was fully awake an hour later, wondering what woke her.

The night was very warm. Her light gown clung to her. Kate was snoring heavily. The moon was up, and Damaris, restless, went to the window. The air smelled of grass and trees—at Booth's the farm-yard was far off enough not to afflict the senses—mingled with something else, sweet, disturbing. It was tobacco smoke— Booth was smoking a pipe to soothe his own sleeplessness in a room not far away.

She tried to go back to bed, to sleep, but that sweet fragrance wafting through the night came and caught her. Hour followed hour. Booth could not sleep this night; he sat waiting, thinking— thinking what? she wondered, yet knowing that he thought of her.

She got up and paced restlessly, marvelling that nothing could disturb the sleep of young Kate, who had laboured hard and long, and whose young body cared as yet but little for the heats of autumn or the pangs of love. The great old clock downstairs tolled the hour—one, two—and Damaris felt she could stay cooped up no longer. Perhaps she would walk a little in the garden; among the flower-beds there might be some breath of coolness, a fragrance that would soothe.

Putting on a muslin gown and slippers, she crept from her room. It was not far from the stairs, but Booth's door was open and he saw her pass. She walked a turn round the garden, and he met her there. Still calm enough, she was about to talk of the closeness of her room, her lack of desire for sleeping, but when he was at her side, the words died on her tongue. For a moment they stood together on the path. He lightly touched her arm; despite the hot and humid air she shivered. She looked up at his face. It was as she had seen it—so long ago it seemed now—on her first night at Towpath Farm: touched by moonlight, noble, distant. But now she saw his eyes, and they were not distant; they were blazing down with an ardent love that could not be denied.

He put his arm about her, and they walked to the house; not quickly, not with the eager tread of two young lovers, but with solemn steps that took in the full import of what they did; not with the wild recklessness of youth, but with a strength of love so great that it faced all meaning, all consequence; and were it to bring them hell itself, that risk was taken and conquered in their loving.

His room above the gardens was bright with moonlight and full of the scents of flowers and the sweet tobacco smoke. Slowly, seeking her implied consent at every move, he loosed her garments from her and stood marvelling at the beauty that trembled before him, silver-naked like the goddess of the moon.

His strong hands, now so tender and so gentle, traced lightly every line of loveliness. This plain man of New England, with eye and heart attuned to a spare, unrelieved harshness, was drunk with beauty and turned her graceful, delicate form before him, enchanted as if by the sight of Venus herself. She was glad to reveal herself to him in ways perhaps no woman had before in this country of the chaste and shamefaced. Having been taught by a past master in the arts of the erotic, she now used that knowledge to make Booth forget the sin he was committing in the joys that were to be theirs.

The girl who had been ravished by her husband, seduced by d'Egremont, was now a woman bestowing herself freely and with pride upon the man she loved. He clasped her to him, the small space that had been between them suddenly intolerable, and closed her eyes with an embrace and rained long kisses up and down her body while she yet stood, worship and lust mingled in a human torrent of desire. He lifted her in his strong arms as though she were a child, stroking her head and crooning soft and broken love words in her ears as he carried her to lie on his bed. With one last long and searing look, he took her body in his hands, no longer with the delicacy of worship but with embraces crushing, bruising in their urgency, making her his own, taking all the authority of possession, knowing her in the age-old language of the Bible. Her breasts, her hips, her thighs were his, given up at his demand with all the eagerness of woman's warmth. The closest inward foldings of her body opened like a flower in the sun as his swift, hard body entered deep into her own, thrust on thrust that brought pleasure and exquisite longing rising to the very peak of searing consummation that blotted out the world, in the discovery of a joy that lifted her essential being beyond anything she had ever known or encompassed at the same moment that it seemed her very self was lost.

He looked down on her, his hard bright face softened at the

mouth with gratified desire, proud, strong, exalted as she was herself.

'You are my wife now,' he said simply, in all the arrogance of his possession. 'And I will not let you go. You will leave here, but you will leave with me. You are mine, Damaris.'

And he bent down towards her and took her once again, in all the heat of passion long denied and all the hope of fulfilment yet to come.

CHAPTER

52

Long before light, Damaris rose. She had not slept; the happiness that had flooded her body and exalted her spirit had not influenced her mind or changed her decision—except perhaps to make her more resolute, more strong.

She dressed in her own room by the light of a candle shaded so as not to wake the sleeping Kate and then paused at the door of Booth's room, gazing upon him, one last look, the soft candlelight showing her his face, vulnerable in sleep, as he lay in a profound unconsciousness close to that of death. Death for her, she thought without sentiment. She had known for a long time what she must do; it only remained to do it.

Quickly, quietly, she put the horse to the shay and made her way to Duckworth's long before the stage might be expected. Mrs Duckworth was already up and about and showed no surprise at Damaris's early appearance. Arrangements were made, with the help of Rufe, for Damaris to get a place in a coach that was travelling to New Haven. There was no need to explain to Mrs Duckworth about this surreptitious flight and her avoidance of the stage. In Mrs Duckworth's eyes she saw the same wisdom that she would have found in Lady Gratton's: Damaris must not be followed and found; Booth must be protected for his own good.

The letters came in with the stage, and Damaris was surprised to find among them another letter for her from the Marquis. She was to meet him at a place called St Augustine. He regretted that he could not wait for her in New Orleans, which was a charming city—they would return there soon—but for reasons of great moment, he wished to change his planning ground to a place out of the control of the United States. 'Some of General Jackson's old army colleagues are showing too much interest in my doings here. I will gather my forces away from prying eyes—but more of that later.'

He gave her detailed instruction as to her journey, which was to be by sea. Damaris had already planned on leaving by ship from New Haven—all she had heard of stage travel in this country had convinced her it was something to be shunned even if she were not bent on avoiding pursuit. Yet she had a strange pang knowing she was to leave the United States. It made the separation seem, not painful—her feelings were quite numb, though the knowledge of pain to come was there—but even greater, more final.

She thought of Jean-Philippe, his passion to be some new Bonaparte as insane to her as the shrieks and cackles of old mad Sarah, and wondered why she felt that she must join him. But she could not think where else her duty lay, and she sat down in Mrs Duckworth's parlour to write a last letter to Booth, to say good-bye—the pen hung in her fingers; she could find no words. It was easiest, at last, to write very little. If he was hurt, perhaps it was as well. He would forget her sooner.

'I leave to join the Marquis. My place is at his side—forget me. Please do not try to follow—I go to Spanish Florida.'

She hesitated, and some fear of d'Egremont's mad notions, some new loyalty to the country that had sheltered her, made her add: 'I think he has some strange scheme of conquest in Mexico—he caught infection from your Aaron Burr. Doubtless it will come to nothing. Perhaps at last we will return to France. Damaris.'

Never was a letter more designed to lose a lover, she thought.

She bade her friends farewell quickly and was soon on her way to the port town. The sun was up as she pulled away from Litchfield, but she saw little of it; the tears that clouded her vision lasted her long journey and until she had set sail, leaving New England behind her, remembering what she had felt and thought the day she had landed, a new country before her, a new life, a new love.

The port slipped away, shrouded that day in mist as Newfield had been in rain; she left the United States as unceremoniously as she had entered, with no one to say farewell; no tall figure had appeared miraculously on the dock to call her back again, to pit his passion against the strength of her resolve. Forced to stay at an inn two nights before she could get passage down the coast, she had lain awake waiting, hoping for that which she told herself she did not want and would not have, her pillow wet with tears because the man she loved had not discovered the place where she was hidden, had not defied her command but had taken her words to mean exactly what she had said. As it must be, she thought, but with no lightening of the spirit.

The voyage was long and slow, with the ship stopping at many ports along the way, and then she had to change ships in the southern coast city of Savannah. The numbness caused by her sudden separation from the people she had known and loved—the end of the life that the transplanted Englishwoman had made, the severing of the new roots—wore off, and all the pain followed. It made a dullness of spirit, a lethargy that caused her to sit in her cabin, unheeding of new sights and sounds, just as d'Egremont had done on the *Bonne Chance*. She made no new friends in her voyaging and stirred in her ship-mates only chivalry and pity—the beautiful frail Marquise seemed unfit to travel, and men wondered that this lady was bound for such a place. For in east Florida there was much disturbance. The Spanish were no longer in control; the Americans were settling, with few rights as yet as settlers; the English were trying to drive out the Americans; the Indians were raiding the settlements. But the lady was going to join her husband, and no one could interfere with that.

At least, they could assure her, the worst of the almost tropical heats would be over, and the chiggers and mosquitoes were no worse than in any swampy land. She listened, not caring very much. For the first time the spirit that had supported her so long failed. During the long journey she had begun to cough again; the sea breezes suited her ill. She remembered her Aunt Gratton's fears for her concerning the Mayne weakness but felt a curious indifference. If she was to die, then she would die. Every man and woman born must die, and she had lived long enough. Her life had always been a burden, first to her mother, who failed to recover from her birth; then to Lady Gratton, who had become, much against her wish, a foster-parent for so many years. She had brought no joy to the Earl, and her name was probably a curse to her own children. Booth she had left to believe she was what Mrs Hatch had always suspected—as indeed she was. Only d'Egremont could want her now, d'Egremont, to whom she felt as cold as she had once felt to the Earl—it seemed to be her fate. Perhaps that fate would not last long.

Autumn was drawing to a close when she reached the old Spanish city. The journey had been long, with many delays. The captain of the small vessel that dipped along the Florida coast was anxious to have done with his voyage—wild storms, he told her, rose from these regions, hurricanes that took many lives and were much feared by all the men at sea. Damaris had little curiosity. As she prepared to land, the weather was still sultry; the sandy peninsula before her was uninviting. The Castle of San Marco, rising behind the crumbling sea-wall, struck her grimly; behind it the setting sun glowed red as blood.

She, with all that was hers, was taken ashore, where she was surprised to be met by a dashing, handsome youth. D'Egremont, she learned, had been sending to each ship that called, so eager was he for her arrival. He would have been there that very day, her escort, who introduced himself as Robert Juneau, explained—'but M'sieur le Marquis is very busy now, you understand. In fact, he is about to set off south—but he will explain that to you, no doubt.'

He took her through streets narrower even than the by-ways of London, overhung by the balconies that decorated the old Spanish houses. When they reached their destination, a house almost in the shadow of a great cathedral, she was relieved to find it comfortable in the Spanish style—it had been the house of a hidalgo, she assumed. The servants were soft-stepping Negroes, who at Juneau's question led them silently towards a high-arched salon.

The double doors were thrown open. Damaris's first look was obscured; the shutters were closed and the room was dimly lit. A group of men were standing round a long dining table covered with what she perceived later were huge maps, pointing and conversing quietly. Then, as she entered, they sprang back. There was a wild whoop of joy, and before her suddenly was Jean-Philippe—Jean-Philippe, who had become to her a misty ghost—laughing, talking excitedly, restored to all he had ever been, straight and tall, his eyes full of mischief, welcoming her with exuberance and love.

He left her with a quiet woman to wait upon her, telling her she must rest because tomorrow they were leaving—'We go up the river for a space. I need a little privacy,' he said, and grinned. 'But you will see all. *A bientôt,* Madame.'

She slept fitfully in the silent room, the comfortable bed, her body having grown accustomed to the movement of a ship, the sounds of wind and ocean and men working on the deck. Later the maidservant came to help her bathe and to put on one of her new dresses, white satin over figured white gauze. It was strange after so long to sit before the looking-glass and have her hair arranged by deft and gentle fingers; she submitted to the attention with little interest in her looks, but she saw the approval in the eyes of Jean-Philippe's friends when she went down to dine.

She spoke and ate a little, the candlelight enhancing her beauty, with Jean-Philippe proud and gay. The men regarded her with an interest she thought almost excessive—she could not know that Jean-Philippe, faced with the necessity of explaining a wife he had not heretofore mentioned, had blithely told his friends in New Orleans of the arrival of his Marquise, whom he had believed lost at sea when she left England to join him after Waterloo.

The deception amused him and made his eyes, sparkling from his plots and plans, even brighter. He observed the skill with which Damaris parried the puzzling questions of his friends—she had no idea of what he had told them, and it amused him to leave her in the dark for a while. How could he have thought for a moment, he reproached himself, of a dull *jeune fille* like Eugénie d'Aubrecourt!

It was a relief to Damaris when he left her at the door of her own room.

'You are tired from your travels, Madame.'

D'Egremont as a lover had always been keenly aware of and attentive to his mistress's feelings, except at times during his illness; she appreciated his return to that delicacy. Now he found himself first in company, a leader of men, all his old self-esteem had been restored—and more. He would no longer be offended by her less than eager reaching for his love. Probably, she thought with a certain cynicism, he was fatigued from amorous exercise in New Orleans. Which was true, in part, for Jean-Philippe had enjoyed himself vastly of late with two married society ladies of impeccable Creole families, a celebrated actress, a singer, and a dancer, as well as a young slave girl in the household where he had resided, a girl so white that he told his friends she was whiter than many ladies of the European aristocracy, and whose position had lightly touched his gallant heart.

But none of these affairs had dimmed his appetite for his renewed life with Damaris, and his concern for her health and welfare was much greater than she knew. He remembered suddenly the London talk of the dreaded weakness in her family. When his project was accomplished he would take her to the mountains and restore health to her frail beauty.

Although he was in a fever of excitement, nevertheless he travelled cautiously so as not to overtire his lady. The place for which they were bound was indeed away from prying eyes, a hacienda built by a don from Castile, abandoned when England took Florida, inhabited briefly again by a Spanish family after 1783, and now owned, she learned, by Jean-Philippe.

She arrived there, still feeling the same incurious lethargy that had accompanied her from New England, with a mixture of some relief and much concern. The house, now known as the Chateau d'Egremont, was large, luxurious, elegant, and comfortable, already well supplied with black servants from New Orleans to make her physically easy. For the rest, she was very troubled.

Jean-Philippe had raised an army, and they were being outfitted and trained here, kept for the most part on an island in the river, hidden from the notice of the Spanish, the English, and certainly the Americans. The army was composed mainly of young men of Louisiana, the dashing Creoles of New Orleans providing the officers. These gentlemen dined at her table, and a group of more gay, charming, reckless young men she had never met. They combined all the qualities of the dandies and the bloods with a wild martial audacity that to her was something new. They were as blithe about conquering an empire as the men she had known in London were about the prospect of an evening at Watier's. Plantation life, she saw, had produced a new sort of gentleman, the hotheaded young aristocrat brought up on the *code duello,* restless now with the imposition of a government he had not chosen, longing for a chance to try himself in battle.

Jean-Philippe was open about his plans. It was, very simply, to take Spanish America for his own. 'It is too easy, Madame. Certainly someone will do it—the Spaniards have no stomach now to fight. It is only a question of who will be the victor. There is no chance to take. I have been much with the Gachupines, the Creoles, and the clerics of Mexico—they will welcome me with open arms. They no longer trust the mother country; there is hatred of the new constitution. They want no democracy to turn their hard-won land to a peasant's paradise. I have but to appear with an army, and it will be mine.'

Damaris listened.

'And the Americans?'

Jean-Philippe waved impatiently. 'They are fighting among themselves. Only General Jackson perceives what is happening— and he has too many enemies in Washington to act. Your New England friends, those codfish-eaters, would rather lose New Spain to me than see him fight his way into the presidency.'

There might be truth in that, Damaris thought, remembering the fulminations of Simon Hatch.

'But what of Louisiana? Your friends are all from New Orleans —that is now part of the United States.'

D'Egremont shrugged. 'Louisiana must do as it will. If I have all of Mexico, I will be satisfied. And there is all of South America—' But his gaze slid from hers. 'Those young men are my best officers. Since Jackson took New Orleans they have not known what to do except to drink, wench, and gamble—I have given them a purpose in life,' he said, and laughed. 'You see me, a social benefactor, Madame. But they are not my sole allies. The English are giving me assistance, and even, if you would believe it, some gentlemen from Spain. They give me funds.' He laughed again. 'They will support anyone to keep the Americans out. And the Indian tribes fight with me.'

'The Indians?' Damaris said, puzzled.

'This country has many Indians—mixed breeds from different tribes, mostly Creeks together with some runaway Negro slaves. Seminoles, people call them. They are good fighters. The Creeks were pushed out of Georgia; the Negroes are claimed by the slaveowners—they will fight against the Americans.'

She saw little of Jean-Philippe in the day, and at night she excused herself from the assembled company early, wearied by the talk of conquest, riches, and power to come. In the quiet of her room she wondered if they could succeed. It was true that the great men of Mexico might welcome them. A firm rule would be preferable to the threatening revolution. Jean-Philippe claimed Bourbon blood—his reign could be thought legitimate. But would he win? He was no great general. Although he was trained as a soldier, he had fought little; his life had been spent mostly as a courtier and the darling of the London salons. And yet she saw the plotters at the table—Englishmen, Spaniards, Creoles, a Scottish merchant, pirates, adventurers. She did not, could not know.

Nor, unfortunately, could she care very much. She felt sad and empty, as though she had brought her body to this place but some vital part of herself had been left far behind. Her days were long and tedious, and her nights—when Jean-Philippe visited her room she felt again as she had felt on her wedding day. She forced herself to do what was expected of her, but the embrace of the gallant Frenchman, once so deeply longed for, now was painful to her reluctant flesh. Jean-Philippe was not the mad old Earl, yet once more, though she consented, she felt ravished. No matter what she told herself, her body knew that she belonged, heart and soul, to Booth and her relationship with d'Egremont was true adultery.

Jean-Philippe, restored to all his amour propre, considered her lack of ardour a result of the weakness that had overtaken her and for a time was at his most tender and most kind. He was, in fact, surfeited with too lusty embraces, and the more distant manner of the Countess did her no disfavour at this moment in his eyes. The Cool Countess! She must, indeed, be his Marquise.

It was a relief to Damaris when he told her that soon he must go away for a time. He was travelling south to one of the great cities of Mexico to meet some important gentlemen and put the finishing touches to their plan.

'Then we will march. All the strongholds will be ours without the need to strike a blow. All Mexico will be ours before the winter sets in—and you will be an empress, Madame!'

He seemed to have quite forgotten Lord Malfrey, who might yet be alive. She observed that in all his activity he had failed to inquire about her legal spouse. A flash of her old humour overtook Damaris—it was so like Jean-Philippe to want to make her his empress before he remembered to make her his wife. She was quite wrong—he had not forgotten. The Earl's death would be better than a divorce, and Jean-Philippe wished he had made sure of it before he had left London. If the Earl lived, d'Egremont thought, once his main business was accomplished, he would arrange something. He had come a long way from the Jean-Philippe d'Egremont who would kill only in a duel or a battle. All of life was the battle to him now, and one more death merely an event in that battle.

Eventually, as days and nights passed, the suspicion came to him: was Damaris's mind lingering on that other man? Was it yearning for his rival that made her blue eyes as chill as northern lakes, her body like winter to his ardent touch? Jealousy did not destroy his love; he was too sanguine now to think of failure, but the once laughing lover became an imperious possessor.

In the nights when he lay at her side, tears would come; her throat would constrict, and she would try to muffle her sobs. Whether she would be empress of this unknown, undesired country, she could not know, but she was very sure that she felt herself to be no more than a slave, without the freedom even to use her own body as she would.

It came to her that she must leave d'Egremont. She had been right to go to him; nothing else would have kept Booth from pursuing her to his own ruin. But now she must go. D'Egremont had no need for her; now in his hour of glory, he would have all the women he could possibly desire at his command. She had discovered at last his deception in New Orleans and his sudden blithe announcement of a wife saved from the sea. If she had not come, she soon would have been forgotten. In her unhappiness she was not quite fair to Jean-Philippe.

What she should do, she thought, was to go home. The war there was over; her crime of aiding the enemy might be forgiven or forgotten. She longed to know how her children fared. It was not necessary to embarrass the Earl or her family—she would travel as Damaris St Cloud. In England, if all went well, she would make no attempt to re-enter Society. She would find a little country cottage where she could live, obscure, unknown, and yet aware of what happened to her children, and be visited perhaps at times by her aunt. Possibly she could have a school again, or if she could not teach, she might earn her bread by her needle.

Certainly she could not stay here, in this strange place, dressed as she was in luxury, heaped with gems and served by slaves, feeling like a creature neither living nor dead, her very presence proclaiming a passion she could not feel, a love that had long since died. Her passion for Jean-Philippe had changed in his illness to a sisterly or maternal love. Now, seeing him restored to all the full vigour of manhood, she no longer responded to his charm. His daring now seemed a mania, his courage, recklessness. The young men he swept along in his train—she knew their activities were treasonous, no matter that Jean-Philippe, their leader, owed no allegiance to the United States, or that the little army was outside their sovereign territories.

His desire was all for power and glory. In her mind she could not help comparing him with that other man, whose own wants were simple and whose thoughts and time were for the people on his land, who had no desire to be raised above the rest but wished to join them in a happy, free republic. D'Egremont seemed still a child, a spoiled and perhaps now a lucky child, but she could not wish a great empire be entrusted to his care. She would not betray him, but she had no desire to share his glories. She was not a slave, she thought; like the mill girls of New England she was a free woman, and she would go.

But then she found she was not free and there was no chance for her departure.

CHAPTER

54

Jean-Philippe was a happy man when he rode away from the Chateau d'Egremont. He was bound first for St Augustine, where he was to meet some men from Mexico before travelling south. He had spoken no more than the truth when he had told Damaris of his welcome there. The men who ruled had crushed the heart of a republican rebellion with the execution of its leader Morelos the year before. In the upper classes, some measure of peace was being restored. The native-born Creoles, ever jealous of the privileges of the Spanish Gachupines, were now willing to make common cause with them to rid themselves permanently of the republicans. The clerics, faced with taxation of church property, became their allies. They needed a general whom they could all trust, an army and an emperor with some claim to legitimacy. The Catholic d'Egremont, an officer of Napoleon with Bourbon blood, seemed ideally suited to their need.

The plan was simple enough. Since Joseph had been deposed in Spain and Ferdinand VII restored, the control of all New Spain was weakened—neither the liberals nor the conservatives trusted this cruel and cowardly king. His own troops wavered in loyalty. When d'Egremont advanced with his army, city after city would be opened up to him; the Spanish garrisons, sparse and poorly led, would find themselves waylaid and hampered at every turn.

D'Egremont's 'army,' a small collection of troops, would, he thought, have trouble finding fight enough to satisfy their lust for battle. He smiled, for he saw his chief battles being with that army. Many of the gentlemen of Louisiana had joined him not from the desire to conquer Mexico but to free Louisiana from the United States. They fondly hoped their first battle would be at New Orleans. But d'Egremont had no thirst to fight the Americans —for a time, at least. Although he affected to despise General Jackson, in truth the westerner was the one man that d'Egremont respected as a military commander, and he had little desire to pit his few quickly-trained troops against Jackson's men.

Like any general, d'Egremont thought, he now had to be a diplomat and persuade his young hot-heads to establish their base first on Spanish territory before they took on the power of the United States—a nation of peasants and shopkeepers but a nation that, with Jackson in command, would fight. As emperor, he would quickly grant lands and palaces to his men and find them rich Spanish wives. That would quiet them for a time at least, until he was ready to expand. New Orleans had been a most agreeable city. It would be well to have it in the new empire of the d'Egremonts.

He would like to show it to Damaris—she must be longing for society other than that of his 'generals.' There were some people not too far from the hacienda, within a day's drive—very few Spaniards, some American settlers—but he had given orders to

keep his Marquise on the place. Frighten her with tales of croco-
diles, he had said cheerfully, but keep Madame at home. He wanted
no visitors, no curious American eyes near his plantations to catch
a careless word from slave or servant about the encampment on the
island in the river—social life must wait.

If there was another reason why d'Egremont was content to
keep his lady immured, he was only half-conscious of it. A certain
freedom for women had been part of the way of life in France and
England, but he had been much of late with the men of Spain.
Their fiery jealousy for their women, a wish to keep them from the
too-free gaze of other men, to control their movements, now appealed subtly to d'Egremont, the man whose pride had received
such blows in New England. There Damaris had controlled their
lives; there she had chosen to stay, her eyes looking with favour
upon his rival even as he, Jean-Philippe d'Egremont, had left on
his journey to the South.

His lady would be the most gorgeous in all of Mexico; her
jewels, her dress, her carriages, the very palace he would build for
her—all would enhance her matchless beauty. She would be royal
—but she would be bound to him as though he held her by a silken
cord around her lovely neck; he would touch that cord and she
would do his bidding.

Yet the gay young men of New Orleans had not perceived the
change in the heart of their leader. They understood that Madame
la Marquise could not travel unescorted about this country—and
they knew that the Marquis could not welcome visitors so near to
the island that was now an army camp.

But they were brought up in the tradition of gallantry to ladies;
they knew ladies loved society and were sorry as day followed day
and the lovely Marquise, pale and despondent, lay on a chaise
longue by her window, pining, they believed, for balls and company as ladies would. At night, after their days of exertion in the
field, the commander, Robert Juneau, and all his swashbuckling
lieutenants talked the matter over but could come to no decision,
even with the help of the fine old French brandy with which they
were well supplied. They could hardly give her a ball with no
other ladies, nor could they take her visiting against the orders of
the Marquis.

They tried their best to amuse her with tales of New Orleans,
but since she had learned that she was, to all intent, a prisoner,
these young men, charming as they were, appeared to her as

gaolers. She was going to be taken to Mexico whether she would or no. She understood what these young men did not, that d'Egremont had become almost a Spanish don—or a Turkish pasha. She would be his wife, she thought grimly—the chief wife of a harem. An ornament to his household, a valued possession. When he returned, she determined to ask him for her freedom, but she already knew that her request would be denied. She meant something to Jean-Philippe—a European treasure he had brought to the New World. He had become a man to acquire vast possessions and certainly was not yet ready to let go.

Three weeks had passed and Jean-Philippe was still in St Augustine. His cause was advancing so smoothly that it was decided he need not travel south until he went at the head of his troops. It amused him to linger audaciously in the city that was still the heart of the remaining Spanish power, and he preferred intrigue to the drilling of the troops, so well managed by his subordinates. Juneau showed brilliance as commander; the men were already in good fighting shape and awaited only the last contingent now being rounded up in western territory to further swell their ranks.

The young men who had not known how to entertain the Marquise were diverted one morning by the sight of a caller arriving at the gates of the Chateau d'Egremont. It was not at all the kind of visitor who might be expected to call on the august Marquise; she was obviously a farm woman, the wife of an American settler who had moved onto an abandoned Spanish plantation and was working it with his family—land that had once been cultivated by perhaps fifty slaves.

Her name was Sue Bascomb. She wore a sun-bonnet and a calico dress, and she had brought two of her children. She had driven up in a rickety waggon drawn by two plough-horses who certainly looked too weary to make the journey back to her place, which was 'downriver a far piece.' Hardly dangerous, Mrs Bascomb might amuse the *souffrante* Marquise who was after all English-born, they thought, and she was shown up to that lady's boudoir almost as soon as her presence was announced.

The Marquise was clearly delighted with her visitor, and the men withdrew about their affairs, glad at their small success.

'I heerd there was an English-speaking lady, so I came to call,' Mrs Bascomb said with no ado. 'In this country I gets hungry for the sound of another woman's voice. It is right lonely on our plantation. Mr Bascomb, my husband, Ma'am, he don't care for visiting the dons, and the English have been stirring up a rare lot of trouble. But they said you were French, so Mr Bascomb said I could come and pleasure myself a little. Not that I would care if you were a heathen Chinee, because it is three months since I went a-visitin'. Then Mr Henry Bascomb—he's brother to my husband—he says he thinks it ain't safe for no ladies travelling by themselves with the Indians stirred up as wild as they can be. So Mr Bascomb told me to bide here, and he and Mr Henry will come and take me home when they get through fishing in the creek. So if it be comfortable for you, Ma'am, I will bide here for so long.'

Damaris was smiling. For the first time since she had come to Florida, some of the lethargy that had weighed upon her lightened. Sue Bascomb was square-faced, sturdy; she had freckles and faded red hair that obviously had once flamed like that of her young son, Johnny-boy, who grinned up impishly at Damaris and who could have been Rufe's younger brother. The girl, Mary Anne, was about four years old, fair-haired, blue-eyed, and shy. Damaris thought of her own Griselda, and her numbed feelings melted into pain.

She begged Mrs Bascomb to be comfortable and sent her maid, whom she would not think of as a slave, to bring refreshments. D'Egremont had made sure his retreat was well supplied and the servants brought chilled white wine and tiny, delicate French cakes to tempt the appetite on a warm day. Sue Bascomb's eyes were wide at all the luxury she saw, especially Damaris's gown of silver lace and her sapphire ring, but there was no envy in her glance; her hands rested lightly on her children's shoulders—her jewels, Damaris thought with an envy of her own.

To the children's joy, she filled their hands with cake and bade them play by the fountain in the court-yard below. Free from her charges, Mrs Bascomb chattered happily, and Damaris, as she learned more about her visitor and the brothers Bascomb, quickly formed a plan. Before an hour had gone by, she knew all Sue Bascomb's history. She had been born in a new settlement in the Southwest Territory, now the state of Tennessee, in the mountain country to the east. The winters had been hard, and they were plagued by Indians. Then Sue had married Mr Bascomb and gone to live down South. But Mr Bascomb's place was small, and it was scarcely worth working; there were too many big plantations with their hosts of slaves bringing in big crops. 'So Mr Bascomb and his brother took the notion to come down to Florida, where crops grow almost by themselves, folks said. And the livin' here is easy, Ma'am, if it wasn't for the trouble with the runaway niggers and the Indians. Folks down here were ready for anything at all until, praise the Lord, Colonel Clinch cleared out Negro Fort last July. It was the English set the Indians on us in the war, Ma'am, and now them pesky tribes don't take it in their heads to stop.'

Damaris felt she owed an apology on behalf of her country, but since she was supposed to be French, she said nothing. She understood then little of what Mrs Bascomb told her. All the interest she had felt in a new country when she had landed in Connecticut had gone and not yet stirred again since she had left the United States. The Chateau d'Egremont had seemed but a stage stop on a further journey that she had no wish to make. From her window she had seen strange flowers and curious birds and never asked their names; she had learned little of runaway slaves and less of Indians. Certainly none of the d'Egremont slaves showed any signs of wanting to run off; they were house-servants, well trained and hardly likely to take to the wilds. Some of them were almost white, especially the young French-speaking girl Mauricette, who waited most particularly on Jean-Philippe.

Mrs Bascomb talked of Creeks and Seminoles, of strayed field-hands, and then, staring at Damaris hungrily, begged for news of slippers and whether elegance now required long sleeves. Damaris obliged her by displaying some of her new wardrobe, purchased by Jean-Philippe in New Orleans, and Sue Bascomb's eyes glittered. She touched the garments, examined them closely, and sighed.

'Oh, I do wish, Ma'am, that I could have just one to copy! Why, I could be talking to you for days on end, and yet my plaguey husband will be here in no time at all because he wants to get me back before sundown.'

Damaris was brave in her new resolution.

'I am all alone here now; my husband is in St Augustine and will be detained—I don't know how long. Perhaps, if you would be so good—I could come back with you and stay a day or two before I go to join him? I will pack some trunks, and you may copy all the gowns you wish.'

Sue Bascomb looked up, for once speechless with delight.

Recovering, she proffered the requested invitation quickly.

'It would be a pleasure, Ma'am—why, the greatest pleasure to me since the Birkett family that was our neighbours took up and went back to Cook County. But we live real plain, Ma'am; we have no house like this. Though it is a good house,' she said, her spirits rising. 'We have no servants, but it's a decent place, and room to spare. Time was we thought Mr Henry Bascomb would take a wife, but he never did.'

Damaris assured her that company was all she required and quickly set the maids to packing some trunks. She did not know exactly how she was going to do it, but somehow she would use the arrival of the Bascomb men to effect her release. From the Bascomb house she would make her way to the coast. She was glad now that she still had her jewels; they would be her means of going home.

The Bascomb men arrived as Sue had predicted—tall, broad, sunburned, and armed with rifles. They were pleasantly courteous to Damaris and delighted to take her home.

'Come and pleasure yourself, Ma'am,' they said, gratified that the lady, the wife of the owner of a great and apparently flourishing plantation, should be so eager to accept their hospitality.

When Damaris's trunks were carried down and loaded on the waggon, Robert Juneau, returning from the island, gazed upon them with surprise and misgivings. He had been told to keep the Marquise on the place. But he could hardly tell the lady, who had been *ennuyée* for so long, that she could not visit a near neighbour, especially as she was escorted by this sturdy pair of armed men.

Nevertheless, the trunks looked ominous—the Marquise was not leaving for a day or two. Juneau, with a whole campful of men at his disposal, hesitated. It was not only the prosaic, bluff manners of the Marquise's prospective hosts that stayed him, nor the homely manners of the American woman with her children. Juneau, a Frenchman at heart, was all gallantry and had quickly become *épris* of the exquisite Marquise. It had not escaped the young man's eye that there was a certain coolness in the lady's manner to her husband; and he had seen the irony in that deep blue gaze as it dwelt upon the pretty slave girl, Mauricette. His chivalry was stirred. He was in duty bound to defend d'Egremont in war, but not in love. If a lady wished to give her husband a reproof, that was her right. Juneau bowed over the lady's hand

and let her go her way. That night he proposed a toast to the company, somewhat muddled but clear in his own mind, to the beauty of the women of France.

55

Damaris, with the idea of freedom growing in her, found her interest in life reviving. She watched the lazy-flowing river whose path they followed, so different from the rapid-falling rivers of New England whose torrents provided the energy for their busy mills. The mills—but she would not allow her mind to follow that path and concentrated on her surroundings. Along the way were handsome trees with leathery green leaves, and Sue told her of the 'purty big white flowers that smell real sweet' that they bore every spring, 'bull-bays, we call 'em—some folks say magnolia.' Of all the birds she saw, Damaris recognized only a grey-blue heron. She asked about a beautiful white creature like a curlew and a brilliant scarlet bird larger than a heron, but she learned nothing. The Bascomb men were interested only in game birds, animals, and fish, and this was the sole subject of their conversation. Shooting and fishing, it appeared, was much more to their taste than farming their many acres—as it was with much of the English squirearchy, she thought, amused.

The Bascomb house, when she first saw it, looked strange indeed. It was built of logs, set up off the ground on a slight rise, and appeared to be two houses under one roof. The Bascomb brothers roared with laughter as she gazed, trying not to look surprised, and told her that this was a shot-gun house.

'When Indians come round you can shoot off a rifle or a shotgun in the passage and not mark up the walls,' they said with pride.

The house was certainly built to be useful if not beautiful, and the passage from front to back made for coolness as well as safety.

But Damaris wondered somewhat uneasily how often the Indians might visit with such intentions as warranted the rifles, and what she learned from the Bascombs was not reassuring.

The Indians were 'all a-fired up.' Now that the war with the English was over, no one knew who was 'riling 'em,' but the Bascombs thought it was still the English at their tricks. The Bascombs had a deep distrust and dislike of the local Indians, many of whom had come from a warlike tribe that had given much trouble in the state of Georgia and had drifted further south after their defeat.

'Creeks, half-breeds—seems like the strongest and meanest came down here, joining up with runaway slaves. They raid any lonely farm-house, and no man can leave his women and his children alone at night. Folks in St Augustine might crave an independent republic, but I say let General Jackson take this place for the United States. He'll take care of the Indians, and a man will be able to go up-river fishin' without coming back to find his wife and chillun' dead and scalped.'

This speech was the longest she was to hear John Bascomb make, and it certainly was alarming enough. After that, the men were taciturn and Sue was loquacious. Another daughter, Polly, almost twelve years of age, large and blonde like her father, had prepared a simple meal, and they sat down to eat—without the grace that Damaris had been accustomed to in her New England days. The chief part of the meal was the fish that the Bascomb men had caught that day, small white fish with delicate flesh, very good to eat. Damaris congratulated Polly on her cooking, and she blushed rosy-red—she was as bashful as Johnny-boy was bold, and for the rest of the evening she continued to blush every time she caught Damaris's eyes, while her brother followed the visitor about, telling her stories of his courage and prowess against Indians.

'Don't you worry none while I'm here, lady,' he said. 'I'm as good a shot as Uncle Henry already. Them Indians won't make no fuss round me.'

His parents observed him fondly, his uncle with a little less enthusiasm. The shot-gun house was clean if very crude—even the furniture had been made by the Bascomb men. They had brought little with them from Georgia, Damaris thought—but perhaps they had lived very simply there. Sue Bascomb did show her with some pride the 'coverlids' that she had brought, cotton quilts made in patches, of a sort that Damaris had seen in New England, sewn with much labour by the women and given sometimes as wedding gifts from mother to daughter.

Damaris was anxious to be on her way and longed to ask the friendly Sue for the use of her waggon to reach the coast, but her hostess was so hungry for female company that she had not the heart to speak of leaving quite so soon, and the next morning, when the men had gone about their occasions, which seemed to be not work on the plantation but another fishing expedition, she brought her new gowns out for the eager Sue Bascomb and her daughter Polly to try to copy as they could, and she herself lent her best efforts to fashion the stiff calico into the pleats and folds meant for *mousseline de soie*.

Gladly would she have given a gown to each of the diligent seamstresses, but the buxom Sue could never squeeze into a gown meant for the slender Damaris, and even young Polly was already full twenty-five inches round the waist. But Damaris took one of her simpler white muslins and fell to work setting in ribbons and letting out seams.

The exuberant Sue talked as they worked and promised to show Damaris round the place when it 'cooled off some' in the evening. Not that there was much to see. The Bascomb place had once been a large plantation, but now it was much overgrown. Though John and Henry talked of the clearing they would do, the practical Sue had her doubts.

'Not while there's fishin' and trappin' rabbits and 'possum and pleasuring themselves,' she said gloomily, 'same as they did back home. Truth is, Ma'am, that this here is a cotton and sugar-cane plantation and no good unless you have the slaves to work it. We had three slaves back in Georgia, but they was mostly sick and idle, and Mr Bascomb sold 'em off 'fore we came here. Mr Bascomb, he ain't fond of slaves nohow, but I don't see no cotton getting planted. The Bascomb brothers, they'll just scratch a few acres here same as they did at home, as far as I can see, and it did me no good to come to this place where I don't have no friends, and nothing but Indians on my doorstep. No, Ma'am,' she said, sighing, 'with the fish fair jumpin' out of the rivers and all them varmints just sittin' waiting to be shot, I don't see the Bascomb brothers stirrin'. If it warn't for Polly and me we wouldn't have no dairy herd. My Polly, she's growed to be a right help to her mammy.'

Polly, quiet as her father, blushed again, her feet and ankles squirming in embarrassment while she looked as though she would like to hide under the pile of calico. The little girl Mary Anne, who in her own home chattered like her mother, though her words were not always clear, now clung to Damaris's skirts, emboldened to claim her as a friend. Johnny-boy had gone with the men. He was younger, smaller, and more slight than Rufe of Duckworth's inn, but his red hair and green eyes were a persistent reminder of Rufe—and other things. Her night in the little bedroom under the Bascomb roof had been filled with thoughts and feelings, not so much of her new freedom and the problems of her future, nor of much relief as yet from being free of d'Egremont, but wrenched with sadness for those other things—all that she had left behind in New England. Even the mild air that came through her window had brought memories of another warm night, Booth's face in the moonlight—but she had to put those thoughts away.

Sue Bascomb was good for soothing female foolishness. This woman, who was trying to hold onto a place in the wilderness, making a life for her children though she was threatened by savages and protected only by two men who liked to live much as Adam did before he had eaten the apple, made her own sorrow of abandoned love seem mere girlish folly. She doubted whether the busy Sue had time to think if she still loved John Bascomb; she fed him, clothed him, worked his land, and worried only that he might break a leg or catch the fever.

Yes, her own sorrow was mere foolishness, Damaris thought. She had done what she must do and should forget her girlish sighings. And after all this lecture to herself she had stayed awake all night crying into her pillow, for although her sorrow might be foolish, it was very real, raw, and painful and would not leave by being bidden. And the second night, though she slept a little from sheer weariness, was not much better than the first.

The next morning, which began very early, before daylight, there was the sound of quarrelling. Damaris tried to stay tactfully out of earshot, but in that house it was hardly possible. The Bascomb brothers, it seemed, had decided to go further up-stream, south of the big island, where there were rumours of fish in great shoals. It was too far to go and return comfortably in one day, and they proposed to take the women and children with them. Sue had no wish to go. Camping was nasty; there were snakes and scorpions; she had her work to do at home; she could not leave her guest who would not go with them. And who was to milk her cows?

The Bascombs muttered something of a neighbour from the other side of the river who might be persuaded to take care of the 'pesky critters' for a day. About their guest, they were abashed. Even the happy Bascombs, when they thought of it, could hardly envisage a lady like Damaris squatting by their campfire.

Not wishing to cause a family dispute, Damaris spoke to Sue and told her that she wished to go on to St Augustine, which was the truth. Sue fought the idea vigorously. She was sure the Marquise had meant to stay at least another day, and in any case she could not travel without the men; it would be too dangerous by far. Besides, they had not yet finished contriving all the calico, and by herself she could never fix that muslin, which brought Polly, who was longing for her new dress, to the point of tears.

Defeated, the two Bascomb men said that they would manage to get back that night. And they would take the lady to St Augustine any time she pleased. Johnny-boy, to his mortification, was left behind to 'watch the ladies' and spent most of the day, in gloomy importance, sitting with a rifle across his knees.

'You can see, Ma'am,' Sue said with resignation after the men were gone, 'that they don't figure the plantation business hardly pressing. Still, in spite of them two Bascombs, we will have a good quiet day to finish up. I daresay that the Marquis will be right anxious to see you in St Augustine.'

The women worked on the dresses at the plain pine table. Damaris had been touched to see how carefully they watched the needles—manufactured goods were not so easily obtained by the settlers. Even little Mary Anne held a needle as though it were one of the crown jewels. Mary Anne now sat on Damaris's lap, and Polly watched her shyly as if a fairy princess had stolen upon them, gazing almost with awe at her dress of pale blue gauze, looped and braided at the hem, with deep blue ruffles of heavy silk, and at her little flat satin slippers, until her attention was caught by Damaris's simple summer necklace, lapis lazuli with a clasp of diamonds. This necklace Damaris had worn only at Brighton, but the girl from the remote, rough plantation craved the ornament with a sudden, passionate attachment like that of a first love.

Damaris saw her almost-hypnotized state and smiled. The necklace was suitable for a young girl, and she determined to make Polly a present of it when she left.

The Bascombs, altogether, were something new to Damaris. She had known no one like them before. They had none of the driving energy of the New Englanders—even Sue, who did far more than the men, would give up in the afternoons and go to take a rest. Certainly, the weather was still warm, even though they were full into November—winter touched this place but lightly, she had heard, and that year the summer heats had lingered. The Bascomb men lived for all the world like poachers, poachers in a paradise with no gamekeepers and no laws of venery. They were happy if their womenfolk were not—it was Eve, as always, who was not satisfied with Eden.

Sue talked as she worked, telling Damaris stories of her girlhood days. 'I was right purty,' she said with some complacence and apparently little regret for the loss of that youthful bloom. 'Even if I was red-headed and freckled some. I was nigh on the most popular girl in the settlement.'

She sighed reflectively.

'I was a-courted by Jim Hind, who had the place next to ours. A real fine man was Jim Hind, but I knowed him all my life as well as my own brothers. Then John Bascomb come along. Trapping beaver, he was then. Lord, he was big and strong, and he'd been to places far off and was as different from my folks as night is to day.'

Polly was listening round-eyed to the story, already, Damaris thought, with a feminine longing for romance.

Sue giggled. 'Well, Mr Bascomb, he had his eye on me right away. We were courtin' before my mammy and pappy could turn around.'

Her face grew soft with her happy memories, and Damaris could see suddenly that she had been very pretty, with Johnny-boy's bright colouring and a sweetness of her own.

'He gave me a beaver pelt,' she confided, 'the best he had—my, it was the softest, prettiest thing. Even a lady like yourself would have been proud to wear it. But my pappy, he told me not to go a-marryin' with the likes of Bascomb. Folks like him make poor husbands, he said, and he went on powerful about Jim Hind, praising him to the skies. But I was real stubborn,' she went on, shaking her head. 'My, I was stubborn. I am real happy that none of my children turned out stubborn like me. My mammy used to say that I must be part mule. I was real stubborn to marry Mr Bascomb, who was a stranger to us, but so fair and handsome and with such great strong arms—'

She gave another little sigh, bit a piece of thread from the reel, and tied a knot carefully.

'My pappy, he were right,' she said sadly. 'Why, I bet Jim Hind has a fine big farm by now, and here I am with snakes and all manner of mean crawly things. But I have my Johnny-boy,' she added with a return of her ebullience, 'and when he's growed he'll make a farmer sure. And I have my good girls—well, look at Polly now!'

Polly, who at last was fitted in the muslin dress, which had been shortened and broadened to the fullest possible extent, made an unexpectedly pretty sight.

'Cleans up right well, does Polly,' her mother said with maternal pride. The stout young farm girl was transformed by the floating layers of delicate white gauzy stuff, cunningly contrived to make her waist look small. The neckline was quite low, as fashion dictated, and Polly's fair young body already showed a hint of the breasts that were to come. She looked almost a belle and, seeing herself in the looking-glass, was struck quite dumb. For once her docility fled; she refused to take the dress off at her mother's behest and went peacocking about the room, trailing her elegant skirts on the somewhat rough wooden floor. The women laughed, watching girlish vanity suddenly springing into life.

The men did not return by the dinner hour. Sue showed little surprise, and the women ate alone, talking of St Augustine and Sue's pleasure at the thought of seeing the city. As dusk gathered, Sue began to get nervous. She was sharp with Polly, who, suddenly showing a stubbornness to match her mother's, refused to take her new dress off even while she washed the dishes; and she grumbled when Johnny-boy went out, brandishing his rifle, to meet the men.

'Time he was abed. He won't be gettin' up to do the milkin',' she said, but Damaris felt uneasily that the cows were not Sue's only concern. Damaris had concerns of her own. The men had planned to go past the island now full of d'Egremont's men. Certainly Juneau and his lieutenants would not be pleased if they saw two American settlers drifting by, observing with their country-trained eyes, going on to talk to their friends up and down the river.

Now she felt she should have prevented them from going. Yet how could she have done it? Confess an army was gathering, perhaps to make war on the United States? She could imagine the fresh, stolid countenances of the Bascomb brothers, the stares from their light blue eyes. Suddenly her head ached; she thought that she would go to bed. Yet she was as restless as Sue, restless and afraid.

She realized that Sue was listening to sounds, the croaking of frogs, the cries of birds, the long-drawn-out hooting of the owls back and forth from somewhere in the spreading wilderness.

'Those owls are very noisy,' she said at last.

Sue gave her a look she did not understand.

'Almost bad as them pesky tree-frogs,' she muttered.

She jumped up, almost knocking the lamp over and, to Damaris's surprise, dropping her needle to the floor without bothering to pick it up.

'Take that dress off, Polly,' she said. 'Time we were all in bed. No call to be sittin' here with the light burning for all to see and those men not traipsed back yet, worthless as they are. I'm going out to look for Johnny-boy. He's probably down at the creek in back, looking for the men to come down-river.'

Polly was sobbing. She muttered indistinctly that she would not take the dress off and she would not go to bed.

Sue paused to glare at her daughter. Her nerves seemed strained to the breaking point, and Damaris thought this might be the moment to try to help.

Quickly she loosed the clasp of her necklace and put the ornament round Polly's firm young neck. The sobs stopped as if by magic, and Polly looked up at her, the light blue, tear-drenched eyes suddenly wide with hope and delight.

'A present for a good girl,' Damaris said, smiling.

Polly's sunburned hand reached up and touched the blue stones on her white bosom with something like a caress. Her tears gone, she turned to her mother to be admired, but Sue's attention was not on her daughter. She was standing where she had paused, her hand resting on a chair-back, her head lifted, listening to the hooting sounds that seemed to be coming closer. Her nostrils were twitching—for no reason Damaris thought of a small animal she had seen in the woods of Heron, aware of the approaching dogs of a shooting party.

A crack resounded, drowning for a moment the hooting noise.

'Johnny-boy,' Sue said. 'He's setting off that gun.'

She ran forward; the door opened up to meet her. At once the little room was full—full of Indians who rushed in, hooting, hollering, flailing hatchets. So many bodies were crowded into the small space that Damaris could see only part of what was happening: whirling figures, dark skins. . . . She sat frozen with terror; then she heard the scream of a child near her feet. Dropping down, she looked through the forest of legs, but Mary Anne was not to be seen; then she caught a glimpse of fair hair under the table. She hushed Mary Anne and heard Polly cry. A tall Indian with a hatchet dripping blood had grabbed the girl, daubing the white muslin red. With a shriek, Sue appeared at his side and fell upon him, trying to tear him away. The hatchet lifted, swooped down, and clove her neck in two. Damaris felt herself grow faint; Mary Anne was whimpering; she crouched down and pressed her hand over the child's mouth, begging her to be still and silent.

Someone was screaming, a high, long, sustained note that cut through the whoops and yells. Where was Johnny-boy with the gun? Damaris looked for Polly, but she could see nothing by the lamplight except the jumping, hooting Indians and their leaping black shadows on the wall. A flutter of something white disappeared through the doorway.

'Johnny-boy,' Damaris screamed, her desperate mind conjuring up the boy with the rifle waiting in the shot-gun passage, and then she saw the men gazing at her as she moved into the light.

Mary Anne jumped up and tugged her skirt. Damaris took her in her arms and held her close so that she would not see her mother's head where it had fallen on the table by the lamp, dripping blood onto the pile of calico. An Indian, turning, saw Damaris with the child, reached towards her, and tearing Mary Anne away, dashed the fair head to bits. He grabbed Damaris by the shoulder; she expected at any moment to feel the hatchet's blow on her own head. But another Indian, who had been staring at her, spoke in words she could not understand and came closer, looking into her face. He spoke again, with some authority, for the howling mass of men grew quieter, and still. Then one by one they began to murmur. It seemed that they might be quarrelling. The man who had caught her tightened his hold; she could smell his body. He was young, very dark, hard, and strong. The other man was older, with grey-streaked hair. He wore beads and seemed to be the leader. With an imperious gesture, he waved the younger man away. Then he touched Damaris's forehead. The men muttered and quarrelled again.

One of them lifted the lamp and made to hurl it—they were going to fire the place. Damaris stared, not knowing if she was to be burned alive. The old man spoke and gestured. Whatever his words were, they brought anxiety—something had made the men afraid, she thought, but what? They piled through the door without waiting to fire the house, the young man dragging her with him, his hand in a cruel grasp upon her wrist. Outside, the first thing she saw in the thickening twilight was another Indian with a rifle. Johnny-boy, pale, his arm soaked with blood, was tied with thongs. His red hair stood up from his face as he gazed at her like a man staring at the dead. Polly, stumbling over her muslin skirts, was being driven forward by the clubbing of the hatchets like an animal going to the slaughter.

Damaris, dragged and pushed along by the quarrelling Indians, suddenly was seized with the idea that she must not leave Sue and Mary Anne. She looked back wildly at the open door in time to see two braves stepping out, attaching something to their belts. Sandy curls, fair curls. Darkness rushed upon her, but she was not allowed to faint; pulled until her arms were nearly jerked from their sockets, she could not find the blessed relief of unconsciousness. Her slippers lost, her feet already bleeding from stumbling over roots, she was dragged off with Johnny-boy and Polly. Night fell, but they went on, deeper and deeper into the pine woods, away from the world of white men, prisoners of the savages.

Sometime that night the Indians stopped in a clearing in the woods and set down to make camp. Whatever fear had made them rush off from the Bascombs seemed to have left them now. They lit a small fire and cooked some meat. Damaris lay flat on the earth, exhausted, with jerking pains in her legs—she had never walked so far or so hard before, on and on, long past feeling that she could not take another step.

She could see Polly glimmering in her white muslin on the other side of the small camp, and Johnny-boy with her. Johnny-boy was propped up against a tree. She had seen him losing blood along the way and wondered how long he could live. The moonlight gave them a white, unearthly look.

After the Indians had eaten, she saw them go out and break branches from the trees and build a great heap of firewood. She wondered why, with a prickling uneasiness, for the night was not cold. They fed the fire until it rose in bright flames lighting up the clearing, and she saw that in the center there was a grove of dark cypress trees. The men began a kind of singing and whooping that sounded to her like *ai-ai-ai!* and then started to dance, a long intricate dance with curious mime, accompanied by the strange shrieks.

The older one left them and came over to where she lay. He offered her a piece of burned meat, and she was shaken with a fit of nausea. The water he gave her was brackish, but she swallowed a little and bathed her face. Then he took her hand and led her round the cypress grove and ceremoniously offered her a fallen log to sit on. To her shock—if anything could shock her further—he spoke to her in English.

'You name?'

At first she did not comprehend; he mouthed the words strangely, but when he repeated them the meaning dawned on her.

'I am the Marquise d'Egremont.'

He nodded his head, looking gloomier than ever.

'I knew it. I have heard. The lady of the eyes like Miami—great blue water.'

He seemed irresolute, as he had looked at the Bascomb house. She knew they had not intended to surprise her—it was the Americans they wished to destroy. Yet it was strange that the name d'Egremont was familiar to this savage—strange that he spoke in her own tongue. Perhaps he was a half-breed; she had heard there were many such. Although his skin had looked dark to her in the house, certainly it was much lighter than that of the young man who had pushed her along the way.

His feet shuffled in the dirt. She guessed that he was puzzled about what to do with her. Perhaps he had wanted to leave her behind—she remembered that he would not allow the house to be burned. Then something had happened to make him afraid. Perhaps—her heart beat quickly—perhaps he would be willing to release her now. The quarrel of his tribe was not with her. He and his men could be far away before she would find her way back through the forest—if she could ever find her way. But the children —she looked at his face, searching in the strong carved features, the dark strange eyes, for some hint of compassion.

'You can let me go,' she said. 'Me—and those children. They have never harmed you.'

'Children!' He laughed. 'That boy killed three braves. He will pay the price.'

Dismayed, she saw that her words had goaded him to anger, and decision.

'You—you are my prisoner. I am Chief Coacoochee. I am your master, and you will go where I go. Your name will now be Okahumpka, Bitter Water. Perhaps I take you for a wife. Black Bear claimed you, but I am still the chief, although he thinks to take my place. I let him have the other, good strong wife.'

'But she is just a little girl,' Damaris pleaded, but his talk with her was over. He bound her wrists and ankles, the thongs digging deep into her flesh.

He turned and looked back at the cypress grove, where the flames were casting up a flickering light. He muttered something, but she caught only her new name, Okahumpka. His arms clasped her body and he dragged her further off, until she was almost out of earshot of the constant *ai-ai-ai!* of the dancing men. Then he left, and for a while she lay wondering what was happening and trying not to think.

Suddenly there was a scream. It was followed by another and then another, long, agonized, hardly muted by the distance. The Indians went on yelling and stamping, but the screams from the single voice pierced through their din. The screams came faster; Damaris pulled against her bonds, but they were tight; then she tried to bury her head in her lap to deafen the awful sounds that went on and on, the shrieks of mortal agony, quick and shorter now. She turned and twisted, choked with sobs, her wrists and ankles wet with blood as she strained against them, not knowing her own pain.

When at last the screaming stopped she lay back exhausted. Her mouth was full of blood from the biting of her lips, and she felt that she could never cry again. Before the sun rose, perhaps she slipped for a moment into an exhausted sleep, for Johnny-boy seemed to stand before her, his red hair flaming, his arms stretched out towards her, pleading. 'Okahumpka, Mother,' he said, but she was tied and helpless.

At the first streak of light, the old chief came towards her. He loosed the thongs and bade her rise. When she could not, he pulled her roughly to her feet. At the touch of his hands on her shoulders she began to scream. She did not want to scream; she was afraid to be noticed by the other Indians; she was afraid of the thin high sound of her own voice, but it came, and went on and on until the woods rang with the sound of her screaming. He slapped her sharply and poured water on her face until the screaming stopped.

'Come,' he said. 'We move on.'

The braves were stirring; she could see their dark forms moving like shadows beyond the cypress grove. Damaris would not walk past that grove, not if she had to die on the spot. She might as well die now with one swift blow of the hatchet that hung at the chief's side, the blade catching the first glimmer of day-dawn. Another night the fire might be for her. The chief saw her glance and pulled her forward, avoiding the place where the fire had been. Damaris kept her eyes full closed, and her stumbling and falling angered the chief, who struck her sharply, muttering in his own tongue. When she opened her eyes again, she was clear of the cypress grove and a distance into the pine wood.

For a moment she thought she saw snow; the ground, the tree-trunks, and some branches were dotted with white. She was so dull and incurious she accepted the idea of snow, but then she saw it was only in one place. Unwilling to see, to think, she saw anyway. It was muslin on the branches, white muslin, muslin brought from England, a present from the Countess of Malfrey to—She turned on the chief with hate, and then she saw Black Bear grinning at her. The pale sunlight caught the blue stones around his neck, the long fair curls hanging from his belt.

Damaris groaned and tumbled down to the ground in a helpless fit of weeping.

'You said—his wife,' she protested, stupid with grief. 'The child—'

'The girl not burn,' the chief said sulkily. 'Black Bear took her for wife. But after—he hate white people. His mother black woman; white people took her for slave. Come.'

Damaris determined not to move; she would die there, with the others. But Coacoochee was her master, accustomed perhaps to recalcitrant female slaves. He rained blows upon her with a cold persistence; he was not angry but business-like. At last it seemed humiliating to lie and be whipped like a dog before the grinning men, and slowly, reluctantly, she got to her feet.

The chief snorted with satisfaction and spoke some words in his own language to the men, who moved on.

He gave her a push. 'We go,' he said.

And she went, deeper and deeper into the woods. Halfway through that long day, she knew she could go no further. The way was hard, her ankles were still swollen from the thongs, and her feet bled from the rough ground until she was leaving prints of blood. The Indians must have felt very safe from pursuit, because her trail worried them not at all, and they took their time and paused to shoot a deer along the way. While they were butchering the deer, the chief took her to a stream to bathe her feet and rest awhile. He offered her some dried corn to eat, but her mouth was dry and her stomach rejected the hard morsels.

Damaris had no idea where they might be or if any white men might be following, searching for them in the woods. The house had not been fired; no other settler would have seen smoke and come to see what had taken place. The Bascombs—where were they? Perhaps taken prisoner by Jean-Philippe's own men.

The chief saw her glances and understood.

'No white men come,' he said briefly. 'White men send. Give many goods. You, only trouble. We go far, no more goods. Oka-humpka,' he added, looking upon her with dislike.

White men send. Sue Bascomb had said the English set the Indians onto the American settlers. Were these decisions made in London? she wondered, light-headed. Did the Earl of Malfrey solemnly advise His Majesty's secretary of state for war, as they drank a glass of sherry at Watier's, to send a party of avenging Indians to carry off his adulterous wife? And burn her son, he has red hair, he is no Malfrey—and she laughed hysterically until she was soundly cuffed once more.

They made camp early. The men were riotous as they ate the venison and drank some potion that seemed to make them drunk. Damaris, bound again, was huddled by a tree. Tonight she was their only prisoner—was it her turn for destruction? The English wife of a Frenchman might be merely another white woman before the night was done. Perhaps the old chief would come to claim her as his wife—but she did not think so. There was a certain fear in his eyes when he looked at her, a fear she could not understand. If one of the men came, it would be Black Bear; she was sure of that.

She made a silent prayer and then felt shame for her praying; no prayer had saved Johnny-boy from the flames, no prayer had saved Polly from the savage rape before the hatchet had fallen on that round young neck. She had given Polly Bascomb a fine gift— bridal gown, grave-clothes. If she had not gone to the Bascomb house, would Sue have gone with her men, taking the children up the river to safety? Or would Jean-Philippe's followers have killed them all? She shuddered, for her sins surrounded her at every mental turn, standing tall like iron bars, like the pine trees that were her prison.

Perhaps it was fitting that she die here at the hands of savages. She had brought nothing but trouble and torment wherever she passed. At least she had saved Booth, she thought. By running away, foolish as it had been to go to d'Egremont, at least she had saved Booth's reputation, his dignity, the value of his life. He must think the Marquise d'Egremont too fine a lady to give herself to a private citizen with his way to make in a new territory. Let him think so, even though this fine lady—if she lived—was to be an Indian squaw.

She listened to the men snoring after all their revelry. When morning came, they would move again. The chief had told her that when they reached their destination, she must begin her work. She would gather firewood, skin animals, and cook the meat. Work as a wife, in fact. Black Bear had heard him, and his eyes had glittered. Damaris understood little about these people, but the look of Black Bear she understood. Whatever the chief said, she knew that Black Bear would claim her. His hatred for white women did not prevent his gazing on her flesh in the tattered remnants of her gown with an appreciation not so different from that of other men, but with a cruelty plain in his desire, a madness in his lust.

The night seemed very long. Too fearful to sleep, she lay wondering if Black Bear would wake before the others, afraid that if she closed her eyes she might find that he had come over the grass-strewn sandy earth, as silently as these Indians could, to appear, tall and malevolent, at her side. Then there was the rustling of small pre-dawn sounds; birds were calling. The men, worn out from their revelry, still slept. The first light came in through the trees; a flashing creature flew above her, bright as the parrot once sent to the Earl from Martinique. It had sat in a golden cage at Heron and called, 'Pretty Polly, pretty Polly.' She shuddered, cried; and because her eyes were so very tired, her lids rolled down slowly.

There was a step, feather-light upon the grass. A hand was on her mouth, a strong arm gripped her. In complete and utter terror, she would not open her eyes, but the grip was real, not nightmare, and her lids moved up without her volition to see that the man who held her, tight enough to crush her bones, was Howard Booth.

CHAPTER

57

The events of that long day, and many days thereafter, would always be clouded in Damaris's mind. With all her terror and pain, she had given small attention to the discomfort of the biting, suck-

ing insects of the place, and the fever broke upon her just as all
her other danger had passed.

She remembered seeing Booth and thinking first that she was
dreaming or mad. Later he told her she had tried to make him
leave; it was not safe, she had said; she was not safe. But he had
carried her off, out of range, while the army men and the militia
rounded up the band of braves. She had been taken in an army
waggon to St Augustine with Booth beside her, holding her—it
seemed through all her days of illness, spent in a modest villa, that
he never left her side. When she was well enough to leave her bed,
she sat on the long, tree-shaded balcony, and he cared for her with
the patience of a nurse and gave her the long cool drinks rich with
cinchona, the specific for her fever, until the nightmare lifted—as
much as it would ever lift.

At first she asked few questions. The horrors she had seen almost overpowered her mind. Mary Anne's mangled body, Sue's
chopped like butcher's meat. The torment of Johnny-boy and
Polly—the recollection was too much to be borne. She had no wish
to get well, to remember; the fever-induced visions, horrifying as
they were, somehow were preferable to reality. But she did recover, clutching now and then at Booth's hand and always hearing
his voice say quietly, 'I am here.'

She began to sleep, true sleep, and at last had to open her eyes
to the world and admit to herself that all that had happened had
happened; it was now the past, and she was still living. Booth's
hand was in hers; she knew that he was real, that he had been
there in the forest and had brought her out.

'How did you find me? Why did you come?'

Not at once, but a little at a time, he let her know what had occurred, saving the darkest part until the last, when she was returned to full strength and he thought that she could bear it. He
had left Litchfield to follow her almost as soon as he received her
letter from the Duckworths, believing her to be in some danger if
she accompanied d'Egremont on his wild adventure. This adventure also struck Howard Booth as being dangerous to the United
States. His journey had taken longer, as he had travelled over
land, stopping on the way to talk to General Jackson, who was
negotiating payment with the Creek Indians for the recently-ceded
territory.

General Jackson, who never waited upon the government in
Washington, had his own system of spies among the Indians and

had already heard about movements of men and supplies on the St Johns River, and about the Frenchman who was the leader of the pack. The letter that Booth showed him made his decision prompt; he sent a detachment of his own men, and letters to the commander of the nearest U.S. Army post. He mentioned casually that he had no authority to do any of this, but American lives were in danger, and 'by the Eternal!' he swore he would do what he could to save them.

The army men had surprised d'Egremont's troops on the island. They were without a leader, as Juneau, growing nervous when the Marquise did not return, had gone to find d'Egremont to tell him of his wife's departure. The camp was broken up, and the officers taken into custody. There was an outstanding charge of murder; the bodies of the Bascomb brothers were found in new-filled graves. Investigation later proved that the shooting had been done by a wild, nervous young man when the Bascombs were found poking about curiously.

Then Booth had found that Damaris was not at the Chateau d'Egremont, and learned where she had gone. A few picked men had gone with him down-river to the Bascombs; he had seen all that was there. Two scouts and the soldiers had gone with him into the woods. After all, the trail had not been so easy to follow, but the tiny scraps of silk and gauze that had caught on the trees had helped along the way. At the cypress grove he thought he had come to the end. He had seen the charred body on the pyre, the naked, mutilated body of a girl. A scrap of blue gauze and then a bloody footprint had kept him on the trail—though when he saw her twisted form lying by the tree he had first thought her dead.

If only he had reached them one night sooner, Damaris thought in an agony of mind that was hardly bearable. If Jean-Philippe's murdering band had not killed the Bascomb brothers and had let them go their indolent way home—but the Bascomb men were dead. Booth lived, and must be thanked. She thanked him, in a low voice full of tears, reaching up towards him with a hand still trembling and too weak to hold.

But her mind was clear enough to know that Booth was keeping something back. Something dark, she knew, and dreadful, because after all the other horrors, he was still afraid to let her know this last.

'What of Jean-Philippe?' she said suddenly. 'Where is he?'

'We'll talk of that later, Damaris,' Booth said, turning from her to gaze out over a quiet court. 'You must get your strength.'

'Is he to be shot?' she asked steadily.

'He could not be judged a traitor,' Booth said slowly. 'He made very sure of that. He owed no allegiance to the United States and was not on United States territory.'

'Then what?' she said.

'Let us not talk about it,' he pleaded, 'not now. Let it wait.'

'I must know,' she said. 'Uncertainty would be the worst.'

'Your husband is a murderer, Damaris,' Booth said at last. His face was very stern. 'It was he who paid the Indians to raid the American settlers. The chief who led the raid and took you off had learned from d'Egremont's men that the Bascomb brothers were dead, and he took his opportunity. That chief did much business with d'Egremont—he must have been embarrassed to come upon his wife.'

Now Damaris clearly understood the quarrelling in the shot-gun house. Certainly the old chief had wanted to leave her behind; Black Bear, his strong young rival, had refused. She found she was not at heart surprised to learn what d'Egremont had done. Many times she had heard him talk of clearing the area from prying eyes —only she had not known what that meant. Juneau—did he know? Certainly he had not known of that last raid: he would never have let her go down-river.

'What will happen now to Jean-Philippe?' Her lips were stiff; it was hard to say the words. Jean-Philippe and his dream of empire. Mary Anne, her skull stove in. Polly, whose curls had danced on Black Bear's belt. . . . The soldiers had returned the necklace to her. She would rather have thrust her hand into a nest of snakes than to have touched it, and she left it to be buried with Polly in her pine-shaded grave.

'Your husband is dead, Damaris,' Booth said gently. 'He was killed by my hand.'

She looked up, staring.

'We met at the Bascomb house. He had been here in St Augustine, and one of his men had come to tell him that you had gone there for a visit. D'Egremont rode back—most hastily, I gather—to come and take you away. It was in fair fight,' he went on, his voice steady. 'I challenged him—it had to be done.'

Damaris's eyes were wide.

'But Jean-Philippe is an expert marksman.'

'He had seen the bodies,' Booth said slowly, 'and you were gone. When we took our paces, he saw your slipper on the path. His shot went wild. Mine went through his heart.'

He left her then, and she was alone in the long grey twilight, to think of Jean-Philippe, whom she had loved, and listen to the tree-frogs, the same sound she had heard at the Bascomb house, with the hooting of the owls that were no owls. Jean-Philippe dead. And by Booth's hand.

Booth was gone for several days. There was business to be done: the matter of the murdered Bascombs, and affairs surrounding the death of d'Egremont. For that wild and reckless adventurer had made a will; he had acquired a pleasant sum of money, and owned a house in New Orleans as well as the Chateau d'Egremont. All of this was left to Damaris, la Marquise d'Egremont, *née* St Cloud. While she was kept to her room, Booth took care of everything. Damaris was not sure if the legacy was hers by right, but it meant she would not go to England without funds. If she was a pariah, at least she would have bread. Damaris's thoughts returned to the mystery of Jean-Philippe—careless Jean-Philippe who had made a will; the crack marksman whose bullet had gone wide when he saw her slipper on the path. And all this time her strength was returning, and she knew that soon she must be gone.

Booth returned, happy to see her stronger and in looks. He told the news, carefully, trying not to revive old hurts. The 'liberating army' except for the murderer, was to go free. No one had authority to take them back to the United States for trial, and Booth conjectured there would be little stomach for it when the news penetrated Washington. There had been little success or glory in the earlier trial of Aaron Burr. D'Egremont was dead, his New Orleans officers, knowing they were now marked men, would probably remain discreet for the rest of their lives. The rank and file were probably just looking for a war—

'They will most likely follow Jackson when he comes to take this land for the United States,' Booth said wryly.

'You think that he will?' Damaris asked, startled.

'I have no doubt. When he finishes his present business haggling with the Creeks. In a year or two, all this will be United States territory.'

Jean-Philippe had been right, Damaris thought. Spanish America was a prize for the taking.

She noted the inflexion in Booth's voice when he spoke of the general; his admiration for the great man was somewhat ambivalent. He had defended him in New England against the wrath of men like Simon Hatch; in this very room he had praised his decision and his swiftness to act when he learned of danger. But Jackson was a famous fighter against the Indians, and she knew that Booth thought of the Indians in a way different from other men—or women, she thought with a shiver, for she now felt as the Americans did. Her horror at the savages could not be erased by Christian thought or mitigated by love, as Booth's had been—love for his boyhood sweetheart, 'Becca.

He understood her thought—there was a quickness about Booth that his slow voice, his unhurried manner, could cause an observer to overlook.

'I don't speak to criticize the general,' he said. 'It is his given duty to be sparing with the public monies. But these people have lost much. I hope this is to be the end of their losses.'

He spoke as though this hope was not sanguine.

The thought of Indians brought back all that had happened; Booth saw her turn white and shudder uncontrollably.

'Don't think I make light of your suffering,' he said remorsefully.

'Not mine,' she cried in passion. 'The boy—his screams—Polly—little Mary Anne—she was still clutching at the needle and her mother's head was on the table—'

It was too much. She sobbed again, and Booth, stricken, gently caressed her head until she quieted.

'It is too soon to speak of these things,' he said. 'Only remember—it is not the Indians alone who have been brutal. Perhaps,' he said, sighing, 'there is no quarter between warring peoples who lay claim to the same land. And our people will go further,' he added soberly, 'whether the men of New England consent or no. Jackson is right in his way; we can't leave the South and West to be taken by any European adventurer, a Napoleon, a d'Egremont, a Laffite—or even a Scotsman with a vision.'

She had never seen him serious so long—except in her delirium. Suddenly she wondered what she might have said in her raving, what he had learned, and she forgot the talk of politics, conscious only of his hand resting on her head. He had come for her; he still wanted her. Without conceit, she knew that now he meant to offer marriage, believing her free, only waiting perhaps for her to recover—or to forget that he had killed d'Egremont.

They spoke meantime of little things, the laws that tied for a time the property in New Orleans. Booth, certain that Damaris would not return to the Chateau d'Egremont, had collected her possessions—even her jewel case which had been found in the Bascomb house. Robert Juneau, who had prudently decided to remain in Florida for a time at least, offered to buy the chateau just as it stood.

'I cannot sell the slaves,' Damaris said. 'They must be set free.' Booth nodded in approval.

'They can stay with Juneau as free servants if they wish,' Damaris went on, thinking that Mauricette, no doubt, would be persuaded to stay. Robert Juneau was most attractive. But at least she would have the choice.

Soon the papers were all signed; the work was done. She was well enough to travel now. One evening when Booth came to her— a warm and languorous evening—she determined to tell him she must go. Yet she could not think how to tell him. Why, she thought, weary of her long deceit, should she not tell the plain truth? That she had been d'Egremont's mistress, not his wife; that she was married to another man; that she was in truth a loose woman whose reputation in her own country was now so vile she feared to venture back; that if he married her she would be a shame to him for all their lives. She knew she would not tell him— to protect him from his own love and folly, and because she could not bear to see the look that would come upon his face, the love remaining, the respect diminishing. This son of the Puritans— when he took her in his arms, would he think of her wantonness with another man? Would the look of passion turn to stern disgust as it had on the face of the Earl?

She could not bear to live through that again. Never had she truly felt herself besmirched by the Earl's madness; she had had no part in the evil that had turned his love to torment. But to have Booth look upon her so would be a living death.

She would leave him, and she would leave him coldly. There would be no more pursuit; the Cool Countess of Malfrey knew well how to contrive that. She would freeze his love and send him home—to marry Verity and be happy after all.

'You will marry me now, Damaris.' He spoke, his thoughts far from her own. 'I know it can't be easy; mine was the hand that killed your husband. Yet it must be. Take all the time you need, but tell me you will marry me at last.'

His voice, soft, pleading, pierced her heart. He had taken her hand in his own, the lightest touch that made her skin feel like silk warmed by a dancing fire. Through her sadness spread delight, and the body that had been dead to sweet sensation vibrated with desire.

It was dusk, though no lamps were yet lit. The long windows were open to the terrace, and the mild air that drifted into her room was touched with sweetness from strange late blooms. A slender moon touched the treetops, and in its spell Damaris once more reached out to tempt the man she loved, answering his question not with words but with all the new-found ardour of her body. His soaring ecstasy matched her own, and they drank thirstily of each other's love like two creatures, long parched, drinking at the spring of life itself.

Dark came, the golden moon rose high; Damaris watched its stately traverse as Booth slept. They lay warm and trembling in each other's arms, naked as the lovers in Eden, and only Damaris knowing she must be cast out. She touched his proud head, the sturdy sinewed neck, the powerful line of shoulder, the strong arms that had carried her away from hell itself. Fear touched her at the memory; he was instantly aware, and his arms grasped her, drawing her to him again. 'This time you will not run away,' he muttered, confident, before his mouth sought her own and she yielded to his embrace with grief lacing her pleasure; for it was true—this time she would not run away. She must do the work of parting, and even as she shuddered in deep joy, she knew this night of love would prove her wanton and that she must be content to have it so.

Book Four

THE RETURN,
1816-1817

58

Damaris took the ship to New York City and then obtained passage on the packet to Liverpool. The accommodations were comfortable, and for the winter season the weather was mild enough. The strong westerly breezes served to send the light ship swiftly across the water.

She walked on deck daily, and gradually her vigour was restored. It was strange to see her face in the looking-glass in her cabin, still so young and curiously unaltered from all her adventures—she felt almost cheated that she was touched with no sign. She had brought no harvest home from all her scattered seed of harsh endeavour, nourished as it had been by tears and the warmth of glowing love.

Travelling as Damaris St Cloud, she kept apart. She had no wish to talk of her life in America or to invent a lie. There was time, too much time, for memory and reflection. With youth and health on her side, the harshest of her memories faded; no longer was she woken in the night by the sound of the boy screaming; the sight of a girl in white muslin no longer made her faint.

But there were other memories, as painful in their own way, that did not fade, that did not need a dream to bring them back. She would stand in a place she made her own, away from all others in the stern of the ship, watching the grey water; and on the rippling waves she would see again the house in St Augustine, her room above the court-yard with the strange flowers and vines. On her last night there she had waited in that room, sleepless—waited until Booth had left her with words of love at daybreak.

Then she had sprung up, swift to act, her plans complete. Servants were sent, her passage booked, arrangements made to get herself and her luggage to the dock. All had gone speedily; most of her trunks were still packed, and the women servants were set to work upon the rest. While they laboured, a coiffeur was sent for, and he cut and curled her hair in the English fashion that she had not worn since she sailed on the *Bonne Chance*. She dressed for travel with great care; she would appear as a *grande dame*—no one knew better than the Countess of Malfrey what great distance could be contrived with dress and all the appurtenances of a lady of the *ton*. She chose a dress of dark blue taffeta with a high arched collar, long sleeves, and a richly-braided girdle made of gold. A matching cloak hung from her shoulders, and carefully on her new coiffure she placed a hat, wide-brimmed, of satin straw, trimmed with puffs of dark blue ribbon that shaded half her face and threw into relief her imperious profile. She looked at her reflection, almost satisfied, then put on all her rings and added last her sapphire bracelet, until she was as hedged about with all the signs of wealth and station she could muster.

On the ship the sailors called from the rigging to the deck, but she did not hear them. She was listening again to that quick step on the stair of the house in St Augustine and peering once more into the looking-glass of the dressing-room to see Booth enter her sleeping-chamber, his eyes bright with happiness, his arms filled with flowers. He looked about, and though the door was open, he did not recognize for a moment the much-accoutred lady who was turned towards the glass, the shadowed countenance in the elaborate Spanish frame. Then their eyes met.

'Damaris!' he had said, shocked. Her trunks were all about her; a servant was at the door, already carrying them down. 'What is this?' Before he asked, the knowledge was clear in his face.

Leisurely she chose a pair of long gloves and then turned to face him.

'I regret—I cannot marry you, Mr Booth,' she had said in her soft voice, but with the coolness proper to the Countess of Malfrey. 'Now that the Marquis is dead and all is settled, I can return to my home. You understand, after he had fought for Napoleon, I had to leave my country. But now nothing stands between me and the life I have always known. It is a life dear to me. The pleasures of Society in Town; the charm of my family estate.'

The flowers had fallen from his arms. He looked at her with an expression in his eyes she could not fathom.

'And perhaps the children whom you left?' he said ironically. 'You did make mention of two children while you were delirious.'

For a moment she was still. He said nothing more, watching her, she thought, like a cat with a mouse. What more had she said? she wondered. She would not have mentioned the Earl of Malfrey. Poor man, he was rarely in her thoughts.

'My children, yes,' she said deliberately. 'Although in England we see little of them, you know. Life there is not as it is—in the colonies.'

He looked at her as though he was trying to reconcile this woman with the girl that he had known.

'No,' he said at last, 'I can't believe this. You are play-acting for some reason; use your sense, Damaris. I have arranged for a minister to marry us today. I know you love me; you have shown me that, here and in Litchfield.'

She had wanted to break down then, to weep and to fall into his arms. Instead she turned away and opened up a small travel case, took out a crystal flask and, gazing in the glass, dabbed the sweet scent on her ears. She replaced the flask, toying with the gold clasp of the case until she had her voice under control.

'Mr Booth,' she said, 'you saved me twice, once from abuse by the mob of countrywomen, once from the Indian who wished to take me as his wife. I am not suited for life as a squaw, nor am I suited to be your wife. I am grateful to you, and I have shown my gratitude.'

He had started at the word squaw, and she realized he believed she was taunting him with a reference to his 'Becca. So much to the good. His face was dark. For an instant she thought he would strike her. Then he laughed. She would much rather have been struck than to have heard that laugh.

'And so you are going now, Madame,' he said, just as Jean-Philippe might have done.

She nodded, and waved to the servant to take the last of her things.

'I had a present for you,' he said. 'Never mind its purpose, it will serve as well for a farewell gift.'

He reached into his pocket and took out a jeweller's box, a small box that perhaps held a ring—but it was not a ring that he removed. Glittering in the morning light were her earrings, the diamond and sapphire earrings that he had sold for her—or so she had been persuaded—long before.

'I always thought they suited your blue eyes too well for them to go to someone else,' he said coolly. 'I still think so.'

He took her chin in his hand, and his grasp was not tender.

'What pretty perfumed ears,' he remarked, and hung the jewels on them. Slowly he turned her head from side to side. 'Very pretty. You belong together.'

He released her, watching her with a faint smile. The way was clear for her to go; the last of her goods was gone.

'But the money—you were so kind—I will repay you. Let me make you a draught—'

Her poise was shaken; she found herself stammering.

His smile broadened. He stood before her, calm and nonchalant. He looked up and down her body, his gaze resting on the curves of breast, hip, and thigh with frank appreciation.

'Don't trouble yourself, Ma'am,' he said affably. 'You have paid me already, most handsomely. I have no complaint, none at all.'

He laughed, took up his hat, and left, and the sound of his laughter floated back from the staircase after him. He had left her standing there confounded, and it had not been the son of the Puritans but the Regency belle who had remained, scarlet and in tears of shame.

A cloud passed before the sun, and suddenly the wind felt cold. Damaris moved off from the stern rail and resumed her daily pacing round the deck. The other passengers gazed at her, some surreptitiously, others with frank stares; the young lady, pale, lovely, and remote, who travelled unattended, excited a lively interest. She took her meals alone, and they had no chance to gratify their curiosity except to watch her on her solitary walks.

Damaris had thoughts enough to occupy her. She could, with great mental discipline, put the past away. Her grief would remain, but she did not need to let her mind strengthen her emotion. It was hard, for there was an irritation of the spirit to make the grief persist, to prevent it from sinking under the surface of every conscious thought. The sting that pricked her sensibility was the manner of her leaving—she could have borne the loss of Booth's presence if she could have kept his respect. If only he could have thought her dead—she had been right to kill his love, but it was a bitter rightness. Then she berated herself, for it was better that he had no memory of tragic love but was free in heart and soul to love another. Yet the sting remained.

Still, new problems were upon her, crowding her mind as the ship drew close to England. How would the Countess of Malfrey be received? What did people believe had happened? It was certainly known that she had fled with d'Egremont the spy after Waterloo. The Countess was thought to be dead, perhaps, or hiding with her lover, far from home. Was she still thought of as a traitor? Christmas had passed while she was on the ship, and the New Year. Now it was 1817; the war was long past; emotions had cooled, perhaps. She was almost sure her life no longer was in danger; when it was known that the Marquis, Napoleon's spy, was dead, his mistress would seem of small importance.

Unless her husband wanted that revenge. She knew now that the Earl had survived the duel. While she had waited in New York for the Liverpool packet she had seen newspapers, and one small item of the foreign news had been that the Earl of Malfrey had completed a mission to Louis XVIII in Paris.

Yet she could not believe the Earl would want her shot. For him the important thing would be to avoid more scandal. Perhaps he had divorced her; if not he certainly would do so on her return. If she lived quietly, obscurely, somewhere in the country, she believed she would not be persecuted—but would she be allowed, ever, to see her children? As she paced the decks day by day, she tried to consider, to be rational.

No matter what she wished to believe, she was certain the Earl would never let her see the children again. She had done them too much harm already, she thought soberly. Her son could overcome the disgrace of such a mother; the future Earl of Malfrey would be rich and powerful enough to assume his rightful place. For Griselda it would be far more difficult.

Then there was the vexing question of where she should go when she landed. Angelhurst had been given to her, a present from the Earl. After a divorce, perhaps it reverted to him again. She did not know. But probably she would not be welcome there. The country folk, though not as puritanical as the farmers of Bantam and Litchfield, would not be happy to have a disgraced, divorced wife come among them as lady of the manor.

When she sold her jewels, and with the money she had received from d'Egremont, she would buy a little house in some remote place, and seeking no society, making no friends, she could live out her days. Her obscurity would be her safeguard. She would be like Cassandra at Greystones. The wheel had come full circle.

Only, she told herself when her heart threatened to sink in the misery of her prospects, she had consolations that Cassandra never had. There was Aunt Gratton, who, however angry she might be with her niece, so carefully reared and yet wilfully choosing disgrace and ruin, had a strong sense of right and justice. She would not try to do what never could be done, to bring her niece back into Society; nor could Damaris suppose she would weaken her own position by much attention to the divorced Countess; but Aunt Gratton would give her news, from time to time, about the children. Decently, quietly, but it would be arranged.

Sometimes at night when she was sleepless in her berth, her body swaying with the brisk light motion of the ship, her mind preternaturally keen, she thought again of the night in the pine forest when all was lost, the Bascomb children dead, and it had seemed that her sins had risen round her strong and tall as trees and that there was no way to escape from that encirclement. She had thought to make a clearing afterwards by righteous acts; she had given up her love; she was ready to pay the penalty for all her treacheries as Englishwoman, wife, and mother. She prayed she had not deceived herself once more, that her journey would not be the means of bringing further misery upon her family, her return from the dead not reform but one more piece of self-indulgence, worse than the rest for being cloaked in piety.

She did not, could not know. It would have been better, perhaps, if she had died there in the forest with the children, if she had not survived after the death of all the Bascombs—better yet if she had died in New England from weakness of the lungs. The Earl, she was almost certain, would wish her dead rather than returned. Her children no doubt would grow up to wish the same. Rising from the berth that was no resting place, she dressed and walked out on the deck to feel the force of the cold wind, to watch the waters, bright, dark, then bright again in the fleeting moonlight.

The sailors on the night-watch observed her silently. There were other troubled souls besides her own that rode the ocean; there was a sympathy, an understanding among the men of the high seas. They respected her privacy, but from them some acceptance, some spiritual solace flowed, and without her conscious knowledge she was soothed enough to go below and sleep at last.

At Liverpool she took the stage for London. She could think of no better thing to do than go to Aunt Gratton—from her she would learn all she had to know. In the bustle of the port she had little time to look about her, but once on the stage she was very aware of being back in England once again, and there was a pleasure mixed with all her fears and sadness at this strange homecoming.

She had to remind herself that she had not been away so very long, for what struck her with great force was that she, who felt a lifetime away from the Damaris who had left, saw a country that seemed not changed at all. She was certainly back in England! The stage was so comfortable, so swift, the pike-road so excellent, the inns where they paused so luxurious. When she had left, all this had been part of the natural order of things; now England, under its grey cloud, with raindrops glistening in the hedgerows, appeared a well-managed place indeed.

Before she felt prepared, they entered London. It was late in the day, and Damaris lodged at the stage-coach inn. Next morning she was up long before the sun. She had to possess herself in patience; one did not go calling at such an ungodly hour. Her dress was chosen with care; Lady Gratton would not be appeased by an old or modest gown, and she donned a striking ensemble from her new French wardrobe, a deep blue *gros de Naples* and a cloak trimmed in rich sables. Then she ordered breakfast and even ate a little but soon sprang up in impatience—part dread, part hope, but beyond containing—to take a hackney carriage and ride about Town until, at ten o'clock, she could call on Lady Gratton.

The streets were brisk and full of life. The warehouses on Oxford Street were bustling, the building of Regent Street was going on apace. Some early riders cantered round the Park; now the holidays were over some members of the *ton*, not country-lovers, had hastened back to Town.

A few people glanced up, surprised to see a lady of such fashionable aspect in a hackney carriage, but Damaris was sure she saw no one she knew, or who knew her—no recognition followed the curious glances. So far, the return of the Countess of Malfrey was causing little stir. At Lady Gratton's modest house on Green Street, she dismissed the carriage and approached the door with a fast-beating heart and a tremor of nerves.

The porter who greeted her was new at his post. Obviously he had no knowledge of who she was. When she asked for Lady Gratton, he told her that the house was closed. Her ladyship had been abroad. Since her return, she had been living at Great Heron and at Malfrey House.

Damaris thanked the man and left, without leaving her name.

Of course, she might have guessed. Doubtless the Earl had taken Lady Gratton to be guardian to the children. Her plans quite overset, Damaris walked distractedly round a few streets and squares, trying to think what would be best to do. Almost certainly Lady Gratton and the children would still be at Great

Heron. The woman who had faced the Indians brandishing their tomahawks knew she could not bear to go down to Great Heron and be turned back from the gates.

Women of fashion did not promenade about the streets unattended, and she was attracting curious looks. Worse, she had wandered absent-mindedly into the masculine sanctuary of St James's, where the club windows looked out upon the street and respectable women were rarely seen. She glanced at the bow window of White's, as she had done once before with the Beau at her side, in the character of Desmond Midnight. Had she ever committed such follies? Almost she expected to see Alvanley grinning behind the glass, though that was hardly likely at this hour.

Her feet took her where her mind had refused to go. She stood at the high wall before Malfrey House. Unable to go forward or back, she saw through the open gate a familiar morning scene. The house itself looked strange; there was crêpe at the windows, the hatchment was over the door, but the servants were sweeping the carriage drive as usual at that hour. Then they paused on their brooms, looking up at a ghost from the past.

The great front door was opened. Damaris, nodding in some kind of acknowledgement of the hum of voices muted with all the politeness of the well-trained household, was drawn forward to mount the steps and enter through the hall, following a solemn servant to the morning-room where Lady Gratton sat on her long sofa waiting to receive her.

CHAPTER

59

Nothing had changed in that room since the two ladies had parted; it was like a stage-set revisited. But now there was a difference, Damaris saw; Lady Gratton was dressed in black so unrelieved that it spoke of mourning. The traveller was struck quite dumb, but it was of no consequence. Lady Gratton, as always, was fully in command.

'You are looking well, Niece,' she said calmly. 'Have you breakfasted? Then some coffee, I think, Burroughs, and see that the Countess's cloak is taken at once to Mrs Chambers. And have Lady Malfrey's room prepared—it will be required shortly. Sit down, child.'

Damaris sat, still incapable of speech.

When the servant left, the aunt regarded the niece in her familiar considering fashion.

'The gown is most becoming—but of course it will not do. We must get your mourning ready at once, before you can be seen. The children have been outfitted—poor Griselda looks most solemn.'

'The children—' Damaris had found her voice. 'They are here in Town?'

'The Earl died here in Malfrey House,' Lady Gratton said, 'and so of course we all came up. We go down to Great Heron tomorrow for the funeral; you must come with us of course, so we must be quick about your clothes.'

All Damaris's questions were in her eyes, but Lady Gratton was not to be hurried, nor would she show curiosity herself. The footmen brought the coffee; it was served; Lady Gratton's gimlet eyes forced Damaris to lift her cup and drink, though if she had swallowed poison she would not have noticed then. When the men had gone, Lady Gratton put her cup down on the little table by the sofa and addressed her niece prosaically.

'It is most opportune that you have returned in time for the funeral. That certainly will quiet any wagging tongues. You will want to know about the Earl. He has been ill for some time. He did not come to Heron for the holidays. His political business was of a nature that could not wait—but I fear it was too much for him. His health has never been perfect,' she added, 'since a certain affray at the house of the d'Egremonts. The Earl, you may not know, apprehended a dangerous French spy and killed him but was badly wounded himself. There was some talk about your old friend the Marquis d'Egremont, but he quite disappeared after Waterloo. No one seems to know if he is alive or dead—so difficult for his cousin the Duchesse. D'Egremont House was sold at auction and now is let.'

'The Marquis is dead,' Damaris said tonelessly. 'He died in Florida.'

Lady Gratton's eyebrows lifted. She looked as though she wished to know nothing of Florida—whatever it might be.

'Indeed? But you could hardly know that, Damaris. The Earl died at last, not from his wound, but from the same malady that killed his father, some affliction of the brain,' she went on. 'I have spoken to several physicians, and they tell me that we should not be unduly concerned for the children. These ailments appear in many families but are not always passed on. And the children have your St Cloud blood, Damaris, good healthy stock. Your sister-in-law, Lady Cassandra, still thrives—apart from her nervous complaints. Too much country life in my opinion; such seclusion would make any woman nervous.'

She glanced at her niece, regarded her stiff back, her head held high, and nodded in approval. The hands, tightly clasped, told their own tale.

'Your husband was a great, good man in his way, Niece. We did not choose ill. Everything was done to avoid scandal. D'Egremont was permitted to escape. After the battle we traced you to Ostend but no further. The Earl always believed that you had taken ship and perhaps were lost at sea. But he took great care. He packed me off post-haste to Brussels while the armies were still pursuing Bonaparte and our men were arriving wounded from the field. I went to the house of the Duchesse—fortunately still with the King —to spread the word among the ladies that you had suffered a collapse. Your health, always fragile, was overset by the horrors of war. The Mayne fragility is too well known to need much explanation, but the Earl insisted that I travel on the Continent a full year —it had its pleasures, though I wearied of it after so much time. I could have no companion, of course, and it was necessary to remain in places inconspicuous, not visited by members of the *ton*.'

Damaris listened to this tale, hardly able at first to take it in. It seemed far more incredible than the adventures she had known. No hue and cry, no scandal, no divorce. Yet it made a certain solid sense. The Earl was very powerful, and whatever he thought of her, he had his children to protect. If she were dead, then he would have her die with her name unsullied. If she returned, her reputation was safe and he could have dealt with her as he saw fit.

'At last I prevailed upon him to let me come home,' Lady Gratton said somewhat plaintively. 'I conjured up a retreat, discreet and private, in one of the more remote and unpleasant Alps, where you were resting undisturbed, breathing pure mountain air while you recovered. Attended, of course, by some worthy matron. But I returned only in time to be packed off to Heron—it was most annoying. And then I came to Town merely for his dying—it was not like the Earl to be so inconsiderate. But your arrival is a most fortunate stroke—don't forget, Damaris, about the Alps. I think your mind can be a little misty about the period of your illness—the fever, after all. And whatever people *might* think,' she said calmly, 'it is known that the Earl supported you in everything. That is the important thing. And indeed, Damaris, most of his arrangements for you are in effect unchanged. Angelhurst, your jointure. Malfrey and Great Heron are yours until Christopher comes of age. Of course, the control of all properties and monies was left in my hands. We had no knowledge whether you were living or dead, or if you lived and were discovered, what your situation might be. But if it was possible, the Earl wished you to live in the state to which you are by rank entitled. So fortunate,' she added, sighing, 'that young d'Egremont is dead. Such a pity it could not have happened long before.'

She rang the bell.

'Burroughs, have the Earl and Lady Griselda brought down to see their mother, if you please.'

Damaris's heart felt squeezed as she sat and waited for the first sight of her children. Two small figures dressed formally in black, each accompanied by a nurse, approached her solemnly. At first she would not have recognized them. They were no longer toddlers; Christopher already was a miniature of his father as a young man; Griselda showed the Mayne delicate beauty and yet, in her height and form, brought her mother's mind back to tragic little Mary Anne.

The little Earl bowed, Lady Griselda curtsied, but Damaris, used now to other ways, grasped them to her and hugged tight as though she would never let them go. The children blushed—not entirely with displeasure, she fancied. The sight of Lady Gratton's face, scandalized by her barbarous behaviour, caused her to release them; and very quickly, at that lady's command, the children were whisked away.

Suddenly Damaris was immensely weary. The tension of fear had left her; the relief that should have followed was yet to come.

She knew of her good fortune without feeling it, and then felt herself wicked to think of good fortune while her husband's corpse still lay in the house. Lady Gratton took her to his room, dark with heavy curtains, where the coffin rested, covered by a pall embroidered richly with the Malfrey arms, which glittered in the candlelight. Acorned oaks—the Earl in death as he was in life, a lord of Heron. Damaris prayed silently for this man to whom she had not been able to give the gift of peace—she hoped he had found it now.

Longing for her bed, Damaris found Lady Gratton was still . . . Lady Gratton. She held her niece with her commanding green gaze and stayed at her side while dressmakers hurriedly cut, fit, and basted. It might have seemed strange to Damaris to stand once more in her old room with Chambers, silent, impassive, waiting on her—but Damaris was too tired, too numb to respond to her surroundings.

She felt nothing—except perhaps that she was once more Damaris St Cloud, niece to the stern Aunt Gratton, meekly doing her bidding. Because of the emergency, even Lady Gratton's dinner, by custom sacrosanct, was postponed. It was evening before the business was all done—the sewing women would be up all night working on the gowns, cloaks, and underclothes; the hats were already trimmed.

Before Lady Gratton went down to dine, she ordered soup and bread brought up for her niece, as she might have done for a child, with only a glass of Madeira to acknowledge her adult state. She watched over Damaris until she had eaten every bite and drunk every drop. Then and only then was Chambers permitted to undress and bathe her and to turn back the linen sheets before she was dismissed. Lady Gratton herself held Damaris's night-gown and gazed at her niece's form thoughtfully as she slipped it on her.

'I must set about finding a husband for you, Niece,' she said, as she had done years before.

Damaris looked up, her hand upon the bed-post, startled from her bone-crushing fatigue.

'There must be a year of mourning,' Lady Gratton went on, 'but after that, the sooner the better.'

'I wish no new husband, Aunt,' Damaris said strongly.

Lady Gratton waved the objection away.

'It will be all to one the most sensible thing. This time we need not look for a great fortune or a title. A gentleman of good family with some property would do. A man closer to you in age who will give you a family and new duties. It is not suitable for you,' she said with her keen glance, 'to remain so much in fashionable society, a beautiful young widow with hints about her past. And you have shown yourself too—impulsive,' she said dryly, 'to live without a strong protection. You have caused much trouble, Damaris.'

It was the only reproof her aunt had given her, and she had to accept it silently.

'You must think now of what you owe to Lady Griselda and the Earl.'

It struck oddly against Damaris's ears to hear her son referred to by that title. Little Christopher, her baby, Earl of Malfrey.

'But we will have plenty of time to consider these matters at Great Heron,' Lady Gratton said briskly. 'Sleep well, for we leave early tomorrow.'

When her aunt had gone, the weariness remained but the capacity for sleep had fled. Lady Gratton had extinguished the candles when she left, and the only light came from the dying fire. Thus Damaris's room had always been at bedtime; nothing was changed. And she, who had thought herself so altered—had she changed? She was twenty-one years old, a grown woman who had thought that she was free.

Her first relief at finding she was not a branded spy, cast out from all society, abandoned by her husband and family to total ruin, was ebbing fast. A new fear was overtaking her that after all her experience, nothing had changed. Christopher was another Earl of Malfrey to whom she owed a duty senior to her own wants and desires. Her independence was a fiction; she was once again a ward of Lady Gratton and would be held to do her bidding—for the family's good.

She would not marry at her aunt's command, she promised herself fiercely. Once she had been forced to give herself to a man she did not love. Lady Gratton did not know and would not ask whether her niece had taken another lover, or lovers, after the death of Jean-Philippe. Certainly it was clear from the green gaze that her aunt thought it possible, if not probable, and yet her wish was not consulted.

Still, she would not make another loveless marriage even if she had to give up Society and her position all over again, to go off and live hidden in a cottage and grow as old and mad as Sarah

Kemble, and she cried, for her aunt's strength, for her own weakness, for her long misery without the man she loved and craved with all the passion of her too human heart.

60

After all, there was not much time at Great Heron for private talk between aunt and niece. The funeral procession that made its solemn way to the church at Little Heron, the ancient burial place of the Earls of Malfrey, was long, the coaches filled with the most distinguished men of the day. All who could stay had to be accommodated, and Lady Gratton and Damaris were not only mourners but also hostesses on a grand scale.

Damaris, riding once more through the great Forest of Heron, her children at her side, was moved by the occasion enough to forget her old feelings of loathing for these dark woods and all that they contained. Mr Poyntz, his own deep sorrow apparent on his wan features and in his trembling voice, assisted at the funeral service which was conducted by a bishop. All the village were present, and the church was crowded with men of politics from both Houses and both the government and the opposition. Damaris found that her husband had been respected by men whom she had thought of as his enemies. Lady Cassandra, deeply veiled, was present, but she vanished with her companions when the service was done, overcome by her brother's death. The tall, stout woman, leaning heavily on a servant's arm, looked broken, like a tree torn and buffeted by too strong a gale. She would be now like a woman almost dead, Damaris thought with a shiver, and promised herself that anything which might be done for Lady Cassandra she would do. There were the children; they were her nephew and niece. But in her heart, Damaris did not believe that

Cassandra would be persuaded to simple family pleasures. Rather would she mourn until she followed her brother to the grave.

At Great Heron she was welcomed with honest affection by Betty, plumper than ever, glad to see her mistress in health. She had many tales of her own to tell of battles fought and won against the Heron household hierarchy, but little time then to tell them, as the servants, quiet so long, were now rushed off their feet. The guests, men of affairs once the obsequies were over, talked of their own pressing business—the price of corn was now the subject of great political battle. Damaris found that few questions were asked about her absence after the first general inquiry about her recovered health. 'Travel—convalescence—' were words enough to satisfy—the political men, like the *ton,* would have little interest in hearing a long history of mountains and medicines.

Much of the fashionable world had also attended the funeral, and for once the resources of Great Heron were stretched to their fullest extent. Some of the guests lingered for the shooting in the woods, and she had less time to brood on lost love in concerns about linen, and her aunt could not scold her for her follies while they fussed about the food.

Among the fashionables, to Damaris's great pleasure, was her friend Lord Alvanley, who found a quiet moment to tell her all that had happened while she was away. The men were out shooting, the ladies sat with Lady Gratton in the morning-room, and Damaris strolled with Alvanley in the shrubbery.

'You will find Town sadly changed,' he told her. 'You probably will not have heard, but our friend the Beau fled last summer to Calais—his creditors were at his heels. We had all done what we could, but it came to the end at last. We try to mitigate his exile but I fear he suffers such.'

Damaris was grieved, horrified almost, to think of the elegant Brummel cast out from London life. Society had lost its most sparkling ornament, and she had lost a friend. She would write to him—perhaps visit if he would welcome that; she did not know. He was a proud man. She and Alvanley mourned together, and he told her all the rest of the gossip of the Town. The Carroway divorce had taken place, and Mr Carroway already was remarried to a milk-and-water miss. Poor Leila Carroway, Alvanley reported—while Damaris conjectured whether he had been one of Leila's lovers—had been packed off by her father to a small farm-house in Scotland, under the care of a dragon housekeeper.

Lord Alvanley sighed. 'She was one of the greatest of the high-flyers. Such a pretty woman—all wasted on the oats and barley or whatever it is occupies those grim regions.'

He took a pinch of snuff and added carelessly, 'And there is the mystery of our old friend d'Egremont—how Leila always eyed him! But with little luck, I think. He quite disappeared after Waterloo. *Some* say he went over to Boney, but no one really knows. Most people believe him dead, but it was never proved. Perhaps, after all, he is merely in Calais like Brummel. It transpired he was quite ruined, and his house and everything in it auctioned off at once.'

He gave her a sidelong glance.

'Your husband, I understand, made an effort to purchase it, but he was ill at the time, and the house passed into the hands of a family in the north who would not resell at any price. But they never lived there; instead they leased it for seven years at a good rent to what I suppose we must now call the United States. The Americans use it as their embassy.'

Damaris was puzzled. 'But why would the Earl have wanted d'Egremont House?' she said. 'I heard nothing of it,' she added, remembering she was supposed to have been in communication with her husband.

'It was believed he tried to keep it for the sake of Madame la Duchesse,' Alvanley replied. 'She is not too happy in France. The family estates were not restored—Louis is trying to be liberal. Your husband was kind, after all, Damaris.' Lord Alvanley smiled. His lisping voice, the dandy-like nonchalance of his manner, was belied by the intelligence in his eyes. 'And your aunt, Lady Gratton, is also kind. Her exertions on your behalf have been prodigious—in the Alps.'

'In the Alps,' Damaris murmured, meeting his glance with a twitch of her lips, and they both laughed.

The company thinned slowly, for the shooting was good at Great Heron. But in time Damaris had leisure to reflect that her aunt had indeed been superlatively energetic on her behalf—burying herself abroad for a year had been a large part, but certainly not all of it. The Countess of Malfrey had received letters of condolence, and of welcome home, from all the women in Society, including the feared patronesses of Almack's. Her position, though shaky, was hers to maintain if she was prudent and followed the accepted rule. As indeed she must if she was not to ruin the chances of little Griselda and cause bitterness between herself and her son when he grew to manhood.

Lady Gratton knew exactly what must be done, and with one exception, Damaris was prepared to do it. Anything—except a second marriage. But she would not argue with her aunt as yet. The Duke and Duchess of Camberly had attended the funeral, and Lady Gratton had urged Damaris to bestow every courtesy on her aunt and uncle. The Duke indeed showed a real concern for his niece, suffering, as he believed, under the scourge of consumption. Lady Devereaux, *enceinte,* did not attend. Wilhelmina, poor Weary, had engaged herself to the old Earl of Fosters and was about to become her elder sister's mother-in-law.

Damaris, sorry for the girl, paid her attention and earned at last a grudging approval from the Duchess and a commendation from Lady Gratton. When at last the house was clear of visitors, the lawyers came. There was much business to be discussed and many papers to sign, but Damaris found that her affairs were as her aunt had described succinctly on the day of her return. She could live the life of a great lady—with her aunt's consent. Without her aunt's consent, she could claim nothing. Matters had been most carefully worked out by the lawyers so that if she lived and returned in such case that her position could not be maintained despite all the efforts of Lady Gratton, the family would be protected. Lord Malfrey perhaps had feared her arriving shamelessly with her lover and several bastards. Were it not for the legacy from d'Egremont and what was left of her jewels, she could not have eaten a crust of bread in independence.

Her independence, in the event, was illusory. Her family obligations were bonds of the strongest kind. Although she was a grown woman, she was once more a ward of her aunt. That lady was now gracious, but underneath her pleasant manner Damaris felt her full severity. She did not realize her aunt's happiness in seeing her niece alive and well. Lady Gratton was truly thankful, but like most of such thankfulness, it was quickly mixed with exasperation at the girl who, after such a careful upbringing, had by her extreme folly almost brought ruin not only on herself but all her family. The aunt's gratitude to the Earl for his protection of his heedless wife knew no bounds. Damaris, during the weeks they spent at Heron, was again moved to think it a great pity that the Earl had not chosen Lady Gratton to be his wife. They would have dealt with each other famously, after all.

The lawyers returned to Town. The thoughts of the ladies turned to Town also, and a difference arose between them. Lady Gratton decided that the children should remain at Great Heron, as the Earl had wished, and that their mother should remain with them—the country, she believed, was a much safer haven for her lovely niece than Town. At least, she said, Damaris could stay there until the novelty of her return had worn away.

Damaris had other plans. She did not at all agree with her late husband's notions on the bringing up of children. No longer was she a biddable young wife. She had lived in other countries; she had seen children of different sorts, brought up by different rules. Though the children of the United States were brought up too freely for an English taste, she thought that some liberty was desirable, and that children should take some part in their parents' lives. The girls should not be hidden away until all the glare of their coming-out was upon them, and then be expected to act like women.

She wanted to keep her children with her, at least part of the year. And she had no taste just then to stay secluded—her private grief, which had been less burdensome in company, would return in force, she knew, in the long winter nights at Heron. The place held no happy memories for her. It was much more Betty's home now, she reflected, than her own. She would live quietly in Town, but to Town she wished to go.

Lady Gratton disapproved and for some time held firm. It was hardly suitable for the Countess, in deep mourning, to return so soon to Society. Once in Town, engagements would follow. It would cause talk for Lady Malfrey, long so ill that she could not return to her husband, to re-appear on his death, a healthy, gay widow. Her words made sense, but Damaris was uneasy. She saw that her aunt was no longer sure she would behave with propriety; it was not her love affair with d'Egremont that had so shocked that lady, but her abrupt throwing over of respectability when she had run off to Ostend. That would never be forgiven. There was no way Damaris could convey to Lady Gratton all the horrors of that night, but if she could have done so, it would not have served. Lady Gratton could admit all the claims of love—all except the endangerment of position. With Lady Gratton, as with all Society, that was out of bounds. Leila Carroway was ruined. Damaris knew that if she herself had become an Indian squaw she would not have been more outcast than the headstrong Leila.

Sometimes she wondered, in their quiet days together, that Lady Gratton never by word or look showed any interest in her doings while she had been away. Her aunt must realize that she had been in America from what she had told her of d'Egremont's death, but Lady Gratton was quite content to leave an ocean between herself and any knowledge of that place.

And Damaris saw, perhaps further than Lady Gratton herself, what really was in her aunt's heart. Her great concern now was for her two young wards, the children who had not disgraced themselves and who deserved all their position could offer them. If she could, she would have liked to keep their mother at Great Heron until a suitable marriage could be arranged that would keep her in some other country fastness, fully engrossed, carefully guarded, and out of the way of harm.

Damaris made up her mind that this was not to be. If Lady Gratton had only known it, there was nothing left for her but a life of prudence and caution. But she could hardly tell Lady Gratton that she had taken yet another lover to whom she must be faithful; she would not like to see the look in those green eyes.

Her aunt did not take long in returning to the attack.

'Young Lord Hallbury, that friend of Alvanley's, is hanging out for a wife,' she said one day, reading a letter from Mrs Farthingale. 'His father has died, and he comes into the estate. A fine old place in Northumberland. He has quite given up gaming and settled down—taken up the new farming, I hear. You used to favour him, Damaris, did you not?'

'I am not hanging out for a husband, Aunt,' Damaris replied with spirit. 'The Earl is dead hardly two months.'

'Don't be missish, Damaris,' her aunt said coldly. 'It is not necessary to pretend with me you ever had the slightest affection for your husband; nor indeed did you give him a modicum of respect. Your lover is dead. I must assume you will want another. You are too young to remain a widow. *I* had no trouble, left in that position not much older than you are now, but you have a different temperament.'

Different indeed, Damaris thought. She wondered if her aunt had ever been in love. If she had, no one would know it. Certainly she was a miracle of discretion.

'It is better to marry than to cause scandal,' her aunt said. 'I really cannot see you remaining in Society too long otherwise. Leila Carroway was never as reckless as you were, and look at that family now. She had a child the year she was divorced, and the Carroways claimed it was a bastard. Unfortunately it was a boy, and the case will drag through the courts for years. I was well aware, even before you threw your cap over the mill, that you were being called "the Careless Countess." For Griselda's sake, that name must not be revived.'

At length, the ladies compromised. Damaris would go with her aunt to Town in deep mourning for a month or two, accompanied by her children. She would receive calls and return visits, but she would go to no dinners or evening entertainments and would be seen in public only driving in the Park.

This régime was better than incarceration at Great Heron, but it was hardly of a liveliness to cheer Damaris's mind. Lady Gratton, whose period of mourning was soon over, resumed most of her social life, and Damaris was left, after the children went to bed, to think of her past follies; to live again with a pleasing torment all the moments of her love with Booth, though her cheeks still flushed at the memory of their last meeting. Surely she could have contrived matters better—her aunt was right, she decided at last. She was not a woman who could manage her own affairs. The man she loved despised her and probably was happy never to see her again.

The London twilight was depressing. She would fall asleep in her chair and dream of a New England garden, a Spanish courtyard, flower-scented air, and the strength of her lover's arms, the tenderness of his mouth as it sought her own. Then she would wake, startled, and realize that it was Verity, no doubt, who now received his kisses in all the lawful bonds of wedlock—so much more suited to that upright man than all their guilty pleasures. If he thought of her at all he would probably agree with Aunt Gratton that she was better married to some hearty country squire who would keep her pregnant and in obscurity—as Black Bear might have done, she thought, her humour twisted suddenly to bitterness.

61

The day dawned bright. Before she went down to the morning-room, Damaris visited the nursery, where Griselda was playing with dolls and Christopher was marshalling his troops against Napoleon, to the amusement of the nurses. She reproached herself for her discontent and resolved not to waste her life in useless agitation. In future she *would* be calm and sensible.

Before the morning was over, that resolve had melted as quickly as the sugar-treats in young Griselda's mouth. For while Damaris sat demurely receiving callers with Lady Gratton and Mrs Satterthwaite, a card was sent up to the Countess of Malfrey from one Mr Howard Booth, of Connecticut, from the Embassy of the United States of America.

Lady Gratton's eyes opened wide.

'The Countess is not at home,' she said. 'Burroughs, you must remember that Lady Malfrey is receiving only old friends.'

Burroughs bowed his head. 'Yes, my lady. But the gentleman was most insistent—'

'That is all, Burroughs,' Lady Gratton said in her most glacial manner, and the man withdrew.

Mrs Satterthwaite, who had been quite dull—she sat with the ladies in the house of mourning every day—became animated with curiosity.

'What barbarians those colonials are,' Lady Gratton said. 'He must have had business with the Earl and now no doubt wishes access to his papers. I must leave word with Burroughs if he calls again to refer him to the lawyers. To intrude on a widow in her grief!'

Damaris was in turn stunned, furious at her aunt's dismissal of *her* caller, and in spite of herself amused at Lady Gratton's apparent ability to handle any kind of situation—Mrs Satterthwaite lapsed into boredom at the thought of business. The rest of the morning passed unexceptionally, but Damaris's head whirled. Why was Booth in London? What was he at the embassy? Why did he call on the Countess of Malfrey? Question after question rushed into her mind. She could hardly wait to be private with her aunt, fearful that Mrs Satterthwaite might stay to dine. But she had engagements, and when she left, Damaris made an energetic protest. She was no longer a child and expected to have the privilege of deciding to whom she was, and was not, at home.

Lady Gratton paid no attention to this at all.

'Who is this Booth?' she said grimly.

'A—a friend,' Damaris said, wondering why the words came out so haltingly, 'from—Litchfield, Connecticut.'

'Litchfield—' Her aunt stared. 'I had not known you had made—acquaintances abroad.'

She spoke vexedly. Damaris hardly knew whether to be angry or to laugh. Lady Gratton clearly thought she should have spent her time keeping free of acquaintances not of the *ton*. She had a hysterical desire to explain that Lady Gratton had been within a hair's-breadth of becoming aunt-in-law to Black Bear—but she kept her composure.

'I will see Mr Booth, Aunt, if he calls again,' she said merely.

'But what if he chatters about meeting you in this—Connecticut? Lydia Satterthwaite is an ignorant woman, but even she will know that that is not an Alp.'

This time Damaris laughed helplessly, and Lady Gratton was much affronted.

'I'm sorry, Aunt,' she said. 'I know I have been a dreadful trouble. But I am sure Mr Booth will say nothing to embarrass us —he is a gentleman.'

As she spoke she wondered about her certainty. They had not parted in friendship, rather in enmity; still she was sure. Nor did she know why the day suddenly seemed pleasant, the sun more golden, Malfrey House brighter; why she felt so well, wanting to laugh and cry at the same time, with her blood tingling from the soles of her feet to the crown of her head. Nothing had changed, she told herself—but everything had changed.

The next day Mr Booth sent his name again and was announced by a somewhat nervous Burroughs. The announcement was followed immediately by Howard Booth himself, who had entered behind the servant and was about to brook no denial.

'Your servant, Countess.' His eyes were full of laughter as he bowed solemnly over her hand.

Booth in London was dressed like the men of the *ton* at that hour. He wore trousers and gold-tasselled Hessian boots, a blue coat of exquisite fit, cut away at the waist, and a light buff waistcoat, all of which showed off his lean, strong form to great advantage. His cravat was a work of art. The countenances of Lady Gratton and Mrs Satterthwaite brightened at the impact of so much well-bred manly charm. Damaris felt a strange pleasure mingled with pain to see the man she loved admired by the ladies of London Society as he had been by the maids and matrons of New England.

'I was so sorry, Ma'am, to hear of your loss,' he said, taking in all the details of her mourning with as sad a look as he could muster, and only Damaris noticing the tell-tale twitching of his lips.

Damaris made the introductions and watched the ladies melt in the warmth of Booth's smile.

'You have been travelling in the Alps, Mr Booth?' Mrs Satterthwaite asked with a sleepy look.

'Oh, I have travelled all over, the last year or two,' Booth replied. 'There is nothing like travel, I believe, to broaden the mind. But now I am settled in Town for a time—on a mission of trade, Ma'am. I have ventured to present some introductions. Mr John Quincy Adams of my country was acquainted with the late Earl and has asked me to present his sincere condolences to the Countess and the family.'

'Thank you, Mr Booth,' Damaris said, finding her tongue. 'I remember my husband speaking of your Mr Adams. He always believed that freedom of trade with the colonies would be beneficial to us all.'

Lady Gratton was delighted with the person, the address, and the discretion of this visitor. She was also relieved at this diversion from the usual set of callers to whom they were limited by Damaris's recent bereavement.

The next afternoon, while she and Damaris were driving in the Park, the Countess heavily veiled, Lady Gratton was most gracious upon meeting the charming Mr Booth, dressed in the most elegant breeches and riding a spirited black stallion that he had well under control.

The day was cool and brisk. Town was as yet thin of company. Mr Booth mentioned that his Ambassador had gone on a country visit and he was alone and dull at the Embassy. Lady Gratton had always been able to make great decisions swiftly, and she invited Mr Booth to Malfrey House for dinner. Damaris, in her room preparing for this meal, felt herself trembling. The black dress made her look like a crow, she thought, but there was nothing to be done.

She no longer wondered why Booth was there. She had stopped thinking. All the night before she had lain awake fretting. Had he merely come to tease her, to get some kind of revenge? Had he married Verity before he left? She understood the mission he was on. The gentlemen of New England had been anxious to have their interests represented in any talks on trade. It was natural that Booth should come. It had nothing to do with her. Doubtless his call was from courtesy only, for he had not tried to have a private word with her, and his attention had been on the older ladies. She had passed a wretched night and now looked anxiously at the shadows under her eyes. A widow indeed—she looked older, she thought, than her twenty-one years. Not the woman who—but she banished the recollection of moonlit nights and made her way down to greet her guest, not knowing if he was friend, enemy—or still a lover.

Dinner proceeded in its usual long formal way. The Duke of Camberly, who was in Town without his Duchess, still tied to the bedside of Lady Devereaux, led the company, with Mrs Satterthwaite and a young nephew to make up the table. The Duke had looked sternly at this young man on his arrival, considering he would be poor company over the port, and was heartened to see Booth, who might be a colonial but obviously was a man able to drink his bottle after dinner. His powers of conversation, too, were a welcome addition to what the Duke thought of as the ladies' inanities. He had accepted the invitation to the house of mourning only as a duty and had quickly regretted doing so, wishing that he had gone to his club. But the dinner, always good at Malfrey House, went very pleasantly after all.

Booth spoke little to Damaris, addressing her from time to time with respect, as a gentleman would address a lady in deep mourning, but he was all charm to Mrs Satterthwaite and actually flirted with Lady Gratton, who preened and tossed her head, her emerald earrings dancing. Damaris was astounded, amused, and mortified in turn. Why had he come at all if just to vex her? At one moment her eyes filled with tears that sparkled in the candlelight. Mrs Satterthwaite's nephew observed the tears on the sad young beauty and was struck to the heart with his first experience of love.

Nothing changed when the gentlemen joined the ladies after

dinner. Young Satterthwaite was at Damaris's feet, but the Duke and Booth were very happy with each other's company. And a real cause of misery came to Damaris. While the Duke had a few words with Mrs Satterthwaite, Lady Gratton, her mind on who could know what, inquired pleasantly of Mrs Booth. Booth replied sadly that his mother was dead. 'And I am, as yet, unmarried, Lady Gratton. Though I have an engagement which I hope will soon be fulfiled.'

So it was settled. He was to marry Verity. Suddenly very tired, Damaris excused herself. Her withdrawal from her guests would be forgiven the widow. Booth had come only to tease her, to take a small revenge for her treatment of him in St Augustine. She hoped that he enjoyed it. He laughed, no doubt, to see her ugly; laughed to see her hedged about by her relations, confined as a young girl. Perhaps he would come back, she thought drearily, to see her married off by Lady Gratton to the bucolic squire of her choice—already Damaris pictured this hated husband, red-faced, stout, and tears of vexation wet her pillow, as she believed almost entirely this dreadful future.

The next morning Lady Gratton, smiling, inquired about Damaris's health. She told her that she had sent for the children the night before: for once it was proper to break their rest so they could further their acquaintance with their great-uncle, the Duke. The Duke had been pleased with their good manners, and Mr Booth, she added, remarked on the resemblance of Lady Griselda to her mother—though of course, she added, sighing, 'in reality she favours my poor sister. She was a true beauty, Damaris.'

Lady Gratton had never believed in compliment.

A few days later, Lady Gratton disappeared one morning after breakfast and left Damaris to receive Mrs Satterthwaite alone. A dull business, she thought crossly, for Mrs Satterthwaite was exceedingly prosy, except when she asked questions that Damaris could hardly answer, occasionally referring to d'Egremont, like a cat playing with a mouse. Damaris knew Mrs Satterthwaite was too loyal to the aunt to want to do damage to the niece, but the old lady's curiosity was tormenting.

'And I do wonder what business Augusta has with Mr Booth that keeps her in the library so long,' she said plaintively.

Damaris jumped. 'Mr Booth! I can't imagine—unless, perhaps, they are talking with the Earl's secretary. Lord Malfrey had some interest in matters of trade. There might be papers to be looked at for the purpose of his mission.'

She did not believe her own words. Her husband had been interested in trade, but the work of his life had been the politics of war. Could Booth have asked for an interview with Lady Gratton to betray her? She could not think it. His pride had been hurt, but he was not a man given to littleness and trick. He would tease her, but he would not harm her. But what could he want with Lady Gratton?

Suddenly she felt she could bear her situation no longer. She must see Booth alone. Yet how could she? Not a step could she stir out of doors without at least two footmen and her aunt in attendance. The Countess of Malfrey could not be seen alone visiting the house that once was d'Egremont's—the scandal would break out again, perhaps this time never to be stilled. Almost she felt she did not care—but she must care, for Griselda's sake.

Lady Gratton returned to the morning-room alone, with an unusual sparkle about her—Booth had been gallant to her aunt, Damaris thought, vexed.

'I think we should pay a call this afternoon, Damaris. You too, Lydia. An old friend of ours is in Town. The Duchesse de Langcourt has arrived. Poor Marie—she is in financial difficulties. Louis is not grateful, it seems. She is trying to regain some of her own property that was sold when d'Egremont House was auctioned—her goods should not have been included in the sale—but she is having much trouble trying to trace her things and prove her ownership. The American ambassador has been most kind and has invited her to stay in her old quarters while she makes an inventory of the furnishings that stayed in the house.'

'Devereaux bought her silver writing-desk, and I *told* him it was Marie's. But it went cheap. I hope he has to give it back,' Mrs Satterthwaite said with some complacency.

Lady Gratton nodded in agreement.

'Mr Booth invites us to stay for dinner—the tête-à-tête must be difficult for the poor man. Although the Duchesse is not a relation I think you should go, Niece. She has entertained you many times, and you were her guest in Brussels.'

The idea of going to d'Egremont House to see the Duchesse again put Damaris in a nervous flutter. She wanted to see Marie, but it would be strange to meet her in the company of the man who had killed her cousin. She wondered whether the Duchesse knew that d'Egremont was dead. Then she remembered that Juneau had promised to inform her. There was the matter of the house in New Orleans—certainly that must go to the Duchesse, but there was so much to explain! Her head ached, and she changed from one black dress to another. Verity, she remembered, since she gave up her muslins, had often worn garnet-coloured silks. They had suited her dark looks, turning her sallow skin to glowing olive, softening the harshness of her features, the colour reflecting in her neat brown hair.

The meeting between Damaris and the Duchesse was affectionate. The Duchesse praised her to the assembled company for her courage and coolness during the dreadful days in Brussels. To Mrs Satterthwaite's question, she answered that her cousin d'Egremont was dead, but changed the subject swiftly and gracefully, without a glance at Damaris. Damaris was thankful, and she determined to talk to Booth as soon as possible about the transfer of ownership of the New Orleans house—if she could ever speak to him alone. Several attachés from the embassy joined them at dinner. Damaris knew that once the ladies withdrew, the gentlemen would remain at least an hour over their wine, and after the tea and coffee had been served, Lady Gratton would be ready to go home.

Booth spoke much to Madame la Duchesse. Damaris sipped her wine. The dining-room of d'Egremont House, so familiar, so little changed since last she had been there, began to swim about her head. Behind the footmen with the powdered wigs she seemed to see d'Egremont, smiling. . . . Booth was there yet still in Litchfield. . . . She was waiting in the pine forest. . . .

'Mr Booth.' Lady Gratton's voice was subdued but clear. 'I think my niece is faint.'

Booth jumped to his feet and was at Damaris's side in an instant.

'Please do not disturb yourselves,' he said. 'I will take Lady Malfrey into the garden for some air.'

Supported by his arm, her one wish granted, Damaris recovered before she was touched by the cold breeze in the garden. A servant had brought the Countess's cloak, and Booth wrapped her carefully. They strolled sedately on the path, but Booth's eyes were dancing as he gazed down at Damaris.

'You are feeling better—Lady Malfrey?' he inquired politely.

'Oh, Howard—' All her questions crowded her mind, yet the

great, important question she could not ask. 'Howard—how did you find me?'

'That was easy,' he said cheerfully. 'With d'Egremont dead, it was natural that you would go home to England. And when I arrived here, the whole town was talking of the return of the beautiful blue-eyed Lady Malfrey, who had been away for nearly two years —in the Alps.'

She thought about this for a moment. Was he implying he had followed her? Or was it merely her own great desire that made her think so? She *must* control herself. . . .

'What—what were you speaking to my aunt about this morning?'

'I was asking her for your hand in marriage. I believe it is the custom in these parts.'

'Not necessarily for a widow,' Damaris said, not thinking as she spoke, but with a great joy flooding all her being.

'Ah, yes—a widow. Well, now you are so *definitely* widowed,' he said, grinning, 'Ma'am— I thought I should ask at once. Your aunt was surprisingly gracious,' he added. 'She seemed more concerned about the length of the period of mourning than with losing you at the end of it to a rebellious colonial. Of course, she questioned me at length on what she called my "position." She would have made a good lawyer, Lady Gratton. She discovered all about my family, the number of my properties, and the extent of my fortune in no time at all—and very politely. But I think she was satisfied.'

'But she did not ask me!' said Damaris, perplexed.

'Well, I allow I let her think you were not averse to the idea. She realized we had been—acquainted in the United States. Your aunt is not a fool, Damaris.'

She was struck with wonder. It had not occurred to her that her aunt might see in Booth the strong, solid husband she had envisaged who was to protect her niece from the dangers of Society in Town. Damaris's good opinion of her aunt suddenly increased a hundredfold.

'But Howard,' she said slowly, 'you know we cannot marry. It would be your ruin. That is why I left you so, in St Augustine. And what of Verity?'

'It did occur to me,' he said dryly, 'some time after you had gone, when I had cooled down a little, that you might have had some such fool idea in your head. Of course, I didn't know then about the Countess—will you mind being plain Mrs Booth? As for

Verity, there's no woman I respect more—on that side of the ocean —but we grew up thinking she was to be my sister, and I still feel about her that way.'

He rubbed his jaw reflectively.

'I have an idea she might become my cousin—I had a letter from Wadsworth before I left. Those two are getting on real well. But you don't understand Verity, Damaris. I don't know if you have women like Verity over here. She's smart as paint and has more energy and drive than ten ordinary men put together. My neighbours want me to stand for the Senate, but if a woman could be a senator, Verity would be as good as any man there and better than most. A woman like that could run the country. Verity will marry or not as she chooses, but she'll always have her own busy life. Now you,' he added teasingly, 'you need me to keep you out of fixes. I can see that your aunt thinks so, too.'

The wind blew chill across the garden, and Damaris shivered.

'Let me take you inside before you catch cold,' Booth said. 'You are right pale, Damaris.'

'How could you be a senator if you married me?' she said wretchedly. 'Half the people we meet will know me as the Countess of Malfrey, and the others as the Marquise d'Egremont.'

'They will know you as Mrs Booth,' he said firmly. 'And they might know you are grand-daughter to the old Duke of Camberly. And if anyone knows you had two husbands before me, I don't suppose they'll trouble to find out exactly when the first one died. You worry too much.'

Yet she could not believe that. 'Rachel Jackson—she was innocent compared to me, and yet the scandal has been dreadful—'

'The General survives,' Booth said. 'Poor Rachel, a country-woman with a corn-cob pipe—she is much less able to hold her own than you are, my lady. But no matter.'

He took her hands firmly.

'I will be here for some time. A year at least, perhaps two or more. After that will be time to think about the Senate. But I am a rich man. I can live where I will. Here, if you would like it, Washington, Litchfield. No one will question you in Litchfield, Damaris. That last episode brought them all to shame, and Mrs Hatch, I hear, is quite an altered woman. It is Verity who rules in that family now. You will have no trouble there. If I am senator, well and good. If not, I can live without it. But I have no intention of living without you, my dear, so you must make up your mind to it.'

Damaris stood stock still, watching a snowflake descend to glitter white on Booth's strong brown hand as it held her own. The snowflake trembled and melted from his warmth into a brilliant drop, and her weight of trouble melted as quickly in his glowing, demanding presence. She looked up, with all her questions, all her fading fear, mirrored in her blue gaze.

'Damaris!' He longed to take her in his arms, but there was no privacy in the small garden; servants hovered, and from the windows of the drawing-room the ladies were watching all too plainly. 'You must have courage. We may have troubles, but they are our troubles—we will meet them together. When I leave this place, you will come with me, or I will never go.'

No more words passed between them, but as they returned to the house he was almost certain that Damaris had been won. He saw the ladies in the drawing-room and remembered that the gentlemen would be still at their port.

'There is another drawing-room upstairs,' he said. 'Let us sit there for a moment. You need the quiet,' he added, smiling. 'You were very faint. It has a little oddity I want to show you—I found it when I was poking about for the Duchesse.'

Dream-like, she ascended the stairs to the music room, hearing again in her mind the music of 'Glorious John' while she wondered if she had the courage to do as her lover wished. She could think of no greater happiness and yet—Booth, though now he looked like any gentleman of the *ton,* was still a man of New England, puritan at heart. Would he suffer at the whispers always surrounding the name of his wife? Would he learn to despise her, knowing as he did that she had been mistress to d'Egremont? What other tales might come to him—true, like her scandalous careers as Desmond Midnight, and as an actress; and untrue, like the tale of her being mistress to the Regent, part of the most debauched set at Carlton House?

Her answers trembled on her tongue—yes, then no. Keep the present happiness, some cautious voices counselled, but let him leave at last. Keep the present happiness and make it live forever, her wishes spoke. She kept close to him, unable to think, to choose.

She had not observed, deep as she was in thought, what he was about. Suddenly she realized that he was tinkering with the secret panel—those clever, contriving Yankee hands had found the entrance to the hidden room.

Her eyes were wide with horror.

'Isn't this the damnedest thing?' he said.

He glanced up at the ceiling with the painted figures disporting themselves in all the rites of love. Perhaps it had come to him that she knew this room, perhaps it had not, but he was not to be in doubt for long. Lying face down on the floor was a canvas. Damaris, scarlet, speechless, knew it was the missing portrait, flung there by d'Egremont before his flight, and realized why the Earl had wanted so very much to purchase d'Egremont House. Damaris burned hot as her lover, descendant of the Pilgrims, took the portrait up and propped it against the wall—to observe his lady, rosy, naked, in all the languor of her satisfied and guilty love. She wished that she had died before she had to meet this day.

'H'm.' Booth regarded the portrait carefully. He rubbed his chin in a familiar gesture and glanced at the picture once again. 'I see you know this place.'

He turned and saw her blushes.

'You've hardly changed since then, Damaris,' he said thoughtfully. He gazed at her form wrapped in widow's weeds. 'You haven't taken on a pound.'

He grinned at her in impudent recollection. She had expected displeasure, disgust, shame—anything but this. Relief and happiness welled up in an instant. She could have laughed, laughed for an hour, but instead she threw her arms about him and with all the force of pent-up love and longing reached up to find his lips and end their long and anguished separation.

To her surprise he caught her arms and held her from him. He watched her with seeming gravity, but his lips twitched with a smile he could hardly control.

'Well, damned if I reckon to make love to you, Damaris,' he said in his laziest drawl. 'Maybe this time I'll make certain you're about to marry me first.'

And their laughter, irrepressible, resounded through the house, causing the ladies listening avidly below to raise their eyes to heaven.

Booth took his lady in his arms and, as his mouth found hers, they both knew that their love, whatever came, was theirs forever.